JASMINE CLOSE

SERIES ONE - EPISODES 1 - 25

LINDA DUNSCOMBE

LUNCH TIME LIBRARY

FOREWORD

Most of my readers will already be familiar with the **ongoing** stories in *Jasmine Close* - the soap opera you can read.

Just in case you haven't read any of the other books in the series yet, and you would like to get to know more about the lives and dramas of the residents of this new housing estate, you can find all the books in Series One, Series Two and Series Three on Amazon.

All titles are available to read for FREE with Kindle Unlimited.

If you are already a follower of *Jasmine Close*, I thank you for your continued support, it is very much appreciated.

INTRODUCTION

JASMINE CLOSE
Follow the lives - Experience the drama!
The soap opera you can read

There are twenty-five episodes in the first and second series and the first ten episodes in series three are available. Each episode takes around 25 minutes to read and follows the lives and dramas of the residents moving into the newly built properties in *Jasmine Close.*

∼

Follow the ongoing story:
https://www.facebook.com/jasmineclosecrew

JASMINE CLOSE

SERIES ONE - EPISODES 1 - 25

Copyright: Linda Dunscombe © 2013

Copyright for Collection Series One: Linda Dunscombe © 2022

All rights reserved.

No part of this book may be reproduced in any form or by any electronic or mechanical means, including information storage and retrieval systems, without written permission from the author, except for the use of brief quotations in a book review. Nor can it be circulated in any form of binding or cover other than that in which it is published and without similar condition including this condition being imposed on a subsequent purchaser.

This book is a work of fiction. Names, characters and incidents are the product of the author's imagination or are used fictitiously. Any resemblance to actual persons, living or dead, is entirely coincidence.

Cover Design: Peter Swann(www.peterswann.co.uk)

Collection Cover Design: GetCovers

Editing: Scott MacDougall

E-book preparation: Peter Dunscombe

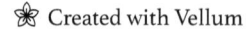

❋ Created with Vellum

EPISODES 1 - 5

JASMINE CLOSE - SERIES ONE

EPISODE ONE
JASMINE CLOSE - SERIES ONE

Jenny concentrated on the music pumping directly into her ears from the headphones. With her eyes shut, she could just about kid herself that she was somewhere pleasant; like on a sunny beach, or relaxing beside the sea. The fact that her left hand was gripping the door handle and her body was totally rigid didn't help maintain the illusion.

'We're here,' Miles said from beside her, in a voice heavily loaded with frustration.

The car stopped moving, and she opened her eyes and looked around her. It was still pretty much a building site. Certainly to the left of her it was hard hats and scaffolding. But all the houses on the right were clearly finished and awaiting their new occupants.

'We're the first in,' her husband said, as though it were something to be proud of.

And maybe it was. They had chosen the house off plan. Miles said it was how you got the best deal. The biggest house in the Close on the largest plot, and they had also put down deposits on two of the apartments from the next building phase as an investment. Miles always had one eye on boosting the retirement fund. Jenny had enough trouble dealing with each day; she left her husband to worry about the future.

She climbed out of the car and fought the impulse to run to the shiny new front door. This was a new start and, armed with the coping strategies her therapist had given her, she was determined to beat the fear.

'Bloody builders. Look at that; talk about shoddy...'

She wasn't really paying any attention to Miles. He would always find something to complain about. It wasn't even that he was a miserable moaner, which he was, but as he frequently pointed out to her, if people did what they were paid to do, then he wouldn't have anything to moan about. He was, unfortunately, a perfectionist, and that made life difficult at the best of times and unbearable at the worst. This was definitely unbearable mode.

'And where is the removal van? It should have been here by now. They left forty minutes before us. Bet they've stopped for coffee and doughnuts at the services...' he looked at his watch and tutted.

'They're entitled to a coffee break,' Jenny said calmly, trying to ease his agitation. The sky seemed to be expanding and the front door was moving further away from her. She tried to do the breathing exercises that she had been taught, but her head was spinning and she could feel the nausea and panic welling up inside her. She walked fast, telling herself she was a calm and confident woman, while not believing a word of it. She reached the door and grabbed the handle gratefully. The door was locked.

'Miles...' She tried to keep the desperation out of her voice, but knew she'd failed when he looked at her with the impatience and exasperation that she had become so used to.

He strode down the path and put the key in the door. He didn't actually tut at her, but she was sure he was making the sound in his head. She entered the house with a flood of relief. It didn't matter that it was empty and impersonal. It was safe, and it offered sanctuary.

'You promised,' Miles said accusingly. 'No more of that nonsense. You were cleared. It wasn't your fault, and it's all over now.'

As if a piece of paper could make everything right, she thought bitterly. But she forced herself to smile. 'I know, but you have to be patient...' he opened his mouth to protest and she corrected herself quickly. 'More patient. My therapist said baby steps.'

'I think the therapist,' he made it sound like a swear word. 'Should stop treating you like a baby. Then you might get over this silly, self-indulgent stuff quicker.'

She should defend herself. She should defend Ally, her therapist, but what was the point? Miles couldn't or wouldn't understand what she went through. What she was still going through. In his world, if you make a mistake, then you learn from it and move on. If only it were that simple.

'Look at the way they've hung that door.' He pulled his ever ready notepad out from his pocket with its little pencil attached and started making notes.

Jenny left him to his snag list and went upstairs. The house had five bedrooms; though why they needed so many for just the two of them, she had no idea. It wasn't even as though they were planning on having children in the future. They were both agreed, no babies for them. The master-suite, complete with walk-in wardrobe and his and her sinks, was at the front of the house and looked out over the building site. It was a large room with plenty of light, but she didn't feel the love. She opened the next door, a smaller room which again had its own bathroom; she thought it would make a good guest room. Across the hall, she entered one of the back bedrooms and immediately knew that it would be her own special sanctuary. It looked out onto the big corner garden and beyond that, the Grand Union Canal. It even had its own small balcony. She saw herself in the summer, sitting in the wooden chair she was going to buy, looking out at the barges on the canal while she sipped her Earl Grey tea and dipped in and out of a romantic novel.

'About bloody time. Jen, van's here.'

Reluctantly, she left the room and her daydreams and went downstairs. She stood in the doorway and watched as her husband made the workman aware of his annoyance at keeping him waiting. She saw a young woman walking along the path holding the hands of two mixed-race children she guessed to be perhaps nine or ten. A boy and a girl, that looked like they might be twins. The woman glanced at her and smiled. Jenny resisted the urge to look away and slam the door shut, and forced herself to smile back. All the time hoping that the woman would keep on walking and not expect to stop and chat. Her mental vibes must have reached the woman, who did indeed do just that.

Jenny watched as the back of the removal van lowered down, and Miles immediately began issuing his instructions. He had directed the boxes and furnishings onto the van in a set order as though it were a military operation and would now no doubt supervise how they were all offloaded.

'Hello, Mrs Fisher?'

Victoria held her hand out towards the woman, who stared at her as though she were a ghost who had just appeared from nowhere.

'Sorry, did I startle you?' she let her hand drop, feeling a little awkward, and instead offered the flowers she was carrying.

'I didn't see or hear you coming,' the woman said.

'But you are Mrs Fisher?'

'Yes.'

Relieved, and still holding the flowers out to the woman, Victoria tried again. She adopted her best, putting you at ease smile. 'I'm Victoria, from the Show Home. Here...' she offered the flowers for a second time and was relieved when the woman took them. 'I just popped along to say welcome to Jasmine Close.'

Victoria was beginning to think the woman might be a bit simple. She was hoping to get a promotional photo, but it wasn't looking particularly promising. She glanced towards the removal van; the men were carrying a large cream leather armchair between them. It was one of those that had a remote control for the recline action. Another man was fussing around and issuing instructions. She assumed it was Mr Fisher; she wondered if she would stand a better chance with him.

As the men carried the chair towards the door, Victoria stepped aside to allow them free access. Mrs Fisher didn't step outside to join her, but retreated back into the house. Mr Fisher followed the men to the door, making sure that they got through without causing any damage. Victoria tried out her smile again. 'Mr Fisher? I'm Victoria, from the Show Home.' This time it worked a bit better in that she got his attention and he shook her offered hand.

'Call me Miles,' he said. 'Here.' He pulled a notebook from his pocket and handed her a list of complaints. 'That's just for starters. I'll give you a full list once I've finished moving in and had time to look around properly.' Without a backward glance, he went into the house.

She gave up on her plan for a photograph and walked slowly back to the Show Home. A car turned into the Close. It was a red BMW with a young female driving. Curiosity made her turn around and watch to see where the car went. So far, apart from the Fishers, only four other properties were occupied, all of them apartments. She knew Flat one, three, five and seven were all owned by the housing association. Five and seven had already moved in, so had three, which was a ground floor, fully adapted apartment suitable for a wheelchair user. Apparently, a Mr Lance had moved in there, but she hadn't seen him yet. And the other occupant was in Flat two, privately owned, but apparently now let out to a tenant.

The Beemer stopped at the corner beside the apartment block and the female climbed out. Victoria wandered across to the building site on the other side of the road for a better view. She knew she was being nosy, but curiosity had always been her thing. She found other people's lives fascinating. The female was tall and slim with the longest legs she'd ever seen, shown off to fall effect by a very short skirt and very high pencil-thin heeled shoes. It seemed she had a passkey. Which was strange. It suggested she was a resident, but Victoria didn't know who, how or where, so maybe she was the tenant in number two.

'You all right, Vic?'

She turned around to face the foreman, Barry.

'You know I can't let you take another step closer without a hard hat,' he said, his blue eyes crinkled against the weak Autumn sun.

'It's Okay, I don't need one. It's you I wanted to see.'

'Yep, it's a bit of a curse sometimes.'

'What is?'

'My irresistibility to women.'

She hit him playfully. 'You wish.'

'I do, I really do,' he said it with a smile, but Victoria suspected he had a bit of a thing for her.

She handed him the snag list from Miles Fisher and pointed across the road. 'More to come, apparently.'

He looked at the list with resignation. 'I'll get one of the lads to have a look tomorrow.'

'Thanks. Don't leave it though, I've a feeling he'll be a chaser.'

'When's your big day then?' he nodded at the semi-detached house a few doors down from the Fishers. 'It's ready and snag free. I double checked it myself.'

Victoria smiled with genuine pleasure. 'Thanks Barry. We move in two weeks. I can't wait.'

It was true, she couldn't. From the moment she'd started working on the development, she knew she had to have one of the houses. It had taken a bit of persuading because her husband, Dave, didn't like change and would have been happy in their two-up two-down terrace forever. But she had lured him with the promise of a dog, something he'd always wanted but couldn't have without a garden big enough and an area where walking it was easier. She showed him the plans and took him for a stroll along the canal and by the time they ended up in the local pub; she knew she'd won him around. The next day she put their name down for the three-bedroom-semi.

Realising that the mystery woman was now inside the apartment block and beyond her vision, she turned around and walked back to the Show Home.

. . .

JENNY LOOKED out over the canal. She felt a sense of peace and calmness that had eluded her for months. Miles was right about one thing; the move had been the right thing to do. Even though it had been less than a week, she felt the house was home, especially the back room she'd turned into her retreat. She didn't think that Miles knew that she had claimed ownership. He spent the first two days in a whirl of organisation, then he went back to work and she rearranged everything how she wanted it. Since he commuted into London every day and left at six and didn't return before eight or nine in the evening, he hadn't really had time to notice.

The Victoria woman had knocked once or twice and she'd seen the odd car go past. She thought she heard the children one afternoon, presumably on their way home from school. But she had managed to avoid contact with anyone, and that suited her fine. Looking across towards the canal, she thought she might like to go for a walk, but knew that she wouldn't. Still, that the thought even existed in her head surely meant something; some tiny wish to return to the outside world. One of those baby steps that Ally talked so much about.

She heard a car pull up and knew it was Miles arriving home. Although he worked stupid hours, he always tried to keep weekends free and to him, it started with an early finish on Friday. She felt a small stirring of irritation that he would be around for the next couple of days, even though she knew she was being unfair. Once, before that awful day, six months ago, she had looked forward all week to Friday evening. They would both get home from work and discard their suits, the uniforms that made them corporate drones. Then into the shower to wash away the city grime, sometimes individually, sometimes together. Then they would order take-away and slob in front of the TV before an early night and sensuous sex.

It was like another lifetime.

'Jen?' she heard the door open and heard him call her name. She planted a fake smile on her face and walked down the stairs.

'I've got a surprise for you.'

She tried to look excited and interested, but in her experience, surprises were overrated. And she had a bad feeling about this one since he was standing by the front door, which was still open.

'Look,' he said, pointing outside and grinning like a schoolboy who'd just scored the winning goal in a football match.

From a safe distance back from the entrance, she stared out. His silver Audi was parked on the drive in front of the double width garage. Beside it was a Yellow Volkswagen Beetle. She felt her lungs constrict as the familiar fear surged through her body. Surely he didn't? Surely he wouldn't.

Apparently he did, and he had.

'For you,' he said, handing her the keys.

She wanted to be pleased and thrilled and excited. She wanted to throw herself into his arm with gratitude at his thoughtfulness. Instead, she burst into tears and ran upstairs to the back room, slamming the door shut behind her.

VICTORIA FUSSED OVER THE DOG, 'he's lovely,' she said. 'We're planning on getting a Labrador.' The couple moving in were going to be her new neighbours, and she was pleased they seemed to be friendlier than the Fishers.

'Sonia Casey, friends call me Son, and that's Paul,' she pointed to a man half hidden behind a huge potted rubber plant that he was carrying. And this...' she bent down to pet the dog, '...is Casper. He's a bit of an oldie now though, aren't you, boy. My husband's had him since he was a teenager.'

Victoria stayed and chatted for a few minutes, then excused herself when she saw a car pull into the Show Home car park. Saturday was often a busy one, and she needed all the commission she could get, what with the house move next week.

It was a flash car, a sports model of some sort. She didn't really know about cars, but she knew an expensive one when she saw it. So she hurried back down the Close.

The driver was climbing out of the car and looking around him as if he was a bit lost.

'I'm coming,' she called, waving at him.

As she approached, she saw that he was short, balding, and probably in his late fifties. He was well dressed and seemed to be in a hurry; he checked his watch and walked a few feet to meet her as though that would save time.

'I'm looking for number two, Jasmine Close,' he said.

'Really?' she replied, doubtfully.

'Yes. Why shouldn't I?' he said, defensively.

'Do you mean you want to see the plans for it?'

Now he looked confused. 'What plans?'

Victoria was pretty sure they were not on the same page with this one, so she took a different approach. 'Are you buying a property, Sir?'

'No,' he was getting impatient and looking nervous. 'I just want you to point me in the direction of number two. Is that really so difficult?'

'No, not at all,' she turned towards the building site and pointed to a plot that had just had its foundations finished. 'There, that's number two, Jasmine Close.'

He looked at the building site and then, without as much as a thank you, he trotted back to his car. Victoria saw him on his mobile as she fussed around the flower beds. Then he started the engine and drove off up the Close. She watched as he went around the corner and pulled up at the end of the cul-de-sac. He climbed out of the car and hurried to the communal door of the apartment block. He pressed the buzzer and was immediately admitted.

She didn't think of it any more until late afternoon when she was locking up, ready to go home. Just one more week and she would be a resident. She had already seen a new dining table that she wanted. They'd never had an actual dining room before and had allowed herself a brief fantasy of sitting down to family dinners. It didn't last long. In reality, she knew that her teenage daughter usually ate, either on the run, or in her room and her husband liked his on his lap with the TV on. She looked up towards her house and waved as she saw Sonia mowing the small patch of grass at the front. It was then that she noticed a man come out of the apartment block. It was another middle-aged man, but not the one she'd seen before. He walked to his car, a black hatchback of some sort, and started the engine.

Sonia's front door opened and one of her young children ran out, chased by the other. Victoria smiled as Sonia stopped mowing to deal with her offspring's argument. It was clearly something to do with a ball. Casper bounded out of the open front door to join them. One of the children grabbed the ball from the other and threw it. Casper chased after it straight into the road and the path of the hatchback, which was going much too fast for a residential street. Brakes screeched, children screamed, and both Sonia and Victoria ran towards the dog, now lying with its front paw at an odd angle.

The car drove off without even slowing down to check what had been hit. Victoria dropped to the ground beside the whimpering animal. Sonia was sobbing and cradling his head in her arms.

'I've gotta get him to the Vets.' Sonia cried.

'My husband will be along soon. He's picking me up,' Victoria said.

'No, I can't wait, but Paul's got the car...' Sonia looked frantically around.

The building site was empty; they downed tools at twelve on a Saturday. Victoria's eyes stopped at the yellow Beetle. She jumped up and ran for the front door of the Fishers' house, banging on it loudly.

'Mrs Fisher, please, we need help, we need a lift.'

JENNY HAD WITNESSED the hit from the master-suite bedroom window. She'd instinctively run for the stairs to go out and help. But her footsteps slowed as she went down towards the door. If only Miles was there, if only they hadn't argued, then he wouldn't have driven off in a huff, and he could rescue the poor dog.

The door banged again. 'Mrs Fisher, are you there?'

Jenny went down the last few steps and crossed the hall. She picked up the keys to the Beetle and even got her hand as far as the door handle. But then the shaking started; a tremble at first, but enough to make her hand fall away from the door. And then; violent, jerky movements throughout her body. The first time he saw it, Miles thought she was having an epileptic fit; he'd manhandled her into the car and driven her to A&E. But it was diagnosed as a panic attack and he'd told her she had to get a grip of herself as though that alone could cure her.

She wanted to help, she really did, but what use was she to anyone. She crossed the hall and sank down onto the bottom step and put her hands over her ears to drown out the noise of her own failure.

The banging stopped; Jenny heard the sound of running heels and an approaching car. She got up and went cautiously into the lounge. She peeped around the curtain, not wanting to be seen. The car stopped, and a man got out. From the gesturing and body language, Jenny thought it was probably the Victoria woman's husband. He lifted the dog and carried it to his car, and then they all piled in, even the kids. Luckily, it was an estate car and big enough to take them all. The driver reversed on her drive to turn around and drove out of the Close.

Drama over, she went upstairs and into the bathroom. She took a couple of pills from the mirrored cabinet and swallowed them with water from the tap, then she crawled into bed, pulling the duvet tightly around her.

It was dark when she woke. She turned over and sleepily reached across the bed. Surprised to find it empty, she opened her eyes and looked at the illuminated clock. It was three-forty-four a.m. She pushed the duvet back and realised that she was still dressed. Without bothering to put the light on, she left the bedroom and went in search of her husband. She checked the other bedrooms first, thinking that he must have slept in one of them. But she found him downstairs in his favourite recliner chair, sound asleep and snoring lightly. She felt a rare flash of love and compassion for him. He was doing his best, and more than that, he was standing by her. She went to the cupboard under the stairs and pulled out a soft fleece blanket, and returned and placed it gently around him. She bent down and kissed his forehead, then went back upstairs to bed.

The following day, Miles left early for a duty visit to his mum up north. He asked her to go with him, although it was clear he already knew her negative answer. No row this time, which was a relief, but she couldn't kid herself that the marriage could survive much more. But what could she do? She took the antidepressants the doctor prescribed. She tried to follow all the techniques that Ally had taught her. What else could she do?

Showered and dressed, she made herself coffee and toast and sat at the kitchen table. She paused, mid-bite, sure that she heard something. She listened carefully. It sounded like a man calling and it was coming from the front of the house. She went to the window and looked out. She couldn't see anything, but heard the voice again. It was definitely a man, and it sounded like he was in trouble. She ran upstairs to the bedroom and pressed her face against the window, searching the Close. And then she saw him, or at least his wheelchair. She looked again and realised that the man was on the floor between two parked cars at the end of the Close.

With no idea what to do, she looked up and down, hoping for help. But no one was about. It was too early for the Show Home and the builders didn't work on Sundays. As if some divine force wanted to crank up the dilemma for her even more, it started to rain, and not a gentle caressing shower, but a full on, black sky, cloud bursting downpour.

Drawing on all her limited reserves she ran downstairs, picked up a jacket from the hook in the hall, paused to look at herself in the mirror and chant at the stranger that stared back at her. 'I am a calm and confident woman.'

Not allowing herself time to stop and think, she pulled open the door and ran.

The pounding rain drowned out her panic. It focused her attention on helping the man and getting him dry again. He was on his side, just beyond the curb, with little space between him and the car on either side. His chair was a few feet away.

'Push it to me,' he shouted as soon as he saw her.

She grabbed the chair and pushed it as near as the cars would allow her to get. He reached out, but it wasn't close enough.

'Shit, shit, shit,' he hissed, shocking her with his anger.

'What can I do?' she asked. The trembling starting in her hands now that she was standing still and not running. 'Can I lift you?'

He gave her a bit of an 'as if' look. She knew he was right. He was a big man.

'try to drag me,' he said.

'What?'

'I need to get closer to the chair so I can lever myself into it.'

She bent down and tugged his arm. Nothing happened.

'Seriously?' he said, with more than a little impatience.

'I'm useless,' she said, the trembling turning into violent shakes. 'I'll go and ring for help.'

'No. Don't leave me.'

As she was about to do so, he grabbed her hand. He was surprisingly strong. He held it tight and looked up into her face. 'Please,' he said, as his strength and will seemed to flow into her own veins and give her courage.

He folded his arms across his chest. 'Now tuck your hands under my arms and pull.'

She had to kneel down on the road in the puddles in order to get the leverage, but it worked. She heaved, and he shifted a few inches. She moved back and repeated the process again and again until he was clear of the cars.

'Put the wheelchair next to me,' he said.

She pushed it alongside him and watched as he reached up to grab the handle. The chair slid away, and he fell back onto the dirty, wet road.

'Brakes,' he snapped.

Brakes on, he heaved himself up and into the chair, then lifted his legs with his hands into position on the footplates. He punched himself on his thigh. 'Useless fuckers,' he said, shocking her for a second time.

The wheels were large and his upper body was strong. He pushed himself around one of the cars towards the path. 'Get us up, can you?'

Jenny hurried around the car. She took the back handles and tipped the chair, putting the front wheels onto the path, then she lifted from behind and he was up and away, pushing himself forward again towards the apartments.

'You coming?' he called, making it a statement rather than a question.

Was she? The rain was slowing, the sky was clearing and her own front door looked a long way away. His door was already opening thanks to a remote device he was pressing.

She ran after him and into his home.

'Bathroom's over there if you want a towel.'

She followed the way his head pointed and went from the open-plan lounge into a large hall and opened a door to a wet room. Several big towels hung on a rail. She grabbed one and started to dry her hair, then she picked up the other and carried it in to him. He was in the kitchen making a drink.

'Tea or coffee?'

'Tea, please,' she replied, surprising herself. Why wasn't she running for home or cowering in a corner?

The units were all lowered to wheelchair height, and everything was within reach for him. 'I'm okay here,' he said, as though reading her thoughts. 'This is my safe zone, you know.'

Didn't she just. She realised she could smell something, not unpleasant, but vaguely familiar. It stirred long forgotten memories; she tried to capture the elusive images from her past, something from her time at University. Then it came to her. 'Marijuana.'

He shrugged. 'Medicinal,' he said, swinging his chair around to face her. 'Wouldn't do you any harm either. Steve…'

'Jenny,' she replied, shaking the hand he offered.

Out of the rain and safe in his home, she could see him properly for the first time. He wasn't very old, certainly younger than her, maybe mid to late twenties. She took the mug from him and shook her head at sugar. She watched as he piled three spoonfuls in his and resisted making any comment. 'What happened?' she asked, not sure if it was acceptable to do so or not.

He wheeled himself back into the lounge, his own mug of coffee on a tray on his lap. 'Some ignorant bastard parked across the lowered curb. I stupidly tried to get down between the cars, failed miserably, hit my head, cut my hand, lost the chair and all hope until I was rescued by my very own lady in red.'

She sat down and smiled at the reference to her top. 'I meant...' she looked at his legs, suddenly feeling embarrassed. 'Sorry, none of my business.'

'No, it's not, but you saved me and that makes us mates. Car accident. Some dopey bitch used my mate's car as target practice. We ended up overturned in a ditch. She apparently span a couple of times and then drove off at speed. My mate, clearly more loved by the Gods than I was, walked away with concussion and a couple of broken ribs. Me? Broken spine...' he stopped. 'What? What is it?

Jenny was sobbing, loudly and uncontrollably. 'I'm sorry, so, so sorry.'

He wheeled closer to her, 'huh?'

'So sorry,' she sobbed.

'For what? It wasn't you who was doing eighty in a sixty zone in a car you couldn't control.' He disappeared and came back with a handful of toilet tissue and a rolled up joint. He handed her the tissue and lit up the marijuana.

She blew her nose and inhaled as he smoked. The gentle aroma wafted up her nostrils and calmed the threatening hysteria. He handed it to her. She shook her head, he insisted, and she gave in.

'I killed a man,' she said, handing the joint back to him.

'Your husband?' he said, closing his eyes. 'He probably deserved it.'

'No, a car crash...' She closed her eyes and for the first time in months, she let herself return to the terrible moments. 'It was a cold and icy February morning,' she said, remembering how pretty it was with delicate snowflakes falling, but she had been in a hurry with a sales meeting to get to.

'Traffic was heavy, and I was getting impatient. I had Miles' voice in my head telling me that I should have taken the train, but I had a pile of reports and papers to take in that day and I didn't want to carry them.' She paused to wipe her eyes and blow her nose, then took a long drag on the joint before continuing.

'Of course, I knew that later, when I got home, exhausted and exasperated, complaining about the traffic, he would say, I told you so.'

'You didn't want to give him the satisfaction,' Steve said through a haze of smoke.

Jenny stood up. Her legs felt a bit wobbly and her head was spinning, but not in a panicky, unpleasant way, more like a disconnected, dreamlike state. She floated across the room and opened a window.

'I wish I had listened, though. The world would be a different place now if I had taken the train that day.'

'Playing the 'if only' game is self-indulgent shit,' he said. 'It will drive you nuts. Believe me, I know.'

She sank back down onto his sofa and looked across at him, knowing that he genuinely did know and he truly understood what she was talking about. She closed her eyes again and took herself back to the tragic story. 'Then the traffic ahead of me opened up a bit as cars filtered off towards the ring road. My lane emptied and the open road beckoned. Well, it was clear at least until the next traffic lights. I was on the inside and a car overtook me on the outside. I turned my head slightly and saw that it was a young lad driving. We both slowed as we approached the red lights and that's when it all went wrong.' Her voice faltered, new tears poured unchecked down her cheeks, her body began to shake, but she forced herself to carry on. 'A car coming in the opposite direction lost control, and it was speeding head on towards us. I swung the wheel sharply to the right to avoid the collision. If the lad had done the same, we might have both escaped uninjured. But through panic or inexperience, he swung his wheel to the left and slammed the brakes on at the same time. He smashed straight into the oncoming car and flipped over twice.'

She looked at Steve. He was watching her intently, her own pain reflected in his eyes.

'I climbed out of my car and ran towards him. His little hatchback was upside down, sitting on its bonnet and he was already dead.'

'It wasn't your fault,' he said.

'The inquest cleared me of any blame. But if I had reacted differently, swung the car to the left instead of the right, or maybe slammed the brakes harder instead of trying to avoid collision. Or...' she paused, he handed her the joint, and she took a long drag, inhaling deeply. 'If I'd simply smashed into the oncoming car.'

'That would have been head on hit and you'd be dead.'

She looked at him. 'I know. But that young lad would still be alive.'

NATASHA WAS EXHAUSTED. The baby had cried half the night and Ed had snored for the other half. The health visitor had told her that when baby did sleep, she should grab some shut-eye herself. Wise words, but then how and when was she supposed to get anything done?

She opened the washing machine door and pulled out the contents into a laundry basket. The sun was out, its rays streaming through the sliding doors. Was it warm enough to dry the clothes? The tumble dryer was so expensive and she hated having damp clothes all around the flat. She unlocked and opened the door onto the small balcony. It overlooked the building site, which wasn't ideal, but the workers weren't there today. A soft, Autumn breeze lifted her hair, and the sun was drying the rain that had fallen earlier. She could hear next door's TV. The kids were watching cartoons. She felt the irritation rise. Something about the woman really put her back up. Their sliding doors were open as well, allowing the noise from the TV to spill onto the balcony.

And not just the noise. Her nose twitched as the unmistakable stench of pot hit her nostrils. She stormed back into the flat. Her husband, Ed, had just crawled out of bed and wandered into the lounge in nothing but his boxers.

'What a night, huh?' he said, stretching his arms out wide. 'Who'd have thought something so small could make so much noise.'

'I'm reporting her.'

'What? Who?'

'Her, she's got kids in that house.'

'You mean Belle?'

'As if that's a proper name! She's smoking pot. Monday morning I'm ringing up social and reporting her.'

IN THE FLAT BELOW, Jenny closed the window and turned to smile at Steve. Her head was still spinning, and she felt a bit like she was walking on air, but it was a good feeling. 'Thanks,' she said.

He was a bit doped himself, but managed to grin back at her. 'For what? I thought you rescued me.'

'I did. But then you rescued me back again.'

'I did?'

'Yep. You listened.'

Jenny opened the front door and looked outside. The sun was shining. Her front door seemed far away, but she felt more confident than she had for months. She took the first step.

'Come and see me again,' Steve called.

'I will,' she replied, and knew that she actually meant it.

EPISODE TWO
JASMINE CLOSE - SERIES ONE

Natasha sipped her tea and let the silence wash over her. It had been another sod of a night and she was shattered. She glanced at the clock. Just five minutes, she could allow herself that, and then she would get busy. She had already filled out her To Do list beside her on the table. It took up the whole page, and she knew she could easily add more. Ed had threatened to tear up the pad, saying it dominated her thoughts. He just didn't understand.

She stood up and carried her mug and plate to the sink, ran the water, put the plug in and squirted Fairy liquid into the washing-up bowl. She heard shouts and squeals and guessed the kids' next door must be fighting. Natasha walked to the balcony. The girl was yelling for her mother at the top of her voice while the boy taunted her for being a baby. Afraid that the noise would wake Amy, she closed the balcony door, shutting out next door's chaos. The children should leave for school soon and she could open it again then.

From the small, pretty bedroom, Amy began to cry. Natasha closed her eyes and fought down her own tears. Was it really supposed to be this hard? She had been so desperate and eager to have a baby, but the reality certainly didn't live up to the lovely little fantasy she used to play in her head. She hurried to the nursery and picked Amy up, smelt the dirty nappy and immediately placed her onto the changing mat. The pink sleep suit was stained from the leaking nappy and her vest was wet. Amy's cry had turned into a full on scream and tears were streaming down Natasha's own cheeks as she struggled to cope. 'Shh, shh, Amy,' she whispered soothingly.

Deciding that wipes were not up to the task, she wrapped Amy in a towel and carried her into the bathroom. She laid the little girl on the floor and filled the baby bath. Amy stopped crying once she was in the water, and so did Natasha. She gently washed her baby and found herself smiling as Amy clutched her finger and held it tight as her chubby little legs splashed and kicked.

Ten minutes later, Amy was clean, dry, and dressed. Natasha carried the baby and the dirty washing into the kitchen. She almost slipped over and had to grab the worktop to support herself. She looked down as the wet seeped through her slippers and onto her toes. The floor was soaking wet and foaming bubbly water was pouring over the side of the sink and down the cupboards.

Natasha dropped the washing and ran for the taps. She turned them off and pulled the plug. Amy, balanced on her hip, started to cry again. She put the baby down on the sofa and hurried to the front door. There was a cupboard outside each apartment. The top door housed the meters, and the bottom one was a storage area where she kept her mop and bucket.

As she pulled the front door open, she heard her neighbours leaving the flat. Natasha closed the door, so it was only slightly open. She didn't want to see Belle or her brats, and she certainly didn't want to have to speak to them and pretend to be polite. But Amy was now howling at the top of her tiny voice and Natasha was desperate to get the water mopped up and to feed her baby.

She could see the children through the crack in the door. They were tall, mixed race, with a father that clearly wasn't around. They were twins, very similar, but not identical. The boy had his head down, staring at his phone, while his fingers clicked compulsively across the touch-screen. Game or text, she didn't know. Hurry! She screamed in her head.

'The baby's crying,' the girl said to her mother.

'It usually is,' Belle replied.

Natasha could barely breathe as her fury boiled with frustration. How dare the woman judge her? She waited and watched until the trio had trotted down the stairs and out of the building, then she dashed for the cupboard and grabbed the mop.

Placing Amy in the baby bouncer, she attacked the water on the floor and mopped and scrubbed until it was shiny and dry, and then she prepared a bottle for the baby. Amy was sobbing now. The screaming had stopped, but her little frame shook with the sobs that compounded Natasha's total failure as a mother. She held the baby tight and whispered soothing words as Amy sucked hungrily on the teat.

It was already nine o'clock. Nothing had been crossed off the list, and she was so tired she could sleep for a week. Balancing the baby with one arm, she reached across and picked up the phone. She pushed in a short number and put it to her ear.

'Yes, can you give me the number for Milton Keynes Social Services, please?' Changing her mind, she hung up and redialled. 'Police please; I want to report a drug dealer...'

JENNY IGNORED the knock on the door, but whoever it was disturbing her they were very persistent. No way was she going to talk to that Victoria woman, no matter how many times she rapped on the door or pressed the bell.

Leaving the sanctuary of her room at the back of the house, she went across the landing and into the master bedroom, where she peered out of the window. It was Steve, the young man in the wheelchair. Pleased that it wasn't Victoria, or one of the new neighbours who were gradually moving in, she left the room and went down the stairs to open the door.

'About bloody time,' Steve said with a wide grin.

'Hello, do you need rescuing again?'

'Hell yeah, I'm bored stupid. Besides, you said you'd come and see me again.'

'It's only been a few days.' Jenny said, she wasn't at all sure if she was wanted to encourage him to drop by anytime.

'Days, staring at four walls and talking to myself.'

'What? So, not only am I your rescuer, but now you want me to be your entertainments manager?'

'Yes, please.'

Jenny found herself smiling. It was hard not to do so with him, but even so, entertainment was not really her thing. Being invisible in her back room was more her style. 'Not today,' she said, attempting to close the door. But the front wheel of his wheelchair was in the way and he didn't seem in a hurry to move it.

'Let's go for a walk. Have you been along the canal?'

'Another time, I'm busy…'

'Yeah, hiding away takes a lot of time and energy.'

She opened her mouth to deny his words and defend herself. But what could she say? It was true, and they both knew it. She looked outside, beyond him. The sky was clear and blue. It was warm and sunny, a perfect September day. The terror must have shown on her face.

'Too much?' he said, more gently.

She nodded.

'Well, how about the short walk to my house? I know you can manage that.'

Could she?

He seemed to think so. 'I know what it's like to have idiots pushing you to do stuff that you aren't ready for. I had well-meaning do-gooders' queuing up at my door…'

'Really, did you?'

'Well, no, but it felt like I did! Everyone had an opinion about what I should be doing and how I should be feeling or coping. But it was all shit. The only one who could decide what's best for me was me.'

Jenny looked beyond him at the wide open world that was

Jasmine Close. She couldn't spend her whole life indoors. Surely, if he was brave enough to go out in his wheelchair, then she should have enough strength and courage to go with him. 'The canal?' she said, fighting down the fear that was lurking in the shadows of her mind.

He wheeled back to clear the doorway. 'Let's do it. Together...'

She put her shoes on and grabbed her door key and, without allowing herself time to change her mind, she stepped out beside him and closed the door behind her. 'Shall I push you?'

'Don't you dare,' he said, with feeling. 'But you can hold on to the handle if you like.

NATASHA CROSSED off two jobs from her long list. She smiled at Amy. The baby was in the bouncy chair, watching, as she dusted and vacuumed around her. If only the little girl was always this good. She put the hoover away and checked her list for the next job. Windows needed cleaning; if Amy stayed happy in her chair, she might even get a couple more finished. The sun warmed her back, and she felt some of the tension ease. She even began humming a tune.

She saw the police car drive up the Close and park next to the apartment block. A stab of sharp guilt pierced her gut. What had she done? The right thing, she told herself. It was for the kids, even if they were brats, they deserved to be free from fear. Drugs and children were never a good mix.

The police were just below her, pressing the buzzer to be let in. She made herself busy cleaning the large sliding glass doors that opened onto the balcony. Her neighbour's door was open, and she clearly heard the police enter the apartment.

'What's happened?' Belle demanded.

Natasha was surprised by the fear in the woman's voice.

'Are my children alright?'

'We've had a report that someone is dealing drugs from this apartment...'

'What? That's crap. Who would say such a thing?'

Natasha felt her face flush and rubbed harder at a barely visible smudge.

'Oh, don't tell me, let me guess...' Belle said, her voice getting louder as she moved towards the balcony.

Her neighbour's doors closed and Natasha could no longer hear Belle or the police officers.

Amy began to whimper and Natasha threw herself into cleaning the window in an attempt to get it finished before her daughter moved on to the full on screaming stage.

JENNY CLUNG onto the wheelchair as though it were some kind of a magical source of strength. If Steve had any view of her diminished mental state, he kept it to himself.

'I'm sorry,' she said, as they made their way back up the Close, the canal walk still an elusive dream.

'So you should be,' he replied. 'you owe me...'

Jenny stopped walking. 'What?'

He stopped and swung his wheelchair around to face her. 'Yep, a coffee at least, and I wouldn't say no to cake or biscuit. My place or yours?'

Her house was nearer. They were almost there already. 'I don't have any cake and not sure if there are any biscuits left,' she said. 'Miles was tucking into them last night.'

'Mine it is then.' Steve said, wheeling ahead of her so she had to run to catch up.

'Ignorant bastards should know better,' Steve said, staring at the police car with annoyance. It was parked across the lowered curb. Either he had to go back down the road to the next driveway or up the curb, which was how he got into trouble before.

'I'll push you up.'

He shook his head. 'I can do it.'

Jenny hovered uncertainly behind him as he tipped his chair back and then launched himself at the curb. For a few seconds, she was convinced he was going to topple backwards. She wondered if she was strong enough to stop him from falling back, but Steve managed to heave himself and the chair forward to safety.

'Impressive.'

'Yep, that's me, the man who can get up a four-inch curb.'

Picking up on his bitter and self-mocking tone, she stayed silent and followed him inside his house.

It was a huge relief to get indoors. The walls made her feel safe, and she knew Steve felt the same. For his brave words, the outside world provided as many terrors and challenges to him as it did to her.

'Stick the kettle on,' he said. 'That cupboard is the goodie store.'

Jenny put the water to boil and rummaged in his cupboards for coffee and sugar. The goodie cupboard lived up to its name and was stacked full of biscuits, cakes and chocolates. She picked out a packet of oaty-biscuits and a box of colourful iced cakes. 'Which ones?' she said, holding them both up.

Steve wheeled himself towards her with two joints in his mouth. 'Later.' He said, taking one out and holding it towards her.

'I shouldn't.'

'Sure you should. A celebration...'

'For what?'

'For being brave, facing the fear and all that crap.'

'Well, I didn't get far.'

He exhaled, and the unmistakable aroma reached her nostrils. He closed his eyes and his body relaxed. 'You tried,' he said. 'Can't ask for any more than that.'

'No, I guess not,' she agreed, taking the joint and settling down on his sofa.

VICTORIA WAS BORED. Her paperwork was up to date and she hadn't had a potential customer come into the Show Home all morning. She had been watching the cars come and go in the Close. One of the houses was due to complete its sale that afternoon and removal vans were expected tomorrow. She flicked through her magazine and looked up when the door opened. She was surprised when two uniformed police officers walked in. 'Hello,' she said, with her best-selling smile. She knew from several years' experience never to discount anyone as a potential buyer.

The male policeman smiled back. She guessed he was early thirties, slightly older than the young woman beside him who looked like efficiency personified.

'We're investigating a report regarding drugs misuse...'

'Drugs. Here?'

'In the Close.' The male PC added. 'Have you seen anything suspicious?'

Had she? Victoria wondered if the frequent flash cars that visited the apartment block counted. She thought probably not, and didn't want to sound stupid, so she shook her head. 'No, sorry.'

The policeman handed her a card. 'Give me a call if you do hear or see anything.'

'PC Clarke,' she said, reading from the card. He smiled again, and she fleetingly wished she was a few years younger and single again. Then shook the thought away as nonsense. Sure, he had eyes the colour of melted chocolate and a smile that could thaw a snowman, but she was a happily married woman. 'How would I know?'

'Know what?' he responded.

'Well, what would count as suspicious? I mean, I don't suppose deals are anything like on the telly when young lads in hoodies look furtively around before swapping dosh for drugs.'

The young woman rolled her eyes, but PC Clarke flashed her another one of his super smiles. 'Anything that strikes you as odd or strange, give me a call.'

Victoria tucked the card into her jacket pocket and peered out of the window, watching them as they walked up the Close and back to their car. Ten more minutes and she could shut up the Show Home and take her lunch break. Often, she didn't bother, but she felt like a walk and a bit of air. Besides, it wouldn't hurt to have a little look around. Not that she really expected to find a syringe in the bushes, but in a few days she would be moving in and she didn't want her daughter exposed to such criminal activity.

. . .

JENNY WAS AWAY with the fairies, as her mother used to say. Her body was limp and totally relaxed. Her pain, fear and ever present guilt belonged to someone else now. She was free and floating in a dream-like state where stress and anxiety had no place and the only noise was the hammering in her head. The banging was an intrusion, and she flinched and screwed up her eyes against the unwelcome noise.

It ended finally, and she became aware of other sounds, voices and footsteps. Then someone was shaking her by the shoulders and, with huge reluctance, she forced her way through the shadows and back into full consciousness.

Jenny opened her eyes and looked into the not very friendly face of a young woman. A few seconds later, she realised that the woman was a uniformed police officer who introduced herself as PC Lipton. She sat up straight and saw that Steve was being quizzed by a male policeman.

'I told you it's medicinal. You try being stuck in one of these...' Steve hit the side of his wheelchair. 'See how you like it.'

'I understand that, Mr Lance, but we have had reports that someone is dealing in these apartments and that is a serious offence.'

'I've never dealt drugs in my life. It's just for me to take away the pain and make my shit of a life a bit more bearable.'

The female PC turned around to face him. 'And what about her?' she said, pointing at Jenny. 'Did she bring her own weed to this little house party?'

Jenny suddenly realised that all eyes were focused on her, and they were expecting her to speak. She opened her mouth, but the only sound that came out was more like a squeak and certainly wasn't coherent.

'Haven't you got any real criminals to catch?' Steve snapped.

'Drug dealers are very real,' the woman said.

Jenny had the impression the young female policewoman didn't like Steve much. PC Clarke put a calming hand on his colleague and walked across to Jenny.

'Are you alright?' he asked.

She nodded and smiled, although she had a feeling it came out as more of a silly grin.

PC Clarke walked back to Steve and nodded. 'Be a bit more considerate of the neighbours...' he pointed to the open window. 'There are children in the flats above you. And from now on, make sure that you keep it for your personal use only.'

The two men looked at each other, the woman tutted with annoyance.

'Have you got a problem with me?' Steve demanded.

PC Clarke cast a warning gaze her way. 'No, she hasn't.'

PC Lipton bent down to Jenny and touched her shoulder. 'Stay away from him,' she said quietly, her voice barely more than a whisper. 'Don't let him drag you down with him.'

The two officers left and Jenny struggled to her feet, swaying slightly as though she were on a boat and trying to find her sea legs. 'Think we'd better have that coffee now?'

NATASHA NEEDED FORMULA. She thought she had another tub in the cupboard, but she couldn't find it anywhere. There wasn't enough to last until the morning, so they would have to walk to the chemist. She did toy with the notion of texting Ed to fetch it after work, but if he forgot or picked up the wrong one, then they would have an even unhappier baby than usual. With Amy tucked under one arm and the pushchair folded up under the other, she hurried down the steps and out of the apartment block.

With one hand, she opened up the pushchair and placed Amy inside. She was just strapping her in when the door opened and Belle came out.

'Who do you think you are, making up stories...?'

Natasha stood up and looked at her neighbour coldly. 'I was thinking of your children. Maybe you should be doing the same.'

Belle flew at Natasha, pushing her. 'You cheeky bitch!'

Natasha was so shocked she lost her footing and fell backwards, crashing into the door of the downstairs flat. She managed to save herself from landing on her bottom and steadied herself. But then the door behind her opened inwards, and she tumbled into the apartment, landing on her back and staring up into the surprised faces of the man in the wheelchair and the woman from the big house down the road.

'Come in, why don't you...' he said, curiosity and sarcasm in his voice.

She scrambled to her feet. 'Sorry,' she mumbled, hurrying back out to the pushchair. Amy was thankfully unaffected by the altercation and was looking around her contentedly.

'What's going on?' The wheelchair man asked, following her out.

'She attacked me.'

'This spiteful skank called the cops on me,' Belle said and then added. 'With vicious lies.'

'What's going on, Steve?' The woman from down the road asked, sticking her head out of the apartment door.

'You called the police?' Steve said, staring at Natasha accusingly. 'Why would you do that?'

'She was smoking dope with kids in the flat. It's not right...'

'Liar!' Belle stepped threateningly close. 'I've never touched drugs.'

Natasha held her position.

'What's going on?' Victoria said, hurrying towards them.

Belle waved her finger at Natasha. 'Keep out of my business.'

'Mine too,' Steve added, staring at her crossly. 'Actions have consequences, you know.'

Natasha picked up the buggy with her daughter still inside it and hurried back into the apartment. She almost dropped the pushchair as she tried to open the door. Victoria rushed forward and held it for her. She carried it upstairs and put it down to unlock her door, dashing in before the ever ready tears came rushing back again.

. . .

'That was mean,' Victoria said to Steve and Belle. 'Ganging up on the poor girl like that.'

'What does she expect? She set the police on me.' Belle replied, before walking away.

Steve turned in his wheelchair and went back into his apartment, leaving Victoria alone on the path. She saw Jenny Fisher hovering in the doorway and thought, what an unlikely alliance they made. Hardly compatible friend material, but then what did she know? She couldn't make the woman out at all and as for him, well, that was the longest conversation she'd ever had with him.

Victoria walked across the Close to the building site. It was lunchtime, and the workers had downed tools and were congregated around their vans, munching on sandwiches and drinking strong tea from thermos flasks. One of the younger lads whistled as she approached. His name was Tom, and he was obviously an outrageous flirt.

'Knock it off,' Barry said, smiling at Victoria. 'I was going to pop and see you in a bit. Can you come and have a look at the phase two plans with me? I just want to double check which ones have been sold off plan.'

'Yeah, no problem. Have you got a key to the apartments...' she said, pointing across the Close.

Barry dug into his pocket. 'Here. I need it back, though; the lighting in the hall is still messed up. I think they'll have to rewire part of it.'

'I'll bring it straight back,' she said, taking the key and walking away.

Victoria let herself in to the block through the communal doors and went up the stairs. She tapped on the door and waited. She could hear the baby screaming, so she knocked harder. After a few seconds, the door opened a crack and the young woman, Natasha Jones, looked at her suspiciously.

'May I come in?'

For several long seconds, Victoria thought the door was about to be closed in her face. 'Please,' she added gently.

The door opened properly, and Victoria followed Natasha into the apartment. It was large and light and absolutely immaculate. The baby was still crying, despite the mother's attempts to soothe her. On the coffee table was a list with a big bold heading TO DO at the top and a page full of jobs with only the top four crossed off.

'Is she teething?'

Natasha looked surprised, as though the thought hadn't occurred to her. 'She's only four months.'

'My daughter was cutting her second by then.'

'Really?' she said, doubtfully.

'Oh yes. I had to stop feeding at three months because she used to use me as a teething ring. Look how red her cheeks are.'

'I thought that was the heat.'

'Yeah, probably a bit of that as well. Have you got any teething rings?' Victoria could tell the answer was no. Her sympathy, already stirred, went into overdrive. She guessed the woman was late teens, only a few years older than her own daughter. Didn't she have support? Partner or parents? Victoria didn't feel she could ask. 'Put your finger in her mouth; see if you can feel anything...'

Natasha ran her finger over the baby's gums and looked at Victoria in surprise. 'It feels rough.'

Victoria smiled.

'I've got Calpol. Would that help her?' Natasha went to her kitchen cupboard and pulled it open. It was as tidy and organised as the rest of the house.

'Shall I hold her for you?' Victoria said, holding her arms out. Natasha handed her Amy. It felt strange and slightly exhilarating to hold a baby again after so many years. She cuddled the infant tight against her and rocked gently side to side. The crying eased to a whimper and Natasha fed the baby the medicine through a dropper.

Natasha took Amy back again, and the baby started to cry.

Victoria could see that the young mother was close to breaking point. 'She'll settle when the medicine takes effect. Maybe when she goes to sleep, you should have a quick nap yourself. It is exhausting dealing with a teething baby.'

'I will.'

Victoria knew the words were empty and the minute baby Amy went to sleep, Natasha would be ironing or cleaning. There was nothing she could do to help, and she had to get back to work. She paused at the door and made one last attempt. 'I'm moving into the Close at the weekend. My daughter is almost sixteen and available for babysitting if you want a break anytime.'

'Thanks,' Natasha said, her hand on the door ready to shut her out the minute she crossed the threshold.

Victoria walked down the stairs and out of the building. Barry waved at her, so she crossed the Close and handed him the key back.

'Everything alright?' he asked.

'Yes, of course,' she said, wishing it were true for Natasha and her baby. 'I've got ten minutes before I have to open the Show Home again. What is it you want me to look at?'

'Let me grab the plans,' Barry said. 'I'll meet you over there.'

The phase two building site was behind the apartment block, so rather than walk through the building site which would require a hard hat; she crossed the Close to go around the flats on the residential side. There was a pathway that ran between the apartment block and the first house in a row of four terraced properties. A red Porsche roared up the Close and stopped at the end of the cul-de-sac. She paused at the edge of the path and watched as the driver climbed out. He was a smartly dressed middle-aged-man who was short, overweight and with far too much hair that looked suspiciously like a wig. He didn't even glance her way, just walked briskly to the apartment doors and pressed the intercom.

Unfortunately, she couldn't see which buzzer he pressed. He didn't speak at all. The door clicked open, and he pushed it and disappeared from her view and into the block.

Victoria walked up the path. It went nowhere, just an overgrown wilderness, but she knew that eventually, it would lead to the new houses, a small play park and the community centre. She had seen the artist's impressions of the architect's plans, hard to visualise now as she looked around the wasteland. In a week or two, the area would be cleared, ready for the initial work to begin. She dodged a wasp as it buzzed around her head. It was lazy and slow as they are in Autumn. Something caught her attention. She stood still and listened, a yelping noise, an animal in distress. The grass was very long, and it was hard to see much at all. She followed the sound further into the undergrowth.

'Bugger,' she hissed, as her tights caught on a bramble.

'Vic?'

Barry approached from the opposite side of the apartment block. 'You alright? Stay there, I'll come to you.'

'Listen,' she said, standing still and trying to isolate the sound of the animal.

'Bloody wasps, think you would have seen the last of 'em a couple of weeks ago. Reckon there's a nest, so watch yourself.'

'Can't you hear it? It's an animal. I think it's hurt.'

Barry listened, and the yelping sound came again. 'Might be a fox.' He said. 'Mind it doesn't bite you, it could have rabies.'

'Rabies! We don't have that here.'

'You say that, but I watched a documentary...'

'Barry!'

'What?'

'Shush!'

Victoria edged closer. She was behind the apartment block and working her way carefully through the waist high grass and brambles.

'Bloody shush me, woman...' Barry mumbled, as he made his way towards her.

Victoria knew him well enough to know that he wasn't really upset. This was the second site they had worked on together. Victoria's foot slipped down a hole and she cried out in pain. Barry ran towards her and supported her while she pulled her foot out. He peeled back the grass to reveal a deep crevice several inches wide. She eased her foot out and tested it, wriggling it carefully before trying to stand on it again. 'I'm okay,' she said, with relief.

'It's this mini heat wave and lack of rain. It's a sod in Milton Keynes. We don't have dirt. The whole city is built on clay.'

'Listen,' she said, bending down. 'It's coming from down there.'

Barry knelt down and peered into a hole, and then he stuck his arm down, wriggled it around a bit as the yelping became louder.

'What is it?'

Barry lifted his arm up from the hole, and a furry face was pulled through.

'It's a kitten,' Victoria said, as the rest of the animal was eased out of the hole.

Barry looked at the crying, wriggling scrap of fur. 'Don't know if it is. I reckon it's been stuck there a while, might be older than you think.' He handed it to her.

'It's probably full of fleas,' he said cheerfully, standing up straight and ruffling its chin.

'Poor little thing,' Victoria said, holding it close and hoping he was wrong about the fleas. 'I wonder if it's been chipped...'

Barry didn't answer; he had his back to her and was staring in the open French doors of apartment number two.

'Barry, that's an invasion of privacy,' she said, tapping his arm.

'What the...' he stopped himself short of the expletive and turned his head to face her.

Unable to resist, Victoria glanced across at the apartment and her mouth opened in surprise. The man from the Porsche was stripped naked and attached to some wooden contraption that looked like a piece of medieval torture kit. 'Do we call the police?'

Barry shook his head.

'But he's in trouble.'

'Of his own making, I think. Look...'

A woman appeared from another room. She was tall, scantily dressed, with stripper shoes and holding a whip.

Barry shook his head. Whether in sympathy or envy, Victoria wasn't sure. She turned around and hurried back towards the path, clutching the kitten that was now purring loudly in her arms. Back at the front of the building, she turned to the foreman who had followed her. 'What do we do?'

He shrugged his shoulders.

'Very helpful.'

'Better get the cat checked out by a vet,' he said. 'I'd better get back to work. We'll have a look at the plans tomorrow.'

Victoria walked down the Close back to the Show Home. She was late opening, her tights were ruined and her arms were itchy. As if that wasn't enough, in a few days, she was moving into her dream house on a lovely new estate with a drug problem and a flat offering kinky sex.

She carried the cat into the kitchen and opened the back door. She set it down on the patio and poured a drop of milk into a saucer, placing it beside the animal.

'What have I done?' she said, with feeling.

BELLE STOOD outside the school gates and tried to relax. It was no good getting all paranoid again. Just because the police had been round didn't mean anything. She hadn't been charged; they hadn't taken her picture, and there was no reason why her identity would be uncovered. The male PC had been kind and sensible and clearly believed that she was telling the truth. It was the other one, PC Lipton, who could have caused the trouble. Suggesting a visit from Social Services just to check she was coping.

She nearly screamed at the woman to keep her nose out and leave them alone. But she had managed to keep calm and sound reasonable. She was pretty sure that PC Clarke would keep his colleague in check.

Belle looked around her, checking that all the faces were familiar. She was very observant and had a great memory. A stranger at the gate would always make her wary, but today there were none. Still, she felt unsettled, and thought that maybe she should start looking for a new place to live. The thought filled her with dread; her poor kids had been moved around the country from school to school. It wasn't fair. They liked Milton Keynes and had settled in well, especially since they got the lovely new flat. If only that silly cow next door had kept out of their lives.

She forced herself to smile as her daughter, Tamsin, ran towards her. 'Where's your brother?' she asked, more sharply than she meant to.

'He's coming,' Tamsin said. 'His phone was confiscated, so he had to go and get it back after class.'

Belle smiled brightly and waited until her son, Kyle, came out, head down, engrossed in some game.

Later that evening, as she was putting them to bed, Tamsin looked up at her with big brown eyes that really had seen too much pain for one so young. 'I like it here Mummy,' she said.

Belle turned the light out and went to close the door.

'Not all the way, Mummy.'

She left it slightly open and went around the apartment, checking for about the tenth time since they got in that everything was shut and locked and completely secured. All she wanted was to be left alone so that she and the children could be safe. Was that really too much to ask for?

EPISODE THREE
JASMINE CLOSE - SERIES ONE

Victoria looked at the vet. She was a young black woman who barely seemed old enough to be qualified. The cat looked ready to bolt and was hunched down with the Vet holding it firmly by the scruff of the neck.

'It isn't chipped and has no collar or name tag. It is a neutered male, undernourished, but otherwise unhurt. I've given him a jab of antibiotics, and this cream is to rub on his swollen lip.'

The vet looked at her expectantly.

She reached out to take the cat. 'Thanks,' she said, not at all sure what to do with the animal. 'Any idea how I can find the owners?'

'Put a description on our notice board; circulate it with RSPCA and the Cat Protection League. Although, I think you'll be lucky to get a response, without a microchip, it's very hard to match animal and owners.'

The vet was holding the door open. Victoria felt a bit disappointed, although she wasn't really sure why or what she had expected. Carrying the cat, she went back to reception with the intention of doing a card for the board. But a small, mean looking dog barked at the ball of fluff in her arms. The cat did a flying leap behind the counter, went under the receptionist's chair and hissed at anyone who tried to coax it out.

'Doesn't seem to like you much.' The middle-aged receptionist said, looking at her suspiciously, while she knelt on the floor and made soothing noises. 'Perhaps you'd like to settle the bill while you wait for kitty to come out of hiding.'

Victoria stood up and dusted her skirt down. She lived by the principle that if you worked in sales, then your appearance was important. Looking smart told the potential customer that you took pride in yourself and the job. She had to be at work in twenty minutes and the dusty cat fluff look was not the one she was aiming for!

'Fifty-five pounds and fort-six pence, please.'

'How much?'

'Fifty-five...'

'No, I heard you; I just can't quite believe it.'

The receptionist raised an eyebrow; it needed plucking and looked like a caterpillar going uphill. The mental image made Victoria giggle; she stifled it and rummaged in her handbag for her purse.

'It's not even my cat,' she muttered, annoyed. 'Isn't there some kind of fund for treating injured strays?'

'Oh yes. We'd never let an animal suffer.'

'Great, so I don't have to pay then?'

Now both eyebrows did a dance. They really were extraordinary. 'Of course you have to pay.'

'But he's a stray. He's not my cat.'

The receptionist pressed a few keys on the computer keyboard in front of her and looked at the screen. 'Mrs Pickles, you rang up yesterday evening and booked an appointment for this morning. That doesn't sound like an emergency with a stray to me.'

'I rescued him yesterday, but by the time I finished work and was able to telephone, you had no free appointments. This was the first time slot you had available.'

'Even so, here he is, registered on our computer as your cat.'

'I looked after him last night, that's all; he doesn't even have a name.'

'Commendable, I'm sure; I suggest that you get him insured to save you the embarrassment of struggling to pay next time you bring him in.'

'I'm not struggling to pay,' Victoria snapped, her temper threatening to blow. 'I'm resenting paying. There's a difference.'

A queue was forming behind her, and various owners and pets were getting restless. Victoria was pretty sure she wasn't going to win this one, so she removed her debit card from her purse and shoved it into the payment machine, silently praying that she did have enough money in the account. She would hate to see the receptionist's smug expression if it was declined. Besides, then she would have to pay the bill on her credit card and her husband Dave would spot it and demand to know what it was. He hated cats and claimed that he was allergic. She'd got away with hiding the animal last night because it was her husband's darts evening, which was code for the weekly piss up with the lads. He stumbled home and straight to bed and was still snoring when she got up and left the house that morning with the cat under her arm.

She entered her pin and showed no sign of relief when approved flashed on the screen. The receptionist gave her a look that she was sure was mocking her. With as much confidence and flair as she could manage, given the circumstances, she walked around the counter, bent down until her head was under the receptionist's chair and level with the fluffy face of the animal and said. 'Time to go, cat,' in her firm voice, not used since her daughter was a child. Green eyes stared back at her and then the cat crawled out of its hiding place and into her arms.

Victoria was very glad she didn't have far to drive since the cat was on the prowl and being very distracting to her. Luckily, the traffic was light, and it only took her ten minutes to make the trip back to the Show Home. It still made her ten minutes late, though, which was annoying, as she hated not being on time for anything, even work. She parked the car and opened the door; the cat leapt across her lap and onto the gravel car park. He ran for the bushes by the street sign and settled down underneath it.

Victoria climbed out of the car and smiled at the young woman taking photos of the Show Home.

'Hello Sasha, you're early. Thought you were coming this afternoon?'

Sasha was one of the junior reporters on the local paper, the MK Herald. Victoria had been pushing for a feature about the new housing site, and Sasha had reluctantly agreed to come along to see her.

'I was passing. I'll take some shots, but like I said on the phone, I can't promise anything, Victoria. We have new housing sites throwing editorials at us all the time and, without a new angle, it doesn't really register as news.'

Victoria unlocked the Show Home and walked in. She knew Sasha was right, but the very fact that there were so many other new sites was why she had to try. A feature would make her development stand out and that might mean potential sales, meaning more commission for her.

'People are moving in now,' she said to Sasha, who followed behind her. 'Want a coffee?'

'No thanks, I can't stop, I've got to get to the shopping centre. Someone has stolen one of the Concrete Cows.'

'Why? It's not like you can sell it on eBay.'

Sasha shrugged her shoulders. 'Publicity stunt maybe, or a dare. Who knows?'

'One of my apartments is fully adapted for the disabled and a young guy in a wheelchair has moved in…'

Sasha looked vaguely interested.

'And an elderly lady is moving into the one next door this morning.' She offered hopefully.

Sasha shook her head. 'Sorry, Victoria, but Social Housing is not a new story, all new-builds have them. I'll take a couple more pictures before I go, then we have them ready if a newsworthy story presents itself.'

Victoria put the coffee percolator on and then went back outside. Sasha was leaning down, fussing the cat.

'Not yours, I assume?'

Victoria shook her head. 'No, but the little bugger just cost me almost sixty quid.'

'How come?'

Victoria explained how she and Barry rescued him from the deep ditch. She left out the bit about the going's on in Flat number two, which was not the kind of attention the site needed.

'Poor little mite,' Sasha said, fussing over the purring animal. 'So no chip and no report of a missing cat like him?'

'Nope, and no one to pay for his Vets fees or upkeep.'

'You'll have to give him a name,' Sasha said.

The Show Home phone started to ring. 'Better get that,' Victoria said. 'Thanks for coming out.' She dashed into the office and picked up the phone. It was an investor enquiring about buying a couple of properties from Phase Two.

GEMMA SIGNED out of school and hurried towards the bus stop. It was a risk. The secretary could decide to check with her mum that she really did have a dentist's appointment, but that was unlikely. She was pretty good at forging her mum's signature. The note looked authentic, and she was fairly confident she would get away with it. She wasn't a habitual bunker, so the school would have no reason to doubt her.

Alex had offered to pick her up, but she knew too many people around the school that could see her. Not only staff and teachers, but her friend's parents, or even her parent's friends. So it was agreed that she would get a bus to the dentists and he would pick her up from there.

The bus arrived almost immediately, and she climbed on and paid her fare. Some drivers would see the uniform and question why she was leaving the school. But not this one. He was hot and fat and bored and clearly couldn't give a stuff who got on his bus or why. She walked to the back and settled herself in the corner. She got her phone out and texted, - TEN MINUTES – then she took her tie off and undid a couple of the buttons on her blouse. She pulled the bobble from her hair and made herself busy with make-up. It was a shame she couldn't ditch the uniform altogether. She had considered going home to change first, but it was her dad's day off and besides, she had to go and see her mum later that afternoon to look at the new house. Whilst she could probably get past her father with some story, her mum was another matter altogether. So the uniform stayed on and she had until around four o'clock to spend with Alex.

She had no idea where he would take her. She'd only been out with him a couple of times and this would be the longest time that they had spent together. He was older; obviously, all the lads her age were losers. Alex had a job and a car. Her friends were beside themselves with envy.

'You know he'll want sex.' Abby had said.

'Yeah, I know,' she'd replied. She'd thought about pretending it was no big deal. But Abby was her best friend, and they told each other everything, so Abby knew that for her it would be the first time. But that was okay. She was ready. She was fifteen. Lots of the girls had already done it and one from her class even had a baby.

It might as well be with Alex. She saw him waiting for her. He was standing by his car, smoking. She got up as the bus slowed for the stop; her stomach was quivering as though a hundred tiny butterflies had just emerged from their cocoons. She stepped off the bus and looked across at him; he looked her up and down and smiled. She'd been checked out before, but with him it was different and she felt her cheeks flush with pleasure, excitement and anticipation.

VICTORIA WAVED as Sonia came out of her house, the two young children trailing behind her, two boys, Adam and Joshua. She didn't know their ages, but knew they were both preschool and from what she'd seen of them, they were a bit of a handful.

'When do you move in?' Sonia asked.

'Saturday,' Victoria replied 'I've got a couple of days off to get packed.'

'Oh, the worst bit.'

'Yep, still at least this house is bigger, must be a nightmare to downsize.'

'You looking forward to moving into the Close?'

'I am. My husband is still a bit hesitant, he'll come round. It's my Gemma that's the worry; she really doesn't want to move.'

'Kids adapt. How old is she?'

Victoria smiled as she thought about her daughter. 'Fifteen.'

'Oh, one of them,' Sonia said, with a serious expression that quickly broke into laughter. 'A teenager!'

'Yeah, you're not wrong there. Although, aside from the not wanting to move bit, we don't have many problems. She's a good girl.'

Sonia didn't look convinced. 'Show me a teenage girl who's good and I'll show you a very clever liar.'

Victoria was shocked and shook her head.

'Just kidding,' Sonia said, unlocking the car and pulling the door open for the children to climb in. 'I'm sure your Gemma is a little angel.'

Victoria watched as the woman drove away, feeling a little unsettled. Of course, her daughter was no angel, but she knew her daughter and Gemma was a sensible girl. No way would she get herself into the kind of mischief that the papers were full of. Loud music, a bit of back-chat and hormonal outbursts. That was the extent of her daughter's terrible teens.

She waited to cross the road to see Barry. A removals van drove past, heading to the apartment block. She watched it park at the end of the Close and then looked down as the cat rubbed against her legs. 'Hello, you,' she said. 'I suppose we will have to find you a name.'

The construction site was fairly empty. She looked around her and spotted Barry at the far end. He was talking on the phone and sounded a bit irritated, not at all his usual jovial self.

'You all right?' she asked, walking towards him as he finished his call.

'Construction politics,' he said, shoving the phone in his pocket. 'I guess it's the same in every industry. Sometimes, I think the only way to get a bit of peace in life is to escape to a deserted island.'

'Don't really see you as the Robinson Crusoe type.'

'I can grow a beard. You can come if you like. Be my man-Friday.'

'Tempting, but no, think I'll stick with Jasmine Close.'

'You're probably right. Besides, I get motion sick just staring at the sea, so a small island isn't really the answer.'

'So where is everyone?' Victoria asked. 'You haven't had a health and safety inspection?'

'No, thank God,' Barry said, with feeling.

Victoria understood his fear. A surprise visit often resulted in a site shut down for some violation or other. Nearly always something stupidly preventable, like one of the lads not wearing a hard hat or high vis jacket. Or some protocol or paperwork not dealt with correctly. Barry badgered the building crew constantly about safety, even so, there was always someone who thought the rules didn't apply to them.

'It's Phase Two plot that's the trouble.'

'But I thought that wasn't due to start work until next month?'

'It's not, but I stupidly sent a couple of the lads with diggers round to make a start on the scrub area. That was it. Word got around and suddenly the whole crew is finding stuff to do there.'

Victoria frowned. She didn't get it.

'The floor show, in Flat Two...' Barry said.

She still didn't really get it.

'Half-naked, pretty strumpets, flashing their bits and indulging in hanky-panky with no interest in privacy or modesty.'

Victoria thought about the middle-aged-man on the torture wheel and shuddered. She looked over at the apartment block and saw a very nice Audi parked outside. The occupier certainly had a lot of visitors. 'You don't think...'

Barry nodded vigorously. 'Indeed, I do.'

'A brothel?' She hardly dared say it out loud; it seemed impossible, and so shocking, that such a thing would be happening there, on her lovely new estate.

'Either that, or it's a film set for a porno channel.' He scratched his head and looked older than fifty-five, the age she knew him to be. 'I believe in live and let live...'

'Now you sound like a Bond movie.'

'All right then, live and let shag, but I don't know how I'm supposed to get these houses finished on time if my workers are otherwise entertained.'

'I'll see if I can find out who owns it. I think it might be a regular investor and I don't suppose they know what's going on.'

Barry nodded his thanks and walked away, presumably to try to prise his workers away from the free peep show.

Victoria still had ten minutes before she had to be back at work, so decided to say hello to the new occupant in Flat One. All she knew was that an elderly lady was moving in.

Careful to avoid the remaining puddles from last night's downpour, she started to cross the road then jumped back quickly as a motorbike roared round the bend, straight through the puddle which sprayed all up her legs and suit, spattering her with dirty, muddy splashes.

The cat had sensibly leapt back away from the road and remained dry and clean, but Victoria was soaked.

MARY MARTIN LOOKED around her and wanted to cry.

She wouldn't, of course, no point in tears. They changed nothing.

'It's lovely, Mum. See, told you there was nothing to worry about.'

Mary wanted to retort, 'you live here, then.' But she didn't. She kept quiet. Her daughter-in-law was annoying, patronising, and she suspected not terribly bright, but her son loved the woman for some unfathomable reason and so that made her family and family was important.

'Did you hear me, Mum...?' Candice said, louder and slower, as though addressing a child.

'Yes,' she forced herself to reply. 'Lovely.'

'I'll put the kettle on, shall I? I made sure that everything we need for a nice cuppa is in my car...'

Mary wondered if a bottle of brandy was also in the car because that's what she really wanted, but no point telling Candy Bar that. She smiled to herself. Candy Bar, was the name Oliver, her Great Grandson, had named his aunt, because in his words. 'She's sweet to start with, but then you stuff your face and it makes you sick.'

'See, there's that smile. Tea will be ready in a tick and then I'll make sure the van is unloaded properly and help get you settled. I've told Jim not to expect me home anytime soon; he can sort his own dinner out tonight.'

Candy Bar left the room, still rattling on about the rubbish that made Mary want to scream. She knew she was an ungrateful cow, but felt one of the privileges of age was being grumpy. Getting to your eighty-eighth year had to count for something.

A woman tapped on the open front door and entered, calling, 'hello,' without waiting for an invitation. Mary was about to tell her to get lost when she saw the scruffy cat following behind. It looked rough, like life had been a trial, and immediately her face broke into a smile. She leant down and petted the animal, which responded by purring loudly.

'Hello and welcome,' the woman said. 'I'm Victoria, from the Show Home.'

'Hello, Victoria from the Show Home, and who's this?'

Victoria looked at the cat and shook her head. 'Not sure really, we rescued him from a ditch and he's trailed along behind me ever since.'

'No name? No owner?' Poor little thing, Mary thought, dumped on an estate where he doesn't want to be, just like her. Mary looked at the woman in front of her. She guessed her to be late thirties, still trim, and obviously kept herself in shape. She was groomed and wearing a suit and would be very smart apart from the stains splattered all over her. 'Looks like you've been in a mud flight and lost.'

Victoria glanced down at herself. 'Sorry for my appearance, don't know about a mud fight, but I'd certainly like to get my hands on the bastard on the bike who did this.'

'Someone say my name?'

Mary smiled from the inside out, as her whole body cheered up. 'Jack, I wasn't expecting you.' She would never admit to having favourites, not even to herself, but her grandson, Jack, would be a close contender if she did. He so reminded her of her late husband, another Jack, who never took life too seriously and knew how to make everyone around them feel special.

'Hello, Gran,' he said, bending down to kiss her cheek. 'So this is the dungeon the family has condemned you to is it?'

Mary nodded her head vigorously. 'It's dark enough to be a bloody dungeon.'

'These really are lovely apartments,' the Show Home woman said, sounding offended. 'They have been built with sustainability and conservation in mind. The heating bills will be very...'

'Enough,' Mary said, unable to stand the lecture any longer.

Jack looked at the Victoria woman and favoured her with one of his smiles. 'Don't be offended,' he said. 'Gran lived in her home for fifty years and was a bit reluctant to leave it. This could be a palace and she'd still be a bit unhappy and unsettled.'

Mary watched as the woman's stance softened slightly. Jack was a charmer; it was a gift and a curse. Over the years, he had many girlfriends, not that he ever paraded his conquests in front of her, but she heard the stories from the family. But it was all so easy for Jack. The grass always seemed greener as soon as the next pair of long legs and firm breasts were in front of him.

It would take a special female to tie him down. She smiled to herself; he was so like his granddad. She realised the pair were looking at her expectantly.

'I was just telling Victoria that you and Grandpa were married for almost sixty years...'

'That's amazing,' Victoria replied, glancing up at him through her mascara.

'Yes, well, all good things come to an end,' she said, refusing to let sadness drag her into melancholy.

'He died last year,' Jack said.

Mary wanted to send the woman packing. Jack was there to see her, not Show Home lady.

'You must miss him terribly.' The woman said.

'I do. I miss the sex.'

'Gran!'

Mary smiled at Jack, who shook his head at her in mock irritation. It was worth it to see the look of shock on Show Home lady's face, and it did the trick.

'I'd better get back.'

Jack walked her to the door and Mary heard him as he said. 'Don't mind her; she's trying to shock you. She'll settle in here once her pictures are up and the furniture is in.'

Mary didn't hear the reply as they went out of the room. Would she settle in? She wasn't so sure; to her, it seemed like God's waiting room. She had been sent there to die. The house, that lovely old cottage that was full of memories, was sold and the money was stashed in the bank. This was where she was supposed to fade quietly away, but the mischief within her stirred. She wasn't ready. True, she missed her Jack, and wanted to join him, but heaven could wait. She was going to have a bit of fun and create some chaos before she headed for the pearly gates.

She looked down as the cat purred and rubbed against her legs. 'See, I've made one friend already.'

VICTORIA WALKED BACK to the Show Home. The car park was empty, sales were slow. The call from the investor earlier wasn't great; he said the incentives weren't good enough to tempt him. It was a pity that the paper wouldn't do a feature. The site needed a boost, and so did her bank balance. She glanced at her watch. It was almost four. Gemma should be popping in soon to have a look at the house. She really wanted her daughter on-side. It was a good move for all of them, yet she was the only one who thought so. Dave could be a lazy git sometimes and she knew that his reluctance was mainly down to a dose of can't be bothered-ness. But she thought her daughter would enjoy the new, bigger house and didn't understand the lack of interest.

In the Show Home she tried to tidy herself up a bit, but rubbing the splattered mud made it worse, and her tights were beyond saving. She pulled them off and washed her legs. She didn't really approve of bare legs with a suit, but it was a better look than the mud. She had a spare blouse hanging in the wardrobe. She knew how easy it was to spill a mug of coffee or bite into a doughnut and watch the jam drop onto your top. Not that she would ever buy them, but Barry had a fondness for sugary cakes and would sometimes buy a bag and insist that she join him. So she changed into the clean top and looked in the mirror. Nothing more she could do. The mud on her skirt was now smudged rather than splats, and her jacket was pebble-dashed with brown flecks and water marks.

She felt the anger simmering inside towards the biker, but to be fair, he had apologised when they were outside of the apartment, and he did have an amazing smile. But sorry and a smile don't dry clean clothes or magic away muddy marks. With a final look in the mirror, she left the bedroom and went downstairs. She heard the door open and placed her welcome smile on her lips.

'Hi, Mum,' her daughter said, waving her hand and grinning like she was a hamster with a shoehorn in its cheeks.

'Alright?' she asked, looking at her daughter suspiciously. She was so used to the whole sulky, surly or bored indifference routine that bright and bubbly suggested something was wrong.

'Of course,' Gemma replied. 'So which one is our house, then?'

Victoria locked up the Show Home and led her daughter down the Close to the three-bed semi-detached property that they were moving into in three days' time.

'Looks nice,' Gemma said.

It was the first time her daughter had seen the actual house. She had been with them the first time Dave came along to the site, but other than the show-homes, the whole area had been a building site. They had looked around the Show Home and chosen a plot from the plans.

Victoria unlocked the door and led her daughter in.

'Do I get first choice of bedroom?' Gemma said hopefully.

'Sure, so long as you don't pick the one with the ensuite.'

'Not fair,' Gemma said, wandering around the lounge and from there into the spacious kitchen. 'It's bigger than I thought.'

Victoria beamed, pleased that it was getting her daughter's approval.

'Knock, knock...' Sonia said, walking through the open front door. 'Measuring up?'

'Just showing my daughter around.'

'Hi, I'm Son, I live next door.'

Gemma smiled at the woman. 'Gem,' she said.

'Gemma,' Victoria corrected.

'Do you babysit, Gemma?' Sonia asked, stressing the full name with a slightly mocking glance at Victoria.

'I have done a couple of times.'

'Perfect. Once you are in and settled, I will introduce you to my two little brats.'

'Sick...' Gemma said before heading up the stairs.

'I think that's the new, cool,' Victoria replied, watching her go. She looked at her new neighbour; she wasn't at all sure about the woman. She thought, and hoped that they could be friends, but there was something about her, like, who calls their own kids brats? 'How's Casper?' she asked.

'Healing well, he was lucky that your husband arrived and we could get him to the vets so quickly. Nice man, your Dave.'

Victoria nodded her agreement. 'He has his moments.'

'Pretty girl, your Gemma,' Sonia said, glancing up the stairs. The carpets weren't down yet and they could hear her shoes as she wondered around the rooms. 'Must be a worry...'

'Worry?'

Sonia was on her way out the door; she paused and turned. 'Yeah, you know, with all the teenage pregnancies.'

And with the dreaded P word left hanging in the room, Sonia was gone.

'I want the bedroom at the back,' Gemma said, skipping down the stairs.' Although, I still reckon I should have the one with the ensuite.'

'Dream on.' Victoria looked at her daughter, Sonia's parting words hanging in the air and haunting her with their implications. Surely it wasn't possible. Gemma was only fifteen; she didn't even have a boyfriend, did she?

The cat wandered into the house and rubbed against her legs. Her daughter bent down to fuss over the animal.

'Cute, is he the neighbours?'

'No.' She'd forgotten about the bloody cat. What was she going to do with it? She couldn't just leave it out to fend for itself all night. Or could she? She'd never had a cat, so she wasn't sure; she knew they were independent creatures who did roam the streets after dark, but what if it turned cold? They were enjoying a late Indian-summer, but it was September and once the sun dropped, so did the temperature. She looked at the small furry feline. Did cats get cold? She didn't know, but she knew that somehow responsibility for the animal rested with her and she couldn't go home and be happy knowing it was alone on the streets. She couldn't ask Sonia, not with a wounded Casper in the house, and then an idea hit her.

'Lock up for me,' she said to her daughter. 'I'll meet you at the Show Home in a few minutes.' She bent down and picked the cat up and hurried out of the door.

GEMMA LOOKED at the keys in her hand; there were three for the front door, two for the back and two what looked like garage keys. They were on a ring with a little label, PLOT 8, and underneath her mother had written – mine – next to a smiley face. Gemma twisted the keys around the ring until one of the back door keys came off. There was a gate at the side of the house that gave a way into the back and the garden was already fenced. It was perfect.

Her date with Alex had been amazing. He drove them out to Brickhill woods, and they had wandered round hand in hand until he stopped below a tree and kissed her. She worried a bit that he might want to do it there because if she got grass and dirt stains on her uniform then mum would go mad. But he didn't. After the kiss they had a picnic, well a couple of cans of lager and two packets of salt and vinegar crisps really, but it would be a full on picnic when she told Abby later.

Abby had told her that he would probably want to do it in the car, which apparently wasn't that comfortable or easy. Not that Abby had done it, but she had an older brother and a sister, so knew a lot more about sex stuff and boys than she did.

But this time, her best friend was wrong. When they got back to the car, he kissed her again and this time his hands went up her top and under her bra. But then he stopped and looked down into her eyes. 'I can wait,' he said.

'I don't want to wait,' she'd replied, even though she wasn't totally sure she meant it. But she absolutely one million per cent did not want to lose him or for him to think she was just a silly little girl.

'We'll wait until we can find somewhere to do it,' he said, seeming pleased with her answer.

She smiled and looked at the back door key. It was perfect, well maybe not quite, since there were no beds or even carpets, but it was warm and private and empty and had to be better than the car. She pulled her phone from her pocket and texted him – *tonight x*

'YOU CAN'T HAVE A CAT,' Candice said impatiently. 'You can hardly look after yourself, let alone an animal.'

Mary looked at her daughter-in-law with annoyance, but since there were still a lot of boxes to unpack and she hadn't had her dinner yet, she decided not to tell her what she really thought.

'Just for tonight,' the showroom lady said holding out a packet of cat food and a feeding bowl.

'I think it's a great idea,' Jack said, clearly not afraid to cross the Candy Bar. He looked at his aunt and smiled. 'It'll be company for Gran on her first night alone in her new home.'

Candice tutted, but even she wasn't immune to Jack's charms. 'Just for the night?' she said to Victoria, who nodded. 'She's an old lady on a pension. She can't afford the upkeep of a pet. It's not just the food, but vet bills are astronomical.'

'It's true, they are,' the Show Home lady agreed, glancing at Jack as though she couldn't help herself.

Mary was silently fuming. She had a small fortune in the bank. The cottage had sold quickly, and for a good price despite the economic gloom. Why the hell couldn't she spend it on a cat if she wanted to? She was tempted to start a sodding cattery, and then the Candy Bar might have something to complain about.

'I'm sure it won't be any bother for one night,' Jack said.

'Thank you,' Victoria said to him.

I'm having the animal, Mary snapped in her head, knowing she was just being jealous and possessive. She didn't like the way Jack and the Show Home woman looked at each other.

The cat jumped up onto her lap and nuzzled at her arms. Mary smiled and stroked his soft fur. One night my arse, she thought to herself, deciding right then that he was there to stay. The animal purred loudly, and she took that as his approval.

GLAD THAT THE cat situation was temporarily sorted, Victoria hung the keys that Gemma gave back to her on the rack. She pressed the answer-phone to check her messages, hoping that the investor had changed his mind about the two apartments. There was only one message.

'Hi, Victoria, Sasha here, just to let you know I had a bit of inspiration about your feature and amazingly, the editor loved it. Better still, we had a bit of late space to fill, so I managed to get it into the last minute deadline. Didn't have time to run it past you first as it has now gone to press, but hope you like it. Talk tomorrow.'

Victoria had no idea what story Sasha had managed to come up with and didn't really care. Anything that gave a sales boost would be welcome. She opened the door and Gemma followed her out towards the car. 'So, did you like it?'

'Oh yes,' her daughter said, smiling. 'It's almost perfect.'

Victoria was delighted. Sonia's cynical words popped into her head, but she dismissed them. Plenty of time to worry about that in the future. Gemma was still her little girl, and she had nothing to worry about.

EPISODE FOUR
JASMINE CLOSE - SERIES ONE

Annabel Bailey parked the car and looked around her. Despite the early hour, workers were already on the construction site. She opened her door and reached in to grab the large supermarket bags from the back seat. She picked up three, closed the door, and locked the car. There was a baby was crying in one of the flats on the first floor, but apart from that, the residential side of the Close was still sleeping and silent.

Annabel let herself into the communal hall and walked along the corridor to apartment number two. She unlocked the door and slipped quietly inside. The irritation that had shadowed her ever since the phone call yesterday evening burst into full-on anger. It was worse, much worse than she had expected.

The kitchen window was wide open; it might as well have a 'come in, help-yourself' sticker on it. The kitchen was a total disaster zone, like a take-away bomb had exploded across the work surfaces. She dropped the bags onto the floor, then filled the coffeemaker and turned it on. Caffeine was definitely at the top of her must-have list. She went into the lounge. Pizza, panties and alcohol! It had obviously been a good night. She followed the trail of discarded clothes into the first of the two bedrooms.

Tammy was sleeping soundly. Her mass of dark curls tumbled across the scarlet pillow as she snored lightly. Beside her was a young lad, probably early twenties, with dark blonde hair. His face was liberally littered with silver studs in his ear, nose, lip and eyebrows.

Annabel slammed the door and watched as the pair woke up. The lad sat bolt upright, looking around in bewilderment. Tammy opened her eyes and pushed herself up on her elbow.

'Annabel?' Tammy murmured, her full lips curling into a smile. 'What time is it?'

The lad threw the covers off and rubbed the sleep from his eyes. He was butt- naked, as was Tammy, who slid out of bed and looked uncertainly at Annabel.

'Time you were gone,' Annabel said to the lad. 'As for you...' she looked crossly at the girl in front of her. 'Get yourself dressed, we have trouble arriving in less than two hours...'

'Ooh, is Mr Smith coming in for a spanking?'

'No, I've cancelled all today's bookings. The letting agents are coming to do an inspection and we have got to get this place spotless and respectable.'

'Good luck with that then.' The lad said with a smirk.

Annabel gave him her sternest look, the one she had perfected over many years dealing with ditsy women and horny men. He picked up his pants and left the room; Tammy blew him a kiss and giggled.

'You can start clearing up in here,' she said to Tammy, 'and put some clothes on. Where's Miranda?'

'People are sleeping,' the girl in question said, appearing in the doorway behind her. 'Oh, hello Annabel, what are you doing here?'

At least Miranda wasn't naked, not completely at any rate. She had underwear on, although it was very flimsy. Annabel was aware that the curtains were open. Luckily, the bedroom looked out on to a wilderness, but there was evidence that building work had started out the back and it wasn't hard to work out how the girls had got the unwelcome attention. 'What part of keep a low profile didn't you understand?' she said, looking from one to the other.

'But they like it,' Tammy said, glancing over her shoulder at the windows. 'Sparko said we bring light to his very dull day.'

'One of the electricians,' Miranda said, in answer to her unspoken question. 'He came in to fix our lights.'

'And did the light need fixing?' Annabel asked sceptically.

'Yes.' Tammy replied indignantly. 'That's why we invited him in.'

'The bulb needed changing,' Miranda said, a bit sheepishly.

'It's good,' Tammy butted in. 'You're always complaining about the cost of advertising and Sparko said he would tell everyone about us. You know, spread the word.'

Annabel groaned and wished she did something easier, more sensible, and less stressful, like being a brain surgeon. Moaning at the girls was just a waste of time. They had a lot to do and little time to do it in. Somehow, they had to transform the place into a nice, residential flat share and convince the letting agent that the only thing the workmen had witnessed was a bit of partying. She went back into the kitchen and poured herself a coffee. She pointed to the bags she'd carried up from the car. 'Cleaning stuff and normal things...'

'Normal?' asked Tammy.

Miranda was rummaging in the bags and pulling out pictures, toiletries, and groceries. 'Yeah silly, most people don't have cupboards and drawers full of condoms, lubricants and baby oil.'

Annabel sipped the coffee gratefully. 'Right,' she said. 'Let's get to work.'

VICTORIA WALKED from the bus stop towards the housing site. She only had the car on Dave's days off, not that she minded. The bus was easy enough, and he usually picked her up at the end of the shift. Soon, it wouldn't be an issue at all; she would live just a hundred metres from the Show Home. And although eventually, the site would be completed and she would be moved on to a new one, that was at least two years away.

She was surprised to see Sasha waiting for her in the car park. 'Everything okay?' she asked.

Sasha held out a copy of the paper. 'Hot off the press, thought you might like to see it. I was just about to push it through the door; I'm on my way to Stony Stratford, several burglaries, all targeting the elderly or disabled.'

'That's terrible.'

'Yeah, I know... here...' Sasha opened the paper and pointed to the page.

Victoria smiled. It was a picture of the cat, sat underneath the Jasmine Close street sign with the headline – HELP US NAME THIS CAT – the article told the story of the animal's rescue and how he had adopted the Close as his home and needed a name.

'This is great, Sasha, thanks.'

'I'll let you know the outcome.' She started walking away, then paused and turned. 'Do you know Al Copeland? From the Bucks News?'

Victoria shook her head. 'No, we do all our advertising in MK Herald and I only deal with you for features. Why?'

'He's probably winding me up. We were at school together and it was always a pretty competitive relationship. He's been hinting about a big story on the new housing site.'

'Could be a different one. There are so many going up in MK at the moment.'

Sasha nodded, but didn't look convinced. 'Maybe, although I definitely got the feeling it was here. He was fishing to see if I knew anything. Have you got any idea of any story he might be chasing?'

Did she? Surely it wasn't the brothel? How would he know about that? 'No, sorry,' she said, feeling bad. Sasha had just done her a favour, but she really didn't want Jasmine Close to be the subject of negative headlines and would do anything she could to keep a story like that out of the papers. The letting agents were doing a surprise visit on the premises that morning and so hopefully that would put an end to the going's on, anyway.

'Let me know if you hear anything? I hate losing out, especially to him.'

'Of course.'

Victoria watched her drive away and then went into the Show Home. If the feature created a fresh burst of interest, then she wanted everything to be perfect. She pulled the vacuum cleaner from the under-stairs cupboard and set to work.

ANNABEL LOOKED around her with a satisfied smile. The place looked clean, tidy, and boringly normal. Her boot was bursting with sex toys and paraphernalia, but that was safely locked away out of view. Everything visible in the apartment was legal looking and legitimate, including the girls. She had thought about sending them out for the morning, but decided that would look more suspicious and give the agents a reason to return to talk to them. Much better to front it out now, with her to watch over them, and steer the ditsy pair away from trouble. She glanced at the clock. It was almost eleven. 'Any minute now…' she said to the girls.

Tammy had her mane of black curls tied back in a ponytail and was wearing jeans and a short-sleeved blouse. Her nose had screwed up in distaste when Annabel had handed it to her to wear. 'Even my mum would refuse to put that on.' She'd said.

But Annabel had insisted, and it was perfect. It covered up the girl's assets, but the soft silky, material hinted at what lay hidden. It was modest and sexy at the same time. She wanted the girls to look understated, but at the same time they were young, attractive women, and so dressing them like nuns wouldn't be convincing.

Miranda was shorter, slightly plumper, but with a tiny waist and large breasts, she was wearing leggings, boots and a long tunic style top that showed a bit of cleavage. Her blonde hair was straight and sleek and her make-up was minimal.

The doorbell rang right on time. 'Remember,' she said, 'be surprised…'

'I didn't know we were due an inspection,' Annabel said, after the two men had introduced themselves as being from the letting agents. 'We were just about to hit the shops.'

'I'm sorry, Ms Bailey, but we've had complaints.' The older of the two men said, not looking sorry at all. 'We need to come in and check for ourselves.'

Annabel stepped aside and let them pass. 'What sort of complaints?' She followed them into the lounge.

Tammy had her back to them. 'Are you ready yet, Annabel?' she said, turning round. 'Oh, hello...' she said. 'Who are you?'

Both men stopped and stared. Annabel was so used to seeing Tammy that she tended to forget just how stunning the girl, in fact both the girls, were. 'These gentlemen are from the letting agents. Apparently they've had complaints.'

'About us?' Tammy said, looking as though she were about to burst into tears.

'No, no, of course not,' the young man said, earning a scowl from his older colleague.

'Yes, about you.' The older one said firmly. 'We've heard some disturbing reports about immoral goings on.'

'Are you talking about sex?' Miranda said bluntly.

Annabel thought about offering the men a seat, but she was enjoying watching them squirm as they stood staring from one stunning girl to the other. She was sure the younger man was blushing. He was certainly feeling uncomfortable.

'I didn't know we're not allowed to have sex. Is it banned under the terms of the tenancy?' Miranda continued, clearly spurred on by their embarrassment.

'Of course not,' the older man said. 'That would be ridiculous.'

'Oh, thank goodness for that,' Tammy said, dropping down onto the sofa and smiling. 'I do so enjoy it, don't you?'

The poor young man nodded his head, totally besotted. The older one was lost for words. Annabel decided it was time to step in. 'I'm not sure what the problem is here gentlemen, the three of us flat share...'

'There are only two bedrooms,' the older man said, thinking he'd caught them out.

'Oh, we share,' Miranda said, smiling at Tammy.

Annabel actually heard the poor younger man gulp. 'I must

admit, like most youngsters, they do like to party. I'm sorry if that's caused problems for the neighbours. Have they been too noisy?'

'It's not the noise that's the problem. We've had reports that an illegal and immoral business is being conducted from these premises and that most definitely is against the terms of the tenancy.'

'What?' Tammy said, looking confused.

'He's calling us prostitutes,' Miranda said, coldly.

Tammy started to cry. Miranda comforted her. The young man looked mortified, even the older one looked uncomfortable.

'Mr...?' Annabel adopted her sternest glare, the one she'd been told could defrost a freezer.

'Tyler,' the older man said. 'Sorry, I should have given you a card.' He belatedly pulled one from his pocket.

'Mr Tyler, you are very insulting. My friends and I pay our rent and keep the place nice. I admit, I have been away for a few days and they told me they had some friends over for a few drinks. I know them well enough to realise that might be an understatement. However, as I understand it, we live in a country where drinking is legal and so is sex. I do not know how you can pass judgement on a group of young, consenting adults having fun.'

'You can look in our drawers if you want,' Tammy said between sobs, clearly trying to be helpful.

'That won't be necessary,' Mr Tyler said. 'It's possible we have been misinformed.'

'Yes, sorry,' the young man said, staring at Tammy.

It was all going so splendidly, Annabel was debating whether to demand an apology for the girls from Mr Tyler when the exterior buzzer sounded. Miranda looked at Annabel, her eyes wide with the question - who?

Tammy glanced at the clock. Annabel followed her eyes. She'd cancelled all the appointments for the day, but she knew well enough that men on a mission didn't always engage their brains. Eleven thirty meant it was probably Mr Smith impatiently pressing his finger on the buzzer.

'Expecting someone?' Mr Tyler asked with undisguised pleasure.

'No, not at all,' Annabel said calmly. 'Excuse me a minute.'

'Oh, I think I'll come with you if you don't mind,' he said.

Obviously she did mind, but he followed her to the door, anyway. 'Hello?' she said into the intercom that linked the apartment to the outside of the building. 'Can I help you?'

'Mr Smith for Tammy,' the voice replied.

'Push the door,' she responded, pressing the button that would allow him into the building. Her mind was racing with possible explanations, but none of them seemed credible. In the seconds it took for Mr Smith to race to the apartment door, the best she could come up with was that he was Tammy's boyfriend and they called each other Mr and Mrs Smith as a joke. She knew it wasn't terribly credible, especially since he was old enough to be her father.

'Mr Smith, is it?' Mr Tyler said, smugly staring at the door, waiting for the evidence to knock on it.

'Yes,' Tammy said, from behind them. She stood up, blew her nose and looked at the men defiantly. 'He's my daddy's solicitor. I texted him and asked him to come because of the awful allegations you were making about us.'

Annabel looked at the young woman with new respect. She'd always thought of Tammy as being the dumb one, but that was pure genius. Mr Smith (not his real name, obviously) genuinely was a solicitor. It might just work.

The door knocked, and Annabel pulled it open. The short middle-aged-man, with thinning hair, glanced past her and immediately registered the two suited men behind her. 'Mr Smith, thank you so much for coming at such short notice.' She held her hand out and took his to shake.

'Glad to help,' he said, showing none of the bewilderment he must be feeling.

'Oh, it's awful,' Tammy said, running towards him. 'They are saying terrible things...' she pointed to the letting agency men.

'Can I ask what your occupation is, Mr Smith, and what business you might have here?' Mr Tyler asked pompously.

'Yes, I'm a solicitor, and I'm here at the request of my friend to defend his daughter against allegations that I understand are unfounded, unsubstantiated and frankly highly libellous...'

Mr Tyler's attitude changed. He looked worried, but put a brave face on it. 'Just doing our jobs, Mr Smith, allegations have been made, and we had to check them out.'

'And now that you have?'

Annabel pulled the door open for the men.

'We will be on our way. I'm sorry for any distress caused,' he said, not looking sorry at all.

Annabel closed the door behind them and stared in happy amazement at her girls and Mr Smith. 'Thank you,' she said to him. 'But how did you know?'

'I texted him,' Tammy said, grinning. 'While you were letting him in and grim and grimmer were watching you.'

'You are a genius,' Annabel said, meaning it.

Mr Smith didn't look so happy. 'Not sure they bought it, to be honest,' he said. 'I reckon you should start looking for new premises.'

Annabel nodded. It was a shame, though; she liked the location and the flat. 'I'm going out,' she said. She owed lunch to her friend from the letting agents who had tipped her off the night before. It paid to have well positioned friends in her line of business.

She looked at the girls. 'No more free floor shows,' she said. 'Keep the blinds closed when you are entertaining and keep your clothes on when you're not.'

She picked up her bag and left the apartment.

VICTORIA LED the couple up the street. She was pretty sure they were going to buy, but they wanted to see the layout and size of the three-bed-semi. She understood how difficult it was to appreciate a property's full potential just from floor plans. The Show Home was larger, a four-bed-detached. They liked the quality and the finish of the build and since they had one child and another on the way; they felt the three-bed was a perfect size for them and just about within budget. She knew she would have to throw in an incentive or two, but that was okay. Amazing how free carpets or solicitor's fees paid could seal a deal.

She unlocked the front door and led the way inside. Her own carpets were being laid later that day and that would make the move seem real and imminent.

'I like this,' the lady said. 'Is it a south-facing garden?'

'Yes,' Victoria replied. 'But the plot I'm suggesting is a corner one with a bigger garden.'

'Is this one not available?'

'No,' she said firmly. 'This one is mine.'

Victoria never tired of saying it. She was very excited. Her packing was well under way and she had the next two days off work to complete it and get moved in.

She led them upstairs and showed off the size of the main bedroom with its walk-in wardrobe and en-suite bathroom. Then she opened the door to the second bedroom and stopped in the doorway. On the floor, over by the window, were several empty cans of lager and a McDonald's bag. 'I'm so sorry,' she said, embarrassed, hurrying over to pick up the rubbish and silently cursing Barry and his men.

Twenty minutes later, with the purchase agreed, and the couple gone, she hurried over to the building site. 'Your lads nearly cost me a sale,' she said crossly, when Barry walked across to see her. 'What the hell are they doing drinking, anyway? And in my house!'

Barry stared blankly at her.

'I thought it was all finished. You told me it was snag free.'

'Your house...' he was clearly confused.

'Yes. Keep up, Barry. What work have they been doing there?'

He shook his head. 'None that I'm aware of. It's all done for you.'

Victoria looked at him. 'Well, someone has been in there, I have the lager cans to prove it.'

'I'll have words,' he said. 'I can't allow alcohol, far too dangerous on a building site.'

Victoria nodded. 'Thanks,' she said, walking away. A car drove past and parked at the end of the Close. She assumed that the agents' meeting had gone well and that the problem of apartment two would soon be over, making a mental note to ring the owner herself later and see if he had heard back from them. She was confident that the lease would be ended and they would evict the girls and their equipment.

Natasha carried Amy and the pushchair down the stairs. Ed said she was silly not to keep the buggy in the large space under the staircase. The kids' next door kept their bikes there, alongside some sealed boxes belonging to the girls in flat two, and Ed stored his golf clubs. She thought that he was the crazy one and was convinced they would be nicked and sold, probably for heroin or alcohol or to feed some addiction. But he always saw the good in people, a trait that was both exasperating and endearing, at the moment mostly the former. He still seemed to be cross with her over the police and the marijuana incident.

'Why did you have to stick your nose in,' he'd said, when she told him about how they had all turned on her. 'You had no proof.'

'I know that woman is hiding something and I could smell the pot.'

He'd rolled his eyes in a way that demonstrated just how annoyed he was and took himself off to the pub. He didn't understand. Why would he? His childhood had been easy, idyllic, in her book. Nice, normal parents, who still cuddled and bickered after forty years of marriage. An older brother who mostly either ignored or teased him, but who would jump in and punch anyone else who did the same, and a younger sister who he adored and who adored him back.

Natasha knew what it was like to grow up at best, ignored and neglected, and at worst, mistreated and malnourished. If only one of her neighbours had stepped in and intervened for her. But like Ed, they subscribed to the mind your own business, rule book and so she had lived her young life in fear and loneliness with an absent father and an alcoholic mother.

She strapped the baby into the pushchair and pressed the button to open the door. 'A bit of air will do us both good,' she said to her daughter, who was sucking hard on the dummy in her mouth. She tried not to think about the list on the table and the jobs that needed doing. Half an hour wouldn't hurt; besides, the air might make Amy sleepy and then she could get on with some cleaning when they got back.

The sun was shining. It really was a lovely September, and she'd always liked autumn. As a child going back to school after the long summer took her out of the house and away from her mother for a few hours every day. Besides, she got a school dinner and sometimes, if she was lucky, she would be given an extra lunch to stuff in her bag and take home with her. There were two options at her school. The hot dinner which she loved and the cold lunch which would be sandwich and fruit packed in a little disposable box. One of the dinner ladies, Mrs Brown, always gave her a cold lunch to take away if there were any leftovers. Natasha had cried all the way home the day Mrs Brown retired.

Up ahead was the Show Home lady, and she didn't want to see her or talk to her, so she ducked into the pathway that led along the side of the apartments and waited until the woman was out of sight. She saw her neighbour leave the building and guessed that Belle was on her way to collect the children. She felt the familiar surge of anger towards her and had to take deep breaths and talk herself down. Ed seemed to be fond of her, though. Natasha had seen him speaking to her several times, and that made everything worse.

'Give her a chance, Nat. She's really sweet and the kids are great fun...'

She'd cut him off, walked into the bathroom and slammed the door. What did he know? All he saw was her pretty face and smile. But Natasha knew that the woman was hiding something.

'Hello...'

Surprised, Natasha realised she was being spoken to. She looked at the man in front of her. She hadn't seen him before.

'You live here?' he said, pointing to the apartment block.

She stared back, as if she was going to tell him, a total stranger.

She released the brakes on the buggy and walked out of the alleyway and on to the Close.

'I'm looking for someone...' he persisted. 'I hear there's been a bit of trouble in one of the flats.'

She paused and turned to look at him. 'Who are you?'

He handed her a card.

'A reporter?'

'That's me, Al Copeland, Bucks News.' He offered his hand. She ignored it.

He pointed across the road to the building site. 'They've given me most of what I need.'

'What do they know?' She said curtly. 'I live next door to her.'

His eyes widened. 'Really? Annabel Bailey?'

'Huh, I knew Belle wasn't her real name. I mean it's not, is it? It's just a Disney cartoon.'

He looked a bit confused. 'I've knocked on the door, but there's no answer.'

Natasha pointed down the street at Belle's departing back. 'Wouldn't be, that's her...'

'Great, thanks. Can I come back and ask you some more questions?'

She wanted to say yes, and was just about to, but then she remembered Ed and his annoyance with her and so she shook her head and walked away.

The man hurried to his car and climbed in. He waved as he drove past her and she saw that in his hand was a camera. She felt a tiny stab of guilt but pushed it away and thought of the children. No one knew better than her how awful life is with a parent who's an addict.

BELLE WAS happy in a fantasy world of her own as she walked out of Jasmine Close and up towards the school. The children had settled in well and apart from the nosy bitch next door; she liked the flat and the area. Tamsin had already made a friend and was asking to stay over. Belle surprised herself by saying she would think about it and meaning it. This just went to show that she was starting to relax and believe that this time they might be safe, despite the incident with the police. If that had gone any further, then she would be packing her bags and running again.

The main road was outside the new housing estate, and she waited to cross it. She knew she shouldn't. Like most of the roads in Milton Keynes, it was a fast, dual carriageway, and not designed for crossing. She would never even consider it when the children were with her. She would walk the extra distance and use the underpass that was available. But on her own, she often took the shortcut and went across the road. It was almost clear. She waited for a silver Astra coming out of the Jasmine Close, turning to pull out and pass, then she started to cross.

It took her ten minutes to walk to the school, a low, single story modern building, with its own playground and sports field. She hoped that Kyle would be inspired to get involved in football or athletics, anything to get his head out of the computer and doing some exercise.

The school was up ahead, and the children were already starting to come out. She knew that hers wouldn't be with the first batch of children. Tamsin and Kyle were both dawdlers. Tamsin because she was a dreamer, and Kyle because of his fixation with the games on his phone.

Just up ahead, she saw a man leaning against his car, watching her as she walked along. It was a silver Astra, like the one that had pulled out of the Close earlier. She wondered if he lived there. He was certainly staring intently at her. People were moving in almost every day, so maybe he had seen her even though she hadn't met him yet. She smiled uncertainly, and he smiled back. It wasn't until she was almost level that she saw he was holding a camera. She tried to react as the fear and panic sent adrenaline cursing through her body. But he was way ahead of her and the picture was taken and he was in his car and pulling away before she could do anything to stop him.

Belle stared after the car in shock. What had just happened, and more importantly, why?

'Mum, can I go to Zareen's house? Her dad said it's okay.'

Belle forced herself to be calm and turned her attention from the departing car to her daughter. Tamsin was clutching the hand of a pretty girl and following just behind was a man who she knew was most probably from Pakistan.

'Mummy?' Tamsin said, her excitement and happiness draining away.

'Another day perhaps?' the man said, watching her closely.

Belle forced herself to smile at him and hoped it looked natural and genuine and not at all like the grimace she feared it was. 'Thanks,' she said, glad that her voice sounded normal, at least it did to her own ears. 'Yes, another time, we have plans today.'

Tamsin let go of Zareen's hand and they watched as the father and daughter walked away. Belle knew her daughter was upset and disappointed, but she couldn't take any chances, not after the man and the photograph.

'Where's your brother?'

'Just getting his phone, it was confiscated again,' Tamsin said in a dull, matter-of-fact tone.

No argument, no tantrum or tears, just sad, resigned acceptance from her young daughter. She took her hand and squeezed it. 'I'm sorry,' she said.

Tamsin offered her a small smile. 'It's okay mummy, I understand. But they are okay, you know. I asked lots of questions. Zareen said that her grandfather came to England a very long time ago and her father hasn't even ever been to Pakistan.'

'Oh, love,' Belle fought back the tears. How sad that her young daughter was vetting friends before allowing herself to get too close. 'I'm sure that they are okay and I promise I will talk to Zareen's parents and make arrangements for another day.' Even as she said the words, she had a feeling that it would be yet another broken promise.

Kyle finally came out of the school, his head down, his fingers chasing over the screen of the phone. In her mind, she tried to reason and rationalise why someone might take a photo of her.

'Look, a squirrel,' Tamsin said, pointing just behind them as the animal scampered around by the bushes.

Maybe he was an animal lover, a wildlife enthusiast? It could have been the squirrel he was photographing. But then why did he take off so quickly?

Belle kept her worries in check until the children went to bed, no point in alarming them. When she was sure they were asleep, she picked up her phone and pushed a saved number. 'Hello, Mum,' she said, as soon as it answered.

'What's happened?' her mother demanded. 'Has he found you?'

'I don't know…' she said, before relating the story of the man and his camera.

'It's probably nothing,' her mum said, in a tone that Belle recognised as being exactly the same as the one she used when reassuring her own children. 'Do you want me to come?'

The question hung in the air. She wanted to shout yes. But it was a risk and if she was wrong and it was just a random picture by a random stranger, then her overreaction would mean they would have to leave, anyway.

'Belle?'

'No.' she said, finally making a decision.

'I'm sure it's nothing to worry about, but it won't hurt to be extra careful.'

'I will,' she agreed, although since her life was always about being careful, it was hard to imagine how that could be improved upon.

She said goodbye and ended the call, checked her children and then went around yet again, making sure that every door and every window was shut and bolted.

EPISODE FIVE
JASMINE CLOSE - SERIES ONE

Victoria woke up to the shrill ping from her phone alarm. She groaned and reached out to shut it up without opening her eyes, and then she remembered - No work today. It was finally time to pack up properly for moving. She threw the covers off and sat up, nudging her husband gently. He snorted and turned over. 'Dave!' she said, jabbing him harder in his back. 'Wake up...'

He wasn't impressed with this suggestion and pulled the quilt tighter around him. 'Ten more minutes.'

She knew from previous experience she wasn't going to win this one. Instead, she left him to it and went down to the kitchen and put the kettle on. She heard Gemma moving around upstairs and wondered briefly if she should let her have the day off from school? The thought didn't stay in her head for long, as reality immediately shoved her picture of a perfect happy family back in its box. The truth was, neither her husband nor her daughter wanted this move as much as she did. After an hour or two at home, Gemma would be moaning that she was bored. Victoria knew she would get much more done with her out of the way at school.

'Everything okay?' she said, as her daughter breezed into the kitchen. 'Toast?'

'Nah, not hungry, thanks.'

'Getting excited?'

Her daughter paused, a plastic bottle of milk in her hand, and looked at her questioningly.

'The move,' Victoria said, unable to keep the exasperation from her voice.

'Oh yeah, sure. Be great.'

Victoria handed her a glass for the milk. She blamed Dave. If he was more enthusiastic, then their daughter would be as well. Because he was so indifferent, she could hardly complain at Gemma for being the same as her father. 'Do you want me to pack your room up?'

'No. I'll do it tonight.'

Victoria sipped her tea and watched her daughter leave for school with nostalgia nudging at her. She shook it away and got busy. Kids grow up and parents are left behind. That's just the way of it.

Dave was still in bed and Victoria was on her second mug of tea and had packed up half the kitchen when her phone rang. She glanced at the display and recognised the number as being Sasha's. Strange, since the young woman normally rang her at the Show Home, besides, Sasha knew she had a couple of days off to move house.

'Hi,' she said.

'I can't believe you didn't know.'

'Know what?' she replied with genuine confusion.

'About the brothel.'

Bugger, she thought.

'Al got the story and the picture. He gets the front page slot and I get a feature about a bloody cat! Thanks a lot, Victoria.'

Sasha hung up before she could answer. Perhaps just as well, since she couldn't defend herself without lying and she hated lies. They were so hard to keep track of and so easy to trip over. She did feel bad, though. Bad that Sasha had missed out on the story, and even worse that the story was out at all. That kind of scandal and association wouldn't help her to get sales.

She left the kitchen and went into the hall to fetch her laptop.

The free paper wouldn't be delivered until later, usually in the afternoon, when the delivery boy or girl finished school. It would already be in the shops to buy, but since she was still in her nightclothes, looking online was probably the best option.

It was, as Sasha said, on the front page. She looked at it in horror and rang Sasha.

'What?' Sasha said, clearly still annoyed with her.

'They've got the wrong picture,' she said, staring at the photo of Belle. 'She's a mum in one of the upstairs apartments, and she has absolutely nothing to do with the goings on in flat two.'

BELLE THOUGHT LONG and hard about whether to send the children to school. In the end, she decided her mum was right, and she was probably panicking for nothing. She had been so careful; she couldn't believe that he had found her. So she walked the children to school and talked herself into relaxing. Tamsin was unusually quiet and clutched her hand tightly. She was a sensitive girl and while her brother buried himself in a game, Tamsin would think and fret and worry. 'Have a good day,' she said, when they reached the school gates.

'Are you alright, Mummy?' Tamsin said, launching herself into her arms.

Belle felt terrible. Clearly, she was not doing a very good job at maintaining a worry free environment for her children. 'Of course I am, poppet,' she replied, kissing Tamsin on the forehead. 'I have a headache, that's all. I'll talk to your friend's mum or dad later and see if she can come and play after school tomorrow?'

Tamsin nodded and smiled, although her eyes were still shadowed with doubt.

'Do you want to invite anyone?' she asked her son.

He shook his head and kept walking. She worried about him. Of course she did, but what could she do? She'd even had him checked by the doctor and then a specialist in case he was autistic or something, but the specialist assured her that Kyle was fine. The chaotic reality of their lives meant that making friends and building relationships had been difficult. So much so that he had stopped bothering.

She watched them until they were safely into the school, and then she turned and walked away.

She diverted on the way home to pick up some bread and milk in the local shop. She had only been in there once or twice before and had no idea why the man behind the counter was staring at her in a way that made her very uncomfortable. Handing over a ten-pound note, she waited for the change. She was aware that the two women behind her were whispering furtively to each other. Belle put the change in her pocket and turned to go. The women were in her way and made no attempt to move. She felt the first stirrings of panic, but forced them down and edged past the first woman. Confused and upset, she reached the door and that's when she saw it.

On the newsstand by the exit, there was a picture of her face. Appearing as clear and recognisable as if she was looking in a mirror. It was the front page of the local paper. She snatched a copy from the stand, pulled a pound coin from her pocket, and rushed back to the counter. She didn't wait to be served. The women tutted, and the man mumbled something about manners. Belle didn't care. She could hardly breathe and her heart pounded so loudly it drowned out all other sounds. She practically threw the coin on the counter and ran and didn't stop running until she arrived home.

Safely indoors, she sank down onto her sofa and began reading the page. Tears streamed down her cheeks, blurring her vision. A brothel! Who would say such things about her and why? It could only be her bitch of a next-door neighbour. But seriously, what had she ever done to make her hate her so much?

She grabbed the phone and rang a number. 'Oh, Mum, it's terrible, I've got to go, get out...'

'What's happened? Is he there? Call the police.'

'No, not yet, but he will be soon. I've gotta move today...'

'I'll leave immediately. Be with you by lunchtime.'

She ended the call and dashed to the bathroom to grab some tissue and blow her nose. Then she started to pack, not carefully, but frantically, throwing things into boxes and cases. She wanted to scream with the frustration and injustice of it all, but there was no point. It wouldn't change anything. She remembered an aunt, long dead now, one of her father's sisters saying. 'You make your bed and you have to lie in it.' She never really understood and didn't much like the relative, anyway. But now the words trampled through her mind, mocking her for her stupidity in ever thinking that marrying Mr Mohamed Kahn was a good idea.

Not that she wasn't warned by her friends that he stopped her from meeting. By her family, who he rarely let her see, and even some of his own family. Like his sweet, brave sister before she disappeared to Pakistan and into an arranged marriage.

Fool that she was, she had taken his control and mistaken it for love. She'd seen his brutish, bullying nature, and somehow her stupid lovesick mind had made him seem strong, passionate and committed. But she had paid and was still paying, as were her children.

Thinking about Tamsin and Kyle nearly made the tears flow again. But she fought them back and got on with the packing. She didn't want her children to leave from the apartment. She wanted everything loaded into her mum's car before they collected the children from school, then they could drive straight to wherever they were going. Not that she had a clue where that was yet. If necessary, they could stay in a hotel for a couple of nights. She had money put aside. Her emergency fund was always ready and waiting to be plundered.

The buzzer sounded, and she cautiously went to the intercom. 'Yes?' she said abruptly.

'It's me,' the calm, reassuring voice of her mother responded.

She pressed the button to release the communal door. A few seconds later, she was being hugged by her parent.

'What happened? How did he find you? Where are the children?' her mum said, gently stepping back to look at her.

Overcome by emotion and unable to speak, she pointed to the newspaper on the coffee table. 'That'll be on the internet. If he hasn't seen it yet, he will soon. You know what he's like. He runs searches every day, my name, the children's names, your name, all my friends, even dad...'

Her mum nodded. 'I'm pretty sure I've been followed a few times.'

'Oh, mum, I'm so sorry,' she said, wishing that the past could be undone and time turned back. But then feeling instantly guilty for the thought since that would take away the existence of Tamsin and Kyle, and no matter how difficult her life had become, they were what made it all worthwhile.

'Do they know?' her mother said, nodding towards a picture of the children.

'No. they're at school. They'll be safe there. I told the secretary that under no circumstances are they ever to be collected by their father.'

'How did the story come about?' her mother asked, as she started to pack the kitchen groceries. 'I'm assuming the story has some truth, but they got the wrong person and photo?'

Belle hadn't really thought about it. She'd focused on the impact the picture would have on her family and not considered beyond that. 'Do you think?'

'Yes. Must be something going on in the street. No smoke without fire.'

'I guess. No idea who or where, though.'

TAMSIN STARED at the whiteboard with little comprehension of what the teacher was saying. She didn't like Miss White much, anyway. The teacher was fat and not in a nice way like her Auntie May, who always smiled and was kind and soft to hug. Miss White was solid, like the fat didn't dare to wobble, and she smelt of sweat and onions. Her eyes were tiny beads that were almost black and reminded her of a horrid crow that screeched and scared her once when she was younger.

Something was wrong. She knew it was. Her mum never got ill and didn't have headaches. What if she was dying? Did people die from headaches? She'd seen something on telly where a boy had a pain above his eye and it got so bad he had to go to the hospital. He died. She felt the heat behind her eyes as tears welled and threatened to fall. Could she run out of class? Would Miss White chase after her? Her skin was tingling, her tummy hurt, and she felt sick. The tears refused to stay behind her eyelids despite her squeezing her eyes tightly shut. She felt the heat as they ran down her cheeks and trickled around her lips.

'Miss, miss...'

She heard one of the girls calling the teacher. She thought it was Becky Smith but wouldn't, possibly even couldn't, open her eyes to see. If she couldn't see the class, then the class couldn't see her. Silly and not true, but it felt better to hide in the dark.

'Miss White.' The voice persisted. 'Tamsin's crying...'

The room burst into noise, chairs scraped as fellow pupils swung round to stare. Some giggled nervously, some whispered, some no doubt pointed. She kept her eyes tightly shut and sat still and rigid, afraid to look and see them all laughing at her.

'Tamsin?'

The teacher was close. She could smell her breath just inches away. Tamsin couldn't breathe. It felt as though the bulk of the woman was closing in on her and stealing the air away.

'What is it, child? Are you sick?'

Tamsin managed to nod her head even though it was spinning like she was on a fairground ride, or the rollercoaster at Gulliver's Land where she had stepped off and fallen straight over. Kyle had laughed, but mum had hugged her and sat with her until the dizziness stopped and the path beneath her trainers was solid again. She wished her mum was there now to hug her and tell her everything would be all right.

BELLE STOOD up and looked at the boxes. 'We'll never get this lot in your car,' she said, shaking her head. 'We'll have to leave half of it behind.'

'You thought about where to go yet? You sure it's not worth going to the Council?'

'The best they could do is put us in emergency accommodation, but that will still be local. If he knows I'm in Milton Keynes, he will come here and not leave until he finds me. I have to get out of the city now, before he gets here, otherwise we'll be trapped.'

Her mother looked sadly at her. 'Would he find you if you laid low for a week or so?'

'You know what he's like. He will drag all the family with him and they will stay here and search until they hunt us down.' Belle sat down on the sofa. She so wanted stability for her children, yet every time they started to settle, it was time to run again.

'What about going to May's? I know she would love to have you and surely he never went to her house, did he?'

Belle thought about it and a surge of hope briefly stirred. She loved her mother's sister, and so did Tamsin and Kyle. 'No, it's too risky. He knew of her and I'm sure I talked about how much I loved her house by the sea. He would find us and I don't want to put her at risk.' She stood up again and picked up a box. 'Let's load what we can in the car, then collect the children from school. We'll stay a couple of nights in a motel. I can't think any further than that, really.'

Her mother picked up her car keys and headed for the door.

'We'll go to Aylesbury,' she said. 'It's far enough away and not an obvious choice. I think he would expect us to use the motorway and head to Northampton or maybe the A5 to Dunstable.'

Belle followed out of the door. It was a good choice, although it was still Buckinghamshire. Would staying in the same county be a problem? She didn't think so and it might even help her get housed again, eventually.

They loaded the car with as much as they could possibly squeeze in. Belle could hear a phone ringing above and didn't know if it was her apartment or her neighbour's. She was aware of the curious stares from the building site. She saw the foreman talking to a lady from the Show Home. It wasn't the Victoria woman; it was a younger sales lady although they wore the same uniform of pale blue blazer and skirt with white blouse and sensible court shoes.

She was pretty sure that the curtains from her neighbour would be twitching as well. The bitch must love it to see her run. Belle fought down the anger. What was the point? The damage was done and couldn't be changed.

Belle took a long, sad look around the apartment. There was a lot left they couldn't fit in the car, plus all the furniture that would have to stay. She told herself and her mother that she would have it all collected in a week or two. But in truth, she knew she probably wouldn't. He would have the flat watched, and it was unlikely that she could ever come back or that she would see the rest of her belonging again. 'It's only stuff,' Belle whispered to herself as she picked up her handbag and then closed and locked the door for the last time.

They drove to the school and parked outside. 'Wait here. I'll only be a few minutes,' she said, climbing out of the passenger door.

School security was tight, and she had to press an intercom on the gate before she could even get onto the premises. It gave her some reassurance that a stranger couldn't gain access to the children while on school grounds, but as she knew well, it wasn't really the strangers that needed to be feared.

'Hello, Mrs Cox, are you feeling better now?' the secretary said, looking at her with some concern.

'Umm, I'm fine, thank you...' she replied, a bit confused.

'Tamsin said you were feeling poorly. She really was worried about you.'

'Tamsin?' the hairs at the back of her neck stood to tiny attention as the first slither of fear chased up her spine and lodged in her brain. 'I need to take the children home early.' She said, hearing that her voice had gone all high pitched and squeaky.

The school secretary was a pleasant lady; plump, middle-aged, with kind brown eyes and a caring smile. But at that moment, the only thing Belle felt towards her was a murderous urge. She saw in her eyes the terrible truth even before the words left her orangey pink painted lips.

'But, Mrs Cox, your mother picked them up, about half an hour ago.'

TAMSIN WAS SCARED, and she knew that Kyle was, too. Not that he would ever admit it, but she knew. She reached her hand out and squeezed his reassuringly. After all, she was the eldest, even if it was only by a few minutes. The sickness and dizziness hadn't gone. If anything, she felt even worse now. 'How much further?' she asked the lady, who was up front and driving.

'Not far,' she replied.

'And mummy will be there? At the hospital?'

'Sure.'

Tamsin was anything but sure and felt that the lady wasn't telling the truth. She kept replaying the last few minutes at school, wishing she could rub them out like when she wrote something wrong in her exercise book. Rub it out and start again.

She was in the medical room and lying on the bed. It was hard and not very comfortable. The deputy head, Miss Wong, had made her blow into a paper bag to stop her hyper... hyper something or other. She wasn't sure what the big word was, and it had stopped her head from spinning so fast. She'd heard Miss Wong tell the secretary to ring her mum, and she waited and listened. The room was warm, and she was sleepy. That's when it went all went wrong. She must have fallen asleep, because Miss Wong came and gently shook her.

'Your granny is here...'

'Granny?' she'd said, confused.

Miss Wong looked at her as though she were sad about something and even patted her hand gently. 'You need to be brave, Tamsin; your mummy is unwell, and she has been taken to hospital.'

Tamsin knew that the teacher was still speaking, but she had lost the ability to hear. The roaring in her ears was so loud it drowned out the words. All she knew was that she had to get to her see her mum. She tried to stand up, but her legs buckled beneath her. Then she was lifted up into arms she didn't recognise and was carried to a waiting car. She and Kyle were bundled into the back seat and told to strap up. The granny who carried her was definitely not her Nana, despite being old and cuddly looking. But she told them she had been sent by their nana to take them to the hospital to see mummy.

Kyle had shut his finger in the door once and they had to get a taxi to the hospital, so Tamsin knew it only took ten minutes to get there. But they had been in the car for longer than that. The granny had taken their phones away, and they were on the motorway, driving fast. Looking out of the window, Tamsin saw a sign for Luton Airport and wished that she and Kyle and their mum could fly away to somewhere nice and warm and live happily together. They could go to a place where her mum wouldn't be scared and worried all the time. Kyle and she could make friends and have sleep overs like the other kids at school did. They could have a pet; a dog or a hamster and maybe Nana and Aunt May could come and visit them.

BELLE WAS immobile for a few seconds, paralysed by disbelief. 'No,' she shook her head. 'Where are they? I need them now.'

The secretary looked worried and the door to the head's office opened and the young deputy came out. 'Everything all right?'

'Where are my children?' Belle demanded, her voice all scratchy and high pitched with panic.

The secretary and deputy looked at each other. 'Your mother collected them; she said that you'd been taken ill.'

The secretary pulled up a piece of paper, a typed permission letter seemingly signed by her. She handed it to Belle. She looked down at it a large tear landed on the paper and smudged the ink. It was a perfect copy of her signature. She wanted to run and chase after them, do something, anything, to get her children back. But where did she run to? What way did she chase?

'Mrs Cox?' Miss Wong said, staring at her. 'What is it?'

Belle looked at them through her tears. 'My mum is in the car waiting for me,' she said, knowing that her worst nightmare had just become reality and not having the first idea about what to do next.

'I'll call the police,' Miss Wong said.

'I don't understand?' the secretary cried, stifling a sob of her own and stabbing the computer screen. 'It says here that only you or your mother can collect them. I wouldn't have let them go with anyone else.'

'Didn't the children say anything?' Belle tried to imagine Tamsin willingly going with a stranger. It just didn't seem possible. Kyle would, with his head in his phone, he probably wouldn't even notice. But why didn't Tamsin kick off?

'No,' the secretary said.

'The police are on their way.'

'Tamsin wasn't well,' the secretary added.

'Sick and dizzy,' Miss Wong said. 'And hyperventilating.'

'I rang you and your mother, but got no answer. I left a message and then your mum turned up...' the secretary was openly crying now.

Belle realised that it must have been while they were loading the car. Her mum's handbag was on the coffee table next to her own phone. They had both been so distracted by getting packed up and out of the apartment that neither had checked their phones for messages or missed calls. She thought of her frightened children and was filled with rage against the man who had taken them and even more rage against herself for letting him do so. She pushed it down, buried it deep. The rage would burn inside and keep her focused. She would track him down, she would find her children and when she did, then the festering fury would unleash hell against the man she'd called a husband. But right now, she needed to be calm and get any information that she could to help her.

'Tamsin suffers from anxiety sometimes,' she said, looking at the deputy. 'Is that what it was?'

'Possible. She seemed upset and scared...'

Belle knew it was her fault. She had let her own fears seep across like poison from a festering wound to infect her daughter. And telling Tamsin that she had a headache was probably the worst thing she could have done to her scared and sensitive daughter.

The police arrived and her mother followed them in. One look at Belle told her all she needed and with a cry of dismay, she pulled her into her arms and they clung together while the secretary and the deputy told the two police officers what had happened.

'The best place for you is at home,' PC Clarke said, looking at her with genuine sympathy.

'No, I can't, I need to look for them...'

'He's right,' her mum said. 'Come on...'

'I need you by the phone in case they ring. They have mobiles?'

'Of course, but they are switched off. I've already tried.'

'All the same,' he said. 'That might change and you need to be where your children and we can easily reach you.'

She wanted to argue, but knew he was right. They could be anywhere in the country by now, or worse still, on a plane. 'You have to check the airports,' she said urgently.

He nodded his head. 'We will. Copies of their school photos have already been circulated. Go home and try not to worry.'

VICTORIA PARKED IN HER DRIVE. Well, not actually her drive yet, but it would be tomorrow when the sale was finalised. She saw Sasha across the road talking to Barry and as she climbed out of the car; the cat came strolling past and fussed around her legs. 'Bugger,' she said, bending down to stroke him. 'I forgot all about you.'

She crossed the road and smiled at Barry and Sasha. Neither of them seemed best pleased with her.

'None of my lads have been in your house since last weekend,' he said. 'I've been over myself today and had a look round. It's all secure and no sign of forced entry, but someone's been there. Cigarette butts in the bathroom sink and an empty Mars bar wrapper on the windowsill in the back bedroom.'

Victoria frowned; it was an uncomfortable feeling to think that someone was using her lovely new house illicitly. 'I don't get who or how?'

'I was just about to check the security footage.'

Victoria looked up at the closest camera. 'Will it cover it?' she said doubtfully. She knew that the cameras would be turned on to keep a check on the building site, not on the finished properties.

'No,' Barry said. He turned around and pointed to the opposite end of the site. 'But that one might.'

It was a bit far away, but they might get lucky. 'Let me know please, Barry.' She turned to Sasha as he nodded and walked away. 'I'm sorry,' she said, knowing it wasn't enough, but hoping that the younger woman would understand why she wanted the story kept quiet.

Sasha shrugged. 'I've rung Al. He's fuming because they'll have to do a retraction. I'll try to get a picture of the right girl and we'll run it in next week's paper.'

They both spun round as they were called from one of the apartments. Mary was at the door, but it was another lady who was beckoning them over. Victoria recognised her as the woman with Mary when she'd moved in; she thought it was her daughter or daughter-in-law.

'You,' the woman said, pointing at Victoria as they walked across to the apartment block. 'One night, you said...'

'Candice, stop making a fuss,' Mary said, smiling at the cat as it trotted along behind them.

'You can't expect an old lady to take on the expense of an animal.'

Mary rolled her eyes.

'I am so sorry,' Victoria said. 'I got distracted. It's been a bit busy and I move in...'

'Never mind busy,' Candice snapped. 'What are you going to do about this moggy?'

The cat strolled into the flat, unaware and uncaring of the scorn directed against it. Mary followed him in.

'Mum, stop encouraging it,' Candice said, in an exasperated voice as she stepped back from the doorway and let them inside. 'Please just take it.'

Victoria, followed by Sasha, walked into the lounge. Mary was sitting in an old-fashioned, but comfortable looking recliner chair and the cat was settled down on her lap, purring loudly. Never one to miss an opportunity, Sasha pulled out her mobile and took a picture.

'Are you sure you want me to take him?' Victoria said, looking at Mary.

'No,' Mary replied firmly.

'Yes,' said her daughter-in-law.

'Look, if it's about the money,' Sasha said. 'I think I can help. We've had money pouring into the paper in the last couple of days. As well as suggested names. Nothing like a rescued animal story to tug at people's hearts and purse strings. I'm sure there will be enough to pay for the cats keep.'

'Great, so if you wanted him to stay here with you, Mary.'

She didn't get to finish as Mary looked at her daughter-in-law and said. 'Settled then.'

'I'll come by next week when we've got the name sorted.' Sasha said, checking her mobile and bending down to show Mary the picture she took.

Back outside they saw Belle climb out of a car along with another woman who was older and looked similar enough that Victoria wondered if it was her mother. Behind them, a police car pulled up.

'Looks like trouble,' Sasha said, stating the obvious.

Belle had clearly been crying, Victoria understood. It must be awful to have your picture splashed across the paper like that, especially when it was all lies.

A young lad aged about fourteen sauntered along, pulling a trolley full of the local papers and coming up the road behind him, pushing a buggy, was Natasha.

The lad stuffed a paper through the bottom flat doors and handed one to Belle before carrying on down the road. He handed one to Natasha as he passed her. Victoria saw the young woman stare open-mouthed at the front page and knew that trouble was coming. Sure enough, Natasha sped up and intervened as Belle reached the communal door.

Natasha waved the paper at her. 'I knew it. Women like you shouldn't be allowed to have children.'

Victoria tried to stop Natasha. 'No, it's a mistake...' but the woman shook her off.

Belle turned her head and looked coldly at Natasha. She opened her mouth to speak, but then changed her mind, shook her head and pushed the door open, followed by her mother. They both paused as PC Clarke ran towards them.

'I'm sorry,' he said, looking directly at Belle. 'Two children matching their descriptions were seen boarding a plane at Luton airport.'

Victoria watched as Belle seemed to slump within herself. Her mother grabbed her arm to support her. What the hell was going on?

'The French police went to intercept, but they were too late and the passengers had already disembarked. Their photos have been distributed across Europe.'

'They're gone,' Belle said, her shoulders slumping in defeat. 'He'll be halfway to Pakistan by now and I will never see them again.'

They went inside, followed by PC Clarke and another uniformed officer, who Victoria hadn't seen before.

'I don't understand?' Natasha said.

Victoria shook her head. 'No, neither do I, but it doesn't sound good, does it?'

'I'm going in to see if I can talk to her or the police see what's going on,' Sasha said. 'You never know, a story in the paper might help.'

Victoria was about to follow when Barry called her.

'You better have a look at this,' he said, beckoning her to follow him.

They went to the porta-cabin that acted as his office and the construction base. On the laptop, he had the security film paused. It was a bit far away, but her house was visible enough. It was dark, probably late evening, and two figures were about to go down the side of the property. He pressed play, and they disappeared.

'My guess is they have a key to the back door,' Barry said, leaning across and fast forwarding the film until the same two figures came back the same way, and this time they are clearly visible to the camera. Victoria grabbed the desk for support. She couldn't have been more shocked if it was little green men from mars.

'You all right, Vic?' Barry said, concerned. 'Shall I tell the police?'

'No,' she said, as anger replaced disbelief. 'I'll handle this.'

'You know who it is?' he said, surprised.

'Oh yes,' she said, prodding the screen. 'That's my daughter.'

EPISODES 6 - 10

JASMINE CLOSE - SERIES ONE

EPISODE SIX
JASMINE CLOSE - SERIES ONE

Miles let the music soothe him. He wanted to wipe out all the stress of a very busy week at work so he could arrive home relaxed and ready for the weekend. Things couldn't go on as they were; Jen was not getting any better. The move was supposed to be a fresh start for them both. He had been patient, beyond patient in fact, but despite his efforts, she still hid indoors and refused to face the world. Well, things were about to change. He had indulged her for long enough. He didn't want to be married to a recluse. They used to have fun, and it was about time their were lives returned to normal.

He pulled up on to the drive and frowned at the sight of the VW Beetle. It hadn't been out since the day he'd bought it for her. He switched the engine off and closed his eyes for a second; no point in him going in with a frown and full of negative vibes. He was determined to turn it all around over the next three days. His father used to say if something was worth having, then it was worth fighting for. Miles believed it to be true and had just declared war on everything that was wrong in his marriage.

He picked up the enormous bunch of flowers from the back seat and locked the car door with the fob. He watched a sweet wrapper dance past him, carried by the autumn breeze. He bent down to pick it up and missed as it skipped away again. Then a hand reached out and grabbed it. He stood up and so did they. It was a woman; he guessed about thirty-ish, although he knew he wasn't very good at gauging such things. She was petite and pretty with honey coloured hair and big brown eyes that seemed to dance with mischief as she looked back at him.

'Someone's been a naughty boy,' she said, staring at the flowers.

'I'm sorry,' he said. Was she talking to him?

'I can see that.'

He was a bit taken aback and not at all sure how to take her. 'I haven't,' he said defensively, immediately annoyed with himself when her lips curled into a smile.

'I'm Sonia Casey. I live at number eleven.' She said, offering her hand.

'Miles Fisher,' he said, shaking her hand, which he noticed had a surprisingly firm grip.

'My brats,' she said, pointing behind her to where two young boys stood waiting while tucking into a bag of brightly coloured sweets. She held the captured wrapper up. 'Guilty, I'm afraid.'

Miles watched her walk away, back to her children. She stopped and turned to look at him. 'Good luck.'

'For what?'

'Whatever it is you need them for.' She called over her shoulder.

He looked at the flowers and then went into the house. He straightened the keys that were hanging at an odd angle on the hook in the hall and stood still and listened to the silence.

At first he thought no one was home, which, although it would be disappointing, it would also carry hope. He put the flowers in the kitchen and washed up a dirty coffee cup that was on the draining board, then he walked through the house, checking each room. He found her in the back bedroom. She was on the balcony, asleep in a wicker rocking chair he had never seen before. She looked more relaxed and peaceful than he had seen her in a long while. He smiled as he recalled watching her sleep when they were first together and were both drunk on the passion of their new love. He would pinch himself to make sure it wasn't all a dream, which, in a way, it was.

The accident had turned their idyllic lives into the stuff of nightmares and he had lost her as surely as if she had walked out of their marriage. In a way, that would be better, as he would know how to react and how he should behave. He could be angry and feel betrayed and he could stomp around, alternating between pain and fury. He could cry if he wanted to drown his sorrows in bottles of whisky, or go out and get himself legless or laid. Anything was surely better than this empty, lonely, no-man's-land.

He reached out his hand and gently touched her arm. She stirred and changed position, but she didn't wake. He looked out across the balcony. It really was a lovely spot. In the distance, there was a boat moored up, and a couple were fishing from the front of it. They were sitting on the deck enjoying the last rays of sunshine creeping through the clouds, with their lines dangling in the still water. He envied them the tranquillity of the scene, but he hated boats, even the stationary kind.

Miles looked down at the garden; the newly turfed lawn needed mowing. Soon the mildness of autumn would nudge into the damp chill of winter. Something caught his eye, and he bent down for a closer look at it. On the balcony floor, beside his wife's feet, was a cigarette butt. In total disbelief, he reached out to pick it up. Jenny didn't smoke. Her father had died from lung cancer. Jenny would never smoke. His mind raced as images and fear flooded through him. Was she having an affair? While he thought she was wallowing in self pity and pain, was she actually indulging in hot, steamy sex with her smoky lover?

The butt between his fingers he stood upright again. It was a roll up, and very thick. Surely too thick to be your average cigarette. He raised it to his nose and inhaled, his eyes widening in shocked surprise. 'No way...' he hissed to her sleeping face.

. . .

JENNY FELT SICK. Like she was on a fairground ride. One of those really fast waltzer things that spin you round and round. She wanted to get off, but it wouldn't stop spinning. Miles was shouting at her, loud in her ear. He sounded very angry. She opened her eyes, winced, and quickly closed them again. She sat up abruptly when she realised that cold water was being splashed on her face. She shuddered and yelped and this time her eyes stayed open as she looked into the rage that had engulfed her husband.

'You want to explain this to me?' he demanded, holding the remnants of the joint against her face.

'Not really,' she muttered, drying herself while still struggling to comprehend what was happening to her.

'Tough, because you're going to.'

His face was red. The little vein on his forehead was bulging, as were his eyes. He looked like he was about to suffer a stroke.

'Chill,' she said, stretching and closing her eyes again.

But the chair was rocking violently. 'Oh, no you don't, no way are you going back to sleep. We are having this out. Right now!'

'Right now?' she whispered, as the soft haze of sleep beckoned her.

'Jenny.'

A fresh batch of cold, wet droplets hit her face. Irritation stirred. What was his problem? She opened her eyes again and realised he had a small jug of water and was dipping his fingers in and flicking her. It made her smile and then giggle, although she wasn't really sure why.

'You think this is funny?' He demanded. 'This is our marriage...'

'Really?' she said, staring at the joint in his fingers in amazement. She reached out to take it from him but missed. Her arm didn't seem to go where she wanted it to anymore. It had a will of its own. Her efforts to control the errant limb failed and made her giggle again as her arm hit down on the bannister.

'I can't take much more of this, Jenny. I have no idea who you are anymore or what part I play in your life. I think we might both be better off apart.'

Somewhere inside her muddled head, a voice was telling her to stop giggling and pay attention. But the voice was lost in the sleepy silly fog and her eyes were closing again even before he was out of the door.

SONIA LOVED everything about the Capital, especially in the deserted early hours of the morning. Her high heels made a clicking sound as she trod the grubby, ground down pathway. She loved the smell of decadence and decay and the sight of shadows, silhouettes and flickering neon lights. London was steeped in old world grime and history, sordid and triumphant. The absolute opposite of the organised structures of the new, modern-day city of Milton Keynes.

Her eyes were immune to the sight of drunks and junkies dossing in shop doorways. She could hear the rustle of the rodents as they scurried through the street garbage. The roads were never still, never silent. Black cabs, cars, and even a few messenger bikers were up and out before dawn. But in a city that never sleeps, it felt like the calm before the storm. Morning would bring the shoppers and tourists, the workers and the scammers, but she would be long gone by then.

It had been a good night. Tips had been generous and Hugo, her boss, was pleased. He'd singled her out and complimented her for her good work. She loved the buzz of the casino and the thrill of the deception. Friday night, and sometimes Saturday night, was her secret time. She smiled to herself as she imagined her husband, Paul's, face if he ever actually saw her dressed to impress and working in London. He thought she was busy stacking shelves at Sainsbury's on the night shift.

She had to wait for the Midland train out of Euston. Virgin was the fastest route home, but it was more expensive and an extravagance that she couldn't justify. There were only a few stops, so it still took less than forty-five minutes to reach central Milton Keynes station. In the beginning, she had worried she might be recognised. But time had taught her that the Sonia Casey, wife and mother who wore jeans and flat shoes, was a different person to the Sonia wearing full makeup, high heels and with enhanced cleavage. In fact, if Paul saw her now, he would probably walk past, might even turn his head in curiosity and admiration, but not in recognition. People made associations and in the unlikely event that someone spotted her getting off the train at daybreak, they would never think of mousy Sonia Casey.

She turned left out of the station and walked round to the office block car park. In the far corner were two large industry size wheelie bins, a black one and a green one. With a quick glance to make sure no one was around, she lifted the lid of the green bin, reached in and pulled out a pink recycling sack tied in a loose knot at the top. Clutching the bag, she retraced her steps to the railway station and went into the ladies' toilets.

In the bag was everything she needed to transform herself back into her mousy mum facade. Make-up remover, hair brush, scrunchy, flat shoes and the shapeless, orange trimmed dress that was the Sainsbury's uniform.

Ten minutes later, she walked out of the station carrying a bag for life with all the evidence of the secrets of 'her other self' safely stowed inside. She climbed into the first cab in the taxi rank line and asked to be taken to Sainsbury's. Sometimes she walked as it wasn't very far, but if it was cold or raining, or like today, when she was just tired, then she would pay the few quid for the ride. Her own car was parked in the multi story. If for any reason Paul ever checked up on her, he would find the car exactly where it ought to be. She saw the driver glance at her from his rear mirror. She avoided eye contact and closed her eyes. She didn't want to chat, she just wanted to savour the last, lingering memories of the evening before she reached home and was thrust back into the grinding routine and reality that was her normal life.

JENNY STIRRED AND SHIVERED. She was cold. Opening her eyes, she realised that the door onto the balcony was wide open and she was fully dressed and lying on the sofa in the back room. She sat up and winced. It felt like a steel band had taken up residence in her head. Slowly, she stood up. The telephone fell on the wooden floor. She had no recollection of making or taking a phone call. Bending down, she picked it up and placed it on the desk, then went to the balcony and closed the door. It was cold and barely light. A distant memory stirred. It was important, and she tried to focus, but it was elusive and wouldn't be defined. A fairground ride and rain? Her face had been wet and... Miles. He was there...

Jenny went into the bathroom and then into the bedroom. The bed was neatly made. Empty and not slept in. She tried the guest room and the small spare room, then hurried downstairs into the lounge. No Miles. He wasn't in the study and he wasn't in the kitchen. But a beautiful bouquet of flowers was on the worktop.

She ran to the hall and looked out onto the drive. His car was gone. She walked back into the kitchen and looked at the flowers. It wasn't their anniversary or anyone's birthday and he wasn't prone to buying her random bunches of flowers. So what was going on? She picked them up to smell them and saw the butt of the joint that Steve had given her yesterday.

Jenny picked up the phone and speed dialled her husband's number as the events of last night suddenly flashed back into her head.

'What?' he said, answering almost immediately.

'I'm sorry,' she replied, meaning it.

'For what? For being a drug addict? For shutting me out? Or for giving up on our marriage?'

'A drug addict?' she said, surprised and upset by his accusation. 'One joint and now I'm an addict? I think you're being a bit OTT, don't you?'

'So that was the first time?'

Bugger, she'd walked into that one. 'The flowers are lovely.'

The line went dead.

Jenny made herself a coffee and kept staring at the phone, willing it to ring. But clearly he was hurt, and he wasn't going to make this easy for her. She could hardly blame him. He was right; she had shut him out and as a result she was about to lose him. Was that what she wanted? Things had been pretty damn awful lately, but none of it was his fault. She was the one with the problem and Miles was Miles. True, he was infuriating at times, but nothing new there. She used to laugh at his obsessions and coax him out of his moans and groans. They used to have fun; they used to be happy. Did she really want to throw away the future they might have?

She picked up the phone and tried again. 'I don't want to fight,' she said, not giving him a chance to speak.

'Neither do I, but we've got to talk, Jen, and we have to sort this out.'

'Okay,' she said, knowing it was the truth.

'Good. Well, pack a bag, get in your car and drive to Oxford. I booked us a suite at The Royal. I thought it would be a good place for us to reconnect. It's not much fun on my own, though.'

Jenny was already shaking. How the hell was she supposed to get in the car and drive to Oxford? The silence was deafening.

'You know where I am, Jen. If you really want to save our marriage, then you'll do it.'

He hung up on her again, his words pounding in her ears.

The Royal hotel in Oxford was where he had taken her for a romantic weekend on their first wedding anniversary. He was reaching out to her with the flowers and the getaway. He was really trying. But how was she supposed to get in the car and drive? He was being cruel. She couldn't do it. But if she didn't, then her marriage was over.

VICTORIA HAD BEEN UP since six a.m. and had barely paused for breath. Moving was a hazard that should carry a government health warning. Yesterday, she had packed up the lounge, the kitchen, the bathroom and their bedroom. Dave had promised her he would sort the shed and the garage and Gemma had insisted that she would do her own bedroom. But Friday afternoon, when she went to do a last check around, she found that neither of them had done a thing. Dave didn't come home from work until late and was drunk when he staggered through the door mumbling something about a leaving do and a curry. Gemma stomped up the stairs to her room and barricaded the door, refusing to come out, not even for her dinner.

Victoria still needed to tackle her daughter about the back door key and illicit visits after dark to the new house, and more to the point, who was the boy she was with? But Gemma wasn't easy to pin down and talk to and seemed to be particularly prickly over the last couple of days. Victoria worried and felt guilty because she wondered if it was the move that was causing her daughter's erratic behaviour. She was also aware that Dave had been working a lot of extra hours lately and she had been distracted by the move. It was possible that Gemma was feeling left out and ignored. Wasn't that one of the reasons why kids played up? Was it her inattention that threatened to tip her daughter into being a teenage delinquent?

Victoria decided – fight one battle at a time. Her priority was to get packed up and into the new house. Then Gemma would get her full attention. Whether she wanted it or not.

She spent the rest of Friday afternoon and evening doing the jobs her husband had said he'd already done, broken by bouts of banging on Gemma's door to ask how her packing was going. Eventually, she'd crawled exhausted into bed and straight to sleep, but had woken in the early hours thinking and worrying about everything and anything until eventually, at six a.m., she gave in and got up.

Somehow that morning, it all was packed up and loaded into the removal van. She had cleaned and scrubbed the house ready for the new owners and had only paused to take a short, nostalgic walk around the building that had been their home for the past seventeen years.

As they followed the removal van into Jasmine Close, she felt the stress and irritation seep away and be replaced by excitement. A brand new home! She glanced sideways and smiled at Dave, but his eyes were fixed on the road and a frown became firmly settled across his forehead.

The removal van pulled across the driveway, Dave drove past the house and turned around at the end so that he would be parked in the same direction as the traffic flow. It was one of his things. He got seriously agitated if the car was parked on the wrong side of the road.

'Watch out,' she screeched, as the yellow Beetle belonging to the Fishers suddenly reversed out of the drive.

Dave swerved to the right to avoid the car. He hit the horn, and the VW stopped abruptly.

The cat darted across the road, narrowly avoiding being hit, and the Beetle shot back into the driveway.

Dave parked outside their house. Victoria jumped out and walked quickly back up the Close to the Fishers' house. 'Hey,' she shouted, as up ahead she saw Jenny climb out of the car and run for her front door. 'Wait.'

But she didn't stop. As Victoria reached the house, the front door slammed shut in her face and, despite her ringing the bell and banging on the door, Mrs Fisher refused to open it.

The cat was fussing round her legs and meowing loudly. She bent down to pick him up. 'I think you might have used one of your nine lives up, cat. You hungry?' She said, turning around and walking back to her own house. She paused and wondered if she should go and see Mary to check that she was coping. But it was still early, and she had no idea what time a lady of nearly ninety might get up. Besides, the removal men would be after a brew, and she wanted to supervise the offloading of the van.

She waved to Barry on the building site, put the cat down and hurried to her lovely new house.

Jenny gripped the telephone tightly. The Show Home woman had stopped banging on her door and had finally gone away. What an idiot to think that she could drive again, ever. Miles was wrong to ask her to do it. She simply wasn't safe to sit behind a wheel.

'I'm putting you through now, Mrs Fisher...' the voice on the telephone said.

'Hello, Jenny, how are you today?' Ally, her therapist said, in her soft, soothing voice.

'Miles has left me. I nearly had a crash, I don't know what to do…' she began, before pouring out everything that had happened.

'Well, first, you were very brave getting in the car. That in itself is a hugely positive step…'

'But I nearly crashed.'

'But you didn't crash. Baby steps, Jenny. Getting behind the wheel was a big leap forward…'

'If I don't drive to Oxford, then I lose my husband.'

'I doubt that…' she said. 'Even so. He's looking for you to make the effort, to show that you care enough to try. Tell him what happened and I'm sure it will be all right.'

'Really?' Jenny said doubtfully. 'He was so angry.'

'And why was that, do you think?'

'Because of the dope? He said I shut him out, had given up on our marriage.'

'And have you?' Ally asked.

'No. Of course not.'

'So get on the phone and tell him that.'

Jenny ended the call and stood up. She needed a coffee, but knew that putting off talking to Miles would only make it harder. Ally was always easy to talk to and never got angry or annoyed at her or made her feel stupid. Miles might not be so understanding.

VICTORIA ISSUED instructions and followed the delivery men as they carried her possessions into the house. She knew she was getting on their nerves, but she didn't care. It was her house, her stuff, and they were being paid to do the job. Gemma had barely spoken a word all morning. She had been texting and had sloped off to the garden to take a phone call for about twenty minutes. Victoria had the feeling her daughter had been crying. But any attempt on her part to comfort or talk to her was shrugged off. Dave was in the garage, putting up a shelf unit. She would much rather he helped with getting the living areas unpacked and habitable, but he was in one of his moods and so probably best if he kept out of her way.

'Knock, knock,' Sonia said, walking in through the door and into the lounge. 'How's it going?'

Victoria pulled a face and glanced around at what should be, but showed no sign of being, her new lounge.

'Yeah, I get it, silly question,' Sonia laughed. 'How about I make us all a cuppa?'

'That would be great, thanks.' Victoria replied, glad that her new neighbour hadn't offered to help her with the unpacking. She didn't want a stranger going through her stuff and having any say about where anything should go.

'Front bedroom,' Victoria said, as the removal men shuffled in carrying a large chest of drawers.

'Don't you just love Ikea,' Sonia said, watching it go past.

Victoria nodded, not sure if it was a compliment or an insult. Was Sonia saying her furniture was cheap? She wanted to be friends, but she was never sure about the woman. She picked up the black sack that was full of scatter cushions and dropped them onto the sofa and half expected a comment about DFS and interest free credit.

'Hello, I'm Sonia Casey. We didn't get introduced before when you came to the rescue of Casper.'

Victoria went into the kitchen; her husband had just come through the back door and was shaking the neighbour's hand with more enthusiasm than was necessary.

'Casper?' he said, looking confused.

'The dog.' Victoria said to him. 'The one that was run over.'

'Oh yeah, right,' Dave replied, the penny finally dropping. 'How is he?'

'Recovering well, thanks to you.' Sonia had finished making mugs of tea and pointed to them, 'I haven't sugared any. I'd better get back to my little brats. Shout if you need anything or if I can help at all.'

'I will,' Dave said.

'Thanks,' Victoria replied, scowling at her husband.

Sonia paused at the door. 'Silly me, nearly forgot, I came over to invite you to a barbecue tomorrow. A 'welcome in' type thingy.

'Oh, thanks, but...'

'That would be great,' Dave said with a huge grin.

'Lovely. We'll do it early, say about four? Better bring a jumper, it gets chilly in the evenings, although we do have one of those heaters.'

'Why did you say yes?' she demanded of her husband as soon as Sonia was out the door. 'We have everything to unpack and sort. Besides, you hate getting friendly with the neighbours.'

He put two spoonfuls of sugar from the open packet into a mug and stirred. 'Depends on the neighbours,' then he took his tea and disappeared back to the garage.

JENNY PUT the phone down and rewarded herself with a coffee. Ally had been right. As soon as she told Miles that she had tried to drive, he was happy and said he would come home to fetch her himself. A tiny part of her had hoped he would still be angry and tell her not to bother. The idea of a weekend away in a hotel, even one as lovely as The Royal, was terrifying. Would he want her to go down to the bar or the restaurant? What if he suggested a walk? They both loved Oxford, with its history and heritage, stunning architecture and beautiful waterways. Last time they were there, they'd spent hours wandering around hand in hand, popping into old bookshops and weaving through the tourists and the students and into one of the many bars for a glass of wine. How could she make him understand that everything had changed? That she had changed and no matter how much he wanted it, she was probably never going to be that carefree again.

She glanced at the kitchen clock, an expensive china plate with ugly thick thistles that she hated. A gift from Miles' mother, who had no taste and too much money. Allowing for traffic, it would take him an hour, maybe less, to get back from Oxford. She searched for ways to keep him at home and forget about going away, but dismissed them all. Even if she offered champagne and sex, he would want to leave straight afterwards. She knew him too well. Once a notion was fixed in his brain, nothing would shift it. Besides, he had paid the money and although he wasn't exactly tight, he could certainly be described as careful and no way would he waste a hotel booking that was already paid for.

Somehow, Jenny would have to find a way to cope. She thought of Steve and his stash of marijuana. It wasn't the answer; she knew that, but even so, she did briefly think of running to his flat for a quick puff and a few of his unique words of wisdom from him. Instead, she went upstairs and put her relaxation and meditation CD on, lay down on the bed, and closed her eyes.

'I am a calm and confident woman…' she chanted over and over, knowing that it was a lie.

Victoria watched the removal van drive away. The house was a tip, but at least everything was in now. Gemma was in her room, hopefully unpacking her boxes, and Dave was having a kip on the sofa. Apparently, putting up garage shelves was exhausting work. The cat was at her ankles again, so it seemed like a good time to go and see Mary. 'Come on, puss.'

'House all Okay?' Barry shouted, as she walked past the site.

'It will be,' she replied, without stopping.

She knocked on the door of Mary's flat. The cat's meowing grew louder, as though he knew food was on the other side of the door, which he probably did. From what little she knew, cats were supposed to be intelligent creatures.

She could hear movement from inside the apartment and after a few more seconds, the door opened and the cat shot straight into the house.

'There you are,' Mary said, with a tut. 'I was calling you all evening. If you hadn't had your tackle chopped off, I'd think you were out with the ladies.'

Victoria stood in the doorway, not sure what to do. The old lady hadn't acknowledged her at all, barely even glanced her way. Mary had followed the cat into the kitchen and left Victoria standing there.

'Don't lurk in the doorway like a dummy,' Mary said, as if reading her mind.

Victoria stepped inside and walked through the lounge to the kitchen. It was well fitted out with gloss white units that gave an illusion of space and plenty of natural light with a large window that was on the wall at the side of the building. She had been in the flats before anyone moved in, even though most of them were social housing and therefore not available for her to sell. Despite them being a reasonable size, she had thought they were dark and a bit depressing. But Mary was lucky having the extra side window, the benefit of being in the end apartment.

The cat leapt up onto the worktop while Mary opened a packet of food and squeezed it into a bowl. Victoria stepped forward and took the bowl and put it down on the floor.

'Thanks, can't bend down as easily as I used to.'

'He's hungry.'

'Well, he didn't come in for his dinner last night, I shouted till my throat hurt. Mind, I don't suppose it helps that he doesn't have a name. Calling 'cat' at my door isn't very explicit, is it?'

Mary walked back into the lounge and sat down. She walked slowly, like she was in pain and it was a struggle. Victoria wondered what it must be like to be so old. Did you still want to live on? Or did you reach a stage in life when the pain was no longer worth the gain?

'Sasha will be here on Monday or Tuesday to give you the name from the newspaper vote, and she'll have the money raised as well. I don't know how much it will be, but I thought perhaps you could use some of it to fit a cat flap in the door. That way he can come and go as he pleases.'

'Huh, typical male then. That's what they all do. You married?'

'Yes.'

'You know what I mean, then.'

Did she? 'No, Dave's not like that.'

Mary smiled. 'Of course he's not.'

Victoria headed to the door. 'See you next week then.'

'A cat flap would be good,' Mary said. 'As long as it's not one that all the neighbourhood cats can run in and out of. I'm not running a bloody free for all.'

'Of course not.'

'Oh, and if you see that young hooligan next door, tell him not to be so bloody noisy. He was crashing around in there at five a.m. this morning, woke me up, he did.'

Victoria closed the door behind her. She had been longer than she intended and had so much to do at home, but it didn't seem right that Mary was being woken up by inconsiderate behaviour. Maybe she should knock and check if he was all right and see if she could say something subtle about keeping the noise down.

A little way along the Close, Mr Fisher's car pulled into the drive. She was tempted to go and tell him what a danger his wife was on the road. But he walked quickly into his house. So she turned away and walked to see Mary's neighbour.

The door was slightly ajar. 'Hello,' she called, tapping on it. Then she saw the broken glass on the pavement. It was from the front window, or at least where the front window used to be. Now it was just a big gaping hole in the wall with curtains flapping around it.

Victoria rushed into the apartment. 'Mr Lance?' The front room was a mess, literally turned upside down. Looking around her in growing horror, she pulled her mobile phone from her pocket. 'Police…' she said, hurrying into the hall, heading for the bedroom and almost falling over his upturned wheelchair. 'I need to report a break-in.'

Steve was still in his bed. An overhead hoist hung down just above him. The room was in an even worse state than the lounge. Every drawer, every cupboard had been ransacked. 'Mr Lance…'

He didn't move or respond. His eyes were shut; a tingle of fear ran up her spine as she stepped forward to prod him. 'Oh, God,' she cried into the phone, 'better send an ambulance, too. I can't rouse him.'

. . .

Jenny made it to the VW. She strapped herself in and forced herself not to grip the door handle. She had promised Miles that she would try, really try, to make the weekend work. He, in return, promised that he would be more patient and try harder to understand the demons that stalked her. They agreed they would go away and talk. Be honest with each other and reconnect.

Miles climbed into the car and started the engine. She turned her head and smiled at him. She didn't want to be alone. They owed it to each other to save their marriage.

'We can be happy again,' he said, leaning across to kiss her. 'I'm going to make sure of it.'

It sounded a bit more like a threat than a promise, but that kind of negative thinking wouldn't help. So she took a deep breath and kept up the positive chanting in her head.

As they pulled out of Jasmine Close, the sound of fast approaching sirens threatened to send her into panic mode again. What if the house was on fire? Or was somebody hurt? Should they turn the car around and return to check on the Close and their home? But Miles put the radio on and turned the volume up. He changed gear and put his foot down on the accelerator, making it very clear that there was no going back.

EPISODE SEVEN
JASMINE CLOSE - SERIES ONE

'Is he all right?' Victoria asked the paramedic as he came out of the apartment.

'Yes, he'll be fine.' The young man said. 'Was it you that found him?'

She nodded.

'Do you know if he has any support? Carers? Family? Friends?'

'No, I've barely spoken to him. Everyone is new here. I've seen him with the lady who lives in there.' She pointed to the Fisher's house. 'But I don't think she's in at the moment. Are you taking him to the hospital?'

'No, he isn't hurt. He could probably do with a cup of tea and something to eat, get his glucose levels up.'

'I can do that,' she said, glad to be useful.

The paramedic climbed into the ambulance, and it drove away. Victoria knocked on the open door and pushed it open. 'Hello...'

Steve was dressed and back in his wheelchair. She had no idea if he got there himself or if the ambulance crew helped him. She had never stopped to think about it before or to question how he might cope with everyday stuff, like getting washed and dressed. He was a tall, young man, but looking at him now, she thought he seemed as though he were smaller, shrunk down into his wheelchair. He might not be physically hurt, but she knew pain when she saw it. He had the look of a wounded animal, and like most hurt or cornered creatures, he was lashing out.

'Bugger off,' he shouted at her, before turning to the police officers. 'You can go too. Just leave me alone.'

'Can I make him a drink?' Victoria asked the policeman nearest to her, wishing it was PC Clarke. 'Am I all right to touch stuff?'

'You can make him a drink...'

'Probably a good idea.' The other one said.

'Don't mind me; I'm just the spastic in the corner.' Steve snapped.

Victoria was embarrassed and felt awkward. She didn't know what to do. She filled the kettle and switched it on to boil.

'Mr Lance, we are trying to help.' One of the policemen said.

'I didn't ask you to. I don't want help; just get the fuck out of my house.'

The policeman looked at his colleague, who looked at Victoria; she shrugged her shoulders, not having a clue what to do or how to respond.

'Am I invisible?' he said, staring at them each in turn. 'You think because I'm in this...' he hit his fist on the side of the wheelchair, 'that I have no rights? Get out of my house. Now!'

Victoria reluctantly walked out of the door. So did the policemen. Steve pressed his remote, and the door slammed shut behind them. She looked at the older of the two men; he was probably late thirties, with a worried frown that seemed to be a permanent fixture on his face. 'That's it?'

'Not much we can do if he won't let us.'

'We'll get in touch with ASCAT...'

Victoria looked at him blankly. 'Who?'

'Adult Social Care Access Team. They'll get his social worker to look in on him.'

'I'll get someone to call back later, see if he'll be willing to give us a statement then.' The older one said. 'Not much else we can do. At least he wasn't hurt.'

'Doesn't he have an emergency cord or something? Someway to call for help?' she asked, thinking how awful it must be to be alone and helpless.

'He said he slept through it all. Took a sleeping pill and didn't see or hear a thing.'

'Is that even possible?' she couldn't imagine sleeping so soundly that you could be oblivious to everything. 'What about fingerprints and stuff?' Victoria called after them as they walked to the marked police car.

The older one shook his head. 'He's a victim, not a perpetrator. Nothing we can do if he won't let us. We've had a spate of these attacks all over the city. They always target the weakest and most vulnerable.'

Victoria walked slowly down the Close, torn between anger, disbelief and disappointment. She paused at the Fisher's house. The Audi wasn't on the drive, but it was still worth knocking. If Jenny Fisher was home, then she might be able to help Steve.

But there was no answer; the woman was either out with her husband or ignoring Victoria's knock. Without any idea what more she could do, she went back to her unpacking.

THE WEAKEST AND the most vulnerable. That's what the PC had said, and that's how he was defined now. Steve Lance, the weak, vulnerable frigging man. He looked around his apartment, it was trashed. Couldn't be more damaged if a tornado had come through the window and set up camp in his lounge. Where was Jenny? Why hadn't she come? Surely she would have seen the police car and the ambulance? Perhaps that prick of a husband wouldn't let her come and see him, or maybe she was having a shit day herself. He wheeled himself into the bedroom; it was just as bad, possibly even worse than the other room. The thieving bastard had taken everything that had value and smashed, for the fun of it, anything that didn't. The photo of his mum taken just months before she passed away was on the floor. The frame was damaged; the glass was smashed, tiny shards glistened beside the larger, jagged pieces, deadly for the tyres on his wheelchair.

This was supposed to be his safety zone, but not any longer. He might as well leave his door wide open with a neon 'come in and rob me' sign stuck above it. Given the ease with which the bastard broke in and his total inability to do anything about it. Everything he had been told at rehabilitation about living a worthwhile and independent life was crap. Just lies and bullshit. He desperately needed a joint, but knew that his stash would be gone. The drawer that he kept them in was upside down on the floor.

Deciding that everything was about as bad as it could be anyway, he decided it was worth a closer look. He tipped himself out of the chair and winced as his shoulder hit the wooden floor, and, using his elbows, he dragged himself across the floor. He reached into the drawer and turned it over; the box he kept his gear in was open and empty just as he knew it would be.

OXFORD WAS BUSY. The roads, the pavements, even the hotel reception. Jenny was trying, really trying, but she could feel the panic seeping through her veins like a slow acting poison. She needed to get to the room, and fast. Her breathing exercises and mental positive chants would soon be overwhelmed by her fear. But Miles was behaving as though time had turned back and they were the young loved up couple enjoying an anniversary break.

'Shall we get lunch? We can go out or eat here. The restaurant has had a complete makeover and they've brought in a new chef. He apparently was runner-up in one of those TV cookery things.'

'Lovely,' she said, barely listening and certainly not caring. 'Can we go to the room first?' she fought hard to keep her voice calm.

'Of course, we need to dump your case. I'll run it up. You can wait here if you like?'

She had to turn her head and look at him to check he was serious. Apparently he was. 'I'll come,' she said, wondering how it was possible for him to be so unthinking and unaware. Did he really believe that everything was all right now just because he decided it would be?

They travelled up in the lift to the suite on the top floor. It was the same room that they had stayed in before and she was touched that he had gone to so much trouble to make it a memorable weekend. There was even a bottle of champagne chilling in an ice-bucket beside two flute glasses and a bowl of strawberries.

Jenny felt safer in the room, less fearful, and more in control. Room barely did it justice as it was so much more than that. The bathroom had a large, corner spa bath, the bedroom had an enormous king-size fourposter bed and there was a lounge area with two soft deep sofas, a huge TV and a mahogany desk.

'This must have cost a fortune.'

'You like it, though?'

'Of course I do, what's not to like?' she said, meaning it as she began to relax.

Miles put the case beside the wardrobe and crossed the floor to stand in front of her. 'I do know,' he said, taking her hands and raising them to his mouth to kiss them tenderly. 'How hard these past months have been for you. But there comes a time when the past has to be left behind. We have to find a way to move forward, Jen...'

'I know,' she said.

'Good, so how about that lunch?'

'I'm not really hungry. I'd settle for a few strawberries, especially if we had them with bubbles.'

'You want me to open the champagne?' Miles said, pulling her closer against him; his eyes alight with interest and the first stirrings of long forgotten passion.

'You could, but I was thinking of those bubbles.' She looked towards the open door of the bathroom.

'The hot tub?'

'It's big enough for two,' she said. As his lips closed over hers, she pressed herself against him and felt him respond. It had been a long time for both of them.

. . .

STEVE MANAGED to drag himself back towards his chair and heave himself up into it. His arms were bleeding from the splinters of broken glass that had lodged like little daggers into his skin. The doorbell rang. He groaned and ignored it; he didn't want to see anyone, ever.

'Mr Lance...?' An unfamiliar voice called through the gap that used to be his window. 'Mr Lance, are you in there?'

Why couldn't the world leave him alone?

'Mr Lance, I'm Sharon Stanza from ASCAT. Please open the door otherwise I will have to climb in through your window and I really don't want to do that.'

He pressed the button to open the door. He was curious to see if she would do as she threatened, but either way, he was certain she wasn't going to go away. He knew a couple of the ASCAT team. Social workers had helped him to find and move into the adapted flat. They had put him in touch with the housing association and also with occupational health, who had a say in the adaptations and wheelchair friendly adjustments. Although in his opinion there was nothing friendly with a wheelchair and the two words should never be used together in the same sentence. The last social worker to visit him had tried to persuade him to have daily carers in, and had been surprised by his adamant refusal.

He wheeled himself from the bedroom and into the lounge as Sharon Stanza came through the door. She was huge, and he was pretty sure that any attempt on her part to climb through the window would result in her needing to be rescued herself.

'Thank the lord for that!' she said with feeling. 'Don't know about you, but I need a cup of tea and a choccy biscuit.' She headed straight for the kitchen. 'You do have choccy biscuits, I assume?'

Surprising himself, he grinned and pointed to the goodie cupboard.

She pulled it open and stared inside. 'Oh yes, my kinda man.' She took out a new packet of chocolate hobnobs and opened them, helping herself and biting into the top one. She licked the crumbs from her fingers and put the packet on the worktop before turning away to make the tea.

Steve wheeled himself over and helped himself to a biscuit. He was on his second before he realised that the round, podgy face of Sharon Stanza was sporting a smug smile. She piled sugar into both mugs and stirred. She placed his on a tray and rested it on his lap, then carried hers into the lounge and lowered her considerable bulk down into the leather armchair. He hoped that she would be able to get out of it again. He didn't fancy having her lodged in his lounge forever.

'So,' she said, staring at him intently. 'Were you really asleep?'

'Yes,' he snapped, staring at his tray as though it held the answer to all life's mysteries.

'Steve...' she said quietly.

He raised his eyes and looked at her. She had pale blue eyes that were remarkably clear and seemed to cut straight through all his denial and all his crap. He was sure she could see right into his pained and mangled soul. 'No,' he whispered, his skin flushing as the fear and humiliation flooded through him.

'Bastards,' she said, surprising him. 'Don't you wanna just string 'em up by their balls?' She shook her head and several chins wobbled like the raspberry blancmange his Gran used to make him. 'Sorry, not being very PC am I by assuming it was a male?'

'Oh yes,' he said. 'It was a man.'

'And what are you going to do about it?'

Steve was surprised by the question. Actually, he was surprised by just about everything to do with the woman. 'What can I do? I'm useless...' he remembered the police from earlier. 'Weak and vulnerable.'

'True,' she said. 'If that's what you believe, then that's what you will be. Or you can decide not to be a victim and fight back.'

'Right, so next time someone smashes their way into my house and steals or destroys everything I have, including my last pathetic thread of dignity, I'll leap out of bed and make like Bruce Lee shall I?

Oh, no, I almost forgot I can't do that because my sodding legs don't work!'

'Steve, life is full of shit challenges. We all wish for a better deal. Inside this lump of lard is a Cindy Crawford body pleading to be let out...'

He found himself smiling again; she certainly wasn't like any social worker he'd ever met before.

'But I know, she knows, and I expect even you know that it's never gonna happen. I have to accept that I will never be a skinny model and you have to accept that you can't walk. After that, we have two choices. Moan and be miserable or deal with it and make the most of the life we have.'

'What are you, social worker or philosopher?' he snapped.

'A bit of both, really. I'll organise someone to fix your window and get this mess cleared up. I can get a support worker in to stay with you tonight if you like.'

'I don't need a babysitter.'

'Of course you don't, but I thought you might like the company.'

'Best then, if you don't think at all!'

She heaved herself up from the chair and walked to the kitchen to get the packet of biscuits. She offered him one; he shook his head. She sat down again and took a large bite. Crumbs fell off and disappeared into her blouse. 'I know that you have personal care twice a week and domestic help once a week. I'm sure you've been told that you would qualify for daily care, possibly even for a personal assistant...

'Are you still here?' He said irritably. As if he wanted someone fussing round him all day long.

'All right, I get it. No care then. But keep it in mind. I'll go. Call me if you need anything.'

'Can you make these work again?' He looked down at his legs. 'If not, you might as well piss off.' He felt a bit bad, but he hadn't asked her to come.

She seemed unmoved by his rudeness. 'The police are sending

someone from victim support.' She stuffed the remains of a biscuit in her mouth and then stood up again.

'I thought you said I shouldn't let myself be a victim.'

'I agree it's a bad name choice, but it is a good service. They can offer practical help and counselling.' She put the half-eaten packet of hobnobs on his tray. 'You have to think about how to move forward from here, Steve.'

'I have,' he said seriously.

'Good...'

'Yeah, I'm gonna get myself a gun.'

GEMMA STRETCHED and opened her eyes. Her head hurt and she felt sick and not just from the Malibu and Coke that Abby had kept topping her up with.

'Did you see Mel making out with Kevin's mate?' Abby said from beside her. 'I saw Mike give you his number. You gonna call him?'

Gemma wished she were at home, in her old house, in her own bed, so she could wander down the stairs in her PJs and Mum would make her hot chocolate and buttered toast. She didn't want to do the whole party post-mortem. She wished she hadn't gone to the stupid sixteenth. She hated Kathy Parry, so why had she allowed Abby to persuade her to go and even more stupidly why had she taken Alex? He had been off with her for days, being evasive, ignoring her texts and then when she did speak to him he was cold and argumentative.

'Come on, Gem, don't be a mardy cow. You knew it couldn't last with Alex,' Abby said, as though reading her thoughts. 'He's hot...'

'Too hot for me, you mean?'

'Well, yeah, really. He's older, he has a job, and he's got a car...'

'And now he has that fat bitch, Lauren.' Gemma sobbed, unable to stop the tears as she remembered seeing him snogging Kathy Parry's older sister.

Abby turned onto her side and pulled a tissue from under the pillow and handed it to her. 'You can't blame him. Did you see her boobs? Kathy said they cost thousands, she had them done in London, the same clinic that the stars use.'

'They were fake?'

'Of course they were fake,' Abby said, laughing. 'I'm gonna get mine done when I'm eighteen. I've already started saving. Honestly, Gem, you're such a baby sometimes. You won't keep a boyfriend until you wise up a bit, you know.'

'I really liked him,' she sniffed into the tissue.

'Yeah, I know,' Abby said, cheerfully throwing the duvet off of the bed. 'Come on, get up, we can go into the centre and get a McDonald's breakfast, I'll text Kevin, he asked me out last night, see if he can get hold of Mike and meet us there.'

'I can't,' Gemma said, climbing off the double bed. 'I have to go home. Mum only let me come out last night if I promised to go back this morning to unpack and sort my room out. You can come if you like. Help me.'

Abby pulled a face that made it clear how she rated that as a plan. 'How about McD first, then I'll help you later?'

Gemma shook her head. 'Nah, I can't. Mum's on at me anyway. I better get back.'

'You're fifteen, Gem, not five. You can't jump every time Mummy calls.'

Gemma picked up her bag and walked onto the landing and into the bathroom. Was Abby right? Her Mum could be a pain, and she was a bit stricter than some of her friend's mothers. But she didn't nag too much, and she was easy to get round, like when she'd really wanted those jeans in New Look that were half price.

Truth was, she didn't want to go to the shopping centre. She didn't want to go out with Mike and most of all she was scared of bumping into Alex with his arm draped all over fake tits, Lauren.

NATASHA ROCKED Amy back and forth. The sun was shining, but it had no warmth to it, so the doors onto the balcony were closed. She heard Ed put the kettle on. She looked out of the window and watched as Belle left the apartment building and climbed into a waiting car that Natasha recognised as belonging to the mother. They drove away and out of the Close.

'You spying again?' Ed said nastily from behind her. 'What are you accusing her of this time?'

Natasha continued to rock her baby and tried to shut out his words and his tone. She felt bad enough already. She didn't need him to be constantly digging at her. And it wasn't just him. Everyone looked at her as though she were the one who had abducted the children.

She walked into the nursery and placed Amy down on her cot. What kind of world was it where those who try to do the right thing become the accused and the oppressed? 'I was only trying to help,' she whispered to her sleeping baby.

Ed had made himself a coffee and switched the sports channel on. She looked around for another mug, but there wasn't one. 'Thanks,' she said.

'For what?' he replied, not looking up from the TV.

'For absolutely nothing.' She snapped, walking into the kitchen to make her own drink. She washed up and cleaned the worktops, then walked back into the lounge. 'You can't keep having a go,' she said, looking at her husband, not understanding why he, of all people, wouldn't support her.

'Because of you, that poor cow next door has lost her children.'

'I got it wrong, but I was trying to help.'

'Keep your nose out of other people's business, Nat. That's the way to help.'

'You're wrong...'

'Oh, here we go again, when you were a kid, blah blah bloody blah! Give it up. Not every single mum is an alcoholic like yours,' he stood up and stormed out of the flat.

Natasha watched him go. An image of her mother popped into her head. She tried to push it away. Memories were painful and never welcome, but this one was insistent – she was very young, probably only about six. The dress she was wearing had been a birthday present sent through the post from the grandmother she'd never seen. It was short and tight, barely fitting at all, but she didn't have many clothes and it was one of the few pretty things she possessed. She was hungry, so hungry that she dared to go into the back room where her mum was with the latest boyfriend. Her mum was in a good mood. She had a cigarette in one hand and a bottle of vodka in the other. She was sitting on the man's lap, giggling like a schoolgirl. Her mum gave her a rare smile along with some money so she could run to the take-away in the next street and buy herself a bag of chips.

The young Natasha had cradled the hot greasy paper packet close against her as she hurried home, savouring the smell. She would have stopped at the park to eat them straight away, but a group of older kids were hanging round the swings and the roundabout. So she waited until she got indoors before opening them up and tucking greedily into them. They were delicious, fat and greasy, soaked in vinegar with lots of salt. But she didn't get far. In fact, she only ate about four of the lovely golden brown chips before the man, whose name she never even knew, came out and grabbed the packet from her. She'd stood in the doorway watching as he scoffed them all, her own mother helping herself to a few.

'Oh, give her some,' her mum had said, seeing her in the doorway. So he threw a small handful at her as though she were a dog. They landed on the floor at her feet and she had to drop to her hands and knees to pick them up and eat. An hour or two later, her tummy rumbling noisily, she went in search of food again. The kitchen cupboards were pretty empty, as was the fridge.

The door to the back room was firmly closed, and she knew that if she disturbed her mum again, she'd likely get a slap. The neighbour smiled at her sometimes and had even given her some sweets once. Driven by the growling in her tummy, she ran out of the front door and down the path to the next-door neighbour's. She had to stand on tiptoes to reach the bell, but she managed it and waited, hopeful that the lady might make her a sandwich or give her a packet of crisps.

Suddenly she was picked up and thrown over the shoulder of her mum's boyfriend. He was strong and rough and she'd cried out. He'd shouted at her to shut up and carried her back home. She saw the neighbour watching from the front window, a worried frown on her face.

The young Natasha was locked in her room. She kept hoping that the lady from next door would come and knock, to check that she was all right. But the neighbour didn't come, nobody came, and Natasha was shut away in her room for the rest of the day and then into the long night.

'Thanks, love.'

Victoria smiled at her husband as he took the mug of coffee and sipped it.

'I'll make a start in the bedroom,' she said ten minutes later. 'Can you unpack these kitchen boxes for me?'

'Yeah, in a bit,' he said, heading for the door. 'I'll do it when I get home.'

Victoria stared at him in disbelief. 'You're not going to football training?'

'Course I am.'

'But what about the house and all the unpacking?'

'Yeah, later...' he repeated, opening the front door.

'Dave!' she shouted, as the door slammed shut and he was gone. She looked at the boxes piled up in the hallway; most of them were for the bedrooms. She knew that her husband's later was code for never. If she wanted her lovely new home to be unpacked and sorted, then it was down to her to do it. She wasn't even angry, not really, more a feeling of inevitable disappointment. She bent down and picked the first box up. The doorbell rang. She put the box down again and opened the door. Sonia breezed in.

'Lovely morning,' she said, looking from Victoria to the boxes and back again. 'Did I just see hubby heading out? Is he doing a bunk to escape the unpacking?'

Victoria was about to defend him and then changed her mind. Why the hell should she? She had been making excuses for him pretty much since they met. 'Yep, football training. Apparently, it can't possibly be missed.'

'Sounds about right. I hope he'll be back for the barbecue...'

'Food and drink? I'm sure he will.'

Sonia laughed and nodded her head in understanding. 'I came to ask if you needed any help.'

'Oh, no, I'm fine.'

'I get it; you don't want someone else going through your boxes.'

Victoria shook her head. 'No, that's not it at all.'

'Sure it is,' Sonia grinned. 'I'm just the same, it's a violation of privacy, a bit like having a stranger go through your drawers. We all have our little secrets.'

Secrets? Victoria didn't have secrets, did she?

'I'll leave you to it, but shout if you change your mind.'

Victoria picked up the box again and started up the stairs. She almost made it to the top when the doorbell went again. She put the box down on the landing and ran down to open the door.

'Hi,' said Paul. 'Son sent me to carry some boxes up the stairs for you.'

'Oh, no, really, I can manage.'

'She said you would say that,' he replied, stepping into the hall and picking up the first box. 'But gave me strict instructions not to take no for an answer.'

He was already on his way up the stairs. It seemed she had no choice, so she picked up the next box and followed him up.

'Thanks,' she said twenty minutes later, when the hall was empty and the boxes were all stacked in the relevant bedrooms.

'You're very welcome. Anything else you need shifting?'

She shook her head.

'I'll see you later, then. I've been told to fire up the barbie at four, food should nicely charcoaled thirty minutes later.'

Victoria made herself a coffee. Paul seemed really nice, pleasant looking and easy going. She didn't really want to go to a barbecue, but both he and Sonia seemed genuinely friendly and welcoming.

She heard her daughter arrive home and called out. 'Gemma? Did you have a nice time at the party?'

Her daughter walked into the kitchen. There was a sadness surrounding her and Victoria instantly felt guilty. Was it because of the move?

'Want a hot chocolate, love?' she said, getting a mug out ready and switching the kettle on to boil. 'I've got some marshmallows?'

Gemma smiled and nodded. Was now the time to question her about the back door key? She tipped the sachet into the mug, added the water and stirred. 'Everything all right?'

'Yeah, of course,' Gemma replied, a bit defensively.

'Was the party good?'

'S'alright,'

'Who was there?'

Gemma shrugged and took the drink from her.

'Were Kathy's parents there? I haven't seen her mum for ages.'

'Yes, they were there. If you want a report, you can ring Mrs Parry and ask her. I'm sure she can give you an account of what I ate, drank, and who I danced with.'

'That's not why I'm asking.'

'Yeah, it is. You're always checking up on me. Always wanting to where I am and who I'm with. I'm not a kid anymore.'

Victoria stared after her daughter in shocked surprise. It simply wasn't true. Yes, she could be a bit strict, but surely it was her job to keep her daughter safe. She gave Gemma a few minutes to calm down and then she went upstairs and knocked on the door before entering.

'Oh, come in, why don't you?'

Victoria decided to ignore the rudeness. Her daughter was sitting on the bed, hugging her knees. Her eyes were red, and a scrunched up tissue was beside her. The bed was about the only thing not still packed away and that was only because Victoria had made it up for her daughter the previous evening.

She wanted to go to Gemma, pull her in her arms and hug away the teenage angst, but she knew it wouldn't be welcomed. 'I can help you unpack if you like?'

Gemma lay down with her back to Victoria. It wasn't going well. Victoria decided she would scrap the softly, softly routine and try the direct approach.

'Why did you take the back door key and sneak into the house? And who were you with?'

Her daughter turned over and looked at her, then the tears began and she was sobbing. Victoria sat down on the bed and stroked her daughter's hair. 'What is it, love?'

'He dumped me.'

'It seems you were right.' Victoria said to Sonia at the barbecue, later.

'I usually am.'

'Gemma had a boyfriend.'

'Obviously,' Sonia replied, topping her glass up from the jug of Pimm's. 'Pretty, fifteen-year-old girl.'

'Hmm, seems I've been a bit blind.'

'Well, don't beat yourself up about it.'

'It just doesn't seem possible that my little girl is all grown up and has, or had a boyfriend. Apparently, he dumped her. She's very upset.'

'Broken hearts heal quickly at that age. She'll bounce back as soon as the next teenage hottie asks her out.'

Sonia sat her two boys down on the picnic blanket and gave them each a sausage smeared with tomato sauce and wrapped in a soft, white roll.

'I suppose I'm going to have to give her the talk,' Victoria said, staring at the boys and remembering her Gemma as a little tot. It didn't seem possible that she was almost an adult.

Sonia laughed at her. 'The sex talk?'

Victoria nodded.

'She's nearly sixteen, not sure there's anything you can tell her. In fact, she could probably tell you a few things you didn't know!'

'No, Gemma said nothing happened.'

'And you believe her?'

'Of course.'

Paul, apparently oblivious to the conversation, offered her a sausage. Victoria took it, grateful for the diversion, and thanked him.

'Is your husband coming?' he asked her.

'So he says,' she replied, holding her mobile phone up. 'On his way.'

'What about your daughter?' he said, holding up a fork with a sausage on. 'I've got plenty. Take something into her if you like.'

Victoria finished her drink and Sonia immediately filled it up again. She was going to protest; she still had loads of unpacking and sorting to do and was back to work tomorrow. But then she thought, sod it, why not? She deserved a couple of stress-free hours.

Dave arrived an hour later by taxi, so she knew he had been drinking. He planted a slobbery kiss on her cheek before plonking himself down on one of the Casey's garden chairs and tucking into the plate of food that Paul handed him.

Victoria stood up. 'I might just go and check on Gemma,' she said, wondering why the ground beneath her feet was moving.

'Here, take her this, Paul said, handing her a plate with a burger and a bun. 'Hold on, I'll put some sauce on.'

'Mind your step,' Sonia said, holding up the empty jug of Pimm's. 'It catches up on you after the first few glasses.'

Victoria carried the plate down the side of the house and out through the gate. Was she pissed? Surely she hadn't had that much to drink?

She looked up the Close, towards the apartment block, and thought of Steve Lance. Maybe she should go check on him? Not that he seemed to want any help, but even so, it would be the right thing to do. She could even offer him the burger, plenty more where that came from, she could go back and get another one for her daughter.

It was getting dark, and the autumn air was chill. She shivered and upped her pace, pleased that she was able to walk in a straight line. She was fine, not drunk at all. She paused at the Fisher's house; the Audi still wasn't on the drive, but something was wrong. She stood and stared, trying to work out why alarm bells were ringing in her head. Then she realised that the side gate was open. She took a few steps closer. Mrs Fisher might be home and in the garden, the gate being opened wasn't really a big deal. Yet she knew that it was. She knew that the gate was never left open, and that something was not right. She pulled her mobile phone from her pocket and pressed in 999, 'I'm reporting a possible break-in,' she whispered. She heard noises coming from the garden, so she gave the address and then hung up.

Clutching the plate, she tiptoed down the side of the house and peeped around the wall at the end. A figure was standing by the back door, a pottery flowerpot in their hand. They were tall and wearing jeans and a jacket with the hood pulled up. Given the height and build, she was pretty sure it was a man. It looked like they were just about to smash the glass to break in. Images of Steve's house flashed into her brain and anger surged, overriding her normal caution.

Victoria charged at the figure, who swung round in shocked surprise as she hurled the plate and the burger at him. The missiles hit him in the chest, then she launched herself at him in a rugby tackle that took them both plummeting to the floor. Her attack took the man totally by surprise and for a few brief seconds, she had the upper hand as she landed on top of him. Her advantage didn't last very long though, as in one swift strong movement she was rolled over and he was astride her, his hands pinning her down.

'What the...!' he yelled, staring down at her.

Victoria screamed and struggled.

They both heard the noises behind them. The man stood up as Miles Fisher ran into the garden, followed by his wife.

Victoria got unsteadily to her feet, she opened her mouth ready to tell the Fishers to grab him and hold him until the police arrive. But the man jumped in first, taking her totally by surprise.

'Miles, call the police. This crazy woman just attacked me.'

She was struggling to engage her brain. The ground was moving and her head was fuzzy. She really wished she hadn't drunk quite so many glasses of Pimm's. 'Wait,' she said, bewildered, a horrible feeling creeping up on her. 'Do you know each other?'

'Yes,' Jenny Fisher said, running to the man and hugging him tight. 'This is my brother, Brett Anderson..'

EPISODE EIGHT
JASMINE CLOSE - SERIES ONE

Belle stayed close to the wall. She didn't want to be seen until she knew it was safe and her sister-in-law was alone. She knew that if Mo's older sister was seen talking to her, then it could cause no end of trouble for Shaz, and so it was best to be cautious and keep a low profile. This was pretty much her last hope. She had been to every relative and every property that she knew her husband and his family had links with. Nobody would cooperate with her, no surprise there, of course, but she had to try.

The primary school was old, possibly even from the late nineteenth century. Belle had only been there once before, many years ago. For all she knew, Shaz might not even work there any longer. It was different now. Security fences had been erected around the perimeter and the gates were locked. She glanced at her watch. It was eight-fifteen. Surely the caretaker or some member of staff would open up soon, ready for the start of the school day.

A car slowed down and then stopped. Belle made sure she remained out of sight. The driver, a well groomed female, probably in her late thirties, climbed out of the vehicle and unlocked the school gates before driving into the car park. Belle waited until the woman entered the building before she slipped into the grounds.

Belle found herself a hiding place between the large wheelie bins at the edge of the staff car park. It was perfect. She could stay out of sight, but had a clear view of every car as it parked. Teachers began to arrive, and so did the children. She had to fight back the tears as she saw them kissing their parents goodbye at the gate before skipping into school. She had to stay focused and be positive. Tamsin and Kyle were relying on her to find them and bring them safely home. And she would do so, however long it took and whatever she had to do, she would get her babies back.

The car park was almost full, and it was nearly nine, it seemed that her sister-in-law no longer worked at the school. She needed to get out of the gate before it was locked up again, so she slipped out of her hiding place and made her way around the parked cars. As she approached the exit, a dark blue hatchback drove in through the gates and Belle clearly saw the driver was her husband's sister.

The hatchback pulled into a space, and the woman got out of the car. Belle hurried towards her and called her name. Shaz swung round in surprise.

'Belle?'

'Overslept?' the stern voice of the lady who had unlocked the gates demanded.

Belle ducked down behind a car.

'Sorry, Miss Cole, I had an early dentist appointment. I emailed your secretary and I don't have a class for the first period.'

Miss Cole gave Shaz a glare before heading to the security fence to close and lock the gates.

'What the hell are you doing here, Belle?' Shaz said, making a show of getting books and her briefcase from the back of the car.

'He's taken Tamsin and Kyle.'

'I know, I heard. I'm so sorry.'

'You've got to help me…'

Miss Cole walked past; she paused, glanced at Shaz and tapped her watch before going back into the building.

'I can't.' Shaz said.

'Please, who else can I turn to?'

'I'm late; I've got to go in. I'm sorry, Belle, I really am, but what can I do?' Shaz closed her car door and pressed the fob to lock it.

Belle grabbed her arm; the tears, never far from the surface, overflowed and ran unchecked down her face. Shaz seemed to soften; she leaned in and whispered. 'There's a pub, The Crown, in the next street. I'll meet you there at lunchtime. Twelve fifteen...'

VICTORIA HAD BEEN TEMPTED to call in sick and it wouldn't exactly be a lie. Her head felt as though an army were marching through it despite the Nurofen she had taken. Added to the hangover was the humiliation and total embarrassment from yesterday's fiasco. How was she ever going to face the street again? She buried her head in her hands and groaned. The door to the Show Home opened, and she forced herself to look up and smile. The smile froze on her lips and she felt the tingling burn of a blush dash across her skin. She stood up slowly, wishing she had a magic wand so she could open up a hole under her feet and disappear into it.

'Jen said I'd find you hiding in here,' he said. His accent was American; she hadn't noticed it last night. He was also taller than she remembered him being.

'I'm not hiding. I work here.'

'Yeah, she said not to expect an apology.'

'Me apologise to you,' she snapped, embarrassment quickly being replaced by anger; 'you had me arrested!'

'You assaulted me.'

'Bit of an exaggeration,' she said, moving closer to him.

'What, so lobbing plates and burgers and then throwing someone to the floor is your way of saying hi, is it?'

'Now you're being ridiculous.'

'Ridiculous? I think you're damn lucky I didn't get you charged.'

'You still let them handcuff me and take me to the station, though, didn't you?' The only small saving factor was that it was Sunday and therefore Barry and the builders weren't on site to witness it. 'Why didn't you speak up then instead of pointing your finger and making wild accusations?' She jabbed his chest with her fingernail.

He stepped closer to her and grabbed her hand, holding it tight. The anger between them was charged with something else, something undefinable and even scarier than being arrested. Victoria felt as though the surrounding air was suddenly sucked away and she could no longer breathe. He yanked his hand away and stepped back. The silence engulfed them as they looked into each other's eyes. The Show Home door opened and the strange moment ended as Sonia breezed into the office.

'Hi,' she said, thrusting her hand out towards him. 'I'm Sonia Casey, and I saw you coming out of the Fisher's house, so I'm guessing you're the mystery man who caused all the trouble last night.'

He took her hand and shook it. 'Brett Anderson,' he said, before glancing at Victoria. 'Sometimes it takes two, you know.'

Sonia grinned at him.

'We are not finished,' he said to Victoria before walking out the door.

'Yummmeeey.' Sonia said, watching him go.

Victoria sank down into her desk chair and buried her head in her hands again. She felt like she'd just been run over by a bulldozer. Her hands were trembling and her breathing was erratic. 'He's insufferable.' She snapped. 'And actually, so are you. What the hell was in that Pimm's last night?'

'Hey, don't blame me because you can't take your drink. I totally get why you might want to tackle him to the ground, but what possessed you to throw the burger at him?'

Victoria groaned again. 'How do you even know all this?' Obviously her humiliating arrest had been witnessed, but how did they know the embarrassing details?

'Miles told Paul early this morning. Apparently, Brett's clothes are smothered in tomato sauce.' She started to laugh. 'I only wish I'd been there to see it.'

Victoria certainly wasn't ready to see the funny side. 'Did you want something other than to revel in my misery?'

'Actually, I came to rescue you. I saw him walking down the Close and come into here. I figured it might be a bit confrontational, so I came to break up round two. Although it wasn't quite what I expected...' Sonia paused and looked at her. 'You seemed to be pretty close.'

The phone rang, making Victoria jump. She picked it up, grateful for the interruption.

Sonia shrugged her shoulders. 'Saved by the bell,' she said, as she left.

'How did you get on?' Jenny asked, as Brett walked through the door.

'The woman is...' he paused, searching for the word. 'Interesting.'

'Well, I did warn you she's very annoying.' She poured him a coffee from the percolator and added milk. 'Miles likes her, but I just want to run and hide when I see her coming.'

'From what I've heard, you want to run and hide from everyone,' he said.

'You've been talking to Miles.'

'He's worried about you.'

Jenny led them into the lounge and sat down. The weekend hadn't exactly built bridges between them, but maybe a rope ladder had been built, which was a start. His expectations for her had been too high and her fear was too far entrenched to be dropped in a weekend.

'Is that why you're here, Brett? Did he ask you to come?'

'No, you did.'

'I did?' Jenny said, surprised.

He smiled gently and took her hand. Whatever the reason for him being there, she was so glad to see him. Even though they didn't share the same blood, from the moment their lives had collided with the marriage of their parents, he had taken his new position as big brother totally seriously.

'Dad and your mother are away at the condo in Florida. I've been keeping an eye on the New York apartment for them. You left a message on the machine. It was a bit garbled, but you sounded pretty desperate...'

Jenny remembered waking up on the sofa in her room with the phone in her hand on Saturday morning and no recollection of making a call.

'You said Miles was going to leave you. So I went home, packed a bag and got the first flight over.'

Jenny leaned her head against his shoulder, and he gently stroked her hair. 'Thank you,' she whispered.

'Hey, that's what big bros are for.'

'Can you stay long?'

'Not sure yet, I need to make some calls later, see what I can do.'

Jenny sat up and sipped her coffee. She felt guilty for making him come over and even more guilty that she wanted him to stay as long as possible. His life was in America, and she knew it was selfish of her. But he would give a new perspective on what was happening. He would have more empathy and be more patient than Miles, yet at the same time he would tell her when she was being an idiot and it was time to sort herself out.

'So, did she apologise?'

'Did she hell. Fiery lady, that one.'

Jenny turned to glance at him, pretty sure she detected a touch of admiration in his voice.

'She will, though,' he said confidently. 'I'll get a sorry out of her before I leave.'

THE PUB WAS old and worn, but pleasant enough. Over the weekend, Belle and her mother had been to Birmingham and London, looking for information. Her husband's family was large, and they owned many properties. She had wanted to get on the first flight to Pakistan, but she had no idea where to even begin looking for the children. She needed help. Shaz was one of Mo's sisters, the one who got away. She moved from London to Kingston-upon-Thames in Surrey, got herself a job, a flat, and a boyfriend. She was frowned on, if not actually disowned by the family, which was why Belle left her until last, believing that she was the least likely to have information. But there was hope; Shaz must be in contact with someone since she knew the children had been taken.

'Do you trust her?' her mother asked, as they sat in the corner and sipped coffee.

'I have no choice,' she replied.

'Will she turn up?'

'Yes,' Belle held up a flat security card, 'she gave me this so I could get out of the school gate. She'll have to come even if it is just to collect it.'

'I don't want to be negative, Belle, but why would she help you?'

Belle had been asking herself the same question, searching for the words that would appeal to Shaz and make her go against her family. She looked at her mum. 'Because she is a good person and she knows they should be with me.'

Her mother nodded her head, the stress of the past few days showed on her face. Belle felt the familiar stab of guilt for what she had put her family through. But she couldn't undo it and even if she could, she wouldn't, as that would be wiping out her children along with the marriage. And it hadn't always been bad; she had loved him in the beginning, and was pretty sure he loved her back. It all changed after his father dropped dead from a heart attack and Mo became head of the large, extended family. He inherited huge responsibilities and had to live up to the expectations of relatives in England and Pakistan.

'Is that her?' her mother said, nudging her ribs.

Belle looked up as her sister-in-law hurried through the doors.

'I can't stay long,' Shaz said, sitting down.

'Can I get you a drink?' Belle's mum, Maggie, asked.

Shaz shook her head. 'I have no say, no influence with Mo or any of the family now, Belle, you know that.'

'You could tell me where to look in Pakistan.'

'You're not going there?' Shaz said sharply.

'Of course I am. How can I not? But I haven't got a clue where to begin searching.'

Shaz shook her head. 'It's madness. Even if you do find them, what good would it do?'

'I'll bring them home.'

'Right! So you think that the family will just let you take them?'

Belle was getting agitated and upset. 'I'll go to the police.'

'And what will they do?' Shaz said harshly. 'The children are with their father and his family. They haven't been abducted by strangers.'

Belle was shaking with fear and anger. She knew that Shaz was making sense, but she couldn't accept that there was nothing she could do. Her mother was crying beside her, but her own tears were spent. 'The embassy then. They'll help me,' she said desperately.

'Look, I know I'm not saying what you want me to say, but I'm telling you now that the police and the authorities will do nothing to help you take the children from their father.'

Belle stood up. 'With or without your help, I'm going to get them.'

Shaz looked up at her and sighed. 'Give me a few days and I'll see what I can find out. Give me your number and I'll call you.'

'Really?'

'Yes, now I have to go. Promise me you won't go running off to get them before you hear from me.'

'I won't let her,' her mother said solemnly.

'Two days. Then I'm booking my flight.'

Shaz picked up her security card and nodded her head in agreement. She got her phone from her handbag and tapped in the number that Belle gave her, and then she left.

Jenny looked down the Close. It was empty and quiet. Even the builders had stopped for lunch. It was cloudy and cold; autumn was finally nudging the warmer weather away. Not that she didn't like the warmth of the sunshine, but for her clear blue skies made the world expand. She felt safer with dark skies and low clouds.

She had to do it; she had thought about ringing him, but that was the coward's way. It all seemed unfair to her. Miles was being unreasonable. But she had promised, and now she had the unpleasant task of telling Steve. Jenny had been putting it off all morning, telling herself it was no big deal whilst knowing that it was. She took a deep breath and ran; she didn't stop until she was banging on his door.

It didn't open. She bent down and shouted through the letterbox 'Steve, let me in...' she couldn't hear any sound from the apartment and the door stayed shut.

'Poor sod.'

Jenny straightened up and swung round to face Mary, the elderly lady from next door. 'I'm sorry?'

'I expect you are. We all are, all apart from the little shit that did it.'

Jenny had no idea what the lady was talking about. 'Sorry, who did what?'

Mary looked at her as though she wasn't that bright. 'The bastards who broke in.' Mary leaned closer and lowered her voice. 'I'd lay off the wacky baccy dear. It messes with your brain cells and I'm not sure you've got too many to spare.'

Jenny watched her go back inside her apartment, followed by the black and white cat. She didn't even know which bit to respond to first. The insult to her intelligence, or the information that Steve had been broken into. What kind of lowlife preyed on the disabled? She wanted to know if he was hurt. Was that why he wasn't answering his door? But Mary had gone back into her own flat and there was nobody else that she could ask. Jenny bent down and shouted through the letterbox again, but still the door didn't open and there was no sound from inside. Annoyed that her trip out was for nothing and concerned for Steve, wondering where he was and what he was doing, she ran back home.

Brett wasn't around. Jenny didn't know if he had gone out or if the jet lag had caught up with him and he was having a sleep. She made herself a coffee and warmed up a croissant and smothered it with butter and a small amount of apricot jam. And put the coffee and the croissant onto a small tray and carried it up to her room. She settled down on the balcony and bit into the warm, sweet treat. A drop of butter dripped down her chin; she dabbed at it with a tissue and looked out beyond the garden to the canal.

She saw him immediately. She had to squint and concentrate to bring him properly into focus, but it was definitely him. He wasn't moving; he seemed to be stationary, staring into the water. But he was uncomfortably close to the edge.

Jenny knew Steve liked the canal and often went in his wheelchair for a walk along it. She had, on occasions, sat on her balcony and watched him go past and waved as he did so, never sure if he saw her or not. But this was different. Something about the way he was siting. Still and slumped, was unnerving her.

A canal boat went slowly past him and when it was gone, he edged his chair even closer.

Jenny leapt to her feet, dropping the croissant on the floor. 'Steve, no...' she shouted, even though she knew he wouldn't hear her.

He stopped, and she saw another canal boat had just come under the bridge and into view. It was moving slowly, but would be past him in minutes.

Jenny charged down the stairs and out of the door. She ran down the Close and onto the redway at the end of the estate. Fuelled by fear and a surge of adrenaline, she ran towards the canal. The pathway took her a long way round, but she had no idea how to find a shortcut across the scrubland. The area was marked for future development and had a perimeter made up of modern new fences interspersed with thick brambly bushes and hedgerows. If she went in to the area, she wasn't convinced she would find a way out. So she ran around the redway. Unfit and afraid she didn't stop until he was in sight.

The canal boat chugged on, the usually still water in the canal swelling each side of the boat and a pair of elegant swans rode the wave behind it.

'Steve!' she shouted, barely able to get enough breath to make the sound.

He turned his head, and she saw shock and surprise register on his face.

'What the fuck are you doing here?' he said, looking into the murky water.

She took hold of his wheelchair in a firm grip and fought to get her breathing back under control. 'Move back, you're too close to the edge.'

'What are you? My Mother?'

'No, but I am someone who cares,' she said, gripping the chair even tighter.

He looked up at her. 'What, you think I was planning on going in there?'

'No,' she lied, and then sighed. 'Maybe.'

'Well, if I was, you hanging on the back wouldn't stop it, you silly cow.' He wheeled back away from the edge and gave her a small smile. 'But thanks for wanting to.'

Relieved, she sank down onto the grass that grew along the edge of the canal.

'Damn, you are one unfit lady,' he said. 'look at the state of you.'

She couldn't deny it. 'I used to run every morning before work.'

He nodded his head; she didn't need to tell him when that had ended. 'Better get yourself a treadmill.'

'That was a shock to the system,' she said, her breathing finally returning to normal, but the stitch in her side remaining.

'What, me or the run?' Steve replied.

'Both.' She looked at him seriously. 'You weren't really going to…'

'Don't be soft. Not exactly a smart way to go, even with useless legs, I reckon I could swim enough to keep me afloat. I was just admiring the view.'

He grinned, but it didn't reach his eyes. She could see his pain and she understood. Home had been his sanctuary, his safety zone, and that had been stolen from him. She didn't know if his denial was real or not. She knew what it was to feel afraid and how easily depression seeped into the soul and corrupted and corroded everything.

She reached out and squeezed his hand. 'I'm glad,' she said

gently. 'I heard what happened.' She paused, waiting for him to respond, but he didn't. 'Did they hurt you?'

He pushed her hand away. 'Nah, I slept through the whole thing.' He started to wheel away from her.

Jenny got to her feet and ran after him. She grabbed hold of the wheelchair, aware that the clouds were clearing and a small slither of sunlight was sneaking through the gap. She wanted to get home, get indoors, but didn't feel able to leave him. 'Can we go that way?' she said, pointing in the direction of the redway that led back to the Close.

'Don't worry,' he said, heading towards the scrubland, 'I'll get you home. This is a shortcut.'

VICTORIA PUT the broccoli in the pan and turned the hob on. She loved the clean, shiny lines of her new kitchen and appliances. The old house had been exactly that – old. It was small, cramped, and crumbling around their ears. Well, okay, that was perhaps a bit of an exaggeration, but it had needed constant repair and renovation and DIY wasn't exactly Dave's thing. Although, if she thought about it, which she did sometimes, it was a struggle to know what her husband's thing actually was. Other than insisting that parked cars faced the direction of the traffic.

'Hi, Mum,' Gemma said, heading straight for the fridge and pulling out a yogurt.

'Dinner will be ready in twenty minutes,' she said to her daughter, who shrugged and peeled back the lid to eat it, anyway.

'How was school?'

'Fine.'

'Have you finished unpacking your room?'

'Yep.'

'Is it looking nice?'

's'okay.'

Victoria decided that having a wisdom tooth removed had been easier than trying to hold a conversation with her daughter. Gemma dropped the empty tub into the bin and the spoon in the sink. Victoria gave it one more go. 'Everything all right, love?'

'Yep.'

Victoria picked the spoon up and put it in the dishwasher. 'You can talk to me,' she said, knowing she was wasting her breath.

Her daughter paused in the doorway, Victoria looked at her hopefully.

'Mum…'

'Yes?'

'Can I stay at Abby's house Friday night, please?'

'Why don't you have her sleep over here? Show off your new room.' She suggested.

'Mum, it's all arranged. We're having pizza and a Twilight marathon.'

Victoria nodded her head and forced herself to smile. She couldn't remember the last time they spent an evening as a family. If Gemma was home, she was in her room, and Dave wasn't much better. He went to the pub whenever he could get away with it, add that to working late, darts night and football and it didn't leave much time or energy for them to spend as a couple. Was that his fault or hers? She didn't really know. Maybe she didn't make enough of an effort. Somehow life had slipped into routine and habit and the passion had all but disappeared.

'Knock, knock,' Sonia said, coming in through the back door. 'Don't mind, do you? It seems so formal to ring the doorbell all the time, much easier to slip into the garden and round the back.'

Actually, Victoria did mind. She minded a lot.

'How do you fancy the gym?' Sonia said, before she had a chance to put her neighbour straight about the whole back door thing.

'I don't really do the gym.'

'Well, I have two free passes for ten day's trial at the one overlooking the lake. Thought I'd go to the Pilates class tonight followed by a swim. You up for it?'

Victoria shook her head. 'Thanks, but no.'

'So what else are you going to do all evening?' Sonia persisted.

'I have loads of unpacking to do still.' she wasn't sure why she needed to justify her actions. Surely no thanks should be enough.

'Well, the boxes will still be there tomorrow and the next day,' Sonia said, waving the tickets at her. 'I'm going at seven. See you then.'

No, you won't, Victoria replied in her head as Sonia let herself out of the back door. To reinforce the fact, she walked over and turned the key, locking it from the inside, then she went upstairs to get changed out of her work clothes.

Hearing a car, she looked out of the window to see if it was Dave. He was already late and hadn't sent her a message to say that he would be. Only it wasn't him, it was Paul pulling onto the next door drive. She watched as he parked before climbing out of the car. The front door opened and the two boys charged out and into a hug from him. They were followed by Casper the dog, limping, but mobile, and frantically wagging his tail. Then Sonia, who smiled at her husband and lent in for a kiss on the lips. It was such a perfect family picture, almost like it had escaped from a Disney script. Had it ever been like that for them? Neither Dave nor her were the touchy feely types, yet she felt a pang of envy, seeing the Casey's kissing so openly on the street.

A movement caught her eye, and she saw a man jogging up the Close. It was Brett, and jogging was an understatement. His strides were long and fast, and despite her assumption that he was returning from rather than starting on a run, he had barely worked up a sweat. She watched him. For some unfathomable reason, she was unable to drag her eyes away. He was almost at her house when he suddenly and unexpectedly looked up, catching her staring. She stepped back away from the window, but she knew he had seen her and was pretty sure that not only did he have a mocking smile on his smug face, but he also winked at her.

BELLE PUT the kettle on and looked at her mother. 'Thanks for today,' she said, 'and yesterday and the day before...'

'That's what mums are for.'

'Tea?'

Her mum shook her head. 'I must get home. Madge from next door has been feeding the animals, but Barney hasn't been for a walk for days, poor thing. My garden will be full of mess and him and Lulu will be fighting, well, like cats and dogs.'

Belle dropped a tea bag into a cup and added the boiling water. She didn't want her mum to go, but knew that she was being selfish.

'I'll be back, love,' Mum said, as though reading her mind. 'Or better still, why don't you come and stay with me for a few days while you wait to hear from Shaz?'

It was tempting. Her childhood home always felt safe and comfortable. A place where she didn't have to be strong and in control. Her mum would fuss her and spoil her and she could slip back into that childlike state of being cared for again. 'I can't,' she said sadly. 'I have to stay here. This is where the children know to find me. I can't leave here not unless it's to go and fetch them.'

She watched from the balcony as her mother drove away. The baby next door was crying, and she felt an unexpected flash of sympathy for the young mother. She dismissed it quickly enough. The bitch had caused her so much trouble, no amount of sleepless nights could justify what she'd done. She closed the glass doors and put the TV on. Not because there was anything she wanted to watch, but because she hated the silence.

The house was still packed up, ready for the hurried move that never happened. She couldn't go now, not without her babies. She thought about putting everything back to normal so that it would be comforting and homily when she did get them back. But in reality, she knew that if by some miracle she managed to get Tamsin and Kyle back, then they couldn't return to the house, anyway. She sat down on the sofa and closed her eyes.

Victoria sat at the breakfast bar in the kitchen and ate her dinner alone. She hadn't managed to get the dining room table and chair set she had her eye on yet, so the bar stools in the kitchen were the next best thing. She had laid out the worktop with new fancy mats from Next; she had poured a glass of juice for Gemma and opened a bottle of red wine for her and Dave. Only she was drinking alone. Gemma had taken her plate and glass upstairs and Dave had finally texted to say that he would be late.

The cottage pie she had made was barely touched, and she preferred white wine. She'd only opened the red because her husband liked it and she wanted to show him she cared and appreciated him. Only right then, at that moment, she didn't. Her phone vibrated, and she checked the text message. It was Sonia telling her to be ready in five. She pressed reply and was just about to say no, but the word that ended up being sent was 'Okay'.

Victoria threw her dinner in the bin, covered Dave's with clingfilm and put it in the fridge, then ran upstairs wondering what she was doing and what the hell she was going to wear. Gym clothes were not a part of her wardrobe.

Ten minutes later, she was in Sonia's car feeling fat, frumpy, and self-conscious in a pair of old jogging bottoms and a plain white T-shirt. Her neighbour, by comparison, looked slim and trendy in pink and black Lycra; even her trainers matched the outfit. Victoria didn't even possess trainers and had to borrow Gemma's.

'Hubbie not home?' Sonia said, seeing the car wasn't on the drive.

'Working late.'

'Do you worry?' Sonia asked, glancing sideways at her.

'Worry?'

'Yeah, I mean it's easy to say isn't it…' Sonia deepened her voice and did a pretty credible mimic of Dave. 'Honey, I'm working late tonight, don't wait up.'

'He usually texts,' Victoria said, not sure she was enjoying the conversation.

Sonia laughed. 'Even worse! Why do you let him off the hook so easily?'

'What are you saying?'

Sonia pulled into a parking space and looked around her. 'Do we have to pay here?'

Victoria shook her head and pointed at one of the signs that were scattered around the car park. 'Not after six.'

They got out of the car, and Sonia locked it. Together, they walked towards the lake. There was a restaurant to the left of them. Victoria could see people seated at tables tucking into their meals. She tried to remember the last time they had eaten out and came to the conclusion it was on their anniversary two years ago.

'So why do you let him get away with it?'

Victoria dragged her eyes away from the diners and looked at her neighbour. She had never really thought about it before. She shrugged her shoulders. 'If he has to work, he has to work...'

'Oh, my god...' Sonia stopped walking towards the gym entrance and turned to face Victoria. 'You actually believe him, don't you?'

'Of course I do. Why wouldn't I?'

'What does he do? Is he on top of the work food chain? Is he constantly being promoted and given rises and rewards?'

Victoria frowned. 'He works hard to keep his job, times are tough, there's a recession, you know.'

Sonia put her arm across her shoulders, and they started walking again. 'The only people who work late on such a regular basis are the bosses or the wannabe bosses.'

Dave was neither of them, and as far as she knew, he had never gone for, nor been put forward for, a promotion. So what was Sonia suggesting? 'Dave wouldn't have an affair,' she said, the penny finally dropping.

'No?'

'No.'

Sonia shrugged her shoulders and smiled before pushing open the door. 'Okay then, let's do this.'

Victoria followed her into the building, the first nagging doubt of her marriage worming its way into her brain.

. . .

BELLE OPENED HER EYES. She must have fallen asleep. It was dark, and the temperature had dropped. The phone was ringing; she jumped up and looked around for it. It wasn't on top of the charger base where it should be. She followed the sound. It was somewhere around the sofa. She pulled up the cushions and dropped to her knees to check if it had fallen. It had, it was on the floor. She picked it up and pressed the button to answer the call. 'Hello…'

The line was silent for a couple of seconds, and then she heard her daughter's voice. 'Mummy?'

'Tamsin? Oh sweetheart, are you okay? Where are you?'

The line went dead. Frantically, she dialled 1471 to get the caller's number, but it was unavailable. Tears running down her cheeks, she held the phone tight and willed it to ring again. She waited five, ten, twenty minutes. She sat down in the darkness and sent all her love and the power of her thoughts out into the still night air to find her children and let them know she was thinking of them. An hour passed, then two, but the phone didn't ring again.

EPISODE NINE
JASMINE CLOSE - SERIES ONE

Victoria stirred the mug before placing it on the table in front of her husband. 'You were very late last night,' she said, looking at him carefully.

'Yeah, I'm cream-cracker'd,' he replied, sipping the coffee and munching on his buttery toast.

'You seem to be working late a lot recently.' She hated herself. She'd never wanted to be one of those demanding, nagging wives, but Sonia's words had lodged in her brain and had kept her awake half the night, questioning and worrying.

'There's a lot of work on at the moment, so if overtime is offered, I take it.' He looked up at her, his brow crinkling as the frown spread across it. 'What is this? When did you join the inquisition?'

'Just asking.'

'He pushed his chair back and stood up. 'Nah, I don't buy it, Vic. What's going on?'

She didn't want to row and wished she hadn't asked. 'I just realised that you've been doing very long hours and wondered if it was for a reason. You up for promotion or something?'

'The reason,' he said. 'Is that you insisted we move to this fancy arse new house and that costs money, which doesn't grow from wants and wishes.'

'I know.'

'Do you? Seems to me that you live in a little dreamy bubble while I work my arse off to keep it floating.'

He stormed out of the kitchen. She ran after him, but he picked the keys up from the hall table and left the house without pausing or glancing back. Why had she listened to Sonia? Dave was working hard to support his family, and she was making him account for his actions. She wasn't being fair, and she was never going to listen to her new neighbour again.

She went upstairs to get ready for work. There was a tiny little rebellious thought that questioned why he got so upset with her, but she refused to acknowledge it. Instead, she concentrated on straightening her thick, wavy hair.

Victoria left the house early and walked to the local shop. She wanted to pick up some flowers and a copy of the local paper before she opened the Show Home.

BELLE OPENED her eyes as sunlight streamed in through the windows. Her curtains were open, and she was still fully dressed, curled up on the sofa, clutching her phone. She must have slept there all night, and she stood up and stretched. She was stiff and aching and felt lightheaded and a little sick. She realised she hadn't eaten anything since yesterday lunchtime, when her mum had made her have a few mouthfuls from a sandwich. She tried to remember the last drink she'd had but couldn't. Not a proper one. She'd had a few gulps from a bottle of water and a few sips to wash down some paracetamol last night. The last cup of tea she made was still untouched in the kitchen. She knew making herself ill was not sensible. She had to be strong and fit and able to travel anywhere, anytime, to fetch her children.

So she went to the kitchen and filled the kettle to make herself a cup of tea. Her milk was out of date and smelt sour, so she tipped it down the sink and dropped the plastic bottle into the pink recycling bag. Black tea held little appeal, so she looked in the cupboard and found a hot chocolate sachet. She mixed it into the boiling water and stirred the drink until the last flecks of powder had dissolved. Then she pulled out a bag of miniature marshmallows and sprinkled them on top. She carried it back into the lounge and took a sip, which was hot and burnt her lip. She started to cry, not because of the pain, but because it was her daughter's favourite drink. Had she imagined the call last night? She didn't think so, but then maybe when you want something badly enough, you can create an illusion.

The phone rang, making her jump and she spilled some of the liquid down her jeans. It wasn't the house phone which was still beside her, so she searched for her mobile. It was in her jacket pocket and almost out of charge. 'Hello...' she said, grabbing and answering it.

'Belle, it's Shaz. I've got to be quick. I've spoken to Mira. She's going to try to help you. She knows where the children are and they are both well. I'll ring you tonight with more details.'

Belle didn't get a chance to respond as Shaz ended the call.

Her hand was shaking with relief; she felt a surge of love and gratitude towards Shaz and Mira. She had always got on well with them and she knew that helping her would cause problems for them with Mo and his family.

Mira was her husband's youngest sister, a pretty and caring girl, who used to spend all her money on shoes and sweets. Mira loved the bags of pink Percy Pigs from M&S, where she worked part time. Until Mo had arranged a marriage for her with some distant relative, who was apparently much older than she was. Belle had tried to intervene, begged him to reconsider and let Mira live the western lifestyle that she had been brought up with. But he wouldn't budge and it was after watching her young sister-in-law board the plane to marry a man who she had never met that Belle realised it was time to leave the man and the marriage.

The doorbell rang, making her jump again. Lack of sleep, food and drink combined with extreme stress and adrenaline spikes were having a detrimental effect on her physical and mental health.

'Yes?' she said, talking into the intercom.

'Hi, it's Victoria, from the Show Home, please let me in…'

She really didn't want to. She just wanted to be left alone.

'I have something to show you…' the woman added, as though her reluctance was obvious even through the intercom.

Since she was sure that the woman would keep returning until she agreed to talk to her, she thought she might as well get it over with. Belle pressed the buzzer that unlocked the communal door and waited. She could hear the woman's heels as she ran up the stairs and tapped on the door.

VICTORIA HELD the flowers out in front of her and smiled as the door opened. 'Hi,' she said. 'I bought you these.'

'Why?' Belle said, staring at them as though she were being offered something hideous.

The young woman was not making any welcoming moves to her at all. In fact, the door was barely open, and it seemed it was going to stay that way. Victoria tried again. 'Look, I know that nothing can ease the pain you're suffering, but I just thought the flowers would look and smell nice and let you know that people in the Close are thinking about you.'

The door opened a bit wider and Belle took the flowers. Victoria held the local paper towards her. 'I got you a copy of this as well.'

On the front page were the photos of Tamsin and Kyle with a headline asking for help to find them. Belle grabbed the paper from her, dropped the flowers, and ran into the lounge to sit down and read it.

Victoria picked the discarded chrysanthemums up and followed her into the apartment. 'It might help…'

'Doubtful. I'm pretty sure that they are already in Pakistan.' Belle gently touched the faces of her children in the photo, then glanced up at Victoria. 'But thanks.'

'It was Sasha's idea. She's the young reporter, and she did a piece about flat two as well, made it clear that you were in no way associated with their activities at all.'

Belle shrugged her shoulders. 'Doesn't really matter now though does it? It was my picture in the paper that did the damage. That's the trouble with modern media and communications. They make it so difficult to be invisible.'

'Can I do anything? Make you a drink or get you something to eat?' Victoria knew someone in crisis when she saw them. The stained, crumpled clothes suggested Belle hadn't changed or showered for a couple of days. She wanted to help, but didn't really know how she could. What can you do or say to someone whose children are missing?

Belle shook her head. 'No thanks,' she said, standing up and walking to the door.

Victoria placed the flowers on the sofa and left the apartment. She didn't want to go, but clearly there was nothing more she could do. 'You know where I am,' she said, before the door closed on her. She stood still for a few seconds, feeling useless. The sound of Natasha's baby crying spilled out onto the communal landing. She thought how sad it was that the two neighbours were both suffering and yet they weren't able to support each other.

She walked down the stairs and pressed the big green button that released the lock on the exit door. As she was about to walk out, a woman breezed in and threw her a smile. She was tall, slim, and incredibly groomed. Perfect hair, perfect make-up, perfectly painted nails, a tiny waist and an impossibly large bust. She knew immediately that it must be the tenant in flat two.

As if aware of her scrutiny, the woman paused and turned around. 'Can I help you?'

Victoria hated confrontation, but this was her neighbourhood and her livelihood. She searched for words that wouldn't form - something clever and insightful, something that would make the woman pack her bags and leave with her head lowered in shame and contrition. 'It's not right...' was the best she could come up with.

The woman smiled. She really was one of the most attractive females Victoria had ever seen. Although she looked like she'd just stepped out of a Hollywood movie rather than like a real live person.

'Are we talking about the terrible state of the economy? The outrageous child poverty that still exists, but gets pushed from the headlines by budget cuts and political point scoring? Or are we talking about the global warmongering, or the crisis in Syria or riots in Egypt? Or maybe closer to home and the terribly sad abduction of those poor little children...' she pointed up the stairs.

Victoria's mouth opened, but no sound came out. Say something, she ordered herself, but still nothing.

'I'm Annabel,' the woman said, walking back towards her with her hand outstretched.

Victoria shook the offered hand. 'Victoria from the Show Home,' she managed to utter.

Annabel looked her up and down. 'So I see,' she said, before walking away.

Victoria had never thought of herself as slow or stupid, but the encounter with the brothel lady proved she was both. Annoyed and frustrated with herself, she left the building. It was almost time to open the Show Home. She hadn't heard from the letting agents yet about the encounter with Flat Two, but had a feeling they didn't get the result she wanted. Certainly the woman showed no signs of being a lady facing eviction. But surely the negative publicity from the local paper would force them out?

She started walking back down the Close when she realised someone was mowing the front lawn at the Fisher's house. The smell of freshly cut grass made her nose twitch and her eyes tingle. She'd have to call into her house and get an anti-histamine tablet.

She very quickly realised it was Brett pushing the lawnmower. Her cheeks flushed at the sight of him and she wondered if she could cross the road and go to the building site rather than walk past. She didn't want him to know she was avoiding him, but if he hadn't seen her yet...?

Victoria glanced his way and was gutted to see that he was

watching her with a smug, slightly mocking expression, as if he knew exactly what thoughts were chasing through her head. So she had no option but to keep on walking. It would be okay, she told herself. She would nod her head in cool, polite acknowledgement and not stop or pause.

He switched the mower off and grinned at her as she approached. Just keep on walking, she told herself, determined to stay calm. She kept her head firmly forward, but she could see him from the corner of her eye.

'Hi,' he said, looking directly at her.

She didn't want to look at him, so she replied without turning her head. 'Morning.'

'I'm still waiting…'

Did she pretend not to hear him and keep on walking, or did she take the bait and stop? Unable to bear the thought of him thinking she couldn't or wouldn't face him, she paused and turned round. 'For what, exactly?'

He started to walk towards her. Long, confident strides that, for some reason, made her want to run to the Show Home and barricade herself in.

'Why, an apology of course.'

Victoria opened her mouth to protest, but he was barely a foot away from her and his finger came up and touched her lips, shocking her into silence. He smiled, and she realised his mouth slanted slightly to the left.

'Tell you what,' he said, 'I'll drop my need for an apology if you drop the passive aggressive attitude.

'I don't,' she started to speak and then stopped. He was staring at her mouth in a way that stirred up all sorts of unwelcome feelings in her.

'Let's start again,' he said, his voice softer and deeper than it had been before. 'Hi, I'm Brett Anderson, Jenny's brother.'

Victoria looked down at their hands clasped together. It was more of a caress than a greeting, and her stomach constricted with excitement. What the hell was going on?

'You are?' he prompted, that mocking smile back on his lips.

'Victoria from the Show Home,' she said, in a voice that sounded more like a squeak.

'Strange name, but lovely to meet you, Victoria from the Show Home.'

She laughed nervously and removed her hand from his. Their eyes met, and she found herself smiling warmly, even though she had no idea why.

'I knew it was there,' he said, his own eyes not leaving hers.

'What?'

'A real smile.'

'Real?'

'Well, I've seen the scowl and the frown and the scary, fake sales smile.'

'I don't have a fake sales smile,' she said, knowing that she did, but annoyed that he knew it too.

He raised a knowing eyebrow. 'Now that we're friends, how about a coffee? Cutting grass is surprisingly thirsty work.'

She shook her head. 'I have to get back.'

'Another time then,' he said to her as she walked away. She wasn't sure if it was a threat or a promise and had no idea why the idea filled her with a heady mixture of fear and delight.

MARY BRUSHED HER HAIR. The cat was perched on her bed, watching her. 'All right for you,' she said, 'with your thick fur coat.' She used to have a mass of thick brown curls that her husband loved to wrap his fingers in. Now all she had was white fluff. She put the brush down and sighed. 'Look at it now,' she whispered to the mirror. It wasn't even the silver grey that made some old ladies look elegant and graceful. No, her hair had gone completely white and thinned out alarmingly with the texture of cotton wool. 'Maybe I should get a wig,' she said to the cat, who blinked back at her. She stood up slowly and winced from the pain in her joints. The cat stretched and yawned and she bent down to tickle the fur around his neck. He purred loudly, making her smile. A knock at the door turned the smile into a frown.

She walked slowly from the bedroom, moaning and mumbling about how inconsiderate people were. She reached the front door just as it knocked again. 'Stop the bloody banging,' she said crossly, pulling it open.

'Stop moaning, Gran,' Jack said, wearing a huge grin and placing a kiss on her cheek.

'What are you doing here?' she asked, not really caring, just delighted that he was.

'Thought I'd see how you were settling in. Has Candy Bar left you alone?'

She smiled and closed the door. 'She stuck a load of casseroles in my freezer a couple of days ago.'

Jack pulled a face that made it clear what he thought about his aunt's cooking that summed up her own view perfectly. Although she knew she was being mean and should be more grateful to Candice.

'You had breakfast yet?' he asked her, holding up a Co-Op carrier bag. 'I have supplies. Thought I'd do us a fry up.'

'Not sure my doctor would approve, idiot says my cholesterol is too high.'

Jack put the bag down on the worktop. 'I can do it just for me.'

'Like hell. I say stuff the bloody doctor. At my age, I'll take a bit of pleasure when I can get it.'

He pulled a frying pan from the drawer and smiled. 'Full works then?'

She nodded and sat down at the small kitchen table. Her legs weren't what they used to be. She'd only been up for an hour and already they felt heavy and tired. Getting old was seriously overrated, but she didn't feel ready for the alternative yet. Not that she was afraid of the big D, but death was so bloody permanent.

The cat wandered into the kitchen and purred around her legs.

'You kept it, then?'

'Yeah, the girl from the paper is supposed to be coming around sometime with money and a name for him. There was talk of doing a cat flap and getting him chipped.'

'Good idea. Tea?'

'Please, stick a drop of the good stuff in it...' she pointed to the cupboard above his head, 'just a teaspoon or two.'

He lifted out a bottle of brandy. 'Gran, it's not even ten o'clock yet.'

'I won't tell if you don't.'

ANNABEL WAS TIDYING up the apartment. Working girls were pretty much all the same when it came to sloppiness, or at least the young ones were. Allergic to cleaning and addicted to take-aways. She had several rented flats and apartments across the city, with a couple of girls living and working in each. It wasn't ideal and most of her competitors used premises for work without the girls actually living there. It made it easier to keep clean, tidy, and professional, but it had its downside as well. The main one being that you could be closed down by the authorities and evicted on the same day. She knew from experience the financial impact when that happened was terrible. Not just from lost revenue, but also from the property deposit, which the owners never returned. She had only just crawled out of the debt caused by her last eviction and she swore then that it wouldn't happen again. At least not on the same scale.

She used to run the biggest and best known brothel north of London and punters travelled miles to visit her girls. She invested a small fortune into the themed decoration of the property, which was a large Victorian detached house in need of TLC and the owner was a friend who gave her a good deal and was happy for her to do whatever renovations and improvements she wanted. The result had been a sumptuous, sensual palace dedicated to carnal pleasures. The punters loved it. She was proud of it and the girls made a small fortune being so busy. But like all good things, it attracted attention. Not just from the police, who kept a cautious eye on the place, but from competitors who set out to bring her down.

'Morning,' Miranda said, strolling into the lounge in her underwear while stifling a yawn. 'You're here early. Everything all right?'

Annabel glanced out of the large French windows. Nobody was working out the back, but it didn't change the fact that they might have been. 'Put some clothes on,' she said, 'or pull the curtains.'

Miranda disappeared back into her bedroom and returned with a short, flimsy dressing gown wrapped around her that barely covered her bottom. 'Better?'

Annabel nodded. 'Just.'

'Are we going to have to move?' the young woman asked, helping herself to a glass of milk from the fridge.

'Yes, I think so.'

'I like it here, so does Tammy. Taxi only costs us four quid into the city centre.'

Annabel had invested a lot of money in to providing advice for all her girls. She regularly held sessions and brought in experts to talk about life coaching, goal setting and financial planning. She told all of them to learn to drive and invest their earnings. They all received income way above a normal wage, but sadly it flowed as fast as a waterfall, straight out of their purses and into shoes, taxis and takeaways.

She looked at Miranda and was about to give her the learning to drive lecture again, but changed her mind. What was the point when they wouldn't listen?

'They can't prove anything yet,' she said. 'I think, for now, I'll move your bookings to one of the flats in the city centre, but you can stay living here.' It wasn't ideal, but it might work while she decided what to do. She picked her handbag up and looked around the room. 'I've cleaned the kitchen and put the dishwasher on; you need to run the hoover round before your eleven-thirty arrives.'

'SORRY, Gran, but I've got to go as soon as I've washed these bits up for you.'

Mary tried not to let her disappointment show. 'I can manage them.'

'Don't be daft,' he said, picking up the plates and dropping the cups into the warm, soapy water. 'Only takes me a minute.'

'Have you got work today?'

'Yeah, I had a couple of days booked off, but the big boss is over from the States and has called us all in for a meeting.'

'That doesn't sound fair.'

He shrugged, 'I don't mind. The truth is, there's been talk of a restructure for weeks now, so everyone will be glad to know what's going on.'

Mary watched him as he dried the clean dishes and put them away. She must be the luckiest wrinkly in the world. She wished he could stay all day, but knew she was being silly and selfish. He was a young man with his own life to lead and she was grateful that he had any time for her at all.

Jack put his leathers on and picked up his crash helmet. She thought how handsome he looked as he headed for the door. She followed slowly behind.

He paused at the door and waited for her to reach him, then he bent down and kissed her on the cheek. 'See you soon, Gran, behave yourself...'

'Sounds boring,' she replied. 'Not much fun in being good.'

'Couldn't agree more. You are a bad influence.'

He gave her a hug and headed for his bike. She saw a woman come out of the communal door and walk to a parked sports car. Mary saw her grandson turn his head and saw his eyes light up in admiration and his lips turn up into that killer smile of his. She felt an irrational surge of jealousy towards the woman with her thick, glossy blonde hair and long, slim legs.

Her hearing was pretty damn good, especially for an old bird of almost ninety, and she had always resisted a hearing aid. But at that moment, she wished she'd said yes when Candice had tried to persuade her to get one fitted.

Jack had twisted right around to talk to the woman. The tart was clearly flirting and fluttering her lashes at him. They shook hands and were much closer than they needed to be. Mary took a few painful steps out of the apartment with every intention of breaking them up and sending the flaunting, floosy packing. But a workman had parked his van down the road and was now standing in front of her, blocking her way, and her view.

'Mary Martin?' he asked, looking at her.

'What do you want?' she said irritably, trying to see past him.

'I'm from KittyKare. I've been asked to fit a cat flap for you.'

Mary heard the roar of her grandson's motorbike as it fired into life. She stepped sideways away from the irritating man and raised her arm to wave. Jack waved back, although she wasn't totally convinced it was directed solely at her. She sent the woman her sternest glare.

'You are Mrs Martin?' he said.

'Yes, yes, in there,' she pointed to her open front door. 'Well, go on, wait for me and you'll have to charge double time.'

The cat sat in the doorway, blocking the man's entrance and looking at him suspiciously.

'This better not let all the cats in the neighbourhood into my house. I'm not a bloody feline free for all.'

'Don't worry,' he said. 'Only your kitty will be able to use it.'

The cat yawned and walked away towards the building site. Mary turned her head and watched the woman in the sports car drive off, then she followed the man into her flat.

BELLE CLUTCHED THE PHONE, willing it to ring. She had spent hours on her laptop searching for flight options and had several possibilities saved and ready to book. All she needed was the go ahead from Shaz and she could be on the flight to get her babies tomorrow.

She had forced herself to take a bath. She preferred a shower, but was terrified she might miss the phone ringing. At least in the bath, she could keep the landline and her mobile beside her. She found some bubble bath and then cried because the liquid was in a Disney princess plastic container and belonged to Tamsin. Tears aside, the soak in the warm bubbles eased her physical aches and soothed some of the stress away. She felt a tiny thread of hope was clinging precariously between her and the children. All she needed was the call and she could be on her way.

After the bath, she made herself an omelette. Her cupboards and fridge were pretty bare, she hadn't been shopping and most of her non-perishable food was packed in boxes all piled in the lounge. She had to rummage through several boxes marked Kitchen, to find a frying pan. The omelette tasted rubbery and bland. She had nothing to put in it other than a slice of sandwich ham that was curling up at the edges. She couldn't even find the tomato sauce. But she forced herself to eat it all and washed it down with a large glass of water all the time, staring at the phone, desperate for it to ring.

It was late, and it was dark when Shaz finally called her. When she hung up, she immediately booked her flight and then rang her mother, who answered immediately.

'I need to be at Heathrow Airport by lunchtime tomorrow.'

'I'll pick you up.'

'I can go on the coach,'

'I want to take you.'

'Thanks,' Belle said, grateful for the support.

'Try to sleep,' her mum said. 'Tomorrow will be a big day.'

Of course, she didn't sleep, not at all. Belle spent the whole night wide awake, willing her mind to shut down and her body to relax. In the end, at five-twenty a.m. she gave up and went for a run. It was dark, cold, and a bit creepy. Budget cuts meant that the streetlights along the main roads were turned off and only the ones at junctions and roundabouts were lit. But Belle didn't care about the lack of light or the scary shadows or the rustles that came from the trees and bushes that lined the redways. The running pounded the panic from her mind and made the time pass more quickly.

. . .

She closed her eyes as she sat on the plane, torn between the excitement that she could soon have her children home and the fear that something would go wrong. Shaz had been very clear that it was a small window of opportunity for Mira to get the twins and take them to the airport to meet her. Belle knew well enough how closely the family interacted. She understood how difficult it would be for Mira to be alone and to conspire to collect the children from school. Shaz had told her they would have to leave everything behind because Mira would have no valid excuse to pack a bag for them. They would have to go straight from the school to the airport. There were so many things that could go wrong.

Belle looked out of the window. The plane was starting to lose altitude, it would be landing soon. In a couple of hours, she would see her children again.

The man at immigration studied her photo and then looked at her suspiciously. 'What is the reason for your visit?'

'I'm visiting family,' she replied, glad she was telling the truth. Well, almost the truth. She was sure she had seen on TV in a documentary about airports that immigration officers were trained to detect lies. People betrayed themselves through body language. She concentrated all her efforts on staying calm and not showing any hint of the true turmoil she was experiencing. A situation not helped by tiredness. Her body told her it was the middle of the night, but because of the time difference, it was a bright, sunny morning in Lahore.

He stamped her passport and gave it back to her. 'Enjoy your trip,' he said.

Belle had to resist the huge sigh of relief that she wanted to emit and instead forced herself to smile and thank him before walking calmly away.

She wandered aimlessly around the airport for an hour, then she sat and had a coffee that was so strong and bitter it actually made her eyes water. But she needed a caffeine hit, she needed to stay sharp, and exhaustion was attempting to overwhelm her.

Belle checked her watch and headed for the airport exit. The air outside was humid and her senses were bombarded with unfamiliar smells and sounds. Her eyes scanned the cars and then the people searching for Mira and her children.

Like airports the world over, it was busy and charged with a maelstrom of emotions. Excitement and anticipation for the adventure ahead, tinged with apprehension, the fear of the unknown. Everyone was in a hurry, working on a timetable. Flights to catch, passengers to meet and greet – children to collect.

She looked at her watch again and then checked her phone. They were late. What if Mira couldn't get away? Or maybe the school wouldn't let her collect the children? What if Kyle and Tamsin weren't at school today? They might be ill or on a field trip, or Mo might have discovered the plan.

The panic was building up inside Belle. They should be here by now. The plane back to Heathrow left in less than two hours. Boarding would begin in an hour and they had to get through security first. If they missed that flight, then it would be over. Mo would come to the airport and take them back and she would have no help or support to stop him. He was their father and if he said they couldn't leave Pakistan, then they wouldn't.

Her eyes scanned the cars and passengers again, and finally she saw them. Kyle and Tamsin clutching Mira's hands as they walked quickly towards her. It was her daughter who spotted her first. Tamsin let go of her aunt's hand and ran into her arms. She lifted her daughter up and swung her round, smothering her head with kisses.

Still clutching Tamsin, she pulled Kyle into a tight hug. 'I've missed you both so much,' she said, fighting back the tears and mouthing 'thank you,' to her sister-in-law.

Mira was also close to tears, and Belle hugged her. 'You okay?' she whispered. 'You could come with us if you want…'

Mira shook her head. 'I'll be all right, you'd better go.'

Clutching her children tight, afraid to let them go beyond her reach again, she walked with them back into the terminal, followed by Mira. The children were quiet and subdued and Belle knew that it wasn't the time for talking for any of them. That would come later when they were safely back on English soil.

They reached the check-in desk and Belle hugged Mira again. The woman leant down and kissed her niece and nephew. 'Be good for mummy, I'll miss you both.'

Tamsin looked up at Belle. 'Are we going home, mummy?'

Belle smiled and nodded. Tamsin burst into tears. Belle dropped down level with her daughter. 'Don't you want to come home with me?'

Tamsin nodded through the tears. 'I was scared, mummy, I missed you so much.'

'We won't ever be parted again, poppet,' she said, wiping away the tears.

Belle looked at Kyle. He hadn't said a word. Not uttered a sound and was holding Mira's hand tightly. She bent down and looked into his big brown eyes. 'Ready to come home Kyle?' she said gently.

He looked at Mira, who smiled reassuringly and let go of his hand. He nodded his head and reached out to Belle.

Relief flooded through her. For a second, she thought he was going to say no. She knew how badly all the change and moving affected him.

'Go,' Mira said. 'Hurry, they're closing the checking gate soon.'

Belle went to the desk and handed over the three flight tickets. The woman at the check-in counter looked up at her. 'Passports please.'

Mira stepped forward and reached for the children's school rucksacks. 'Cousin Hiba lives in the same house,' she whispered, unzipping the back pockets. 'she promised to get them and put them in the bags this morning.' Mira handed over Tamsin's passport.

Belle gave the woman her daughter's passport along with her own, then turned back to wait for Kyle's.

Mira was frantically searching every pocket, every pouch; eventually she tipped the entire bag upside down onto the polished airport floor. 'It's not here,' she said, her eyes reflecting the panic Belle was feeling.

'It has to be,' Belle said, grabbing the rucksack and shaking it.

'Ma'am...' the check-in lady was demanding her attention. 'I have to close this desk. Are you travelling or not?'

Belle looked at Mira. They both looked at Kyle, who stared passively back at them.

'You have to go,' Mira said.

'I can't!'

'You have no choice. If you don't leave now, then you lose them both.'

'Mummy, are we going home?' Tamsin said, in a small, frightened voice.

'Ma'am...'

Belle looked into the eyes of her son, tears streaming down her cheeks as she pulled him into a tight hug. 'I'll come back for you, I promise.'

He stood still and unresponsive as she let go and kissed his forehead, a horrible, cold chill wrapping round her heart. She'd failed him.

Tears pouring down her cheeks, she walked away and left him.

EPISODE TEN
JASMINE CLOSE - SERIES ONE

'Up for it again tonight?' Sonia asked, as she walked into the office of Victoria's Show Home. 'I thought the Pilates instructor was pretty good, hot too. Not sure I've ever seen such a tight bum on a woman over twenty-five.'

Victoria frowned at her neighbour, not at all sure she had ever thought of another woman as being hot. Did that make Sonia gay? Besides, she was still annoyed with her for putting thoughts of doubt in her head about Dave. 'No...' she said curtly, and then instantly felt guilty and added 'thanks,' since she hated rudeness.

'We could try out the main gym and go on the treadmill or the bikes; they've got those ski machines as well, great for toning your butt and your thighs.'

Victoria shook her head.

'Fair enough,' Sonia said, heading for the door. 'I can see you're busy.'

Victoria looked up from her paperwork. She felt bad about saying no when Sonia was working so hard at being friendly.

Sonia paused in the doorway and smiled. 'We'll just have a swim tonight, then. Be round at seven.'

And that was it. She was gone. Victoria didn't know whether to be flattered or pissed. The woman just wouldn't take no for an answer, but then what else was she going to do that evening? It's not like Dave or Gemma would miss her. She seemed to have become a spare part in her own family recently and she had no idea how it had happened.

Lowering her head, she stared at the paperwork on the desk in front of her. She really wasn't in the mood, but unfortunately she didn't have a paperwork fairy hiding in her drawer that could do it all for her. She groaned as the door opened again. At first she thought it might be Sonia again, but it could be a customer, so she planted a smile on her face and stood up, ready to greet them.

'Oh, it's you.'

'Lovely to see you too,' Brett said, walking into the office. 'I see fake smile has come out to play again.'

'Thought you were a customer.'

'How do you know I'm not?'

'Are you?'

'No.'

'So what do you want, then?' she said, feeling strangely bold and excited.

His eyes rested on her lips, and it seemed like an eternity before he finally spoke. 'Coffee?' he said in a slightly mocking tone.

She felt disappointed and, at the same time, relieved. What the hell was going on? She didn't even like the man; he was responsible for putting her through what was undoubtedly the most humiliating experience of her life. Yet he came near and it was as though the air was sucked out of her body. She felt dizzy and breathless and as silly as a blushing schoolgirl. 'I'm very busy,' she said.

He picked up a site brochure from the table and studied it carefully. 'So if I said that the two-bed terrace house looks interesting and I would like you to take me through the detailed spec and my options, I imagine you would offer me a seat and make me a coffee?'

'Is that what you are saying?'

'I believe it is.'

She looked at him, torn between showing him the door and

playing out his little charade. He smiled and the pile of paperwork was forgotten. 'Milk? Sugar?'

They looked at each other, and Victoria knew that something had changed. It was scary and thrilling, and she knew that the only sensible thing to do was to stop it now. Send him packing and not let him anywhere near her life again. A voice in her head was drowning out the warning by insisting it was only a coffee. But the long forgotten fire in her belly had been ignited and it was clearly reflected in his eyes. Something stirred between them, and she knew it was both exhilaratingly dangerous.

JENNY KNEW she had to talk to Steve. Last night in bed, Miles had asked her outright if she had told him yet. Resting on his elbow, her husband had looked directly at her. She'd wanted to lie and say yes, but she couldn't. Instead, she'd shaken her head in denial. Miles looked at her with the disappointment and irritation that had become such a big part of their recent relationship.

'You promised,' he'd said, before turning his back on her and switching off his bedside light.

From the bedroom window, she looked down on the Close. It was a dull, overcast day, perfect for her to run up to Steve's apartment. Trouble was that she didn't want to. He had helped her, they'd helped each other, and he was the only friend she had in Milton Keynes. But Miles would ask her again and keep on asking until she gave him the answer he wanted. If she intended to keep her husband, then she was going to have to say goodbye to the friend.

She shivered and wished she'd put a proper jacket on instead of grabbing a cardigan to wrap around her. No way was she turning round and going back now, though. That just extended her time outside. She didn't know where Brett was. He had disappeared after breakfast, but not before telling her he was taking her shopping later. She knew her brother well enough to know that it wasn't his idea and felt a surge of anger towards her husband and his manipulations.

A car drove past her, and she saw it stop and park outside the apartment block. A harassed, tired looking woman climbed out and banged on Steve's door. Jenny hesitated; it wasn't a conversation she wanted to have with an audience. On the other hand, it might be good if he had someone with him, as she knew he wouldn't take it well. Besides, she was almost there and if she went home, it could be days before she was brave enough to run up the Close again.

The woman was calling through the letterbox. At her feet was a plastic container with a handle full of cleaning products. 'Mr Lance, let me in.'

'Sod off,' was the response Jenny heard shouted from inside the apartment.

The woman picked up her things and glanced at Jenny. 'Can't help some people,' she said, shaking her head and walking back to her car.

Jenny tapped on the door and was surprised when it opened immediately. 'Thought I was going to have to do some letterbox yelling of my own.'

'Don't be soft,' he said with a smile. 'I'll always let you in. You're a PIG'

'WHAT!'

'Relax, you're a **P**ermanently **I**nvited **G**uest.'

'How did you know it was me?'

'I know that gentle tap tap you do…'

'I have my very own door knock?' she said.

'Yeah. It is as scared and hesitant as you are, yet underpinned with a hint of determination and defiance that makes you so interesting. Stick the kettle on.'

Jenny did as she was told. 'Tea or coffee?'

'Tea and biscuits.'

She made herself busy, unable to look directly at him. She was being unfair to Steve, but she had no choice. Miles was being totally unreasonable, although she knew her husband didn't see it that way. As far as Miles was concerned, Steve was no better than a drug dealer, and he didn't want her to have anything to do with him. In Miles' world, everything was black or white, right or wrong.

He had neither time nor understanding for life's intricate shades of grey.

She stirred a couple of teaspoons of sugar into his mug and placed it on the tray he had on his lap. His hand reached out and grabbed her wrist. 'What's up, Jen?' he asked seriously.

'Nothing,' she lied, with as much conviction as she could manage.

He let go, and she went back to the kitchen to get the biscuits. She could feel the sharp sting of tears gathering in the back of her eyes. She didn't want to hurt him. It was so unfair. 'Was that your cleaning lady at the door?' She asked, opening the biscuits and taking one before handing them to him. 'What's up with her? She tells you off for dropping crumbs?'

'Oh, she's okay, I suppose, thinks she's my sodding mother, though. The social worker organised her. Everyone wants to help me.'

'Isn't that a good thing? At least you have support.' She said it gently, knowing that he hated being fussed over or patronised.

'I know I'm an ungrateful git. But they drive me insane; they all know more about what I need than I do myself. Or at least that's what they like to tell me.'

She knew that feeling well enough. Wasn't that exactly how Miles was treating her? 'Do you see much of your family?' she asked.

'Nah,' he said, pulling another biscuit from the packet. 'Mum's dead, Dad's a tosser and my sister buggered off to Australia years ago.'

Jenny almost sighed out loud. She had to stop the sound escaping from her lips. 'You went through all this alone?'

'You can take that pity out of your voice,' he snapped sharply. 'I'm a big boy now. I can look after myself. I don't need sympathy.'

'No, of course not. I'm sorry if it sounded that way.'

'I'm sorry for snapping. I just get sick of it, you know? Mates?'

'Mates,' she said, standing up to take the mugs to the kitchen. She couldn't do it, she wouldn't do it. Stuff Miles and his judgmental dictates. Steve needed her, and she definitely needed him.

'Have you gotta go?'

She looked at the door and shook her head. 'No, I can stay a little longer,' she said.

. . .

BELLE COULDN'T THINK beyond getting her daughter home. She wanted to scream and shout and demand that someone get her son back for her. But who was that someone going to be? Who could realistically help her? Shaz and Mira had conspired to help and thanks to them, she had Tamsin curled up asleep in the seat beside her. But what about her son? Would she ever see him again? She knew Mo would make his sisters pay for betraying him. Mira and Kyle would be watched closely. It was unlikely another chance would present itself.

She looked down at her sleeping daughter and fought back the tears of frustration. She knew they weren't safe yet. She had to get Tamsin beyond Mo's reach and back into hiding, and then she could work on getting her son home. She had to blank her last image of his solemn face, watching her as she left him. The pain was too great to bear. Did he know how much she loved him? That leaving him was the hardest thing she had ever had to do?

The plane was beginning its descent into Heathrow Airport; she gently woke her daughter up and kissed her sleepy head. She wanted to pull her into her arms and hold her tight, never letting go, but obviously she had to resist and play down the drama. Tamsin was scared and upset enough already. The girl needed stability and normality.

They cleared immigration and had no luggage to collect, so it didn't take long to reach the arrivals exit where her mother should be waiting for them. She stifled a yawn; but had no idea if it was day or night. She wished she had managed to sleep on the plane like her daughter had. The long return flight and the different time zones were adding to her state of near exhaustion. She needed sleep, but after what she had just done, she wondered if she would sleep properly again. 'Can you see Nana?' she said, her eyes scanning the crowd that was gathered around the barrier.

'There's Daddy.'

Belle gripped her daughter's hand tight and searched for security.

She saw Mo leaning on the barrier, watching her carefully. He looked relaxed and at ease. She had an image leap into her head of a tiger she'd once seen on a nature programme. It looked so calm and lazy, lounging in the shade. But its eyes were focused and suddenly it had leapt to its feet and launched itself at its prey, a small monkey that had no chance to escape.

She had to escape; no way was she going to let him take her daughter again. What was he even doing there? She thought he was in Pakistan. She could see a couple of security guards just back inside the arrivals gate, and two uniformed police were a hundred feet away in the direction she needed to go to the car park. Surely, if they ran, he couldn't chase them? They were in England in a crowded place. If she screamed the police and security would be all over him like a rash.

Tamsin was waving and smiling at her dad in a hesitant, uncertain type of way. Belle kept a very firm grip on her hand and walked towards the end of the barrier. She could see her mother up ahead hurrying to meet them and was aware that Mo was also on the move. She didn't want to scare her daughter by panicking or running, but she had to get them to the car and away from the airport.

Belle upped her pace, Tamsin struggled to keep up with her fast stride. Mo was just behind them. She kept her head forward and focused on reaching her mother. She was aware that Tamsin kept glancing behind and heard a small sob escape her daughter's lips. She had always tried to keep her own fear and distrust for her husband away from the children. They knew she took them away from him so that they wouldn't have to go and live in Pakistan like Aunty Mira. And they knew that's why they didn't want to be found. But Mo was still their father, and she had never trashed him in front of them. Her poor daughter was obviously worried and scared and very confused.

Her mother rushed towards her, and Belle handed her daughter over. 'Go,' she said, turning round to face and block Mo.

'Maggie, wait,' Mo called after her mother. 'Please just let me see Tamsin...'

Her mother paused and looked at Belle, who shook her head. Tamsin was openly crying now and people were starting to stare. 'I'll scream if I have to,' Belle said, standing her ground and not allowing him to follow their daughter.

He held his hands out in a conciliatory gesture. 'I need to talk to you, Belle, we can't go on like this. It's not fair to us or the children.' He pointed to a Costa, 'let's get a coffee and be civil and see if we can sort this out.'

'Okay, but they go...'

He glanced at his daughter, smiled, and blew her a kiss.

'Go, Mum,' Belle said. 'I'll get a coach or taxi and meet you later.' She smiled reassuringly at Tamsin. 'See you soon, sweetheart.'

Belle watched them hurry away then she turned to her husband, 'Come on then let's get this over with.'

S*TEVE KNEW* that something was wrong. They might not have known each other for very long, but he felt as though he knew her better than anyone he'd ever met before. Whatever was bugging her, she wasn't ready to share. He wished he had some dope left, but the thieving bastard who broke in took every last ounce and, despite pleading with his supplier, he was still waiting for a replacement stash. He thought it would relax her. She was so uptight and on edge, even more so than usual. He wanted to help her, but what could he do? He was about as much use as a donkey in a horse race.

His house phone rang. He no longer had a mobile, at least not until the insurance coughed up for a replacement.

'You going to answer it?'

'Nah. No one I want to talk to.'

'How do you know?' she said. 'Might be some hot girl...'

'Yeah, right?'

The ringing stopped, and it switched to the answerphone. 'If it's a hot girl, I'll ring her back.' He laughed. Of course it wasn't, it never would be again. He was no use to anyone. It was a friend, Danny, asking if he fancied a pint and a catch up.

'Will you ring him back?' she asked him.

'Maybe,'

'That's a no then.'

'What makes you the expert on me? I said maybe...'

She raised a perfectly plucked eyebrow at him.

'Yeah, okay,' he said, knowing she was right. 'It's a pity call.'

'He sounded like he was genuine. It is possible that he really does want to have a pint and a catch up.'

Was it possible? They used to be great mates, best buds and all that crap until the accident. Then, so-called friends melted away like snow in sunshine. Not immediately, of course. They were all there for him when he was lying in a hospital bed with his severed spine. But once word got out that he'd never walk again. That his legs were fucking useless and he would be stuck in a chair forever. The visits became less frequent and more awkward. For the first time in his life, he knew what it was to be really alone. 'No.' he said firmly. 'Trust me, it's just a pity call or a guilt call. Someone probably asked him how I was getting on and he thought he better check up on me.'

Jenny shook her head at him. 'You don't have to push the whole world away, Steve.'

Didn't he? From where he was sitting, everyone who had ever been a part of his life had either left him or hurt him. What was the point of letting anyone in?

'How about a walk?' he said, knowing he'd had enough of the conversation. Life was shit and then you die. If you're really lucky, you might get a few happy hours thrown in to sweeten the deal. Like Jenny and her friendship.

'I'd better get back. Did you know my brother is over from America?'

He didn't know and was instantly jealous that someone else had a call on her time. He knew it was unreasonable and the bit of him that was still capable of caring was pleased that she had someone else to help her out of the dark hole she'd fallen into. 'Great.'

'It is.' She stood up and smiled at him. 'You should give your friend a call. Go out for that pint.'

He pressed the button to open the door and watched her go. Should he? Maybe she was right. He had let her into his life and would be damn lonely without her. 'Okay…' he called. 'I'll ring Danny back and say yes.'

Mo led the way to the small, busy coffee house. Belle sat down at a table in the corner and waited while he got them coffees. She didn't want a drink any more than she wanted a conversation with him. But all the while he was sitting opposite her, he wasn't chasing after their daughter. Her mother would take Tamsin to Toddington services on the M1 motorway. That was what they had prearranged. If they got split up then they would meet there at the Motel. It was as good a place as any to spend a couple of nights while she decided where to go and what to do next.

'Thought you could do with a sugar hit, so I got you a cake.' He put a plate down in front of her. It was a brownie. 'Your favourite,' he added, with a smile.

She knew what he was doing, turning on the charm, trying to make her weak and vulnerable like she used to be when they first met. 'I'm not sixteen anymore. I'm not that easily bought or impressed.'

'No, but you are still the woman I fell in love with and who loved me back.' He sat down opposite her and reached out to take her hand. She snatched it away.

'History,' she snapped.

'True, but our history is what makes us what we are today. You might want to erase the past, but you can't. It is a part of us both, our lives are interwoven and that can't be undone…' he paused and took a sip of the hot coffee. 'We have two children, Belle…'

'You stole them from me.'

'No, I took back what you stole from me. I am their father and I have rights.'

'You don't have the right to abduct them and take them out of the country.' Her voice was rising, fuelled by anger and frustration. 'I want my son.'

'And I want my daughter.' He looked across the table at her. She knew that look. It was the same one that he had when she pleaded on Mira's behalf. The look of stubborn determination.

She pushed her chair back and stood up. 'This is a waste of time.'

'Agreed,' he said calmly. 'But I have a proposal, a compromise to offer.'

'You don't know the meaning of the word!'

'Sit down and try me.'

She looked at him. She didn't want to sit down, and she didn't want to hear anything he had to say unless it was that he was returning Kyle to her and she was pretty sure that wasn't about to happen.

'Please...' he said more gently, 'for our children...'

Reluctantly, she sat back down.

'How did we come to this?' he asked. 'Is there anything that I can say or do to make you come back as my wife? We could be a family again, all live together.'

'Is this your proposal? A fairy tale, where we all live happily ever after?'

He shook his head. 'No, that was just my long shot, nonsense of course, I knew you would say no, but I had to be clear in my head that there was no going back.'

'Never.'

'Not even for the children?'

'I left you for the sake of the children.'

She saw his dark brown eyes flash with anger. He was a man who liked to get his own way, and being crossed was not something he tolerated well.

'You can throw accusations at me, Belle, but surely even you can't believe that I was a bad father?'

She felt a small niggle of guilt. It was true he had always been loving, even doting, on Tamsin and Kyle. 'They were young; it was the future I was worried about. What you would impose on them...'

'Not this again.' He snapped, openly angry now. 'Mira needed a husband and Hazan needed a young wife...'

'With a British passport,' Belle said, interrupting him. 'You sold her.'

'Always the drama queen. It was a mutually beneficial arrangement. Mira was heading for trouble; she needed a strong husband to settle her down. If you would open your eyes and stop judging, you would see that she is happy now. She has a baby on the way. Did you know that?'

She didn't, but even so, nothing could justify the fact that she was forced into a marriage she didn't want. 'This is pointless.'

'Agreed.'

'What's your proposal?'

He looked steadily at her. 'We have two children...'

Something in his expression warned her that she wasn't going to like what came next.

'I will let you keep Tamsin, and I will promise not to take her or interfere in your lives again.'

'And the catch?'

'No catch. It's simple, really. You have Tamsin and I have Kyle, we have one each.'

He was joking, right? 'Mo, you can't be serious?'

'It's the only sensible way forward.'

'They are twins. You can't split them up. They need each other.'

'They're young, they'll adapt.'

Belle stared at him. He was serious. He meant every word. She pushed the chair back and got to her feet, shaking her head. 'No! I won't let you do this. You're insane.'

'You're being emotional and irrational.'

'Of course I'm emotional. These are our children, they are not a commodity.' She grabbed her bag from the floor and fled. She didn't want to hear another word from him. She headed for the train station. He came after her; she could hear him following her. He reached out and grabbed her arm; she swung round and slapped him. He let go, shocked. She hurried on until she reached the queue for the train ticket.

'Go away,' she hissed.

'Not until you listen.'

'I won't.'

'Then you'll never see Kyle again.'

A sob escaped her lips as she pictured her little boy clutching Mira's hand while his mother and sister left him. 'I'll get a lawyer; I'll take you to court.'

'Aside from the fact that you have been accused of running a brothel…'

'Lies. Even you know that wouldn't be true. The paper did a retraction, an apology.'

'Mud sticks,' Mo said, looking at her coldly. 'Kyle is in Pakistan, Belle. Safe, loved, and with family. We both know your threats are empty. Think about him, he barely speaks, he doesn't interact and keeps everyone at a distance. He needs stability…'

'With me. I'm his mother.'

'And how has that been working out so far? You've done this to him.' He took her arm and pulled her out of the queue away from the curious eyes.

She shook her head vigorously in denial. 'No, it's you, your fault. We couldn't settle anywhere. We always had to hide from you.'

His eyes narrowed. The charm offensive was over. 'And that's how it will be again. You have Tamsin; will you go back to the apartment in Milton Keynes? Of course not, you'll have to move again. She told me about her friends and the school. She likes it there.'

'She'll adapt, make new friends, like a new school.'

He held her upper arms and stared searchingly into her face. 'Look at this rationally, Belle. I'm offering you and Tamsin the chance to go back home and be safe and settled.'

'But I lose my son.'

'You've already lost him.'

Belle looked at her husband and knew he meant every word. The truth crept up on her. She pushed him away. 'You set this up. You let

Tamsin go and made sure that Kyle didn't have his passport.' He made no attempt to deny it. She had been played, and she had lost. 'It will always be like this, won't it?'

'Yes,' he said. 'I have Kyle, and I will keep him. You can have Tamsin and I will leave you both alone as long as you promise not to harass my family anymore and let me bring Kyle up as I see fit.'

She shook her head in desperation. 'He's my son! You're asking me to let go of my boy.'

He looked coldly at her. 'No, Belle, I'm not asking. The deal is already done.'

'Can I talk to him? Write to him? See him sometimes?' she pleaded.

Mo shook his head. 'No.' He turned and left, walking away at speed.

Belle felt as though he had reached inside her chest and ripped her heart out.

Steve finished his pint and put the glass down. 'Another?' he said to Danny.

Danny checked his watch. 'No, sorry mate, I've got to go.'

'Who is she? Do I know her?'

Danny grinned. 'No, mate, met her at work. Do you want me to push you home first?'

Steve shook his head. 'No way, I'll be fine.'

'You sure?'

'Yeah. Get outta here.'

Danny paused and looked at him. 'Do this again?'

Steve nodded his head and then watched his friend leave. It was the first time he had been in a pub since the accident. It felt good to be out again, even though he was sure that everyone was staring at him in the chair. At the Stoke Mandeville spinal injuries rehab unit, they said the feeling would pass, that the more you went out in the wheelchair, the less it felt like everyone was looking. He wasn't convinced he believed it, but Jenny had been right; ringing Danny was a good move. It had been awkward to start with. Danny had skirted around subjects as though he were tiptoeing on eggshells. But they soon slipped back into the banter from their youth. He would be up for doing it again.

'Another?' the barman said.

'Yeah, why not?' Steve replied, thinking he would have one more and then head home. He felt good; better than he had for a long time. And anyway, you can't get done with drunken driving in a wheelchair, can you?

MILES INDICATED to turn into Jasmine Close. He was tired. The traffic out of London had been heavy. An accident on the M1 had caused a tailback several miles long. It was dark and drizzly, the horrible rain that isn't wet enough to have the wipers on all the time, but manages to keep the screen smeared and visibility poor.

He was just about to turn the wheel when he saw Steve coming down the redway that led from the bridge. The chair was free-wheeling and gathering speed. It struck him that while going down looked like fun the getting up must have been hard work.

Miles pulled into the Close and stopped by the curb alongside the Show Home. He pressed the remote to let the window down and watched in his wing mirror and waited. A few minutes later, Steve was alongside him. He felt a surge of anger towards the man, but made sure his voice was calm and friendly. 'Evening,' he said.

Steve stopped wheeling himself. Miles saw he wore fingerless gloves with a leather grip on the palm side. It was an impressive chair, clearly lightweight, probably custom built since it fitted the young man perfectly.

'Been out?'

'I am allowed,' Steve said. 'I don't have a curfew.'

He seemed such an angry young man. Miles wondered why his wife even wanted to spend time with him. But then she had always been a softy with a big heart. It made her a target for losers who would take advantage. 'No, of course you don't. So, have you seen my wife today?'

'Why don't you ask her?' Steve replied, looking at him with open hostility.

'I will, but I just wanted to make sure that you understand. I mean, it's not personal...' Miles watched carefully for his reaction. If he was reading the man's expression right, it was mainly showing confusion, which meant that she hadn't told him yet. Annoying, but not surprising. He knew how much his wife disliked upsetting anyone. He would have to do it for her. 'You have to know that Jenny is very vulnerable at the moment.'

'Yeah, well, she's been through a lot.'

'Yes, she has.' Miles agreed, his own anger rising, as if he needed anyone else telling him what she had been through. What they had both been through. He realised she must have told Steve, talked to him about the accident, poured her heart out in some dope induced therapy session. Why would she talk to the man when she wouldn't say a word about the event to him? He forced himself to smile at Steve. It took a lot of effort. 'Which is why it's best that she doesn't continue to spend time with you.'

'What?'

'I'm sorry, I really am,' he lied, not feeling sorry at all. 'But it is for the best.'

'Jenny's a big girl. If she has something to say, she can say it herself.'

'Can she though? We both know how kind she is. She feels sorry for you.' Miles saw he had hit a nerve and felt a bit of a git, but he was doing for Jenny what she clearly couldn't do herself. 'She doesn't want to hurt your feelings. But she has her own problems to deal with. She just isn't strong enough to take on yours as well. I'm sure you understand.'

'Loud and fucking clear.'

Miles watched him wheel angrily away. He knew it was harsh, but sometimes his wife needed protecting from herself. And really, when it came down to it even though the man was in a wheelchair, he was still just a foul-mouthed dope dealer.

STEVE PUSHED himself as fast as he could up the Close to the sanctuary of his flat. He pressed the button and let himself in. Not that it was safe to him anymore. The bastard who broke in made sure of that. Not only had he trashed and smashed his home, but the callous shit had trampled on what pathetic scrap of dignity he had left.

He hadn't been asleep, of course he hadn't. No sleeping pill could keep his eyes shut through that raid. The thieving bastard had been in his house for ages, even made himself a drink and a sandwich. Once he knew that Steve was in a wheelchair, which he moved out of reach, he had relaxed and made himself at home, picking through the apartment one drawer at a time.

Steve had dragged himself out of bed. The burglar heard the thud when he fell from the bed to the floor. And when the bastard saw him dragging himself towards the chair, he had stamped on his hand and laughed. Then he kicked Steve in the side before lifting the chair up and moved it out of the bedroom. The kick ruptured his catheter bag. Steve was left on the floor, soaked in his own piss and as helpless as a baby.

He had stayed like that until finally, at dawn, the burglar left. Then he crawled across the floor and heaved himself back into bed. He closed his eyes and pretended to sleep, vowing he would never admit the truth to anyone.

He sat in darkness for seconds that became minutes.

That's why Jenny had not been herself earlier. She'd come to see him to tell him their friendship was over. Of course it was. Her husband was right; she shouldn't spend her time with a pathetic spastic like him.

The phone rang. He let it ring out. Danny left a message. 'Had a great time tonight, mate. Good seeing you again. How about doing the same next week?'

Steve reached for the phone, picked it up from the base, and hurled it at the wall. Pity. That's all he was now, the poor sod that everyone pitied.

He wheeled himself into the kitchen and grabbed a bottle of whisky from the cupboard, then went into the bathroom and pulled a packet of prescription painkillers from the medicine cabinet. He put them on his tray and wheeled into his bedroom. 'Sorry, mum,' he said to the photo with the missing glass and broken frame.

Life is shit, and then you die.

EPISODES 11 - 15

JASMINE CLOSE - SERIES ONE

EPISODE ELEVEN
JASMINE CLOSE - SERIES ONE

Gemma heard her phone beep again. Was that the ninth or tenth text in the last five minutes? She knew she should read them, but was afraid that she knew exactly what they would say. Of course she had been warned, but stupidly she'd thought that it was just Kathy showing off and making idle threats. She didn't for one minute know that the vicious cow would actually do it.

She pulled the duvet up over her head and tried to shut out the sound of her mobile. She had been so stupid and hadn't got a clue what to do next. Come off Facebook and change her phone number, obviously. But that wouldn't be enough. How could she persuade her mum to let her move schools? Was it possible to change your name? If she dyed her hair and had it cut really short, that might make her unrecognisable. She'd always fancied being a redhead or maybe even a blonde - weren't they meant to have more fun?

Her mobile started ringing again. Torn between answering and ignoring it, she pushed the cover back and picked it up. It was Abby. Reluctantly, she took the call.

'Oh my god Gem, have you watched it?' Abby said before she'd even said hello.

'No.'

'But you know?'

'Oh yes, Kathy bitch Parry posted a link on Facebook. Everyone's seen it.'

'What will you do?'

'Dunno.'

The phone was silent; for once, even Abby didn't have any answers.

'Thought I'd change my hair...' Gemma said, eventually.

'Not gonna hide who you are though, is it?' Abby replied, not really helping at all. 'I'll talk to my sister; see if she's got any ideas.'

'What would you do?' Gemma asked hesitantly, not even sure if she wanted to know the answer.

'Well, you can't go back to school, that's for sure. Run away perhaps. Yeah, I'd go to London...'

Gemma ended the call and hugged her knees to her chest. Was running away the only option open to her? She'd been to London a few times, a couple with her mum when she was younger and once with Abby when they went to Oxford Street shopping. She didn't like it much. It was loud and busy and dirty. The huge Primark store was great, but they had one in MK now, so they didn't need to go back to London. What would she do there? Where would she stay and how would she live? She had some money saved, nearly five hundred pounds. It was for her driving lessons when she was old enough to get her provisional license. How long would that last? Could she get a job? Would anyone employ her at fifteen? She'd have to pretend to be older and get a fake ID.

She looked around her bedroom. It wasn't home; it was just a room, impersonal magnolia walls and most of her things were still in boxes. She wouldn't miss it and running away would mean she would never have to face everyone at school. Should she leave a note for her mum and dad? Or would it be better to text them once she was safely away?

Her phone beeped again, and she saw it was Abby.

'You need to find a squat,' her friend told her. 'There's a website that tells you when and where places are available.'

'What's the address?'

'Well, it's not Squats R us, is it? You have to be in the know and it's password protected. My sis is trying to find out for you. A friend of hers is a squatter in London. She's waiting to hear.'

'Thanks,' Gemma said, fighting back a sob.

'Hey, don't cry, it'll be fun, an adventure...'

'Will it?'

'Sure. I'll come and see you on Saturday; we can go shopping, go to Oxford Street again.'

'I guess. You think I should go then?'

Abby sighed down the phone. 'Well think about it Gem, what choice have you got? I mean, you can't show your face in MK ever again, can you?'

It was true she couldn't. 'When should I go?'

'Tonight.'

'But it's late, and it's dark. Where do I go when I get there?'

'Well, obviously you'll have to doss in the train station or something for the first night or two. Best take a sleeping bag with you and make sure that your and phone and things are safely stashed away. You need one of those money belts you can hide under your clothes.'

'Perhaps I'll leave it until the morning,' Gemma said, still clutching her duvet tight around her. She didn't want to go to London alone, especially not in the dark. She felt so unprepared.

'Well, that's okay Gem, but what happens when you don't turn up at school in the morning? The secretary will phone your mum and she'll want to know where you are. She'll probably call the police. You know what she's like. And it won't take 'em long to find you on the train or at Euston Station and they'll drag you home and tell you to explain to your mum and dad what's going on. If you go tonight, then you will have a head start. No one will know that you're gone until the morning, by which time you'll be lost in the crowd. It's easy to blend in and become invisible in London.'

Gemma knew it made sense, or at least it did in some crazy way that wouldn't have seemed possible just a few short hours ago. She ended the call and climbed off the bed. Then she started rummaging in boxes for her rucksack. She pulled out a battered old grey teddy that had once been white; she hugged it against her and sniffed, trying really hard not to cry.

THE WHISKY HIT the spot and slightly numbed the pain. Steve fumbled with the bottle of prescription strength painkillers and realised that he should have opened it first before downing half the bottle of whisky. His coordination was non-existent and the child-proof lid was proving to be man proof as well. Eventually he managed to unscrew it, but in his befuddled state, he dropped the bottle and pills scattered all across his bedroom floor.

He threw the now empty bottle in angry frustration and was just about to drop out of his wheelchair and onto the floor to get the pills when his doorbell rang. He glanced across at his bedside clock. It was nine twenty-seven, and he never got visitors in the evening. He didn't want to see anyone anyway, but his curiosity was aroused. Could it be Jenny? Had her jerk-off husband told her what a prick he'd been, and she dashed straight out to assure him it wasn't true?

Steve wheeled himself into the lounge. The bell rang again. Jenny never rang the bell; she did her unique tap tap on the door.

'Steve, let me in...' a weak, shaky voice called through the letterbox.

He pressed the button that controlled the remote, and the door swung open. An elderly lady walked into his apartment. She was bent over like life had weighed her down. She leaned heavily on a walking stick and her hands trembled as if she had Parkinson's disease.

Steve did not know if she suffered from the disease or not, nor did he know how old she was; although he reckoned she must be late seventies, at least going by her thin wrinkly skin. All he knew for sure was that he was delighted to see her.

'Chilly out there,' she said, walking slowly across and sitting down with a shiver on his sofa. 'How you doing?' she sniffed the air. 'Been drinking?'

He nodded his head. 'One or two...'

'Any spare?'

He wheeled back into the bedroom and picked up the whisky bottle from the bed where he'd placed it when he was trying to open the pills. He carried it on his lap back to the lounge and handed it to her. 'Hold on, I'll get you a glass.'

'Don't worry,' she said, taking a long slug from the bottle. 'Only wanted a tot to warm me bones. Wait until you get to my age pet, then you'll know what pain is.'

Steve had no intention of getting to anything remotely like her age. Until she'd knocked on his door, he'd had no intention of getting beyond that evening. But she had something that he wanted and maybe that was worth sticking around for.

'Had a tough day?' she said, lifting her head and tilting it sideways to look at him.

'You could say that.'

'Keep fighting.' She looked at him as though she really cared about him, as though he mattered to her. Which was ridiculous since she they barely knew each other.

'You got a delivery for me, Lou?' he said gruffly, trying to cover the burst of emotions that her words prompted.

She reached down and picked up her handbag. It was old and battered and looked like it had escaped from a black and white movie. Hands trembling, she unclipped the clasp and pulled out a cellophane sandwich bag. Inside was a sausage shape wrapped in silver foil. She handed him the bag.

'Think you might have just saved my life, Lou,' he said, taking it gratefully.

She looked at him sadly with tired eyes that were full of empathy and nodded her head. 'Things will get easier.' She stood up to go.

He wanted to say, 'no they won't,' but he didn't want to upset her by disagreeing. He had no idea why she did what she did, but he was grateful. He had been given her number while he was in the spinal rehab unit. The rumour was that she had lost someone close to her and set up her little business to help people like him. Her rules were strict and simple; she supplied the weed for personal medicinal use only. She rationed the supply and would only deal with people who had severe physical problems. He knew better than to offer her money. He tried that once before and she got very upset with him. 'How did you get here? Can I call you a taxi?'

'I'm okay, I drove,' she said.

He followed her to the door and watched as she climbed onto her electric scooter. He did not know where she lived or how far she had to travel. She put the walking stick on the floor at her feet and her handbag into a basket at the front. She waved at him and then headed off into the darkness.

Steve closed the door, opened the packet and rolled himself a nice fat spliff.

ANNABEL TURNED the music up in the car and tried to relax. It had been a long day. One of her working girls had almost burnt the city centre flat down. Silly mare had put a damp towel in the microwave to warm it for thirty seconds then gone outside for a cigarette. Only she'd put the timer on minutes rather than seconds and only realised her mistake when black, rancid smoke started billowing out of the open window. The girl was on her own. Luckily there were no punters in, but rather than call the fire brigade or unplug the appliance, she rang Annabel and screamed down the phone at her. At the time, Annabel was on a supply run for bulk-buying condoms. It made her realise she needed help. Another pair of hands to help her organise the growing number of girls who wanted to work with her.

All she wanted now was a long soak in a hot bath overflowing with bubbles. But first she had to check on Tammy since the girl hadn't shown up at work that afternoon.

She sped along the dual carriageway towards the roundabout and indicated to turn left. Something caught her attention. A figure disappeared down the redway and into the underpass that went below the road. She wasn't sure why it worried her, but she knew it was always worth listening to her instincts. The trouble was that the underpass would divide into four different routes, and she had no idea which one the figure would take. Cursing silently and longing for the day to reach its end, she cruised slowly round the roundabout, craning her neck to look down the redway at each exit. She had to repeat the process three times and was feeling seriously dizzy by the time the figure emerged. She couldn't tell if they were male or female. Although the street lights were lit above the junctions, further down the road, it got seriously gloomy. Her guess was that the figure was heading into the centre and she knew now why alarm bells had rung. Apart from the fact they were all in black and with a hood pulled up covering their face, they were carrying a bundle and had a rucksack on their bag. She was aware of the burglary in the block of flats and wondered if the thieving bastard had returned for round two.

Annabel pulled into the bus stop lay-by and jumped out of the car, glad that she wore driving shoes as running in her high thin heels was never going to be an option. She was tall and fast, a bit of an athlete in her school days. She had almost caught up with the figure when they realised that someone was after them. 'Wait up,' she called, reaching out to grab them.

They didn't stop and started running faster. But Annabel had the momentum and with a flying leap that ripped her short skirt, she caught on to them. They both fell to the floor, and the figure cried out. Annabel realised instantly that it was a female and a young one at that. She pulled the girl's hood down and recognised her as being a young teenager who lived in the Close.

'Get off me, you bitch,' the girl yelled as she scrambled wildly to get to her feet.

Annabel also stood up and dusted herself off. 'What are you up to?' she said, eyeing the girl with suspicion. Everything about her screamed trouble, especially the black sack that she was clutching. 'What's in the bag?'

'Nothing.' The girl said, looking as though she were about to run.

'So if I took you back to your house right now, you would be happy to explain to your mother what's going on?'

Annabel saw the frightened look and knew that tears were very close to falling. She'd been a pretty troublesome teenager herself many years ago. She changed her tone. 'Look,' she said gently. 'Maybe I can help. If you don't want to go home yet, come back with me and we'll have a chat.'

'I don't know you.'

'I live in Jasmine Close. In one of the apartments. I've seen you; your mum is the lady from the Show Home.'

The girl nodded her head, still looking as though she were about to bolt. 'Please don't tell her.'

Annabel reached out and took the black sack from her. It was soft and light and when she opened it up, it was a sleeping bag. 'Where exactly were you going?'

'A sleepover.'

'Nice try, but you can't kid a kidder. Come on.' Annabel led her back to the car and opened the passenger door. The girl hesitated. 'It's me or your mum.'

It only took two minutes to drive to Jasmine Close. They didn't speak; Annabel decided to save the questions until they were in the light, so that she could see the girl's face properly. Clearly, something was very wrong and if she was reading the signs correctly, the teenager was running away. From what and why, she did not know, but she had every intention of finding out. 'Come on,' she said, leading the way into the apartment block.

Since the visit from the letting agents and the article in the newspaper, Annabel had cancelled all callers to the flat. Tammy and Miranda had to go to one of her premises near the train station to meet their clients. Annoying and inconvenient, but at least she knew she could take the girl in without the risk of any punters being around. She pushed open the door to see the usual mess and chaos that seemed to follow everywhere that Tammy went.

'Sit.' She pointed to the sofa and went into the kitchen to put the kettle on.

'Hello,' Tammy said to the girl as she wandered into the lounge from the bedroom wearing a plunging red and black Basque and little else. 'Who are you then?'

Annabel pulled the curtains and looked at Tammy, her eyes narrowing with suspicion. 'I thought you were unwell today?'

'I am,' Tammy replied, staring at her painted toes.

'You've been entertaining.'

'No.'

'Yes. Who?'

Tammy looked up guiltily. 'Mr Smith.'

Annabel shook her head with annoyance.

'Who's Mr Smith?' the young girl said, staring at Tammy with open-mouthed curiosity.

'Sorry Annabel, I don't like it at the other flat. It's too cramped and too busy.'

Aware of the visitor and just how young she actually was, Annabel decided the discussion with Tammy should wait until later. 'I'm Annabel; this is Tammy. What's your name?'

'Gemma.'

'How old are you, Gemma?'

'Eighteen... seventeen...'

'Try again.'

Gemma sighed. 'Fifteen.' She admitted. 'Nearly sixteen.'

'So what in the world could be so bad that it would make you run away into the cold, dark night?'

'Run away?' Tammy said, shocked. 'Not smart.'

'I had to.'

Annabel looked at the girl; she seemed to be a pretty tragic little thing. Whatever the problem, it was clearly a biggy to her. 'Would you like a hot chocolate?'

Gamma nodded her head. Annabel looked at Tammy, who headed off to the kitchen to make it.

'Tell me.'

'I can't.'

'Because?'

Gemma started to cry. 'It's so horrible and humiliating...' she continued sobbing.

Annabel pulled a clean tissue from the pretty pastel box on the coffee table and handed it to her. Tammy returned with the drinking chocolate.

'Hey baby, don't cry. Whatever it is, Annabel will sort it.'

Annabel was touched by Tammy's confidence in her. 'I'll certainly try.'

Gemma wiped her eyes and blew her nose. 'No one can sort this out.'

'What is it?' Tammy asked. 'You can tell us anything.'

Gemma shook her head. 'You'll be shocked,' she said, pulling her mobile from her pocket.

Annabel resisted laughing. She certainly hadn't had anyone say that to her for a very long time. 'I'll try not to be. Is it something on your phone?'

'YouTube clip.' Gemma pressed a button and handed it to Annabel, who watched for several seconds and then passed it to Tammy.

'You didn't know?' Tammy said angrily.' He filmed this without you knowing?'

'Yes,' Gemma sobbed.

'Bastard should have his balls chopped off!'

Annabel looked sadly at Gemma. 'Your first time?' she asked gently.

Gemma nodded her head. 'Alex dumped me. Now he's going out with the older sister of a girl in my class. I got into a fight with Kathy at school yesterday. I said he only went out with her sister because of her big fake boobs. She said I was just jealous - as if! And that she would get me back, then she posted this...' Gemma started crying again, 'I thought he really liked me, that it was special. I can't go back to school. Not ever.'

Annabel knew what a big deal such things were for a teenager. She remembered how important it was to fit in and not be the target of attention or ridicule. But she also knew the importance of standing up to bullies and finding enough self-confidence and self-worth to fight back and not be put down by them. 'You have to...' she said gently.

'You don't understand, look.' Gemma grabbed her phone from Tammy and opened up her text messages. She handed the phone to Annabel. 'It's even worse on Facebook.'

'I understand.'

'No, you don't. Look at the names they're calling me.'

'We've been called a few ourselves,' Annabel said, exchanging a wry smile with Tammy. 'It doesn't really matter what they say or do, it's how you handle it that counts.'

'Really?'

'Oh yes,' Tammy said. 'The first thing you must do is go onto Facebook and tell the world that he has a tiny dick and is rubbish at sex.'

'Really?' Gemma said again. 'Won't that make it worse?'

'It will be for him. The attention will shift away from you and switch to him and his new girlfriend. She will have to dump him or defend him and all these silly Facebook trolls will have a new target to annoy,' Tammy said. 'Then you have to go into school tomorrow, with your head held high, looking fabulous and without a care in the world. Everyone will think, wow, you are amazing, and he is a tosser with a tiny dick.'

Gemma looked at Annabel, who nodded her head in agreement. 'She's right. It is the only way. Remember the saying – sticks and stones will break my bones but names will never hurt me – I know it isn't really true and often words wound more than a physical assault. But the principle holds true because the words can only hurt you if you allow them to.'

Gemma went into her phone and onto her Facebook page. 'Done,' she said, looking at Annabel for approval.

'Proud of you,' she said. 'Come on, I'll walk you home.'

VICTORIA SIPPED her tea and bit into a slice of buttery toast. She was tired and irritable following a restless night's sleep. Dave was still in bed. It was his day off and he hadn't arrived home last night until gone midnight. But it wasn't thoughts of her husband that had kept her tossing and turning all night, but a tall dark American who seemed to have lodged himself in her head and was dominating her thoughts.

Gemma walked into the kitchen and helped herself to a glass of milk from the fridge and a cereal bar from the cupboard.

'I'll make you some toast if you like?'

'No thanks, I'd better get going, don't want to miss the bus.'

Victoria looked at her daughter. There was something different, but she wasn't sure what. 'You changed your hair?'

'No.'

'Well, you look very pretty this morning,' she said, smiling.

'Thanks mum,' Gemma dropped the wrapper from the oat bar onto the table, waved goodbye and left.

Victoria finished her tea and then hurried around the house, tidying up. She was surprised to see one of the sleeping bags wrapped up in a poly bag in the hall cupboard. She thought they had all been put in the loft for storage. Typical Dave, he rarely did any of the jobs she asked him to do. She wondered if Brett would pop in for a coffee again and knew that she was hoping he would. She went upstairs and re-brushed her hair and applied her lipstick. Dave was snoring loudly, so she turned the bedroom light off, left him to sleep off last night's darts, piss up, and headed for work.

Sasha was in the car park waiting for her as she hurried down the road. 'Hello,' she said, 'what are you doing here so early?'

'I have the money that the readers have given, and the name they have chosen for the cat. I want to get a couple of promotional photos.'

Victoria unlocked the Show Home, Sasha followed her in. 'it might be a bit early for Mrs Martin. I don't know what time she's up and about.'

'That's okay, thought I'd call in on my way to the office. Can you talk to her and get something organised for later, say around three?'

'Yep, I'll text you to confirm.'

Victoria waved to Sasha as she drove away, then she went back inside and put the coffeemaker on. She heard the door open and walked back into the office.

'Fake smile at the ready,' Brett said.

'What else could it be for a fake customer?' she replied, trying to remain cool and calm and failing completely as she felt her cheeks flush.

He grinned, well aware of the effect he had on her, and walked across the room until he was just inches away. He looked into her eyes, his gaze dropped to her lips, and then he took her totally by surprise and gently touched her lips with his finger.

Victoria stepped back, afraid of the intimacy between them. 'Would you like a coffee?' she said, running into the kitchen.

'Sure,' he replied, following her. 'You can tell me what enticements are on offer.'

'What?' she swung round to face him again.

'You mentioned free carpets yesterday,' he said, laughing at her.

'Oh, I can do free fake carpets; I can even offer you fake blinds throughout your fake house. Are you still thinking of the two-bed terrace or are your aspirations bigger now?'

He smiled at her. 'I think my aspirations are very high indeed. Have dinner with me tonight.'

'I can't.'

'Of course you can. You say yes, we go somewhere quiet and cosy and eat delicious food and drink expensive wine.'

She held her hand up and pointed to the rings on her fingers. 'I'm married.'

He took the hand and held it clasped in his. 'But you're not happy,' he said softly.

She shook his hand away. 'You don't know that.'

'I think I do.'

'You're wrong,' she snapped, afraid that he might be right. She folded her arms across her chest.

'When you look at him, do your eyes light up with desire? Does he make your pulse race and your head spin? Do you lay awake at night fantasising about his hands caressing your body?'

'Stop it,' she ordered. 'You're talking nonsense.'

'Am I? That's how you make me feel. I think it's the same for you.'

'I have work to do,' she said, picking up a file from her desk and clinging onto it as a barrier between them.

'Later,' he said, walking away.

'Don't count on it,' she shouted after him.

She sat down at her desk and looked at her wedding and engagement ring. She had been married for nearly eighteen years. Of course, the passion and excitement had faded. That didn't mean she wasn't happy, or that they weren't in love still. She pictured Dave as she'd left him that morning, an image that didn't inspire desire. But that was real life, a proper relationship. What Brett was talking about was lust and fantasy, not the same thing at all. It was fun to flirt, and he did make her pulse race and her body ache with unfulfilled passion, but it wasn't real and she knew that she would have to put a stop to it now before it went any further.

Gemma got off the bus, her phone beeped with a message; she quickly read it and took a long deep breath. It was from Tammy telling her to walk tall. She was terrified, but determined. She knew that a couple of girls on the bus had been whispering about her and one of the lads from year ten had whistled at her. But she knew she didn't want to live in a squat in London and cowering in a corner for the rest of her school life didn't seem like fun, either. So the only way forward was to do as Annabel said and front it out. Her post on Facebook last night had certainly had an effect. The focus did shift onto Alex and Kathy, and Lauren, and away from her. She started to get new text messages and this time, instead of calling her names, they were messages of support and encouragement.

Abby came running to meet her as soon as she reached the school gates. 'Thought you were going to London.'

'Change of plan.'

'Yeah, I saw.' Abby tucked her hand through her arm and led her towards a large group of girls, mostly from their year, although a couple were older. All of them were watching her approach with a mixture of curiosity, some animosity and a collective excitement.

'Did you know he was filming?' Amanda said.

'Was he really crap?' an older girl asked.

Gemma ignored Amanda and nodded her head at the older girl, feeling a bit overwhelmed by the attention.

'What a waste. He looked so hot,' the older girl said, walking away.

'Kathy said he dumped you because you're a slapper.' Kelsey, one of Kathy's best friends, said nastily.

The group went quiet, and all eyes focused on Gemma. She forced herself to relax and smile. 'Well he would, wouldn't he? Didn't want anyone to know that I dumped him for being so crap at it.'

The group whispered and jostled to get close to her, everyone talking at once.

'Hey Gemma...'

She turned around. It was Owen Knight, a boy from year twelve and generally acknowledged as being pretty buff.

'Fancy sharing a pizza with me tonight?'

Owen Knight asking her out! 'Sure, why not,' she said casually, enjoying the looks of envy and admiration that the other girls were giving her.

The bell rang, and they all trailed into class. Abby nudged her in the side. 'I was looking forward to coming to see you in London. Thought it would be exciting, two friends on an adventure.'

Gemma shrugged her shoulders, not sharing Abby's regret. She thought how lucky she had been that Annabel and Tammy found her and put her right.

STEVE'S HEAD WAS POUNDING. Reluctantly, he opened his eyes and realised that someone was hammering on the door. He was in bed, or at least on the bed, fully clothed and if his clock was to be believed, it was morning, unbelievably almost ten o'clock. He had the button that opened the door remotely on a black cord around his neck. But he wasn't at all sure that he wanted to open it. Whoever was there, they were persistent. He listened carefully, aware that someone was calling his name. He recognised the voice as belonging to Sharon Stanza, the social worker from ASCAT. Knowing that the woman would not give in easily, he opened the door to let her in.

'Well, thank the lord for that,' he heard her say, 'beginning to think I'd have to break in. Mr Lance?'

He was clinging onto his overhead grab bar and halfway through a transfer to his chair when her large frame appeared in the doorway. Her eyes darted around the room, taking in the mess of the empty whisky bottle and the pills scattered all across his floor.

'Heavy night?' she asked, although it was more a statement than a question. 'I'll put the kettle on.'

He wheeled himself into the lounge, feeling as rough as he no doubt looked. His mouth was as foul as a rat in a sewer and his clothes were creased and grubby. He needed to shower and change, but most of all, he needed coffee.

Sharon put the steaming mug on the tray and onto his lap, then she broke out the biscuits. 'I can do you something more sensible if you like? Toast or cereal? I assume you have bread?'

'Biscuits fine,' he said, taking one and biting into it gratefully. 'Two visits in one week. I must be on your risk register.'

'Top of it,' she said, lowering herself into the chair. 'I'm sick of hearing your name, to be honest. I've had your cleaner claiming you never let her in and when you do the place such a mess, she can't get it all done. I've had the police telling me you still refuse to give a statement and the lovely lass from victim support said you made her cry.'

He did feel bad about that. She was young and pretty, but so nice and condescending it did bring out the very worst from him. He took another bite of the biscuit.

'Steve...' she said seriously.

It made him look at her. She really did sound worried.

'You need help. What can I do?'

He shook his head. 'Nothing. I'm great, top of the fucking world.'

'Do you want me to see if I can get you back into Stoke Mandeville?'

'Shit no! For what?'

'Well, you were supposed to come away from the spinal unit equipped and ready to cope with your new reality. Clearly, that's not the case, so maybe you need another stint.'

'You're kidding me, right?' he could tell by her expression that she wasn't. 'Jeez, I'm not going back there.'

'Then what?'

'Then nothing. Told you, I'm fine.' He picked his mug up and took a large gulp. It burnt his lip, his hand shook, the drink spilled and scolded his chest. He hurled the mug across the room and started to sob.

Sharon fetched a cloth soaked in cold water to mop up the spilt coffee. She fetched him a tissue and picked up the broken bits of his mug. Then she sat quietly and let him cry it out.

'I'm sorry,' he sniffed when the sobs eventually ended.

'Don't be,' she said. 'You should have done that a long time ago. Now maybe we can start to get somewhere.'

Victoria pushed Mary down the Close in a manual wheelchair. It was a bright cold day and Mary had taken ages, adding layers of clothes to protect her against the chill. The cat was nowhere around, which was annoying. She knew that Sasha would want a picture of him to put in the paper. He was, after all, what the fuss was all about.

Brett waved to her from the Fisher's front door as she walked past. She ignored him.

'You have to watch out for the lookers,' Mary said. 'If you ask me, I'd say he's trouble.'

Victoria wasn't asking her, but she knew that the old lady's words were spot on.

'You can wait in the Show Home until Sasha gets here,' she said. 'No point in getting cold.'

Victoria pushed her into the office and closed the door. 'Want a drink while we wait?'

'You offering brandy?'

'I was thinking tea or coffee.'

'Hmm, do you always play it safe?'

Victoria raised her eyebrows. 'Safe?'

'Yeah, tea coffee, affair no affair.' Mary said, her old eyes dancing with mischief.

Victoria remembered Mary's grandson Jack telling her how the elderly lady liked to shock, so she chose to ignore her and instead made two cups of tea.

Sasha arrived, and Victoria left her to talk to Mary while she went in search of the cat. She looked all around the apartment block and then walked over to Barry.

'Not seen him at all today,' Barry said, crinkling his eyes against the sun's weak glare. 'You alright Vic? You look different.'

'Different? How?'

'Not sure, almost glowing. Rosy cheeks, sparkling eyes, like a woman in love or one who's in a delicate condition. Are congratulations in order?'

'You saying I'm pregnant?' she said, shocked.

He smiled and shrugged, 'No? Oh well, must be the glow you get from seeing me then.'

'Yep, that must be it,' she said, laughing. 'Yell, if you see the cat, he's about to miss his own show.' She walked away, feeling unsettled. She knew she wasn't pregnant. Last time she checked, you had to have sex before that could happen and Dave and she hadn't got it together for months.

She crossed the road and looked up and down the Close. Daft cat had to be somewhere.

'Looking for this?' Brett said, walking out of the Fishers back garden carrying the animal in question.

'I am,' she said. 'Thank you.'

He handed the cat over to her, and their hands and arms entwined. She wanted to drop the animal and wrap her arms around him. Instead, she untangled herself and walked away, back to the Show Home without a backward glance.

Sasha beamed at the cat as Victoria put him down. As though he knew exactly what was expected of him, he padded across the floor and jumped up onto Mary's lap. Sasha took a photo and handed over a cheque for five hundred pounds.

'Wow, that should keep him in cat food,' Victoria said.

'Readers always love an animal in distress story, especially one that has a happy ending.'

'So what's his name?' Mary said, 'I'm sick of sounding like a daft git standing at my door calling for a cat.'

Sasha grinned. 'Say hello to Roy...'

Mary rolled her eyes.

'I like it,' Victoria said.

The cat purred loudly, seemingly giving his approval.

'We had a short list from the readers and then asked our editor to make the final choice.'

'Can we get a picture outside?' Victoria asked, keen to get as much good publicity for the site as she could.

She wheeled Mary out into the car park; Roy still sat contentedly on her lap. And then watched as Sasha took the pictures. It was cold, the Indian summer definitely over. She stuck her hands in her pockets and pulled out a piece of folded paper. Surprised, she opened it up and saw it was a note with a number on it. Clearly a mobile phone number and she knew exactly who it belonged to. He must have put it in her pocket earlier. Question was, what was she going to do with it?

EPISODE TWELVE
JASMINE CLOSE - SERIES ONE

It had been a great day and Gemma knew who she had to thank for that. She got off the bus and hurried home to change out of her school uniform. She couldn't believe she had a date with Owen Knight, and she definitely wanted to look her best. 'Hi,' she shouted as she walked into the house. It was her dad's day off, but he didn't seem to be around, although the car was on the drive. She grabbed a yogurt from the fridge and quickly ate it, then ran upstairs to get changed. A few minutes later she was at the apartment block and ringing the bell for Flat number two. 'Hi, it's Gemma,' she said, speaking into the intercom. The door opened, allowing her to enter. She walked round to the door and tapped it lightly.

'Come in, baby,' Tammy said, opening the door.

If anyone else had called her baby, she would have been outraged, but Tammy made the word sound friendly and affectionate. The young woman was wearing tight jeans and a baggy jumper that, despite being shapeless, she somehow managed to look incredibly sexy. Her long dark hair tumbled around her shoulders and she wore minimal makeup.

'My day off,' she said, as if to explain her appearance.

'What do you do? I mean, where do you work?' Gemma asked,

thinking that she was the most beautiful woman she had ever seen. 'Are you a model?'

Tammy smiled. 'Yeah sometimes. So how did you get on today?'

Gemma handed her new friend her phone and pointed to the Facebook comments. 'Just like you said it would be.'

'Good, so no more running away?'

'No, absolutely no. the hottest boy in the school asked me to go out with him for pizza tonight.'

'Did he now?' Tammy said, lifting her hand up and looking at her fingernails. 'Think we'd better do something with these then don't you.'

Gemma tried not to fidget while Tammy gave her a manicure and painted her nails, and then she tried not to squirm and flinch when the tweezers came out and her eyebrows were worked on. She refused to think about tomorrow and the school's policy regarding nail polish. It didn't matter, she could keep her hands in her pockets all day and if her crimson tipped hands were spotted, then it would be worth the detention.

The door opened, and Annabel entered the flat. She looked surprised and not necessarily pleased to see Gemma sat on the sofa being groomed by Tammy, but she smiled politely. 'I take it you had a good day?' she said to Gemma.

Gemma grinned widely and nodded. 'Thank you so much.'

'She has a hot date,' Tammy said pointing to the nail polish and holding the tweezers up. 'Thought I'd help her out a bit.'

'You look lovely.'

Gemma got the feeling that Annabel wanted her gone. Besides, mum would be in from work soon, so she looked at Tammy. 'Thank you, I'd better get going now.'

Tammy looked a bit disappointed. 'Have you got something hot to wear?'

Gemma thought how much she would enjoy going through Tammy's wardrobe to see if anything fitted her. She would love to look half as amazing as the young woman did. But she knew that the vibes from Annabel were not encouraging. She didn't know what the problem was; the older woman was polite and friendly, just more distant and less welcoming than she had been last night. She nodded her head. 'I have thanks,' she said before heading for the door.

Annabel followed her all the way out to the Close as if to make sure that she really did leave. It upset her a bit, but she tried not to take it personally. Adults were weird and rarely talked any sense, and although Annabel was one of the coolest grown-ups she'd ever met, she was still an adult, probably as old as her mother.

'You're alright now?' Annabel asked her.

'Oh yes, it all worked like a dream.'

'Good, I'm really glad for you, Gemma. If ever you are in trouble, you know where to find me.'

'Great thanks,' she replied, thinking that she had got it wrong and Annabel didn't have a problem with her being there after all.

'But I don't think you should come around to the flat anymore.'

'Why not?' she was upset, she couldn't help it. Not only had they helped her last night, but Tammy had been great, like a big sister, doing her nails and stuff.

Annabel sighed. 'Oh Gemma, I know you think you are all grown up but believe me despite your adventure, or mis-adventure with Alec...'

'Alex.'

'Alex, you are still a lovely little innocent and hanging around at my flat will not do much to maintain that innocence.'

Gemma didn't really know what Annabel was talking about. Unless she meant that Tammy would have boyfriends stay over. She wanted to argue, but despite Annabel's kind eyes and soft smile, there was a determination underpinning it and Gemma was smart enough to recognise that it really was goodbye.

VICTORIA STEPPED outside the Show Home to take the free standing sales sign inside; the wind was already strong and according to the forecast it was set to get worse. Mary's grandson rode past her on his motorbike and waved. She watched him speed up past the building site towards the apartment block. And that's when she saw it. Her daughter, Gemma, was talking to the woman from the brothel. She was so shocked that she stood there staring for several seconds. Then her shock intensified a hundredfold as her daughter leaned in and hugged the woman.

The phone inside the Show Home started ringing, and she was torn between running up the Close and demanding to know what the hell was going on or answering the call, which could be the sale confirmation she'd been waiting all afternoon for. She saw Gemma pull away and walk back towards their house, so she ducked inside and grabbed the phone. It was a sale. A couple that had been in earlier about one of the terraces had decided to go ahead. It made her think of Brett, but she pushed his image away and made arrangements with the wife to complete the paperwork tomorrow. She hung up, closed her computer down and hurried to the door to finish bringing the sign back into the office. Then she grabbed her jacket and keys and locked up the building.

ANNABEL KNEW she had hurt Gemma, but she also knew it was the right thing to do. The young girl had no idea who or what she was dealing with, and Annabel was happy for it to stay that way. Innocence was a precious gift and one she had no intention of destroying. She watched her walk down the Close towards her house and saw the motorbike roar up towards them. She decided to make herself busy at the car rather than go back indoors straight away. She'd enjoyed her brief encounter with the biker when they'd met briefly yesterday. He was attractive and cocky, a combination she always found irresistible.

So she unlocked her car and lent in to get something from the glove box while he parked up and removed his helmet.

'Hello again,' he said from behind her. He had an interesting voice, strong and deep, with a hint of a northern accent.

She smiled and turned around to face him. 'hi, was it John?'

'Jack.'

'Jack, of course.' She was just about to ask him in for coffee when the annoying Show Home woman appeared, apparently having run all the way up the Close given how out of breath she was.

'Stay away from my daughter,' Victoria said, prodding her in the chest with a fingernail that could really do with an emery board work over.

Rarely lost for words, Annabel genuinely was unsure what to say or to do. Obviously, she wanted to defend herself, but knew that she couldn't betray Gemma's trust. So she kept her mouth shut and let the woman rant.

'I won't let you corrupt her. She's only fifteen. What's the matter with you? Don't you have any sense of morality or decency?'

Annabel was quite sure that Victoria would happily hurl insults at her for some time yet, but Jack jumped onto his hero horse and came to her rescue.

'Okay, Victoria, that's enough now,' he said, stepping between them and taking the brunt of the still prodding finger himself.

'Why are you defending her? You know what she is.'

'Obviously a misunderstanding.' Jack stood firm and Annabel's interest in him grew. She couldn't remember the last time a man had actually tried to defend her honour.

'She sells sex.' Victoria threw at her as though it were some shocking revelation.

Annabel shrugged her shoulders. Jack was still acting like a human shield and protecting her. She felt sorry for Victoria. True, she was a narrow-minded nimby, but then so were most of the population. And she was only trying to protect her daughter. Annabel understood that. She might not have children of her own, but she would fight like a lioness to protect her working girls from anyone or anything that tried to harm them. So she stepped out from behind her new hero and looked directly at the other woman. 'I don't know what you think you know, but I can promise you it's almost certainly wrong.' Well, that was about as clear as mud, she thought irritably and tired again. 'Your daughter lost her phone, I found it,' she lied.

Victoria stared at her as she clearly tried to decide whether to believe her. 'Her phone?'

'Yes, I picked it up at the bus stop earlier today. I rang it and she answered, and we agreed she would collect it after school today, which is exactly what she did.'

'Why didn't you drop it into me at the Show Home?'

'I did suggest that, but Gemma was keen to collect it herself. You know what young girls are with their secrets? I think it is the modern equivalent of the locked diaries we used to tuck under our pillows at night.'

'Well, if that's true then thank you,' Victoria said grudgingly.

'You're welcome.' Annabel replied, proud of her quick thinking and credible lie. All she had to do now was hope that Tammy had Gemma's number and could quickly ring or text her with the same cover story.

Victoria gave her one last doubting look before turning round and walking away.

Annabel looked at Jack. 'Coffee?'

'Sure.'

She opened the flat door and hurried inside, with him following close behind her. She had no idea if he knew about her and the infamous flat or not. But either way, questions were bound to be asked. She liked him, and that was rare for her. She spent so much of her life dealing with men and their willies that she found them ridiculous rather than sexy. It was very unusual for any male to make her want to spend more time with them than she had to.

But first, she had to warn Gemma.

JACK LOOKED around him with interest. He had seen the story in the local paper. Who hadn't? But what he didn't know was how much truth there was to it. Either way, Annabel was a beautiful and interesting woman and he was game for a challenge.

The young female in the flat was undoubtedly the sexiest creature he had ever set his eyes on and if the story was true about it being a brothel, then they must be making a fortune because he was pretty certain any man with blood in their veins would pay to have sex with her.

He was disappointed when she went into the bedroom, but the feeling faded quickly when Annabel sat down beside him on the sofa. 'So what do you want to know?' she asked, her clear green eyes assessing him shrewdly.

'Is it true? Do you sell sex?'

'Is it a problem if I say yes?'

'Depends.'

'On what?'

He smiled. 'On whether you're expecting me to pay or not.'

'Seems to me that you're the one with expectations,' she said, laughing.

She was like no woman he had ever met before, and he was pretty sure she was as interested in him as he was in her.

Without a word, she got up and went into the bedroom. A couple of minutes later, the younger female left the flat. Annabel looked at him. 'Hungry?' she asked.

'Very,' he replied.

VICTORIA FELT STRANGELY UNSETTLED by the confrontation. Was it really about a lost phone? Gemma confirmed the story, but Victoria still wasn't happy. Something was wrong. Well, obviously the whole situation was wrong; there shouldn't be a brothel in her lovely new estate. Gemma was hiding something and that worried her, but on the other hand, she knew that all teenagers had secrets from their parents, so maybe she was being paranoid. The uneasiness didn't leave her, though.

She had no idea where Dave was. It was his day off and that meant he was supposed to clean up and make the dinner. But the kitchen looked like a fry up bomb had exploded in it and when she went to the bedroom, the bed was still unmade. She tried ringing him, but his mobile was turned off. There was no note on the side or pinned on the fridge and nothing had been taken out of the freezer.

She went upstairs and tapped on her daughter's door before pushing it open. 'Thought I might order pizza,' she said. 'Bit of a treat for us.'

Gemma shook her head. 'Not for me thanks mum, I'm going out.'

'Where are you going? What about dinner?'

'A few friends are meeting at Xscape; I'll grab a sub or something there.'

Victoria hated being at the stage in her daughter's life where she was excluded, but knew that she had to let her go out with her friends. The Xscape building was an entertainment venue that looked like a giant shiny slug, and on the inside, it was full of shops and restaurants. It also housed the multiplex cinema and the indoor ski slope, and it was a busy and popular place. So she forced herself to smile. 'Be home by ten.'

Amazingly, Gemma accepted the curfew without argument and simply nodded her head before turning her attention back to her hair straighteners.

Victoria walked into her own bedroom and stripped out of her work uniform. The mobile phone number fell out of her pocket. She picked it up and looked at it. She was tempted, of course she was. She put it on the bed while she changed into jeans and a soft red jumper, then with a determined effort she grabbed the number and screwed it into a ball before dropping it into the waste bin.

Back downstairs, she looked in the fridge for something to eat, but uninspired, she closed it again and put the kettle on. A feeling of loneliness washed over her and she had to go into the lounge and switch the TV on to give the illusion of company. She was a married woman with a child. How could she be lonely? She was certainly alone. No sign of Dave, and Gemma skipped down the stairs and out of the front door with no more than a quick wave in her direction. She closed her eyes and thought about Brett and his invitation to take her to dinner. She fought the temptation to retrieve the phone number and text him. She told herself that she was hungry and thinking about dinner, and not about the man.

The doorbell rang, and she leapt guiltily to her feet. Surely her wishes hadn't conjured him up? She told herself she was being ridiculous and hurried into the hall and opened the door. Ridiculous or not, she was disappointed when he wasn't standing on the doorstep, ready to whisk her away.

'You alright?' Sonia asked. 'You look all weird.'

'Just tired,' she said, thinking it was probably true.

Sonia was carrying a bottle of wine, an enormous bar of chocolate and a couple of DVDs. 'Paul is on the early shift, so he's already asleep and the boys are in bed,' she said. 'Thought you might like a mushy one.'

Victoria took the DVDs she was offered and followed her into the lounge. They were all what Dave would term chick flicks and were absolutely perfect for her mood. 'I'll get the glasses,' she said, dropping the films on the table. 'You choose...'

'No Dave?'

'Darts night,' she lied, not wanting to admit that her husband had gone AWOL again.

'Here.' Sonia handed her the chocolate. 'Who needs men? Well, apart from Patrick Swayze, of course.' She opened up the case and took out the Dirty Dancing DVD. 'Okay?'

Victoria popped a piece into her mouth and made herself comfy on the sofa. 'Perfect,' she said, pushing all thoughts of Brett and Dave from her mind. She filled their glasses and then settled down to watch the film.

JENNY SWITCHED the TV off and stared at her brother.

'What?' he said, realising that she was looking at him intently?

'Exactly,' she said. 'What is it with you tonight?'

'Nothing.'

'Liar. You've been checking your phone every few seconds and pacing the floor like a caged animal.'

He sat down beside her and looked contrite.

'Who is she?'

'She?'

Jenny smiled. 'Well I know it won't be a man that's got you so fired up and agitated.'

Brett took her hand. 'Sorry Jen, I came here for you but I've allowed myself to be distracted. Not been a lot of help really, have I?'

'Don't say that. I love having you here, and I don't mind you being distracted. It means that you're not going on at me to go out and do things all the time.'

'Like Miles?'

'Yes.'

'He is a bit full on,' Brett said. 'His motivation is good...'

'But?'

'I don't know Jen? It seems forcing you is a risky strategy, but what do I know? He might have it right and it is the only way to get you better.'

'My therapist says it takes time, and there's no quick fix.'

'Miles clearly disagrees.'

Jenny nodded her head. 'He says she holds me back, indulges me.' She paused and looked at her brother. 'What if this is it?' she said, saying the words that were too frightening to speak out loud to Miles. 'He wants me to go back to being the person who I was before. Is that even possible? Can anyone go back? Surely we all change and move forward throughout our lives.'

'Oh Jen, shouldn't you be saying this to Miles?'

'He doesn't listen, though. You know what he's like? He only ever hears what he wants to hear.'

Brett took her hands and looked at her. 'What can I do for you? How can I make this better?'

'You're here,' she replied. 'That helps a lot.'

He smiled. 'So when are you going to tell me the story of the spliff? So far, I've only heard your husband's very unamused version of events. And who is this Steve guy?'

Jenny felt a stab of guilt as she thought of Steve. She had lied to her husband and told him she had ended her friendship with him. 'I'll tell you about Steve and the spliff if you tell me about the mystery lady who's got you all tied up in knots.'

'Deal,' he said. 'You go first.'

STEVE LOOKED IN THE MIRROR, and a stranger stared back at him. Didn't matter how much he brushed his hair or cleaned his teeth or checked his shirt was clean, he was still the poor sod in the wheelchair. The door knocked, and he heard Sharon Stanza shout his name through the letterbox. He pressed the remote to open the door and wheeled himself out of the bathroom.

'Well, you scrub up well, don't you?' she said, grinning like she'd swallowed a shoe horn.

He rolled his eyes and grunted. The reason he'd agreed to her secret mystery tour was to get rid of her earlier. 'I'm not feeling great,' he said, hearing how pathetic it sounded even to his own ears. She didn't bother to acknowledge it.

A taxi was outside the flat waiting with a ramp at its rear. 'In you go.'

He pushed himself into the vehicle and put his brakes on and let the driver put a seat belt around him. Sharon climbed into the back and spilled across two seats. Her breathing was laboured and she was bathed in sweat despite the evening being bitingly cold.

The engine started, and the driver reversed into a space to turn round and then headed out of the Close. Steve hadn't been in a car since the accident and never in a wheelchair. He didn't like how high up he was. He couldn't see out of the windows and felt like one jolt from a pothole or over a speed ramp and his head would go through the roof. Up until then, he had been ferried around in ambulance transport vehicles with platform hoists and floor fixing systems to clamp the chair firmly in place.

'You alright Steve?' Sharon asked, watching him carefully.

'You gonna tell me where we're going?'

She smiled and glanced out of the window. 'Nearly there.'

Not being able to see out properly, he was struggling to work out where they were. Besides, it was dark, and the roads were largely unlit. Back before his accident, when he was driving, the budget cuts hadn't hit, and the roads were brightly illuminated from dusk till dawn. It all looked so different now.

The taxi indicated, and Steve bent his head right down to see where they were. It was the big School Campus and leisure centre. He looked at Sharon, but she was giving nothing away.

The driver released the strap and lowered the ramp so that he could wheel himself backwards and out of the car. He felt a bit nauseous, sat higher up and swaying around in the wheelchair. He had been very aware of how many roundabouts they had gone around. No avoiding them in Milton Keynes. Roundabouts were everywhere.

He knew his way around Stantonbury, although it wasn't where he went to school a couple of his mates did, and as a teenager, he'd competed against them in football. During the school holidays, they'd all hung around at the leisure centre sometimes and go swimming. He didn't want to be there, he really didn't. Why the hell would he want his nose rubbed in his youthful past? The place was full of memories that evoked nothing but pain and regret. He felt a surge of anger towards the social worker who waddled along ahead of him towards the leisure centre entrance. He stopped. 'I'm not going in.'

Sharon paused and turned round; she shrugged her fat shoulders that sent ripples of wobbles all down her body. 'Your loss,' she said. 'The taxi will be back at ten and it's bloody cold out here.' She pointed just inside the doors. 'The lift is over there. I'll be upstairs.'

He watched her go in and felt a stab of guilt. She'd obviously gone to a lot of trouble, and he was pretty sure it was far beyond what she was paid to do. He didn't want to be there; he didn't want to be anywhere, and he hadn't asked her to drag him out on her mystery tour. She was right about it being cold; he couldn't stay there for the next two hours. There was a bitterly cold wind and the night sky was full of heavy rain stuffed clouds. He tried to remember where the nearest pub was. He was fairly confident it was quite close. Could he go there and then come back for the taxi at ten? Or could he just call his own taxi and go straight home now? He cursed not having a mobile phone. He'd have to go in and ask reception to ring one for him. Were they allowed to do that? Surely they would do it for a spastic.

He heard a sound and turned his head. A wheelchair zoomed past him. He had a fleeting glimpse of a young woman with long brown hair flying out behind her. She didn't stop or pause and went straight into the leisure centre. He saw her wave to the reception staff and then she disappeared into a corridor that he knew led to the changing rooms, the swimming pool and the gyms. Curiosity got the better of him and he wheeled himself into the building through the automatic doors. He paused, not knowing where she had gone. He knew that on the next floor he would be able to look down at the swimming pool and the gyms. The lift was a small cubicle that had obviously been an afterthought for the building. He had to put his finger on the button and manually bring the platform down and keep pressing until the door swung open. He pushed himself inside and then found that he couldn't twist round enough to press the button to close the door and take it up. So he wheeled out and turned round, then reversed in. That was better, but it still wasn't easy. The button had to be depressed the entire time. Take your finger off and the lift stops.

He saw Sharon as soon as he came out of the lift. She was overflowing on a plastic chair, looking down over the balcony with a vending machine drink on the table in front of her.

He wheeled across and looked down in surprise. 'What are they doing?'

'Wheelchair basketball,' she said. 'It gets pretty brutal.'

Steve spotted the young woman who had shot past him outside the building. It was mainly men and just a couple of females. 'Shit,' he said, wincing as two chairs freewheeling at high speed went for the ball and collided. Both men were thrown from their chairs, but no one rushed in to help them. The ball was picked up by one of the women, and the fallen men climbed quickly back into their chairs and carried on. Steve was impressed, more than that he was astonished. He watched the game play out as thoughts and emotions chased through his brain. A tiny dart of hope lifted his spirits. Was it possible to engage in and enjoy a sport despite his disability? By the end of the match, he had extinguished the hope and was feeling angry and manipulated.

The players all wheeled themselves out of the gym. It was still twenty minutes before the taxi was due, but Steve was spent. Without a word to Sharon, he headed for the lift. He waited impatiently for the platform to come up and then saw as it did that the young woman was inside. He moved aside to let her out and ignored the smile she gave him. He went in and pressed the buzzer to go down. Outside, he sat in the cold and waited to go home.

VICTORIA PASSED SONIA A TISSUE. They both dabbed their eyes.

'He's not being fair to her,' Sonia sniffed, before blowing her nose. 'All little girls have to grow up sometime, even Baby…'

'I know, but she was such a daddy's girl. It's hard for her father to see it. He feels let down and betrayed.' Victoria finished her wine and reached for the bottle. It was empty.

Sonia held her glass out for a refill without taking her eyes off the screen. 'Well, what girl could resist Johnny?' She deepened her voice. 'No one puts Baby in the corner.'

Victoria smiled. 'I've got another one in the fridge.' She held the empty bottle up and pressed the remote to pause the film.

She unscrewed the bottle and left it on the side while she ran up to the bathroom. Her mascara was smudged from the tears, so she dabbed at them with a damp tissue, which made it worse. Leaving the downstairs cloakroom, she ran up to the bedroom and got a makeup remover pad to do the job properly. Knowing that the film had more emotional bits to come, she didn't bother to reapply it. She hurried back downstairs and grabbed the bottle of wine from the worktop and then went into the lounge. She topped up both their glasses and popped a square of chocolate into her mouth.

Sonia was in the recliner chair with her feet up fiddling with her phone. 'Honestly, some of the stuff that goes on Facebook.'

'I'm not on there. Can't be doing with it all,' Victoria said.

'You get some funny stuff and it's good for keeping in touch, especially with mates from schooldays.'

Victoria shuddered. 'I couldn't think of anything worse.'

'Really? You didn't like school? I would have thought you'd be one of the popular girls.'

Victoria shook her head. She didn't want to think about those days. Her teenage years had been traumatic, and she was glad to leave them behind. She certainly had no intention of looking back or trying to rekindle old relationships. She pressed play on the film, clutching her tissue, ready for the next batch of tears.

Sonia was still holding her phone and was watching something intently. The colour drained from her face. 'Oh my god…'

Victoria paused the film again and looked at her neighbour. 'What?'

Sonia kicked the foot riser down and stood up. She walked slowly towards Victoria. 'I need to show you this.'

Victoria took the phone, Sonia leaned across her and pressed play. It was a video clip. It started with a lad with his back to the camera, removing his shirt and undoing his jeans. Victoria frowned. 'Really? We have to watch homemade porn now?'

'Keep going,' Sonia said something in her voice that made the hairs on the back of Victoria's neck stand to frightened attention.

The lad removed his jeans and knelt down on the floor beside a half-naked young woman with pale skin and a tiny waist. Victoria fidgeted; uncomfortable watching what should have been a private intimacy. The lad lay down, giving the camera full view of what was happening. His back was still to the camera, but the woman's face was now in view. Victoria gasped and shook her head. 'No!' it wasn't a young woman, it was a girl, her girl, her Gemma. The lad lent down to kiss her and Victoria dropped the phone in horrified disgust.

'I'm sorry,' Sonia said, kneeling down beside her. 'I thought you should know.'

Victoria was angry. She was hurt, and she was upset and, above all, she was terrified for her little girl. 'I'll call the police.' She said, standing up and reaching for the house phone.

'Shouldn't you talk to Gemma first?' Sonia cautioned.

'She might have been raped. When was it taken?'

'It looked like she consented,' Sonia said gently, 'and I think you'll find it was filmed here...'

'Here?'

'Yes, it looks like an empty new building to me.'

'The key,' Victoria whispered as understanding washed over her. 'I'm such an idiot.'

'No, Vic, you're a parent. Your baby girl is all grown up and you, like hundreds of mothers before you, didn't realise.'

Victoria began to cry, 'I should have...'

'Here.' Sonia passed her a tissue and a glass of wine.

Victoria blew her nose and drank the wine down in one long gulp. 'Hand me the phone.'

Sonia hesitated. 'I really think you should wait until you've talked to Gemma. I'm not sure the police will do anything.'

'She's fifteen, underage.'

'Yes, I know, but...'

'No. No buts. He's taken advantage. Look at him, he must be over sixteen.'

Sonia nodded her head. 'Probably,' she agreed. 'But not much older, maybe seventeen or eighteen.'

'Old enough to know better.'

'Young enough to still be ruled by hormones.' Sonia countered.

'Why are you defending him?' Victoria asked angrily.

'I'm not defending him, especially not for filming it. I'm just trying to put a bit of perspective on the situation. You are an emotional mum defending your daughter, I get that. But I'm pretty sure she was up for it, and the simple fact is that teenagers have sex. If you get the police involved, you turn it into a big, big deal. If it goes to court, Gemma will have to give evidence and relive it again and again. He will go on the sex offenders register and that will haunt him and mark him for the rest of his life.'

Victoria stood up. She couldn't listen to any more; all she knew was that he had to pay. She grabbed the phone and started to press in the numbers.

The front door opened, and her daughter came into the lounge. 'Hi mum.' She called happily. 'Oh, hello Mrs Casey.'

'Call me Sonia.'

Gemma looked from one to the other, her smile dropped. 'What's up?' she said warily.

Victoria looked at her daughter and ended the call. Sonia was right. She needed to hear what Gemma had to say first. Did she know about the filming? Surely she must do. If Sonia found it, then it was pretty certain that a social media savvy teenager would have.

'I might leave you to it,' Sonia said, looking from one to the other. 'You've got stuff to talk about.'

'What stuff?' Gemma said warily.

'I'll pick my films up tomorrow; call me if you need to.' Sonia bent down to pick up her phone from the floor where Victoria had dropped it. Gemma glanced at it, and a flash of panic crossed her pretty face. Her cheeks flushed and her eyes lowered.

Victoria barely nodded in her friend's direction; her eyes were focused on her daughter. She felt betrayed, which was, she knew, unreasonable. She also felt guilty for failing to see the evidence underneath her nose. She had been so focused on the move and so busy being busy that her baby had become a woman without her having a clue. Yet all the signs had been there. The stolen key, the video evidence, the tears and tantrums and sulking in her room. Of course, it was a relationship and one that had clearly gone wrong. She simply hadn't been paying proper attention.

'You've seen it.' Gemma whispered, barely able to speak for the tears that were choking her.

'Yes.'

'I'm so sorry mummy.'

Victoria crossed the space that separated them and pulled her daughter into her arms. Gemma hugged her tight and sobbed.

EPISODE THIRTEEN
JASMINE CLOSE - SERIES ONE

Mary was up early. She'd set her alarm for seven thirty and had dragged her aching limbs out of bed as soon as it went off. Leaning heavily on her stick, she went into the lounge and looked out of the front window. It was still there. Her grandson's bike, exactly where he parked it yesterday at teatime, when he came to see her. Only she didn't see him, at least not in person. That tart from the flat behind her got her claws into him and dragged him into her apartment. Well, maybe not dragged, but definitely lured. So it seemed he had spent the night with her and not bothered with his old nan at all.

It was a ridiculous time to be up unless you had somewhere to be, which she most definitely did not. So she went back into her bedroom and crawled gratefully under the covers. She closed her eyes and tried not to feel let down. He was young and single, and she knew she should be glad for any time that he could spare her. And she was, but she couldn't help feeling resentful towards the floosy that had enticed him into her bed. He had been on his way to see her and parked his bike outside her flat and then that hussy had stolen him away.

Mary must have dropped back off to sleep because when she

opened her eyes again it was gone nine o'clock and Roy was sitting on her bed meowing loudly. 'What's the matter with you, boy? I suppose you're hungry?' She fussed around his ears, and the meowing changed to purring. Smiling at the cat, she realised she was grateful for his warmth and his company. Her eyes were damp, and now she was crying. She wiped the tears away with the back of her hand. 'Silly old cow,' she said impatiently. 'Getting all soppy over a daft moggy.'

Roy jumped down, and she pushed the duvet off. She didn't really want to get up, but she knew that once you gave in and stayed in bed in the morning, then the slide to oblivion was fast. Her old neighbour Ted had fallen into that trap. One morning he couldn't be bothered to get up and then, before he knew it, he literally couldn't get up. 'Use it or lose it, Pet,' her husband Jack used to say, although that was his idea of foreplay. She smiled as she thought of him, lord how she missed him.

She put her slippers and dressing gown on and walked into the kitchen to feed Roy, who was getting very impatient and rubbing round her legs so insistently she was sure he would trip her up.

Mary opened a food pouch and squeezed it into a bowl. The cat jumped up onto the worktop and tucked in hungrily before she could put it on the floor. The doorbell rang, making her jump. She walked back into the lounge and opened the door. Jack was on the doorstep holding a carrier bag and grinning widely.

'Someone's happy this morning,' she said, delighted to see him but unable to stop the bitter tone in her voice.

'Breakfast?' he said, holding the bag up and either oblivious to or choosing to ignore her sarcasm. 'You're late up today, nan. How come you're not dressed? You okay?'

'Keep feeding me greasy breakfasts and I'll think you're trying to finish me off.'

He stopped midway to the kitchen, and she kicked herself for her sharp tongue. His smile was gone, and he looked shocked and upset.

'Nan, I wouldn't. I mean, you can't think that.'

'Of course not, don't mind me dear,' she gave him a hug. 'Your granddad used to say my caustic tongue could melt metal. I'm sorry; I don't mean a word of it.'

'I could do you scrambled eggs on toast, no frying involved in that.'

'Don't you dare? I want the full works, including a drop of the good stuff in my tea.'

He smiled. 'You sure?'

'Hell yes.'

She led him into the kitchen. He put the bag on the worktop and lifted Roy and his food bowl onto the floor. Then he put the kettle on and delved into the pot drawer for the frying pan.

'No work today?'

He shook his head.

'Day off or starting later?'

Jack turned his head to look at her. 'No job to go to nan.'

'What happened?'

'Turns out that big meeting was code for – we're closing down the business – all but a handful of staff have been made redundant, and those that get to stay will have to relocate to a site up north.'

'I'm sorry Jack.'

He shrugged and put the bacon rashers in the pan.

'Do you get any redundancy pay?'

'Peanuts really. I wasn't there long enough to get a worthwhile amount.'

'I was only joking about what I said before.'

'I know.'

'But I've got some money, Jack, if you need any help.'

He walked over to where she was sitting and gave her a hug. 'You are the best nan in the world, but I'll be okay, thanks.'

'Of course you will,' she said, deciding that she wouldn't say a word to him about how much she disapproved of the flirting floosy he obviously had enough to worry about.

. . .

Belle walked back to the apartment. The woman from the Show Home waved at her as she walked past and one builder called out 'good morning,' but she wasn't in the mood for being sociable. She let herself in through the outer door and went to her mailbox and opened it up and pulled out the small pile of letters. She looked through them quickly. There was only one that she was interested in. She looked at it in horror. It was addressed to her son, care of her husband at his London address. It hadn't been opened, and the address was crossed out and in big red letters were the words – RETURN TO SENDER.

Belle hurried up to her flat, let herself in, and closed the door. He told her she couldn't have any contact with Kyle, but until that moment, she hadn't really believed him. She knew that even if he was not in the country, he would have known about the letter and it would have been returned on his instructions.

She walked into her son's bedroom and looked around her. She had unpacked all the boxes and put the flat back to normal. She wanted it to be a home for Tamsin, and she wanted her daughter to feel safe and be happy. But without Kyle, they were incomplete, and they both knew it.

Belle picked up her mobile phone and sent a text message, then she pressed a speed dial number. 'Hello mum,' she said into the phone, 'I'm going to see Shaz again. I've asked her to meet me in the pub at lunchtime.'

'I'll pick you up in an hour.' Her mother said.

'No, it's okay mum, I'll get a train. But can you pick Tamsin up from school for me and have her until I get home, please? I'll call into the school and tell the secretary in person.'

Since the children had been taken from the school, security had been tightened, especially where Tamsin was concerned. It had been agreed that no one would take her from the premises without prior face-to-face permission given by Belle.

She said goodbye to her mother and got herself ready to go. She would have to get a train into Euston and then head south out of London, but she wasn't sure how. She could find out easy enough at the station and if all else failed, she would pay for the cost of a taxi. She would willingly pay any price if it got her closer to her son.

VICTORIA TRIED to concentrate on her paperwork in front of her. She had buyers coming in soon and she needed to have it all ready to go through with them. Her mind was everywhere other than paying attention to her computer monitor where it should be.

The shock of last night hadn't diminished with sleep. She felt sick every time she thought about it. Despite Gemma hugging her and crying it out, they hadn't talked, not really, not properly. Gemma had made her promise not to report the lad to the police. She hadn't wanted to make that promise, but her daughter had become near hysterical at the idea. So they made a deal. She wouldn't call the police yet. At least not until they'd sat down, and Gemma explained to her how she was plastered all over the internet having sex. It had been late and her daughter was exhausted after the emotional outpouring, so they agreed that the talk could wait until after school the following day.

Sat at her desk trying and failing to work, Victoria realised that decision like so many others she had made recently was a bad one. In her defence, she had it in her mind that delaying it would allow her to talk it through with Dave first, and that perhaps they could work this one out together. But Dave was not easily available lately. Not for late night talks, nor dinner or even sex. He didn't get home until gone midnight and despite her putting on the light and trying to talk; he was snoring the minute his head hit the pillow. Then that morning, he was up and out of the house while she was in the shower. Clearly, something was wrong. So now she had a daughter to deal with and a husband who was avoiding her as if she were the grim reaper chasing after him.

She closed her eyes and thought about what she'd witnessed with the brothel lady. It didn't add up. She knew it at the time, but had no idea why. Now she was wondering and worrying again and she couldn't stand it a moment longer. She left her computer on but remembered to lock the office door. She grabbed her jacket and hurried up the Close.

'Alright Vic?' Barry called out.

She waved but didn't stop. She saw that the sports car was parked alongside Jack's bike and wondered if they were an item. Did prostitutes have boyfriends? She had no idea how such things worked. All she knew was that the woman was in and she needed to talk to her.

She pressed the buzzer and after a few seconds a sleepy sounding voice answered 'yeah' down the intercom.

'Let me in,' she demanded. 'I'm Gemma's mum.'

The buzzer sounded, and she pushed open the door and hurried in. Upstairs, she could hear Natasha's baby crying and felt guilty because she hadn't checked up on her for a few days.

The door to Flat two was open and held on the latch. She walked straight in. Like the flats at the front, this one was an open plan. She went straight into a large bright lounge separated from the kitchen by a breakfast bar with tall red stools. Sat at one of them was a young woman with long dark curls and wearing oversize pyjamas tucking hungrily into a bowl of cereal.

'Hey, come in. Is Gemma alright? How did her date last night go?'

Victoria stared at the woman in surprise.

The young woman looked up as if aware of the scrutiny and laughed. She tugged at the pyjama top. 'Annabel insists we cover up. This is her idea of a joke.'

Victoria had absolutely no interest in the pyjamas. 'And is Annabel here?' she asked icily.

This time the woman picked up on her tone and her stance; she slid off the stool and hurried past Victoria and into one of the bedrooms. 'Gem's mum is here to see you...'

Annabel walked into the lounge, a large fluffy dressing gown wrapped around her. Her face was bare of makeup and her hair was wet and dripping onto her shoulders. Clearly, she'd not long stepped out of the shower. 'You want me?'

'I want to know what's going on with my daughter.' Victoria demanded. 'And don't give me that crap about the lost phone.' She glanced at Tammy who was hovering in the doorway from the bedroom. 'I know there's more to it than that.'

'Well, if you know, then why are you asking?' Annabel replied.

Victoria didn't know whether to scream or cry. 'Because I don't know what part you played in it.'

Annabel's eyes narrowed, her voice lowered, she was clearly getting angry. 'What exactly are you suggesting?'

Tammy moved into the room and stared at Victoria as though she were some alien species. 'What's she saying, Annabel?'

Victoria wasn't even sure what she thought and she couldn't bring herself to articulate her fears. 'She's only fifteen…' she whispered.

'She's seen it,' Tammy said.

'What part did you play in it? I saw her with you; no way would she hug you like that for finding her phone.'

'Talk to Gemma,' Annabel said.

'I'm talking to you and unless you give me answers, I'm calling the police. She's underage.'

'And very upset and feeling very foolish.' Annabel sighed and shook her head. 'She needs to move on. You do realise that if you get the Plod involved, it will drag on for months, maybe even years.'

'You're saying that to save your own skin?' Victoria cringed. She sounded like bad dialogue in a gangster movie.

'Enough with the veiled accusations.' Annabel snapped. 'None of this has anything to do with me. If you talked to your daughter more and were less bloody judgemental, then I would be blissfully ignorant of the whole situation.'

Victoria was shocked and hurt. 'Gemma can tell me anything.'

'Oh yeah? Well, why was she halfway to London then?' Tammy stopped talking when Annabel scowled at her.

'London?'

'Halfway is an exaggeration,' Annabel said. 'But she was on her way to the station.'

'When?'

'Two nights ago. I saw her in the dark heading for the underpass; she looked a bit sus, so I talked to her.'

'You saying she was running away? She might not have been.' Victoria was searching for a straw to clutch onto.

'She had a packed bag and a sleeping bag.'

How had she been so blind?

'She wouldn't go home, so I brought her back here, and she told us what had happened. Her biggest fear, aside from you finding out, was how to deal with school.'

'Yeah, the social media bullies were already all over it.' Tammy added.

'But one thing we do know about is being judged and called names and how to rise above it,' Annabel said, giving her a look that made her feel tiny and mean.

'I'm sorry, I jumped to conclusions.'

'Yes, you did. She's a sweet girl. Talk to her.'

Victoria opened the door.

'Don't make her feel any worse than she already does,' Annabel said, 'Let her learn from this and move on.'

Victoria walked back to work with the words ringing in her ears.

STEVE BENT DOWN and picked up the post. The only letter that interested him was the one from the bank. He opened it up and pulled out a brand new debit card sent to replace the one he lost when his wallet was stolen during the break in. ''Bout bloody time,' he muttered to himself, tossing the card along with the envelopes onto the coffee table. Then he put his brakes on and lit up a joint from his lovely new stash. 'Thank you Lou,' he said aloud as he closed his eyes and inhaled deeply. He was tired, definitely irritable, and, if he was honest with himself, a bit confused. He knew why Sharon had taken him to Stantonbury last night. She wasn't exactly subtle. What he didn't know was how he felt about it all, or even what she expected him to do next. Did she think that watching a few spastics throwing themselves on the floor would make him happy?

Steve began to relax, and that feeling of deep lethargy seeped easily and gently throughout his body. Then the doorbell rang and dragged him straight back to his shitty reality. 'Piss off,' he shouted.

'Yeah, I was told you'd say that.' A female voice shouted back. 'Now open the sodding door.'

He hesitated, his brain still slow from the drug induced haze. It wasn't Jenny or Sharon or his Mrs Mop. Curiosity got the better of him. He stubbed his joint out and opened the door. The young woman from the leisure centre wheeled into his flat.

'About bloody time, it's cold out there, you know.'

'Come in, why don't you?' He said sarcastically, wondering what the hell she was doing there, and how did she know where he lived.

'I was told you were a slob,' she said, looking round in distaste, 'and what is that smell...' she moved closer to him, wrinkling her nose and looking at him accusingly.

He held the joint out. 'Get over it,' he snapped.

'I wasn't referring to the weed. It's you that smells. Did you sleep in those clothes last night? Seriously, it's tossers like you who give disabled people a bad rep.'

Steve sniffed his shoulder and conceded she might have a point, but what did it have to do with her, anyway? 'Who the fuck are you?'

She smiled, and it lit up her face, changing her from plain to stunning. 'I am your worst nightmare!'

'I can see that...'

She held her hand out. 'Melanie Sykes.'

He shook it warily. 'Steve Lance.'

'Yeah, I know who you are.'

'You have the advantage, then.'

'Just how I like it. You need to shower and change, while I make us some breakfast. Well brunch really...'

'Why?' he had no idea what was happening or why she thought she could order him around in his own house.

'Because I'm hungry.'

'No,' he snapped. 'Why the...'

'Fuck, am I in your house?' she finished his sentence for him. 'Get cleaned up and we'll talk. I can't think straight on an empty stomach.'

Steve looked at her. She was making herself very at home in his kitchen. She knew her way around a fridge, that was for sure. His own stomach made a noise in anticipation of the promised food. Maybe he should have the shower. She was right. He did stink, and then she could tell him what was going on before he booted her out.

BELLE GOT herself a drink from the bar and sat down to wait. The journey hadn't been too bad at all, two trains and the underground. She knew it was probably time she learnt to drive, especially if they were going to settle in Milton Keynes. The new city was designed for cars with its dual carriageways and network of grid roads. Besides, as the children got older, they would need lifts to friends and activities and picking up after nights out. She always thought that Tamsin and Kyle would be safer as teenagers because, as twins, they would have each other. She clung to that thought, unable to visualise a future that didn't have Kyle standing beside his sister.

The door opened and Shaz hurried in. 'I'm so sorry,' she said immediately.

'It wasn't your fault,' Belle replied. 'it was all a setup, anyway; Mo knew I would come after them and he let us take Tamsin.'

Shaz looked shocked and annoyed. 'I should have known it was too easy, really. Mira said that she hadn't seen Kyle since she took him back to his home. She thinks he has been sent to our cousins in Islamabad, but nothing is certain. Mo won't talk to me. I'm sorry, I really am, but there is nothing more that I can do.'

Belle wasn't really hearing anything that she hadn't expected. As far as her husband was concerned, the deal was done. He wouldn't let her get close to their son again. But she couldn't give up on Kyle. She had to keep trying. She pulled out the returned letter and pushed it across the table to Shaz. 'Can you send it to Mira for me? Put it inside another envelope and ask her to pass it on if she ever gets the chance to do so.'

'I'll send it...' the shrug of her shoulders showed what little chance she thought it had of ever reaching its destination.

'I have to try. I left him at the airport. I'm his mother and I left him.'

'Mira told me how awful it was. You had to do it for Tamsin.'

'I know. I need to tell Kyle. Make him understand.' She pointed to the letter. 'It's all in there.'

Shaz nodded and stood up to go; she hesitated and looked seriously at Belle. 'There is one thing that I've heard. Kyle has changed his name. Apparently, he is Mohammed now.'

Belle closed her eyes; she should have seen it coming. 'I chose the name,' she said, remembering the moments after birth, back in the days when they were still blessed with love. 'We agreed to name one each. Mo would choose for the eldest, so he called her Tamsin, and then I named our son Kyle.'

Shaz leant across the table and took her hand. 'He'll always be your son, Kyle. Living in Pakistan, he will fit in better if he's called Mohammed.'

Belle thought of her son and hoped that wherever he was and whatever name he was using, someone loved him and that he was happy.

'Your bacon was out of date and your sausages are frozen. You have no cooking oil and mould growing on your cheese.'

Steve wheeled into the kitchen. Whatever she had managed to cook, it smelt good. 'Anything else wrong?'

'Yes. You're out of milk.'

He could tell by the mess that she had been busy doing something, and his stomach growled in eager anticipation. 'What a mess. You had the cheek to call me a slob.'

'You are a slob and this,' she wave her hand around the kitchen. 'Will all be cleared up.'

She placed a plate on her lap and wheeled across to the lowered breakfast bar. She put it on a mat that he had forgotten he even had and then she went back for the next one.

'You waiting for an invitation?' she said, squirting tomato sauce all over her food.

'What is it?'

'Omelette a la Mel,' she laughed, 'my very own concoction. Eggs with everything thrown in and potato slices fried in butter.'

Steve hadn't realised how hungry he was and decided that given the apparent state of his fridge, it was best not to ask for any more details about what he was eating. So he just got on and enjoyed it. He picked up a mug and looked at the dark hot liquid.

'Black coffee,' she said, 'what can you expect if you don't go shopping?'

He thought about pointing out that shopping wasn't so easy, but then realised that he couldn't use the - can't do- card with her. 'Bit hard to go shopping without any money.'

'Don't give me that. You get benefits and probably accident compensation?'

'Benefits, yes, still waiting on the other, in the hands of solicitors and insurance companies. But what I meant was I had a break in. Some shit stole my wallet...' and just about everything else, he silently added. 'Sharon, my social worker, got me an emergency cash pay-out, but I've only just received my new card.' He glanced at the post on the coffee table.

Melanie looked at him. She had piercing blue eyes that were remarkably clear and seemed to see straight through him. Something clicked inside him. 'You're related aren't you? Of course you are. Same eyes, same bossy, opinionated attitude.'

She grinned. 'Yep, Sharon is my aunt.'

'That's how you know so much about me. I thought it was all meant to be confidential.'

'It is she only broke the rules because she believed you were in trouble and that I might be able to help.'

'Bloody presumptuous of her.'

'Yep, that's her and you should be warned, I'm even worse.'

'Yeah, I can see that. Well, come on then, what big plan have the pair of you hatched to save me from myself?'

Melanie looked him up and down. 'Well, now that I'm not ashamed to be seen in public with you I suggest we go shopping...' she stopped when she saw his expression. 'Or we could scrap the supermarket idea and do an online order?'

'Do what you like,' he said. 'I'm not doing a Tesco's run.' He'd seen wheelchairs in there, back in his other life when he could walk and run, and life was still fun and full of possibilities. He used to be annoyed by the old bats in scooters getting in his way and the worst offenders were the wheelchairs that had a shopping trolley attached to the front. No way was he going to be that saddo person.

'Online it is then.'

She looked intently at him and he squirmed uncomfortably, knowing what it must be like for a germ under a microscope. He had the uncomfortable feeling that's how she viewed him, like a science experiment. Something slightly unpleasant that needed to be dissected and studied. He suddenly felt tired, worn out or worn down.

'Come on,' he said. 'Let's get outta here.' He left the kitchen and opened the front door.

'Wait,' she called after him. 'What about the washing up?'

'Sod the washing up.'

She followed him out. 'Don't you need a jacket?'

He probably did, but the door was closing and she already thought him the biggest prat in the world. No way was he going back in. He realised she had unlocked a car, and was leaning in across the seat to get something.

'Yours?'

'No, I just wanted to steal this jacket from it.' She pulled a dark blue fleece out and closed the door. 'Course it's mine.'

'You drive?'

'That's the general idea. It has hand controls, foot pedals aren't a lot of good for the likes of us.' She wriggled into her jacket with a dexterity that he had yet to master and then she set off down the Close. 'Come on then, where are we going?'

. . .

VICTORIA JUMPED every time the office door opened. Each time she dreaded it being Brett, and then she was disappointed when it wasn't. Realistically the chance of him coming back was a big fat zero. She had sent him away, turned down his dinner invitation and thrown his phone number away. What more was there to say or do?

Besides, she had much bigger issues to deal with, like talking to her daughter and finding out what was wrong with her husband. They had always been fairly independent, never one of those clingy couples who do everything together. Lately, though they could hardly be termed a couple, she saw more of her dentist than she did her husband, and she had good teeth.

She sent Dave a text message saying they needed to talk and could he please try to get home early tonight. But she had heard nothing from him.

Bang on the dot at five p.m. Victoria shut down her computer and finished work for the day. She wasn't looking forward to the talk with her daughter, but she did want to deal with it as quickly as possible. Annabel's accusation that she was judgemental and that Gemma couldn't talk to her had really stung.

She walked quickly up the Close, a taxi drove past her and as she reached her house, she saw Belle climb out of it and hurry into the apartment block. Poor cow, she thought, at least her daughter was still under the same roof. She couldn't imagine the horrors that Belle must face every time she looked into her son's empty bedroom.

'Gemma?' she called as she entered her house. She got no response, but her daughter's school bag was dumped in the hall, so she knew she was home from school.

Victoria went into the kitchen and boiled the kettle. She got two mugs out and made herself a tea and did a hot chocolate for her daughter. Two minutes later, she was knocking on the door.

'Yeah.'

'Yes,' she corrected, pushing the door open with her foot. 'I made you a drink.' She put both mugs on the bedside table and then sat down on the bed. She looked around the room. 'You haven't unpacked yet.'

'Been busy.'
'Will you put your posters back up?'
'Nah, probably not.'

So much for small talk. She looked at her daughter, who was busy texting and not paying any attention to her at all. It had all been so easy when Gemma had been little. How did she bridge the gap that now stretched between them?

She reached out and took the phone.

'Hey!'
'We need to talk.'
'So talk. I'm a female. I can multitask.'

Victoria took a deep breath and silently counted to ten. She realised Gemma didn't want to have the conversation and was therefore pushing her away and being difficult. She decided to just launch straight in. 'Did he force you?'

'Mum, no.'
'How old is he?'
'Sixteen.'
'Gemma?'
'Oh okay, he's eighteen.'

'I suppose that was the attraction for you? Older lad showing an interest, no doubt he has a car and a job?'

Gemma nodded and lowered her eyes, 'I'm sorry mum, he was different.'

'Yeah, I know.'
'Yes,' Gemma corrected her.

They both smiled - small progress. 'Yes,' she said. 'I get it; boys your age can be immature.'

'Dead right.'

'And he was cocky and confident and swept you off your feet. You thought you loved him and believed that he felt the same about you.'

'Something like that.' Gemma nodded looking at her strangely. 'How do you know?'

Victoria smiled. 'Oh love we've all been there.'

'Really? You?'

'Oh yes. Only we didn't have the mobile phones, thank god. Did he use a condom?'

Gemma squirmed with embarrassment. 'Mum, of course we did, I'm not that stupid.' She sipped her hot chocolate, her eyes narrowed. 'Surely you did. I mean, I know you're old, but I reckon Durex is older.'

Victoria hesitated. Was sharing stories a good thing or a bad thing? She wished teenagers came with a clear set of instructions.

'Please mum, tell me, who was he? Not dad I assume?'

'No. This was before I met your father. I was sixteen and Alan…'

'Alan? Really?'

'Yes, what's wrong with Alan?'

'Well, nothing wrong exactly, it just isn't the name of a romance hero.'

'What like Mr Darcy?'

'Better, although I was expecting a bad boy name.'

'Alan,' she said, continuing, 'was eighteen and he had a motorbike. He had a reputation for trouble, nothing serious, but he was known by the local constabulary. I never knew the details. I didn't really care to be honest, it just added to the excitement of it all.' She paused.

'Don't stop, please mum.'

'You don't want to hear this.'

'I do. It makes me feel better, less foolish, to know that you made mistakes as well.'

'Oh sweetheart, everyone makes mistakes.' She drank her coffee; still not sure that telling Gemma about her teenage trauma was the answer. But for the first time in months, they were communicating with more than one syllable grunts. So she put the empty mug down and carried on. 'I was lonely and, I suppose, unhappy. My dad got a new job, and we had to move up north. Birmingham was very different from Surrey, and I started the new school halfway through year eleven.'

'Ouch,' Gemma said sympathetically. 'That couldn't have been easy.'

'I wasn't bullied, but I wasn't welcomed in either. I was on the edge of everything at school and at home mum and dad were fighting all the time. I guess my mother was finding it as hard as I was being uprooted and leaving all her friends.' She paused, surprised at the revelation. She'd never realised that before and her mother had certainly never spoken to her about it, not even later when she was an adult.

'I always thought that you would be one of the popular girls and that life had never been difficult or complicated for you.'

Victoria was surprised. She never felt as though she gave the impression that life had been a breeze, yet Sonia had said almost the same thing. 'We all survive and move on. That's what growing up is all about.'

'So Alan the biker came along and saved you from your teenage misery, a knight on a shining motor bike.'

'Yes, that he did. Or at least for a while, until he dumped me and moved on to the next girl.' Victoria smiled and stood up. 'So now you know, I'm just as daft as you were, but without the filming.'

'Thanks mum. I'm sorry and I promise I won't do anything so stupid again.'

'That's a promise I doubt you'll be able to keep. Talk to me though Gemma, I might be your mother, but I was a teenager a long time ago and some things never change - hormones are charged, girls want a boyfriend and boys want sex.' She handed her daughter the phone back, picked up the mugs, and walked to the door. She paused when Gemma called after her.

'Did you ever see him again? I mean, after he ended it? '

'No,' she lied and walked out of the door. Some secrets were best left in the closet. Such as his reaction when she told him she was pregnant and the abortion her parents forced her into having. No one, not even Dave, knew about that.

She walked into the kitchen and put the mugs in the dishwasher. She checked her phone, still no word from her husband. Despite being annoyed with him, she felt like a weight had lifted. Gemma wasn't talking to her like she was the enemy anymore. That had to be a good thing.

STEVE FOLLOWED her back to his flat. He was struggling to keep up, but no way was he going to let her know that. Her agility and confidence in the chair amazed him. He wasn't going to tell her that either. If he was in the market for hope, then she was certainly a great salesperson. She almost had him believing that there was life after lower body death.

'You live in a great spot,' she said, waiting outside his door for him to catch up. 'You are lucky having the canal so close. I might investigate; see if any of these apartments are still available and if I could get an exchange. Is it a housing association?'

Too out of breath to speak, he nodded his head.

She laughed at him. 'Think you'd better come training with me; look at the state of you.'

'You coming in?'

'No, I've gotta get back. My moggy will be in for her tea.'

'You've got a cat?'

'And a part-time job and friends and a social life. I even have dreams and ambitions.'

Steve opened the door; he didn't want to hear it.

'You are grieving Steve, we've all been there.' She said softly, flicking her windswept hair back from her face. 'It's part of the process. You cry for what you've lost and then you look at what you still have and strive for what you still want.'

'You're a bleeding philosopher like your aunt.'

'Life in a wheelchair is still a life, Steve. It might not be the one you wanted or thought you would live, but if you open your mind to the possibilities, you can learn to dream again.'

'What do you know of my dreams?' he snapped.

'Not much, but I know about mine. I want to travel the world and write about it as I go. One day I hope to get married and have children.' She paused to look at him. 'Why are you shaking your head, Steve? Anything is possible. You just have to alter your perception.'

'Crap.'

'No. you can have almost anything you want. It's there for the taking.' She unlocked her car, and he watched as she transferred herself into the driver's seat. She dismantled the chair beside her and lifted each part across her body, and put it on the passenger seat beside her.

He went in and closed the door. It was all nonsense. Okay, so she could drive a car, big deal. The rest was just wishes, and they only came true in Disney films. He went indoors and wheeled into the bedroom to get his stash and roll himself a joint. The box he kept it in was empty. He looked all round. Had he taken the package out and put it somewhere else? He thought back, retraced his wheeled steps; he definitely put it back in the box and left it on the bed.

Just to be doubly sure, he searched the flat. The kitchen was still in chaos after her cooking, but his weed wasn't there. He checked the bathroom, then the bedroom again, and then turned the lounge upside down. He knocked the letters off the coffee table and as he bent down to pick them up, he realised that his new debit card was gone. He looked and looked again, unable to believe what his eyes and his head were telling him.

Melanie Sykes was just a lying fucking tealeaf.

EPISODE FOURTEEN
JASMINE CLOSE - SERIES ONE

'I really needed to talk to you last night.' Victoria said to her husband.

He groaned into his Weetabix. 'Give me a break Vic, I'm having the week from hell.'

'I'm not exactly at Disneyland myself.'

'No? I thought moving to this place was meant to be your equivalent of a dream location.'

'Dave, you agreed to this house. I thought you wanted it too. I thought you were going to get a dog. I don't understand what's happening. You don't answer your phone or return my messages and you haven't been here for dinner once all week; you get home after bed time.'

'What am I ten?' he shouted, pushing the cereal away and getting angrily to his feet.

'Younger, I would say, given the tantrum you're throwing!' she retorted. 'You know very well what I mean.'

'Well, if I get to bed once you're already asleep, then I don't have to hear you whining and nagging for half the night.'

Dave stormed out of the kitchen and Victoria stood still, stunned into silence. She was well aware that she had many faults, but was she really a whiner and nagger? Until recently, they had always rubbed along fairly easily together, with very little friction. Rows had never been a big part of their relationship. She felt completely lost, with no idea what was happening or why. Surely it wasn't all about the new house? Even though it was what she wanted and no doubt she coerced him, Dave was nobody's pushover and if he was dead set against it, then they would still be in their small terraced house now.

She heard him leave, slamming the door like an angry teenager as he left. She made herself busy clearing up the breakfast dishes. Was Sonia and her insinuations right? Did he have another woman? A month ago, she would have sworn that he was not the cheating type, but maybe there was no such thing as a 'type' and everyone was capable of having an affair, given the right circumstances. She would have to call herself a liar if she tried to deny that Brett was not a temptation. So it was conceivable that Dave's passion had been ignited up by some pretty little flirt in his office.

Question was how to deal with it. Her parents finally gave up the fight and split when she was in her late teens. It had been a tough and traumatic time for them all and she made a decision then that she would do anything she could to ensure that her children never had to go through that same experience. Yet here she was now with her own marriage in crisis. They needed to talk and try to work it out, but how could they do that if he wouldn't cooperate?

STEVE STARED at the telephone in his hand. He felt like a shit, but worse than that he felt like a fool. Although he didn't want to admit it, yesterday had been fun. She was fun. And a small part of him had wanted to believe in the fantasy that she waved under his nose. He didn't understand why she stole from him. It didn't make any sense. Unless he had a sign engraved on his forehead – fleece me, fleece me!

All night long, he had tried to rationalise it by making excuses for her and searching for other possibilities. He failed on both counts and not only did he have to cancel his bank card again, which meant he was still cashless, but worse than that, he had no dope again. No way could he ask for more. The rules were clear, and he had agreed to them. Personal consumption only at agreed intervals. The last drop had been a special one-off exception because of the break-in. Lou would never believe him if he told her he had been robbed again. Hell, he hardly believed it himself.

He knew he had to ring Melanie. Confront her and maybe she would give it back?

She had scribbled her mobile down for him before she left, which was bizarre. Did she think he wouldn't notice the tiny fact that she had robbed him? Maybe she had some magpie compulsion, which she couldn't control. He pressed the numbers into the phone; her writing was strange, lots of long thin lines criss-crossing with elaborate embellishments that resembled a spider's web. Nothing about her made sense, not even her handwriting.

She answered on the third ring. He nearly hung up, but he needed to hear her excuse and, more than that, he needed his stash back.

'So when you said 'anything you want is there for the taking,' you meant it literally.'

'Steve?'

'Yep, otherwise known as a sucker.'

'What's going on? Are you drunk? Or stoned?'

'Huh. I wish.'

'I'm hanging up.'

He looked at the phone in surprise. She had actually hung up on him - he redialled.

'What?' she said, answering on the first ring.

'You know what?'

'Actually, I really, really don't. Either you tell me what's going on in that pea-sized brain of yours or I say goodbye.'

'I want it back,' he said.

'You want what back?'

'Seriously? You want to play games? If you return it to me, then I'll pretend it never happened. If you don't...'

She hung up again.

He re-dialled the number. '... if you don't, then I will report your aunt to social services for giving out my personal data. Data Protection is a big thing, you know.'

She hung up again.

MILES LOOKED up from his desk as, after a brief knock, his secretary, Shirley, came into his office. She put his coffee carefully down on the mat in the far corner away from his laptop and then she handed him a slice of sponge cake with yellow and pink icing. 'From Tessa, it's her birthday today, the big four zero, so she brought cake in for everyone.'

He wasn't even sure that he knew who Tessa was. She might be Johnston's secretary? The shy one with the enormous chest. He couldn't be sure, and he cared even less. The cake looked unappealing, but he took it anyway; it was always good practice to keep the secretaries on side. 'Say thanks and wish her a happy birthday for me.'

'I will. She's having a party this evening; we've all been invited.'

He looked up.

'Oh, you as well, Mr Fisher, except I told her that you always finish early on a Friday, so best not to expect you.'

Shirley really was very nearly the perfect secretary. He smiled and quietly congratulated himself on training her so well. He had a lot of work to get through before he could go home and since he had driven into work, he really needed to get on the road soon. Friday afternoons out of London were notoriously when the M25 lived up to the Tabloids claim, that it was England's biggest car park. 'Thanks Shirley,' he said. 'Best get on.'

He bit into the cake while scanning down his emails. It wasn't a very good cake. The sponge was dry, not enough jam and cream filling in the middle, and the icing was way too sweet. He put it down and pushed it away, and that's when the idea hit him.

. . .

VICTORIA LOOKED up as the door opened and Sonia walked in. She held the door open for a delivery man who was carrying a huge bouquet of flowers.

'Wow, nothing says guilty quite like a large bunch of mixed blooms.'

The delivery man handed them to Victoria and waited for her to sign, then he left with a cheeky wink at Sonia as he passed.

'He agrees with me,' Sonia said. 'You going to look at the message?'

She had a horrible feeling that her neighbour might be right. She pulled the card out from the inside of the cellophane and opened the envelope.

'Well?'

'Sorry.'

'That's it?'

She nodded and put the card down on the desk beside the flowers and tried to remember the times that her husband had ever bought her flowers. It wasn't difficult. A red rose on the first Valentine's Day that they were together and that was only because a man came round selling them in the restaurant where they were eating. All the men were buying and Dave would have looked cheap if he hadn't reached for his wallet. Next time was a bunch of anniversary carnations. They were staying at his parents' home while they waited for the mortgage to complete on their house and the card with the flowers was handwritten by his mum. The third and final time was the pretty posy of pink blooms that he handed her after Gemma was born. She still had a couple of the flowers pressed in their daughter's baby record book. It was the only time that he had turned to flowers without coercion – until today.

'So, do you know what he's sorry for?' Sonia said, helping herself to a coffee from the percolator set up for customers.

Victoria shook her head. 'Not really. We had a row this morning.'

Sonia pointed to the flowers. 'That big a row?'

'No.'

'Must be a woman, then.'

'He wouldn't, would he? I mean, I would know, there would be signs.'

'The signs couldn't be bolder if they were written in multi-coloured flashing neon lights. He stays out late, he doesn't answer your messages, he gets defensive and aggressive when you question him and he sends you appeasement flowers.'

Victoria sank down onto her chair and buried her face in her hands. 'What do I do?'

'I'd ask him straight out.'

'I might, if I ever get the chance to talk to him properly.'

'Well, he's sent you the flowers, so why don't you text him, thank him and say you'll do a special dinner tonight, just the two of you? You can send Gemma to the pictures.'

'She's got a sleepover at a friend's.'

'Even better. Get him home; let him get comfortable believing that the flowers have got him off the hook and then pounce with the question.'

'Surely he'll lie.'

'That's why you need to let him get comfortable first; men aren't so good at lying when you catch them off guard.'

'How do you know all this?' Victoria asked.

Sonia grinned. 'How is it you don't?'

She picked her phone up and sent him a message. 'I'll get the bus straight into town when I lock up. I'll buy some steak, that's his favourite.'

'I can give you a lift. Just bang on the door when you're ready and I'll run you down there. Paul is still on the early shift, so he'll be at home to look after the boys.'

'Thanks,' Victoria said, meaning it.

STEVE STARED INTO THE CANAL; he knew that in the murky depths, there were plenty of fish. He'd seen the size of some of them the fishermen had caught. He felt sorry for the fish and an irrational anger towards the men and lads who chose to sit for hours staring into the water. If he could stand and walk, he thought he would never sit still again.

He moved closer to the edge so he could lean forward in and look down. There were no fish visible, the water was too dark. He wondered if Jenny was on her balcony watching him. He resisted turning around to look, not that he would be able to see her, anyway. The sun was low and shining weakly from behind him. All he would get for trying was sore, watery eyes. He missed her.

'Thought I'd find you here,' Melanie said from behind him.

He swung his chair round in surprise. 'Have you got my gear?'

'Shit, you're like a parrot that only knows one sentence. What are you talking about?'

'You took my roll of weed.'

Her face screwed up, and a deep frown scrunched up her forehead. 'I never did. Why the hell would I?'

She looked shocked, and a little upset, and he began to doubt himself. 'What about my bank card? Or do you deny taking that as well?'

'Are you accusing me of stealing?'

'The bank card and the dope were there when you were in my house and gone when you left – so yeah, I'm accusing you.'

'You are an absolute shit, Steve.' She turned around and wheeled away at speed.

He wanted to believe her. He really did, but how could he? There was no other explanation. She was in his flat and no one else had access. He had resisted all attempts to give a key to cleaners, carers or any other support group that the social team suggested. He didn't want anyone to be able to let themselves in and out. It was his home, his turf, his territory and now it had been violated, again.

Steve wheeled after her but knew he couldn't catch her; she was much quicker than he was. He turned around and went back in the opposite direction. She was going the long way round, sticking to the redways. If he cut across the scrubland, he might just make it back before her. He wasn't sure why he wanted to. If she was denying taking it and he knew she did it, then they were at a stalemate.

He realised that his idea was not such a good one when his wheels started spinning in the mud. Last time he'd taken this route it had been dry and easy to negotiate round the potholes. There had been a lot of rain since then and the builders had been out with diggers churning up the ground, ready to start the new development. He was going nowhere fast. As soon as he managed to free himself from one deep sloshy groove, he was pitched straight into the next. He was getting splattered with mud, which meant his hands were getting slippery and he couldn't grip hard enough to push the wheels forward to free himself.

After what seemed like hours but was probably around thirty minutes, he was only halfway across the scrubland. He was tired and frustrated and furious with Melanie for running off so that he had to go after her and then even more angry that she didn't come back to look for him. He needed his mobile phone and a new surge of fury against the bastard that stole it gave him an enormous adrenaline burst sufficient to free him.

Trying to avoid the huge truck tyre tracks that were causing most of his problems, he made fast progress and, with less than twenty feet to go, the cat from next door leapt out from a wide shallow crevice with a small mouse in its mouth. He hadn't seen the hole and would have wheeled straight into it. 'Thanks,' he called after the cat, turning his wheels away to avoid the hazard. As he pulled to the left, his tyre lodged in yet another muddy groove and he lurched sideways, almost falling out of the chair. He pushed and pulled, and he rocked with all his might, but nothing would shift the chair.

He looked towards the block of flats. His eyes were scanning the windows and balconies for any sign of life. He didn't think that many of the back apartments were occupied yet, although obviously Flat number two was. He'd seen the report in the paper. He focused his visual attention on the ground-floor apartment. He couldn't see anyone but waved just in case. Then a woman moved closer to the French doors and, with relief, he saw her wave back. The relief was short-lived though as the curtains were closed across the doors and he was shut out.

'Shit, shit, shit,' he hissed to himself.

He could hear the sound from the building site; a radio playing, chatter, hammering, a cement mixer churning. If he shouted, his voice would be lost in the general mix of noise. 'Help!' he called out, just in case, knowing it was pointless.

His options were severely limited. He was getting cold and a huge black cloud was gathering over his head. If he was going to die, then he wanted it to be at a time and in a manner of his choosing and not from hyperthermia stuck in a sodding field. Deciding it was time for drastic action, he lowered himself out of the wheelchair and onto the wet, muddy ground. Lying on his back, he twisted around, gripped the wheelchair and heaved it free. The momentum pulled it from the crevice and it swung across his body to the other side of him. He managed to keep a slippery grip and, more amazingly, he managed to drag it alongside him. He struggled to put the brakes on; the skies opened and heavy rain battered down on him. Eventually, he was able to pull himself back into the chair and wheel himself home.

Melanie's car was gone, as he knew it would be. She hadn't bothered to look for him. She'd left him and driven away, no doubt back to her house to chill out with his dope and probably have a laugh with her aunt over what an idiot he was.

He wheeled inside, leaving a trail of mud on the carpet behind him, and picked up the phone and dialled the number for social services. He waited for it to answer and then, with a deep breath and a heavy dose of resentful anger, he spoke. 'I want to report a gross misuse of my personal data.'

It's bloody perfect,' Miles said later that evening to Brett.

'It's terrible,' Brett replied bluntly. 'She'll hate it.'

'What will I hate?' jenny asked suspiciously as she came in from the kitchen.

'I suggested we go out to dinner tonight,' Miles lied. 'I've been told about a new gastro pub that's just employed a new and highly sought after chef. Apparently, he specialises in rare meats.'

'What, undercooked?' Brett laughed.

Miles frowned, taking him seriously. 'No, like ostrich and buffalo.'

Jenny smiled. 'He's teasing you. I've already put the dinner on. Perhaps another night?'

He waited until she had left the room again before expanding on his real idea to his brother-in-law. 'Come on, it's exactly what she needs. Socialising without having to leave her home. Surely that's got to be good for her.'

Brett still didn't look convinced. 'Who would you get to come?'

'Friends, neighbours.'

'Well, from what I've seen and heard, she hasn't made many friends here and she doesn't stay in touch with any of the old ones either. It might be a party for the three of us.'

'Proves my point Brett, she needs this and I need you to help me organise it. Her birthday is on Sunday, so we'll have to get going.'

Brett shook his head. 'Seriously, Miles, this is not a good idea. Besides, you'll never get invites printed now and what about food?'

Miles grinned, pleased with his forward planning and ability to act fast. Feeling like a magician, he pulled a printed card from his pocket. 'I had my secretary Shirley run down to the print room. The rest are in my briefcase and I have an email copy to contact her old friends and work colleagues. As for the food, she found me a caterer that could deliver for Sunday and they can set up a bar and can supply the drinks as well.'

'Sorted then,' Brett said.

Miles didn't miss the tone of disapproval, or was it sarcasm? In Bretts' voice. Jenny was his wife, and he knew her better than anyone, and that included her brother. He wasn't even a real relative, just one because of marriage - a step brother. 'It will be great,' he said, determined to make it so.

'So, what do you want me to do?'

'Two things. I'll take care of email invites, but I need you to go around all the neighbours.' He hesitated as that doped up wheelchair man came into his head. 'Most of the neighbours.' He corrected himself. 'No need to invite the apartment people. Stick to the houses.'

Brett didn't look too impressed, and Miles wondered what Jenny had told him about the dope head. Well, whatever it was, he didn't care. He knew he was protecting his wife, even if she didn't see it that way herself. Meeting some of the other neighbours would help her get out and reconnect with the world.

'The second thing?' Brett asked.

'Take her out on Sunday.'

'Where?'

'Anywhere. Shopping? Lunch? Cinema? Dinner? Anything you like, just keep her out of the house for the afternoon.'

'She hates going out.'

Miles was getting sick of the negatives; he thought Americans were supposed to be a positive bunch. 'You'll find a way,' he said, making sure that Brett knew it wasn't a request. He wasn't at all sure that having her brother staying was helping her. Brett seemed to indulge her in the same way as her therapist did.

'Dinners nearly ready,' Jenny called from the kitchen.

Miles stood up. 'I'll go and get changed. I'll put the invites in your room, and I'll push them under your pillow just in case she goes in there.'

Brett shrugged his shoulders in a resigned type of way.

Satisfied that he would do as he was asked, Miles left the lounge, picked up his briefcase from the hall and headed up the stairs, whistling happily to himself.

ANNABEL LET herself into the flat. The usual mess and chaos greeted her, but she wasn't going to let it ruin her good mood. She could hear the shower running and knew that since Miranda was still at work in one of her city centre flats, it must be Tammy.

She made herself a coffee and sat down to wait.

'Oh hello, didn't hear you come in?' Tammy said, walking into the lounge with a towel wrapped round her.

'You didn't show up again today.'

Tammy tilted her head to one side and pouted. 'I'm sorry Annabel, and it's just that I hate that flat.'

'I know. But you've had clients here again.'

'Only two.'

Annabel raised her eyebrows.

'Okay four, just regulars, and look, I did close all the curtains.' Tammy sat down on the edge of the sofa beside her, wet tendrils of dark hair dripping onto the upholstery.

'I have a new place for you and Miranda. You can move in tomorrow.'

'Just the two of us?'

'Yes.'

Tammy threw herself at Annabel, hugging her tight. 'Thank you. What are you going to do with this one? It's a shame. I like it here.'

'Yes, I do too.' Annabel replied, thinking about an attractive biker who had crawled into her bed for the past two nights. 'I'm going to keep it for now. I'll set up the office from here, I think, and stay occasionally.'

Tammy grinned at her. 'Hmm, I wonder why. Nothing to do with a tall dark stranger, I suppose.'

Annabel had to admit to herself if not to Tammy that her decision had everything to do with Jack. Of course, she had no expectations beyond the immediate business of having some mutual adult fun. She knew herself well enough to know that she was bored quickly and easily. It had occurred to her that he might be useful beyond the bedroom since he was out of work and she needed help, though she hadn't talked to him about it yet.

'Where is the new flat?' Tammy asked, towel drying her hair.

'Bletchley.'

Tammy tutted.

'What's wrong with Bletchley?'

'What's right with it? It's too far away from the centre, and taxis cost a bomb.'

Annabel was used to the moaning. All the girls were the same; she wanted to point out that if they learned to drive, it wouldn't be an issue, besides the amount of money that they all earned negated any real worries about transport costs. 'It is right opposite the train station. I chose it especially for you. You can jump on the train and five minutes and one stop later you are at central Milton Keynes with all the shops entertainment and pizza bars you could possibly dream of.' She held a hand out to stop Tammy from hugging her again. 'Happy?'

Tammy nodded and went back to the bedroom, presumably to get dressed and dry her hair. Annabel looked around her. It was a nice apartment. She would turn one of the bedrooms into an office for now. It would be good to move the money and the paperwork away from where the girls worked. She picked up her mobile phone and speed dialled a number. 'If you want a come round later, I've got a proposition for you.'

BRETT WAS TEMPTED to tell Jenny what her husband was up to. He knew she wasn't keen on surprises and this one would be from her list of nightmares. He watched her fuss around the kitchen, clearing up the dinner things. In her own house, she was safe. He couldn't pretend to understand the trauma that she had been through and was still going through, but he did get how important the sanctuary of her home was. Clearly Miles didn't. Not at all, otherwise he would not dream of opening the doors to every Tom, Dick and Debbie in the street.

'You're getting old, sis,' he said, grinning at her.

'No, I'm not. I've decided, no more birthdays for me, I'm staying put at thirty-four.'

'Good for you. When I reach the big one next year, I'm going to start counting backwards. So in a few years we'll be the same age.'

'But I like having a big brother to look out for me,' she said, smiling at him.

What to do? He really didn't know which wasn't like him at all. His loyalty was to his sister, no question, but Miles was going to a lot of trouble and even though the idiot was so unbelievably wrong, he was doing it for Jenny. Brett was in little doubt that the marriage was in free-fall and the party was Miles' idea of a parachute. Did he have the right to ruin the plan?

'I want to take you out for your birthday on Sunday.'

Jenny stopped wiping down the side and looked at him. 'Is Miles on at you again?'

'No. Well, yes. This is something that I want to do. Remember when I took you out to buy your prom dress?'

'She smiled, 'I do. Mum was ill, so you went into big brother mode and took me shopping, showing off your credit card, as I recall.'

'True, I was proud of it; I'd just completed my first proper development and made a mint. I celebrated with a trip to England.'

'It was a beautiful dress, at least when the evening started, until my date spilled orange juice all down it.'

Feeling like a traitor, he slid off the stool and put his arm around her. 'So, how about it? We'll go shopping; I'll flash my card and buy you something lovely for your birthday.'

She turned to look at him. 'I don't think I can.'

'And if you can't, then we will just drive. Perhaps we can window shop from the car until you see something you like, and then I can run in and buy it for you.'

'Not in Milton Keynes you won't,' she said laughing, 'Don't think they'd appreciate a car cruising through the mall.'

'Then we'll go somewhere else.'

Her eyes narrowed. 'You sure Miles hasn't put you up to this?'

'I'm sure,' he lied, hoping that her husband knew what he was doing.

VICTORIA LOOKED at herself in the mirror. The dress was one that Dave always liked. It was red jersey fabric that hugged her figure without emphasising any of the pinch an inch bits that seemed to be getting slightly bigger with each passing year.

She brushed her hair and re-touched her lipstick. She felt strangely nervous, as though she were getting ready for a first date. It seemed inappropriate to be dressing up for what could be the death chop to her marriage. 'No.' she said aloud. She didn't believe it and wouldn't do so until he told her with his own lips that there was someone else. She paused by the dressing table and picked up a wedding photo of the two of them. They looked so happy then, holding hands and smiling brightly as they dreamed of sharing tomorrows. She knew that even then, theirs wasn't the type of relationship that was driven by hot passion and excitement. Somebody once said that passion dies and friendship endures. She thought it might have been one of her mum's sisters. Anyway, whoever it was, they were right. Friendship was what remained after the first flush of a relationship faded. If you didn't have that as a foundation, then the marriage would collapse. Only she always believed that they did have that and couldn't comprehend how it had gone so wrong.

Victoria went downstairs and checked the dinner. It was all ready and warming in the oven. He had replied with a simple 'ok x' and so she was expecting him to turn up. But he was already late. Not enough for her to worry yet, so she opened the bottle of red and poured him a glass. She had two places set up at the breakfast bar. She wished they had a dining table and could sit down at a romantic meal with flickering candles as the only illumination.

She glanced at the clock and tried not to let doubt or fear creep in. Sonia could be wrong about him having a mistress. Any minute now, he could walk through the door with a smile and an explanation and everything would return to normal.

BRETT RAN ALONG THE CANAL. It was dark, wet and muddy, but he preferred the terrain. Pounding on the roads was never good for joints, and he had already been warned that his knees were showing signs of wear and tear. Crazy in his eyes since he wasn't even forty yet.

He upped his speed and pushed himself harder. He was disappointed that she hadn't rung, of course he was. What he couldn't fathom was how she had got under his skin. She wasn't his type, not one little bit. The woman he dated were mainly glossy groomed girly types, with perfectly manicured fingernails. She was all the girl next door, who nibbled her nails and worried more about everyone else than she did about her appearance. Not she wasn't a looker, but it was low key and understated, and maybe that was part of the attraction. He wanted to see what hid beneath the wholesome naivety.

He ran even faster and tried to push her out of his mind. If she wasn't interested, then that was probably a blessing. He was there for his sister and soon he would need to fly home. His property business was mobile and he could keep up with most of it from anywhere, but only for so long.

He went over the bridge and started the run back to Jasmine Close. He had debated bringing the invites out with him and knocking on doors when he got back. Being out anyway meant he didn't have to find an excuse for Jenny as to what he was doing, not that she ever asked. He just felt driven to tell her.

As he approached the Close, he saw that although lights were on in Victoria's house, her husband's car wasn't there. He wished he had brought a couple of invites with him so that he could knock and say hi. Ignoring the fact that he had sweat dripping from his nose, was covered in mud and probably smelt unpleasant, he realised he had nowhere to put the invites to carry them on his run, anyway.

He slowed down as he approached her house, compelled to turn and look as he went by. She was at the window looking incredibly sexy and, at the same time, intensely vulnerable. He couldn't take his eyes off her and she watched him as he went by and then that stupid cat from down the Close shot in front of him and tripped him over. He fought to stay on his feet, his arms flaying around like a demented idiot swotting imaginary flies. He fell anyway and hit the ground with a loud and painful thud right in front of her house.

VICTORIA RAN to the window and looked out. Was he hurt? He seemed to go down heavily. Should she go out? She saw him stand. Even in the poor lighting of the Close, she could see that his knee was bleeding, and he was limping. She felt a stab of guilt. If she hadn't been watching and admiring him, he wouldn't have been staring back at her, and he would have seen Roy the cat dive in front of him.

She hurried to the door and pulled it open. 'Brett,' she called after him.

He turned round and limped back towards her. 'Hi,' he said, smiling at her ruefully. 'Not my greatest moment.'

'Come inside. I'll take a look.'

He put his arm across her shoulder so that she could take some of his weight. She could feel his body heat pressing against her and was glad of the dim light as she felt a flush creeping across her cheeks. She told herself to get a grip; it was truly ridiculous that a woman of her age should still blush.

He paused in her doorway. 'Perhaps this isn't such a good idea,' he said softly.

She knew he was right, but her body seemed to think that it was Christmas and he was the best present in the sack, just waiting to be unwrapped. She didn't want to let go and found herself leaning into him further.

'I'm very muddy,' he said, breaking into her momentary lapse of control.

She pulled back away from him and looked down at his trainers and his legs. 'Oh, you are a bit, and your knee is bleeding. Hold on a minute.' She propped him up at the wall and hurried inside, returning with a copy of the local newspaper. and opened it up and laid it down to make a path for him into the kitchen. She wanted to tuck herself back under his arm, but thought it might not be a good idea. 'Can you manage?'

'Yes,' he said, giving her a mocking grin as if he was very well aware of her thoughts.

He sat down on the stool, and she bent down to examine the cut. 'It's okay, no stitches required. I'll clean it up for you, though.'

Victoria went upstairs to the bathroom to fetch the first aid kit.

'Looks like you have a special evening planned,' he said when she returned. 'Something smells good.' He looked at her rather than the oven. She didn't tell him that her husband was late and the dinner, along with the evening, was ruined.

She knelt down on the cold kitchen tiles and opened the box. She pulled out a couple of antiseptic wipes and started to clean the cut. It wasn't deep and was as much a gravel graze as anything. 'I think the bruising will be bad tomorrow.'

She held up a small aerosol. 'This is an antiseptic liquid plaster,' she sprayed it all over the affected area; 'it will help it heal more quickly.'

She realised he wasn't really bothered about his damaged knee at all, but was watching her administer the dressing with smug satisfaction.

'I hope you didn't stage that performance.'

'No, that was all down to that damn cat.'

She stood up and looked at him, wondering why he turned her knees to jelly. Was she so starved of affection that she would melt the minute a man paid her any attention? No, she knew it was more than that. It was him. Some heat or chemistry crackled between them whenever they were close. She let her eyes linger on his lips and then move up to meet his intense gaze.

She knew what was going to happen. A small voice shouted at her to step away before it was too late. Instead, she stepped closer. His arms went round her waist, pulling her against him. His lips closed over hers and every inch of her body came alive.

EPISODE FIFTEEN
JASMINE CLOSE - SERIES ONE

Victoria opened her eyes. The bed beside her was empty, and she could hear the shower running in the bathroom. She had no idea what time her husband came home. He must have crawled quietly into bed, as she didn't hear him at all. She stretched her limbs under the duvet and resisted the urge to close her eyes and go back to sleep. She felt warm and snug and happy, and then she remembered why. She had kissed Brett. Well, technically he had kissed her, but that was just splitting hairs. The simple, indisputable truth was that their lips had touched and neither of them pulled away. In fact, the opposite happened. They melted into each other as the kiss lingered and deepened. She savoured the memory, playing and re-playing it in her mind, enjoying every detail, every sensation that the intimacy stirred. She felt her cheeks flush in memory as his hands clasped her bottom and pulled her closer against him.

'You alright Vic?'

She half buried her face under the covers to hide her blush.

'Thought you moaned. Look, I'm sorry about last night. I'm really sorry.'

Back to reality. She pushed the cover down and forced herself to smile back at her husband. 'S'okay,' she said, not meaning it at all, but her desire to talk with Dave had disappeared the minute her lips had locked with Brett's. Now she did not know what she wanted from either of the men, and that was a confusing state to be in. She looked at her husband as he towel dried his hair. He was naked other than his Simpson's boxer shorts. His belly had grown since the last time she looked. Middle-aged spread aided by beers and darts and not enough football or healthy eating.

She knew it was unfair to make comparisons and somehow she had to banish all illicit thoughts and do something to sort out her marriage. As if reading her thoughts, her husband sat down on the edge of the bed and reached out to stroke her hair.

'I really am sorry Vic,' he said, looking at her strangely.

'Sorry enough to tell me what's going on?'

His hand fell away, and the brief moment was gone. 'Work, stress, the move,' he shrugged and stood up. 'Just need a lucky break.' He went into the bathroom and closed the door.

Victoria pulled the covers over her head. Five more minutes, she told herself.

'THANKS,' Brett said, taking the coffee from Jenny.

'You had a very late run last night,' she said, looking at him speculatively.

'Went along the canal. It was good.'

She raised an eyebrow that told him she wasn't convinced, but she let it go. 'What are your plans for today?'

'Oh this and that,' he said evasively. He couldn't tell her he had party invites to deliver that she knew nothing about.

'Okay, spill. Who is she then?'

Despite their chat the other evening, he hadn't told her anything about his infatuation - if that's what it was – with Victoria. Instead, she had filled him in on how Steve, the guy in the wheelchair, had introduced her to the calming properties of marijuana and her husband's reaction when he found her stoned.

He laughed. 'I've no idea what you're talking about.'

She always was perceptive, even when she was a little girl, being introduced to her new stepbrother for the first time. She had looked up at him through her lashes and smiled shyly as she said hello. Then she had reached out and squeezed his hand as though to reassure him that everything would be alright. Of course, he had been a sullen teenager, still reeling from his parents' divorce, followed by the arrival of a new female in his father's life. He had been all set to hate the English woman and have nothing whatsoever to do with her snooty little brat. But in those first moments of meeting the little ten-year-old, Jenny had stolen his heart and he couldn't have been more proud or more protective if she had been a birth sister.

She smiled at him knowingly. 'Alright keep your secrets. I'm going to have a long soak in a very bubbly bath.'

He watched her as she left the kitchen. He still wasn't convinced the party was a good idea, and he felt bad about not telling her about it. Miles was a good guy, doing his best to deal with a situation that he could neither understand nor control. Brett felt he had no choice but to help him. He stayed in the kitchen and waited until he was sure Jenny was fully distracted by the lure of her bubbly bath, and then he went and retrieved the invites from the hiding place in the bedroom.

He started at the top end of the Close, avoiding the apartments, although once again he thought that Miles was wrong to exclude the only friend that Jenny had made so far. It seemed to him that Steve, the wheelchair guy, was probably harmless and if Jenny felt able to reach out and connect with him, then that could only be a good thing. He was tempted to put the invites into the apartments, anyway. But he had agreed he would do it Miles' way, so he walked on past and started knocking on the doors of all the houses.

Of course, he knew there was only one door that he actually wanted to knock on and he was saving that one until last. The fact that her husband's car was on the drive probably also played a part in his decision making.

He knew none of the people that opened their doors to him and, from their bemused expressions, when he told them about the party, they clearly had no clue who Jenny Fisher was, either. He knew the Brits were not always the friendliest folks in the world, especially when it came to dealing with their neighbours. His step-mum had tried to explain it all to him once about an Englishman's home being his castle and all that crap. But his understanding was about as clear as mud. Still, most made polite noises about 'dropping in' and he was sure in Jenny's case it would be the fewer the merrier.

'Ooh how exciting,' Sonia said when he handed her the invite. 'I get to be noisy and suss out if there's any gossip worth hearing. I love parties.'

Brett believed her. There was a mischief lurking in her eyes that he was sure could cause trouble. He liked her and was certain that she would be a lot of fun. But he was also wary. She was the type of woman that warnings were written for. He didn't buy into the wholesome mum act at all.

'Would you like a coffee?'

Did he? He was eager to get to Victoria's. He wanted to look into her eyes and she if they lit up with pleasure and memory or moved away in embarrassment after last night's kiss. He glanced sideways. Her husband's car was still on the drive, and he kept hoping that the man would go out, go play football or go to work or do something. Of course, it was possible that the man was already out on foot or bike or bus, and Victoria could be alone at home thinking about him.

'I'll text Victoria. See if she wants to pop round if you like?'

There it was again - that mischief making glimpse. Was she a mind reader?

'I'll have a quick one if you're not too busy?'

She stepped back to let him in. 'Nope, not busy at all.'

It was clearly a lie as the vacuum cleaner was stopped halfway across the carpet and in the kitchen; the dishwasher was open and part loaded. Toys were everywhere, although no sign of the kiddies they belonged to. She didn't seem at all bothered by the disarray as she put the kettle on. On her fridge was a magnet that read, – Boring women have immaculate homes.

'Paul's taken the boys to visit his parents,' she said.

'You didn't want to go?'

'It's a bit of a trek to Hampshire. They'll be gone all day and I have to work this evening. Sugar?'

'No thanks. Where do you work?'

He saw her eyes take on a faraway look, just briefly, before she smiled. 'Just stacking the shelves in Sainsbury's.'

He thought she was lying, but couldn't explain why he got that impression or why she would be untruthful. He watched as she rang Victoria and multi-tasked by stirring the drinks. She placed one mug down beside him. 'No answer,' she said. 'Maybe she's having a lie in.'

Brett couldn't resist the image of Victoria snuggled up in bed. But aware of Sonia's keen gaze fixed on him, he didn't dwell on his thoughts. He knew that women talked to each other and wondered what, if anything, Victoria had told her neighbour. He hoped it wasn't very much at all; there was definitely something suspicious about Sonia Casey. In her case, the old saying – what you see is what you get – did not, in his opinion, apply.

STEVE FELT DREADFUL. Like he'd been run over by a bus that had turned around and come back for another go. It was obvious that it was his exertions of being stuck in the mud incident yesterday that caused it. Plus, he felt shit because, well, let's face it, he was a shit. He knew how much trouble Sharon Stanza would be in because of him ratting her out. He shouldn't have made the call and dobbed her in. As he lay in bed crippled, not just with a severed spine but with a sickening guilt, he searched for a way back, a chance to undo the damage he had caused. But you can't unsay what has already been said and no doubt Sharon was already facing the firing squad. Feeling bad about it didn't change the fact that Melanie had stolen his stash from him, and that couldn't have happened without Sharon handing out his personal information. He couldn't even light up a dooby to ease him through the stress of it all.

He was sick of staring at his damn door in some vain hope that Melanie would bang on it and tell him everything had been a huge misunderstanding. That she hadn't stolen from him, that she did actually like him and that her aunt wasn't in trouble after all.

It wasn't going to happen.

He thought about knocking for Jenny. He even opened the door and looked down the Close. Her pratt of a husband was home and besides, she didn't want to see him. Nobody wanted to see him.

VICTORIA HEARD the doorbell ring as she stepped out of the shower. She left Dave to answer it and got herself dried and dressed, then went downstairs in need of a caffeine shot. She saw the invite as soon as she entered the kitchen. Dave was sitting at the table reading the local newspaper.

She picked the card up and looked at it.

'Yeah, him from down the Close dropped it in.'

Brett? And she missed him?

'Probably just as well that you were late up,' Dave said, glancing across at her. 'I know I've got to keep you two apart.'

'What?' she said sharply, wondering what he knew, and then thinking, how could he know anything?

'I know the man's a dick. Wonder he's even got the nerve to turn up at the door after getting you arrested.'

How had she even forgotten that? It seemed so long ago and almost from a different reality. 'Yeah, nerve of the man,' she said.

'There would have been sparks flying if you'd answered the door to him.'

'There might well have been,' she agreed with a stab of guilt. She looked at the card. It was tomorrow evening and already her brain was sifting through her wardrobe, mentally trying on and discarding her party dress options, which was shockingly limited. It struck her that they had no social life. They never went out, which was why she had nothing suitable to wear.

'Obviously, I told him we won't be going,' Dave said, folding the newspaper up and finishing his coffee.

'We won't?'

He looked at her, clearly surprised by her question.

'I mean, don't you think we should?' she said. 'Give us a chance to meet the other neighbours.'

'But what about dickhead?'

'I'm sure I'll find a way to cope.'

'I guess you can just avoid him or ignore him.'

Victoria nodded her head, wondering if she had time before tomorrow to get her hair cut and the colour re-touched. 'Yes, I can do that.'

Dave walked towards her and wrapped his arms around her waist. 'I really am sorry for how I've been,' he said, making her feel like the most awful person in the world for kissing another man.

'What are your plans today?' she asked, wanting to hug him back but finding herself gently pulling away.

They both looked round as the kitchen door opened and Sonia stepped in. 'Knock, knock...' she said, walking further into the kitchen. 'Thought we might pop into the centre, see if we can find something to wear for the party. Don't know about you, but I intend to dazzle my new neighbours.'

Victoria hesitated. Money was tight, and they were wiped out after the move. A new dress wasn't really a sensible option. No matter how much she longed to look sexy and stunning.

'Good idea,' Dave said, taking her totally by surprise. 'About time you treated yourself.'

Victoria stared at him. Now she was really worried. Normally, if she said she needed something new, his response would be 'why?' He didn't get the whole 'what you wear matters' thing. As far as he was concerned, unless it was literally falling apart, then it was still fit for purpose, so why replace it? That philosophy extended from knickers to overcoats, the number of times she had heard him say, 'if it ain't broke, don't bin it.'

Even more shocking than his words were the actions that followed. He opened his wallet and pulled out three twenty-pound notes. He handed them to her and smiled. 'Put that towards a party frock, and show dickhead that he's messing with the wrong woman.'

'Dickhead?' Sonia whispered with a grin as Dave left the kitchen.

'Brett.' Victoria replied, still bemused by her husband's very out of character actions. She saw Sonia's questioning expression. 'Well he did get me arrested.'

'So he did.' She pulled the back door open again. 'Ready in five? Debenhams have got 20% off today and I've got a discount voucher for New Look and I really want to look in Monsoon.'

Victoria nodded and watched her neighbour leave. She wanted a new dress, and she definitely wanted to look her best for the party. But she was uneasy, partly because her husband's behaviour was odd and worrying, but mainly because she knew she wanted to impress Brett. She was a married woman who, until recently, thought she was happy. Now, stuck between Dave's disappearing acts and Brett's flattering attentions, Victoria felt confused and lost.

JENNY FORCED herself to smile at her husband; he was so enthusiastic looking at her like a kid seeking approval. She opened the birthday card, which he'd obviously ordered, especially for her, from one of the online companies that provided personalised greeting stuff. It had a photo of a dolphin on the front. It had been taken years ago when they went to Florida on holiday and Miles had surprised her with a day of swimming with the magical creatures.

'Remember?' he said.

'Of course,' she replied. How could she forget? It had been an amazing experience.

'Here,' he pushed a small package towards her.

Jenny opened the box and pulled out a dainty gold chain with a dolphin pendant hanging from it. 'It's lovely,' she said, picking it up, genuinely delighted. She had been dreading her birthday, afraid that Miles would use it to ambush her in some way. She held it up, and he fastened it round her neck, then he lent in and kissed her.

'There's more,' he said, pointing to the box. 'Underneath...'

She pulled out the preformed packaging and stared at what she knew were undoubtedly travel documents. Her fingers started to tremble, and she had to fight to stop the tears that were welling up and waiting to fall. She knew if she tried to pick up the document wallet, then her shaking would be clear and her husband would be annoyed. Please, please be for somewhere in England. Going anywhere seemed like an impossible dream, but the idea of getting on a plane was as farfetched as planning a trip to the moon.

Miles seemed oblivious to her turmoil. He grabbed the wallet excitedly. 'I thought we could go back.' He pointed to the photo on the card. 'Go and swim with the dolphins again.'

'Florida?'

'Yes Florida,' he said slightly sharply, obviously picking up on her lack of enthusiasm. 'Oh come on Jenny, don't tell me you're sliding back into all that nonsense again.'

'Sliding back?' she asked incredulously. 'When did I slide forward?'

'You know what I mean,' he snapped. 'You were getting better, going out doing stuff.'

'I was?'

'Well, if you weren't, you should have been. Damn it Jen, we agreed. In Oxford, you promised to be better.'

'I'm trying,' she said, unable to hold back the tears. 'I don't want to be like this.'

'Good. So don't be then. Decide to be normal again and you will be.'

'As easy as that?' she watched him storm out of the kitchen and wished that she could make him understand just how difficult it was. She looked at the card, 'happy birthday me,' she said sadly.

'Hey, the birthday girl can't cry,' Brett said, walking into the kitchen. He pulled her into a hug and stroked her hair soothingly. 'I take it he's told you then?'

'Yes,' she sniffed.

'I told him it wasn't a good idea, but he didn't want to listen.'

'He never does.'

'Come on, let's get out of here.'

Jenny stiffened. 'I can't...'

He stepped back and looked at her. 'Just the car Jenny, we'll drive somewhere, anywhere. I promise you don't have to step outside the vehicle unless you want to.'

She nodded her head and managed to smile. Why couldn't her husband be as understanding as her brother was? A drive around the area might be good. Just getting out of the house would be a positive thing to do. Besides, she didn't want to spend her birthday hiding in her room trying to avoid Miles and another showdown about flights to Florida. She knew she should be thrilled and before the accident, she would have been. Miles seemed incapable of accepting and understanding that she was a different person now. It didn't matter how much he wanted everything to go back to how it had been before the accident. It simply wasn't going to happen.

'Shall we take your car? Miles said I could borrow his, but maybe yours could do with a run out?'

She thought of her attempt to drive it and shuddered.

'Hey, it's okay. I'll take Miles'.'

'No, you're right. The Beetle does need a trip out, just so long as you don't expect me to drive.'

She picked up her handbag and her jacket. Brett took the car keys from the hook in the hall. She glanced up the stairs, wondering if she should find Miles and tell him where she was going. He would be upset and annoyed when he discovered she wasn't at home. She was used to being on the wrong side of his humour, but she didn't want her brother to have to suffer an extended lecture, so she called up the stairs.

He appeared quickly enough and lent over the balcony to look down at her. 'Great idea,' he said, taking her totally by surprise after she told him they were going for a drive. 'Have fun,' he added as she stood in the doorway waiting for Brett to unlock the car.

'Thanks,' she replied, waiting for him to add something, but he didn't. Maybe he was being sarcastic? He didn't sound like he was. In fact, as she ran out of the house to climb in the car, she was pretty sure she heard him whistling.

. . .

Brett glanced at Victoria's house as he drove past. He hadn't seen her since the kiss on Friday evening and it was driving him nuts. Three times he had been to the house. The first to deliver the invite where he had been forced to hand it over to her husband. He then went back a few hours later when he saw the husband's car was gone, but he got no answer and he felt an unfamiliar sensation that he suspected might be jealousy when he thought she might be out with her husband. The third time was late afternoon when the car was still not there, but lights were on in the house. He rang the doorbell and knocked on the door and after a couple of minutes, a young teenager pulled the door open and looked him up and down with mild curiosity. Of course, he had an excuse ready and waiting if the husband opened the door but the girl, presumably the daughter, took him completely by surprise.

'Yeah?' she said, eventually.

'Mum or dad in?'

'Nah, sorry,' she said, closing the door before he even had the chance to ask if she knew where her mum was or when she might be home.

So that was that. They kiss and then nothing. He had no idea how she felt. He wished he had her phone number so he could text her, but maybe that was risky. Since she hadn't messaged him, he assumed she had lost or possibly even thrown his number away. At least he hoped that was the case, and she wasn't simply avoiding or ignoring him. Either way, he would love to see her tonight. He was confident that she would turn up for the party. Like Sonia, she would see it as a chance to meet her new neighbours. And then he would have the opportunity to look into her eyes and see whether his own excitement and anticipation were being reflected back at him or if she was full of regret.

Of course, he hoped the husband would stay away, but knew that was maybe a hope too far. He pulled his thoughts away from fantasy and grounded them firmly back to driving on the correct, or as it seemed to him, the wrong side of the road and his determined attempts to give his sister a lovely day. 'Where too?'

'No idea.'

He saw a sign for the motorway and turned in the opposite direction. Up ahead, he saw another sign for Woburn Safari Park. Perfect, he thought. They can drive through the animal enclosures. He promised Miles that he would keep her out until early evening; he had no idea how big the park was, but hopefully it would take them a good few hours to get round all the animals.

MILES GLANCED AT THE CLOCK. It was just gone six and, unbelievably, everything was ready. He wasn't expecting Jenny back before seven fifteen. Brett had promised to keep her out and busy until then. He had asked the guests to arrive at seven so that he could hide them and then they could all sing happy birthday to Jenny as she walked through the door. She was going to be delighted. He was absolutely sure of it, well, fairly sure of it. He hadn't really expected her to react so negatively to the holiday tickets. Obviously, he knew she would be wary and nervous about the trip. He had been ready to reassure her it would be alright, he would stay by her side the whole time as they negotiated the airport and security and he had splashed out on business class seats so that they would have space and comfort on the flight.

She hadn't given him or the idea a chance. You would think from her reaction he had suggested a trip to medieval torture chambers rather than a five-star luxury holiday. There was still time, though. It wasn't for another six weeks and he was sure he could bring her round by then. He wished he could simply turn the clock back to that awful day of the accident and insist that she take the train. One simple bad decision had sent their lives into free-fall and no matter how hard he tried, he couldn't halt the downward spiral.

He had to show her that the only way to conquer whatever it was that had her by the throat was by fighting back. Face the fear and all that. He viewed the demons that haunted her as bullies and everyone knows that you have to stand up to them. He only wished it were a battle he could take on for her, but all he could do was push and encourage her and then stand by her side to help her win.

He ran up the stairs to get himself changed and ready. He laid out what he knew was Jenny's favourite dress, ready for her to change into when she got home. He felt excited and optimistic. The party would show her how much he loved her and how hard he was working to reintegrate her back into a normal life. Jenny had to stop resisting him and realise that if she let him, he could help.

She would be so pleased to see all their old friends and to meet the new neighbours, all in the safety of her own home. Soon he would have his lovely happy wife back and one day, perhaps even in six weeks' time, sitting round a pool in Orlando, they would look back and laugh at just how daft she had been.

'THANK YOU,' Jenny said, smiling at her brother. 'I've had a great day, and I hadn't expected that.'

'You are very welcome. I'm sure the McDonald's drive through was the highlight.'

She laughed. 'Well it is years since I last had a burger. I'm sorry we couldn't go to a nice restaurant.'

'Are you kidding? I'm American. I love a Big Mac.'

He turned the engine off and looked at her. 'You're alright with this?'

She didn't really know what he was talking about, but assumed it was the fact that they were home and she had to face Miles after the row that morning. 'Of course,' she said, knowing that it couldn't be avoided. She'd just have to tell him straight that Florida was not an option. In fact, it was probably time she put him straight on a lot of things. She had been tiptoeing around, trying not to anger or upset him, and it hadn't helped either of them. If he couldn't cope with her new reality, well, then it was probably better that they both accepted the relationship was over. Better now than let it drag on until they couldn't stand the sight of each other. If they had to split up, then she wanted it to be as amicable as possible.

'I must admit I thought you would hate the idea,' Brett said as they got out of the car and he locked it with the remote.

She wasn't sure what he was talking about, unless he meant the holiday? 'Don't worry, I'm going to tell him straight that it is not possible. I simply can't do it and it's unreasonable for him to expect me to.'

'It's a bit late for that, isn't it?'

She hurried to the door and put her key in the lock. 'Well, yes, I don't suppose he'll get the money back for the tickets, but that's his fault for booking a holiday without asking me first.'

'A holiday...'

'Yes, Florida,' she said, walking into the hall.

'Oh Jen,' Brett said, touching her arm and looking worried, 'I'm so sorry, I thought you knew.'

'Knew what?' The unease creeping into her bones. 'Oh god, what's he done now?'

'This morning, I said 'I take it he's told you then, and you said yes.'

The door to the lounge opened, and Jenny blinked in confusion. There was music and flashing disco lights, and lots and lots of people.

'Oh no...' she whispered, 'he hasn't.'

But of course he had.

'Surprise.' Her husband said with a grin wider than the Cheshire cats from Alice in Wonderland.

Loads of people launched into singing happy birthday. Miles took her arm and started to lead her into the room. Her eyes darted around a sea of smiling faces.

The panic hit her like a force ten gale. She couldn't breathe, she couldn't move, and she couldn't speak. The noises deafened her. A hundred eyes stared down at her as her legs buckled under her and she felt a stab of pain in her side as she hit the floor. Then the darkness consumed her, and she sank gratefully into it.

STEVE HEARD THE NOISE. Hell, everyone could hear the noise. He went outside to have a look and was surprised to see that it was coming from Jenny's house. It had to be a party. He was pretty sure that he remembered her saying she had a birthday coming up soon. So that was it then. She was having a birthday party and from the sound of it, everyone was invited. Everyone, that is, except for him. So the pratt of a husband had been spot on. She didn't want him in her life. She just didn't have the courage to tell him herself. Nothing said 'stay out of my life' better than a party without an invitation.

Not that he blamed her. She was better off without him. Everyone was.

As if pulled by an invisible string, he headed down the Close. He didn't want to get up close and personal, but somehow he felt compelled to wheel to the driveway. Loud pulsating music pumped out of the open windows. Flashing coloured strobe lights spilled out a garish glow. He could hear laughter and chatter and see people dancing. He hated it; he hated them but most of all; he hated himself.

He turned the chair around. He was cold and miserable, and he could feel just the same indoors, no point sitting in the Close like a kid outside a sweet shop.

He heard a noise above him and looked up. It was Jenny. He couldn't see her clearly, but he had a feeling she'd been crying. Not that it was his problem. He started to wheel away.

'Steve, wait,' she shouted down to him.

He paused; annoyed that she had seen him pathetic and alone staring in at the party nobody wanted him at.

'Please wait,' she said again. 'I'm coming down.'

She ducked back inside, and he pictured her leaving the bedroom and running down the stairs. He had no idea why she wanted to speak to him.

She reached his side and gripped the chair tightly. Under the streetlight, he could see that she definitely had been crying. But more than that, she was pale and clearly hurting and wearing jeans and a jumper. He was confused. Surely it was her party?

'Were you going in?' she asked in a voice laced with pain and edged with anger.

'No. I'm not a gate crasher.'

She looked at him, and her features hardened. 'He didn't invite you?'

A tiny spark of hope ignited inside him.

'Bastard,' she said. 'Can I come back to yours?'

He had no idea what was going on, but thought he might as well go along with it; he missed not having her around. 'Sure.'

'Can I stay tonight? Kip on the sofa?'

'Of course,' he said, wondering what the hell was going on. 'I should warn you though, that if you only want me for my dope, I have none.'

'Really? What happened?'

'It's a long and dirty story,' he said, wheeling towards his flat, delighted to have Jenny beside him.

'Well, I'm not going anywhere in a hurry, so you can tell me all about it.'

DAVE CONCENTRATED HARD, willing the spinning fruits to stop in a line. A cherry, a bar and a melon, no good to him at all. He pressed the button to spin again.

'Dave...'

Somewhere behind him he thought he heard his name called but wasn't certain, so he carried on, his eyes following the fruits as they span.

'Dave, mate!'

Annoyed by the interruption, he swung round; it was John the barman shouting over at him. 'What?' he said irritably, eager to get back to the game.

'I've just rang last orders. You want another?'

Dave blinked. He was confused. How could it possibly be last orders? Surely it was barely evening?

'Beer?'

He nodded his head and fished in his pocket for money. He had none. He pulled his wallet out and opened it, confident that he still had plenty left. Friday night had seen his luck change, which was why he'd missed the dinner and chat that Victoria wanted. He couldn't walk away from a winning streak. But he had made it up to her and given her money for the dress. His wallet was empty. How did that happen? No way had he put it all into the machine. He checked again - nothing. Damn, why had he given her that sixty quid? It wasn't as if she needed any more sodding clothes. He needed that money now; he could turn it into hundreds with one lucky spin.

'Dave, here you go, mate.'

John reached across the bar and handed him the beer.

'I'll settle up in a minute, John,' Dave said, wondering where all the rest of his money had gone.

John rolled his eyes, but Dave wasn't bothered. He needed to get back to the game. He had a few more credits to play, then he would have to pause the game to get some cash out. Trouble was, the ATM was near the gents, which meant walking away from his fruit machine. He had been feeding it all evening, and it was fat from his money and primed and ready to the big pay-out. If he walked away now and one of the lurkers hovering like vultures around the bar stepped in, they could take the jackpot that should be his.

He began to sweat as the panic rose up inside him. What to do? He was on his last two credits. If he didn't get a win now, then he would have to stop. He paused to glance furtively around him. The two lads at the bar looked his way. They knew a payout was due, they'd been watching him all night. The minute he stepped away, they would pounce. He picked up his beer, his hand shook, and he spilt it down on his trousers. His last credit, please, please, please be the winning one.

VICTORIA LOOKED into Brett's eyes and knew, just as he did, what would happen next. The attraction between them was so charged that even his hand on her waist while they danced felt like a thousand tiny fire ants were crawling across her skin. Never in her life had she felt so excited and yet at the same time so afraid. If only Dave had turned up. If he was at the party with her, then she couldn't be dancing with Brett, staring up at him like a stupid star-struck schoolgirl. Where the hell was he? Did he have another woman? Sonia was certain of it and Victoria had to admit it seemed likely. What else could possibly explain her husband's behaviour? The constant late nights, the mood swings the total disinterest in her or the house or even in Gemma. Even when he was at home, she knew he wasn't with her. His mind was somewhere else, and he had probably left it on another woman's pillow.

Brett leant down and whispered in her ear. She knew it was decision time. She never thought she would be capable of having an affair. She thought that you had to be a certain type of person, and was quietly, smugly sure that it would never be her.

Brett stopped dancing and led her to the corner of the room. It was busy, amazingly so. Almost everyone from the Close had turned up, people she only recognised because she'd seen them moving in or walking by or because she had sold them their houses. The music was loud and in the centre of the room; she saw Sonia and Paul dancing together. She envied her neighbour her happy marriage and felt a sudden stab of tears at what she was about to lose. You've already lost it, the voice in her head whispered. Maybe she never had it in the first place. Maybe her entire marriage was a mirage, or at least her perception of it. Like an idiot, she thought they were partners, best friends, lovers and parents. Yet looking back, had it ever been true? They pretty much lived their own lives, and neither of them was open and honest with their feelings. She had never experienced that overwhelming passion that romance books were so fond of describing and was pretty sure that Dave hadn't either. At least not with her.

Brett squeezed her hand and then walked away. She knew where he was going. She was supposed to wait a few minutes and then follow him upstairs. She wanted to; every part of her was yearning to give in to the feelings that were burning through her. Long forgotten sensations. She finished her wine and did herself a refill. She pulled her mobile phone from her bag and checked it. Nothing. He promised her he would be home in time for the party. His promises meant nothing anymore, so why should hers?

She finished the glass and headed for the stairs. Victoria paused and clutched the bannister. She wasn't drunk enough to blame the alcohol. Whatever step she took next, she would have to live with the consequences. If she went up to Brett's bedroom, then everything would change and there would be no going back.

EPISODES 16 -20

JASMINE CLOSE - SERIES ONE

EPISODE SIXTEEN
JASMINE CLOSE - SERIES ONE

Miles looked around him; a party without the party girl didn't really count as a success. Somehow he had cocked it up and instead of drinking and dancing with her old friends and new neighbours, Jenny had hidden away upstairs. He finished his whisky and planted a flake smile on his face as he weaved his way through the partygoers, most of whom he'd never seen before. He paused at the stairs and looked up. Should he leave her or would it be best to try and talk to her? Encourage her to come downstairs and meet everyone. She'd suffered a panic attack, but surely that was over now? He stepped aside to let a lady go past who he'd never seen before in his life. She was swaying and giggling and he was worried she would fall down the stairs. And he was also annoyed that she was upstairs in the first place. They had a perfectly good cloakroom in the hall. He didn't like the idea of strangers wandering around his house. He could feel his irritation levels cranking up higher by the second.

'Lovely party,' she said with a slurred lisp and leaning into him so the full force of her sour breath hit him. Clearly, the cheesy garlic nibbles had been a mistake.

He edged past her without bothering to reply and ran up the

stairs. He tapped on the bedroom door. 'Jen...' she didn't answer. He opened the door, the lights were out. He hovered uncertainly in the entrance and called again, 'Jen, you all right?'

With mounting annoyance, he slammed the door shut and left her to it. He was making an effort. Why couldn't she? Jenny wasn't even trying to get over this ridiculous self-absorbed phase she was going through, and now she had made him look like a complete fool. What must everyone be thinking? He went back downstairs, trying, and failing, not to notice that some fool had spilt red wine on his lovely new carpet, or that the stench of fresh vomit was wafting from the cloakroom. What had he been thinking, letting a bunch of total strangers into his brand new home? He went into the kitchen and pulled out a new bottle of whisky from the cupboard. He opened it and took a long slug, then he let himself out of the back door. He needed to get away. He couldn't bear to see his house being wrecked, and he hated the pathetic looks of sympathy that kept pointing his way.

Bottle in hand, he went into the garden and drank some more. The amber liquid warmed his limbs and dulled his angry brain. Then he went around to the side of the house, through the gate and into the Close. His only intention was to get away. He found himself on the pathway that led to the scrubland that would eventually become the phase two building site. It was dark and cold, and the ground below him seemed to be swaying heavily. He took another deep slug to steady himself, but it didn't seem to help. He leaned against the wall of the end terraced house and huge drops of rain started to fall. His head slumped forward and his legs wobbled. He slid down the wall and closed his eyes.

VICTORIA STRETCHED HER LIMBS. She was warm and snug and naked. It was still dark, and she quickly realised that the bed and the room were not hers. She was also aware that the arm resting across her stomach was not her husband's. 'What have I done?' she whispered into the darkness.

The arm moved, and the hand on the end of it stroked her skin. 'You want a replay?' Brett replied, moving his body close against hers.

Did she? Her body was already responding to his touch, but her mind was urging her to run. 'I have to go.' she managed to say before his lips pressed down on hers silencing any protests.

With willpower she never knew she possessed, she wriggled her body away from him and slid out of the bed. Conscious of her nakedness, she was glad of the darkness as she tried to find her clothes that were discarded all over the room. The curtains were partly open and moonlight eased through the gap, bathing Brett in a silvery glow as he watched her from the bed.

'Come back,' he said softly, his voice seductive and inviting.

'I can't. I must go home. Dave…'

'Probably won't even notice you're missing.'

'Gee thanks!'

'The man is an idiot who treats you with contempt.'

'What do you know?' she said crossly, giving up all attempts to find her bra and pulling her new silk dress she'd bought from Monsoon over her head. 'He's just busy and stressed.' She had no idea why she was defending Dave, but Brett's words hurt, possibly because they were true. Her own guilt was taking hold, and she needed to get home and face her husband. She couldn't take back what had happened, but she could make sure that it would never happen again.

She found her shoes and fumbled with the straps. Brett slipped out of bed, went down on his knees, and buckled them up for her.

'Thank you,' she whispered, her voice husky with desire as her body reacted to his nakedness and closeness.

He stood up and looked into her eyes with that slightly lopsided smile that was already so familiar. He stroked a strand of hair back away from her face. 'Anytime Victoria.'

She thought he was going to kiss her, and she found herself tilting her head and closing her eyes. But he didn't, and she was both relieved and disappointed. It would be so easy to crawl back into the warmth of his bed. The party was over; if she went back now she had to explain herself, so why not leave it until the morning? She had no idea if she was going to tell Dave the truth or lie to him. She had no idea how to deal with the situation. Saying sorry wouldn't cut it. You can't just apologise for having sex with another man. The truth would probably end her marriage, and she didn't want that. The alternative was to lie and keep on lying, and that didn't seem like a great option either.

'Stay,' he whispered, bending his head down to trail tiny kisses around her neck.

'I can't,' she said, stepping away from him while longing to wrap herself up in his hot embrace. She picked up her bag, and without a backward glance, she left the room.

The house was silent. The aftermath of the party littering the floor. She was glad she didn't have the job of cleaning it up. She let herself out of the front door and into the Close. It was cold and dark and drizzling. She shivered and wished she had a coat. Maybe she should have waited until the morning; she could have enjoyed a few more hours with Brett before facing a new day and probably a new reality. But walking back in the morning, the wintery sun would illuminate her guilt and her shame. She was better off slipping home in the shadows.

She put her key in the door and winced at the noise it made as the lock released and the hinges creaked. Was he pacing the floor? Was he worried about her? What if he had called the police? No, she thought, that was silly. He knew exactly where she was. So why hadn't he come looking for her at the party? The lights were out, and the house was quiet. Gemma had stayed at her friend's house, but surely Dave would be concerned or angry, or at the very least, curious.

Victoria sat down on the bottom step and undid her shoes. They had heels much higher than she would normally wear. They would be loud on the bathroom tiles when she got upstairs. She carried them in her hand and went up to the bedroom, steeling herself for the unavoidable confrontation. She opened the bedroom door and slipped into the unlit room. The curtains were wide open; the bed was empty and made. She flicked the light switch on and stared in surprise. Where was he? The car was on the drive. She had passed it on her way in. She went to the window and looked out just to double check.

She went into the ensuite bathroom and stripped off. Her make-up was streaked and her hair was a mess. She stepped under the shower and refused to think about Brett. It wasn't easy; her skin was alive and sensitive, still alert and tingling from their night of passion. She dried herself, slipped on her comfy old pyjamas and cleaned her teeth, then she went downstairs.

Dave was sprawled out on the sofa, fully dressed and sound asleep. She didn't know whether to be annoyed or relieved. She had gone straight past him without realising he was there.

He hadn't known that she was in another man's arms and, for all he knew and apparently cared, she could be dead in a ditch. She stood watching him. He was face down, snoring loudly, one leg hanging off the sofa, and his knee on the carpet. She was tempted to switch the light on, wake him up and deal with the situation head on. It seemed their marriage was in tatters and maybe beyond saving. Why was he asleep downstairs? Had he come home so late that he was afraid to come to bed and be quizzed by her? Was he totally unaware of the fact that she hadn't been sleeping alone in their room?

She thought about Gemma. Their little girl would be the one who suffered the most if they split up. Victoria knew what it was like to watch your parents' divorce and she never wanted that trauma for her own daughter. She tiptoed out of the lounge and closed the door. It seemed her secret was safe. She should be relieved, and she was, although a tiny part of her wanted a showdown, almost needed the confrontation and Victoria wasn't entirely sure why. She went up to the bedroom and climbed into the cold empty bed and wished she were back in the Fisher's house with Brett's hot body pressing hard up against her. She couldn't regret what had happened, but she was determined that it was a once only experience to be kept hidden as nothing more than a memory.

. . .

MILES BLINKED as the sunlight streamed in through the open windows. His head was pounding so badly he was sure he had a miniature army marching through it. He was disorientated. His memory was hazy. And where the hell was he?

He sat up and looked around him. He was in an unfamiliar bed in an unfamiliar room he'd never been in before and all he had on were his boxers. He stared in horror and confusion as he realised he wasn't alone. Curled up beside him was a beautiful young girl wearing nothing but scanty underwear. He leapt out of the bed and stubbed his toe on a small wooden chest. He cried out and hopped around as he clutched his throbbing foot. He realised the curtains were open, and the window backed onto the phase two building site. That meant he must be in one of the apartments. His attention wandered back to the chest. The lid was up and inside there was a strange assortment of what looked like dressing-up clothes and soft toys. He reached down and picked up what appeared to be a nurse's uniform and underneath it in the box were some fur lined handcuffs.

'Takes all sorts,' a soft female voice said from behind him.

He swung around. The woman was indeed young. He guessed around twenty. She was also absolutely stunning, with thick, luscious, almost black hair that fell around her shoulders in curly disarray.

'You into nurses? I'll put it on for you if you like.'

He dropped the dress back into the box and tried to force his brain to catch up with what was happening.

'Nope, not nurses.'

'So, what's your fantasy, then?' she smiled alluringly.

It seemed one part of his anatomy was wide awake and paying attention, and his flimsy boxer shorts did nothing to disguise it. He turned his back on her, feeling embarrassed, and then swung quickly back again as a couple of builders walked into view and waved.

The young woman giggled and waved back at them. Miles sank down onto the bed and wondered if he'd crossed into some parallel universe. 'What the hell is going on?' he groaned.

The woman got off of the bed and walked around to the windows to pull the curtains, shutting out the onlookers. He looked at her and some memory stirred from the previous evening. 'You helped me...' he frowned, trying to piece together the fragmented picture that was beginning to form in his head. 'Yes, you were outside.'

'You were very drunk, and it was raining heavily. I couldn't just leave you to drown in the alleyway, could I?'

'Bit of an exaggeration.'

'Well, not really. You were totally pissed and lying in a puddle.' She shrugged her naked shoulders and smiled. 'What's a girl to do?'

He dragged his eyes away from her and looked around the room. 'So, this is your home?'

'Sort of.'

'What does that mean?'

'Well, I used to work here and sometimes live here, only not at the moment because we have to be careful.'

'That explains everything!' he said sarcastically.

'It does?'

'No. why didn't you just help me home?'

'Well, number one, I don't know where you live and number two, you didn't want to go. You kept banging on about how she didn't deserve you and it would serve her right.'

Miles groaned as last night came into full focus. 'I was mad at Jenny,' he said, mainly to himself. Just how far had he gone to vent his anger? He glanced at the beautiful, barely covered woman in front of him; he hardly dared ask but knew that he had to. 'We didn't?' 'He coughed and cleared his throat. 'Did we?'

'Nah, you were way too pissed.'

He was relieved, although his ego was soothed by the fact such a lovely had taken him on in the first place. 'My clothes?'

'Soaking wet, I had to get you out of them. They should be dry now. I'll fetch them.'

He watched her leave the room. He needed to pee, and he craved caffeine and he wished he smoked; it seemed like the perfect time for a cigarette. He had to get home and assess the damage, not only to his house but also to his marriage. He had no idea why the young woman had taken him in and wasn't at all sure if he should be grateful or not.

She dashed back into the room and threw the clothes at him. 'You gotta go,' she said urgently. 'Out the window, now!'

He stood up and stared at her. Was he still dreaming? Was some huge hairy husband about to come crashing through the door?

She pulled the curtains and was fumbling with the lock.

'I'm not going out the window,' he said, pulling his trousers on. Surely she wasn't serious?

'You are. You must...' she pushed the window open and looked close to tears. 'Hurry, Annabel will murder me if she finds you here.'

'Annabel?'

She was pulling his arm and urging him to the window. She picked up his shoes and chucked them out into the small courtyard garden.

'Hey.'

'Go.'

The rest of his clothes followed the shoes, and he had little choice but to climb out. He heard the front door open, and the young woman pulled the curtains back across the open window, shutting him out.

Glad that the builders didn't seem to be anywhere in sight, he picked up his clothes and ran.

VICTORIA STIRRED a spoonful of sugar into a mug of coffee and then carried it into her husband. He was in almost exactly the same position that he had been in when she got home a few hours earlier. She placed the mug on a mat on the coffee table and then pulled the curtains, allowing the daylight to stream in.

'Wakey, wakey,' she said with a cheerfulness that she was far from feeling.

He groaned and moved slowly, as if in pain. He turned from his front to sit up on the sofa. 'Bloody hell, Vic, what time is it?'

Her eyes narrowed as she studied him. He was a mess. His clothes were muddy and stained and his shirt torn. His lip was swollen and cut and he had a black eye and a graze on his forehead.

'What?' he said, realising that she was staring.

'You,' she replied, dropping to her knees in front of him so that she could have a proper look at his face. 'What happened?'

He touched his lip as though remembering that there was a problem. His eyes shifted away from looking at her.

'Dave?' she reached up to touch the area below his eye. Black was not an accurate description since it was a multi-coloured patchwork of yellow, purple and blue.

He winced and shook her hand away.

'Were you attacked?'

He looked at her then, his eyes suddenly lit up with something undefinable. 'Yes,' he said quickly. 'That's it, I was attacked.'

'Oh, Dave, that's awful. Where were you? Who did it? What happened?'

'Stop with the twenty bleeding questions,' he snapped back at her.

She realised she was being unfair. He was probably still in shock as well as pain, so she handed him his coffee. 'I'll get you some paracetamol.'

As if she didn't feel guilty enough already. While she was in bed with another man, her husband was taking a beating. She truly was a terrible person. She opened the cupboard and pulled out the medicine box. The key was in the lock. When her daughter had been small, it was always been kept secure with the key up high on top of the fridge freezer away from little hands. She took out a couple of painkillers and returned to the lounge.

Dave was sipping his coffee and looked much happier and more relaxed than he had a few minutes ago. She assumed the caffeine was hitting the spot.

'Here,' she said, handing him the tablets. She sat down and waited until he had swallowed them. 'So, what happened?'

'I was mugged...'

'Oh Dave, I'm so sorry.'

'Yeah bastards, there were three of them...'

'Three!'

'Do you want to hear this or not?'

'Yes, sorry, go on.'

'I was walking home...'

'Why?'

'Victoria!'

'Okay, okay, I'm sorry...' she mimed, zipping her lips and waiting for him to continue. Her head was swimming with questions like where was he, why was he walking and how did the car get back on the drive, but she stayed silent and listened.

'They came from behind me. I had no time to defend myself. They were on me like a rugby scrum. The bastards had me on the floor, pinned me down, and nicked my wallet. They gave me a couple of kicks in the guts and then they were gone.'

She waited to make sure that he had finished. 'Do you need to go to the hospital? They might have cracked your ribs or damaged your kidneys.'

'Don't fuss, I'll live.'

'It's lucky they didn't take your ring,' she said, spotting his wedding ring still on his finger. She stood up and fetched the phone.

'What are you doing?'

'Well, we need to cancel your cards and call the police.'

He looked startled. 'I'm already on it.'

'You've rung them all?'

He nodded his head, then clearly wished he hadn't, as his face screwed up in pain. 'Yeah, I cancelled the cards as soon as I got home last night.'

'Well, at least the bastards can't get anything from the bank or credit cards then. What about the police?'

'Not much they can do. They took a report but I couldn't even describe them as it was dark.'

Victoria thought of her poor husband having to go deal with it all on his own, thinking that she was asleep upstairs in their bed. 'Are they coming to see you or do you have to go to them?'

'What, the police? No, I told you, nothing they can do other than log it as a reported crime.'

'That's it?'

'Yes.' He stood up and stretched. 'I'm going to have a shower and get changed.'

She watched him walk away and felt a rare surge of love and compassion. They might be going through a rough patch, but he was still her husband. 'Wait,' she said, running across the room and hugging him. 'I'm so sorry,' she said.

'Not your fault, love,' he replied, stepping back. 'These things happen.'

'But they shouldn't,' she said sadly, wishing that she had never set eyes on Brett.

He left the room, and she watched him go up the stairs. He looked slumped and in pain. It wasn't right that the police weren't even trying to do something. 'I'll phone work. Tell them you're not going to be in today.'

He swung round. 'No,' he said urgently. 'I rang and left a message already, said I would be in later.'

She was surprised, and wondered as to exactly when he had made the call since he was slumped in exactly the same position when she woke him up as he had been when she got home. He must have called at the same time as dealing with the police and the bank.

Victoria went back into the kitchen and looked in the fridge. Perhaps a large fried breakfast would make him feel better. She didn't have work herself that day, which was good. She wasn't at all sure she could cope with being bright and smiley to customers and browsers. She glanced at the kitchen clock, a pretty china plate with a bright red poppy painted on it. Gemma would already be at school; she was going in with her friend and not be home until after four. At some point, she knew she would have to see Brett. Although they barely knew each other, she was pretty sure that he would be around, wanting to see her before the day was through. He didn't know she had a day off; they hadn't done much talking last night. So he would go to the Show Home office first. She couldn't risk him coming to the house in search of her, so she decided the best approach was to get to him first. It was over, that was definite. It was a once only moment of madness and that was what she had to tell him. Trouble was how? She still didn't have his phone number and, of course, regretted putting it in the bin. It was gone now, chucked out, when she emptied all the rubbish into a black sack and put it out for the weekly collection.

Could she go and boldly knock at the door? It might be awkward unless he answered it himself. But maybe she could have a cover story. A valid excuse for being there if either of the Fishers opened the door. She could go and thank them for a great party, but on the basis that the birthday girl had collapsed, and the host buggered off, it would hardly seem sincere. She walked to the front window and looked out. Did he run in the mornings or was activity saved for the evenings? It struck her how little she knew about him. She had no idea what he did for a living or even where he lived. She assumed he was visiting from America, but for all she knew, he could live in the UK. Not that any of it mattered now, because it was over. She wasn't even sure what 'it' was. A brief affair? A one-night stand? For a few short seconds, she allowed herself to wonder what it would be like to get to know him. To go on dates and flirt and have fun. She banished the notion and picked up the phone. She dialled a number and waited until it answered. 'Hello, I want to talk to PC Clarke please.' The least she could do was make sure that the police were doing everything possible to catch her husband's attackers.

Just as the man himself came on the phone, she saw Brett run past the house. She thought of cancelling the call and chasing out the front door in pursuit but quickly realised that she would never catch him, anyway. So she would wait and grab him on his return.

Gemma bent over and heaved into the bushes.

'Gross,' Amy said, standing just behind her.

'Yeah, I feel pretty gross.' she pulled a crumpled tissue from her school uniform jacket and wiped her mouth. She had felt sick and dizzy all morning and actually felt slightly better now that she had thrown up. 'Think I must have a bug.'

'Hope you're not knocked up.'

She shook her head at her friend. 'Nah, can't be. He had a condom.'

'They don't always work.' Amy said matter-of-factly.

Gemma stared at Amy in shocked surprise. 'What? Don't say that!'

Amy didn't seem at all fazed or worried and Gemma felt a surge of anger at her so-called friend. 'I can't be.'

'Oh come on Gem, these things happen all the time. You can soon find out with a test.'

Gemma burst into tears. As if the whole situation with Alex hadn't been hideous enough, now she might have to deal with the pregnancy. Could life really be that unfair?

'Hey, don't cry, it's no biggy.'

'No biggy! Are you insane?'

'No need to shout at me. It's not my fault you were stupid enough to sleep with Alex, the shitface.'

'You told me to. You said he'd dump me if I didn't do it.'

Amy shrugged her shoulders. 'Well, I only pointed out what you already knew. Stop being such a mardy cow.' Amy stopped walking and turned to face her. 'Oh, my god! That's it, you must be pregnant and the hormones have kicked in, making you so stroppy.'

'No.' Gemma cried in terrified denial. 'I'm not.' She knew that school was no longer an option. She needed to get a test and go home. She turned away from the school and started walking back towards the bus stop.

'Gem wait. I'm sorry. Come on, let's go to school and then we can pick up a test kit from Boots in the lunch break.'

Gemma kept walking. She had a longing to see her mum. Could she tell her? They had been closer recently and mum did say that she could go to her with anything. Did that include stuff as awful as this? She felt in her pocket to see how much money she had. Was it enough to buy a test kit? If she got off the bus a stop early, then she could go to the small chemist next to the doctors and buy one. Would it be embarrassing? What if they asked questions like how old was she? Or did she need a parent's permission to buy one? Maybe she shouldn't have got angry with Amy and walked away like that. Amy did tend to know stuff like this.

She saw the bus coming and ran to catch it. The driver looked at her suspiciously but clearly decided it wasn't worth the hassle of questioning her about why she was going away from school. Gemma sat at the back of the bus and decided to go straight home and talk to her mum. She closed her eyes and thought about a comforting hot chocolate her mother would make her while she made reassuring noises and organised a test.

PC CLARKE WAS as helpful as Victoria hoped he would be. Although strangely, he couldn't find any record of the report that her husband filed in the early hours after the attack. He promised to call in to talk to Dave and said he would be there in about an hour. So Victoria had time to go and find Brett on his run and tell him that last night would not be repeated. She grabbed her jacket and her purse. If she needed an excuse when she got back, then she could say she went to the local shop for milk or bread. She had no clear idea of where Brett ran, but given the direction he went, she guessed that he might have taken the redway round to the canal.

She hurried up the path and hoped that she wouldn't bump into anyone else; she really wasn't in the mood for talking. The redway forked with one path leading up over the bridge towards the local centre with the shops and school and doctors' surgery and the other leading to the canal. Way up ahead beyond the bridge, she saw Belle walking back towards the Close, presumably having just taken her daughter to school. Victoria couldn't even begin to imagine how awful it must be for the woman to lose her son like that.

The sound of pounding feet pulled her attention back to her own problems as she saw Brett running towards her. He slowed down and then stopped just in front of her. 'Hi Victoria,' he said, his eyes seeming to be full of mischief and memories. 'You looking for me?'

Her resolve weakened as she stood so close to him. Despite the chill air, he was sweating and although she had seen him approaching fast; he seemed barely out of breath. He was tall and lean and strong and her body was responding just looking at him. 'We need to talk.' She managed to say even though talking wasn't what she wanted to do at all.

He looked at her with a slightly mocking expression. 'Don't tell me it was all a mistake and we can't do it again.'

She frowned. 'Yes, how did you know?'

He took her hand. She looked round quickly, but no one was in sight. The path from the shops curved around before it reached the slope that led up and over the bridge. No doubt Belle was at that point on her walk home and wouldn't be able to see them until she got to the other side of the bridge. They were visible from the road but only just as the path dipped down and so they would only be seen by a someone in a high vehicle.

'Relax,' he said, pulling her back towards the shrubbery that edged the path. 'No one's around.'

She pulled back away him, determined to be strong. 'I can't, we can't. It is over, I'm married.'

'I know. You were married last night, nothing's changed, it's just that the guilt has hit you.'

'Wow, you've done this a few times before then,' she said, feeling a sharp stab of jealousy.

'You came to me last night because you are unhappy in your marriage. I can't believe that's changed in the last few hours. You're just pretending that it has.' He moved in closer and lowered his head to kiss her.

She knew she should push him away and her arms moved to do just that, but somehow they ended up winding themselves around his neck while her lips kissed him back. This is just a final goodbye kiss, she told herself.

. . .

Gemma looked out of the window as the bus slowed down at the local centre bus stop. A few more minutes and she would be home. She wasn't looking forward to telling her mother that she might be pregnant, although it would be a relief to hand over the worry and responsibility. She was too young to deal with a baby; mum would know what to do.

The bus moved on and she stood up, ready to press the buzzer to tell the driver she was getting off at the next stop. She saw a woman walking along the redway and realised it was the lady from the apartment block whose son had been taken from her. Then her eyes moved on as the bus passed under the bridge and she smiled as she two a couple snogging. She blinked in disbelief; the smile slipping into a frown. She blinked and stared, unable to comprehend what she was seeing. Her mum was in the arms of the man who had knocked on the door the other night.

The bus slowed down and pulled into the stop in a daze. She ran down the steps and off the bus, then stood still while it drove away. Had she been mistaken? Surely her eyes were lying. Was she dreaming or hallucinating? Could pregnancy make you crazy? Her mum would never do that, not to dad and not to her. She had it wrong; it was just someone who looked like her mother.

She started to walk towards the bridge that would take her across the busy dual carriageway road. On the other side, she saw the jogger run past. He was tall and fit and moving fast and was followed by a woman who was undoubtedly her mother.

EPISODE SEVENTEEN
JASMINE CLOSE - SERIES ONE

Jenny handed Steve a couple of slices of buttered toast and placed a mug of steaming coffee on his tray.

'Thanks,' he said. 'Did you sleep okay?'

'Yes, thanks.'

'Liar. You look like shit.'

'Thanks,' she said, popping another slice of bread in the toaster for herself. She knew he was right. She hadn't slept at all and had avoided looking in the bathroom mirror, well aware of the fact that her hair needed brushing and the dark circles under her eyes had nothing to do with smudged mascara.

'Wanna talk about it?'

Did she? Probably not. There was nothing more to say. All night long, she'd searched for a way forward that didn't involve tearing their marriage apart. It seemed impossible. She knew it was her fault. She might have survived the accident, but the person she used to be died that day and the new Jenny was so alien to Miles that they could no longer communicate. The relationship was over and they probably both knew it had been over for some time. They were just clinging on in some vain hope that it could be rekindled. But it couldn't. It was over and it was time they both faced up to it. 'Thanks, but no.'

They munched on their toast and drank coffee in companionable silence. She felt comfortable with Steve, perhaps because he had so many demons of his own that he didn't make her feel like a freak. He understood how the past stalked her like some malevolent shadow, because it was exactly the same for him.

They both looked up in surprise as the doorbell rang, followed by heavy banging on the knocker. Jenny felt herself tense in anticipation, assuming that it was Miles who had tracked her down. Not that she would be hard to find. She only had one friend in Milton Keynes. Steve glanced at her, presumably reaching the same conclusion. She nodded her head, knowing that her husband had to be faced at some point. Steve pressed his remote fob, and the door swung open.

But it wasn't Miles. Jenny watched as a young woman in a wheelchair entered the flat at a surprising speed.

'You arsehole...' the woman hollered, wheeling right up close against Steve highly aggressively.

'Hello Melanie,' he said in a restrained manner, not at all his usual cocky, mocking self.

'You got her suspended. Why? Why'd you do it?'

Steve studiously studied his tray as though it held the answers to all life's mysteries. Jenny had no idea who the angry young person was, but she knew she wanted to protect her friend.

'Hello, I'm Jenny,' she said, standing up and offering her hand.

'And I couldn't give a stuff who you are.' Melanie retorted, looking at the offered hand as though she had pulled it out from somewhere unpleasant.

'Hey back off,' Steve said, wheeling forward and ramming into her chair. 'She has done nothing to you.'

The woman rammed him back harder. 'You certainly have, though. What did Sharon do to you other than try to help you, you ungrateful bastard? She cared, you know, wanted to show you that you could still have a life.'

'I'm sorry.'

'What use is that? It's just a sodding word. You can't undo the harm you've done. She's suspended from work and under investigation and all because you are such a miserable coward.'

'That's not fair,' Jenny said, jumping in to defend Steve.

Melanie turned the full force of her scowl on Jenny. 'Butt out, lady. This doesn't concern you.'

Jenny was about to argue back when Steve put a calming hand on hers and shook his head.

'I was annoyed and hurt. You shouldn't have taken my stuff. But I am sorry, if I could unsay it, then I would,' he said.

Melanie stared at him; the anger a visible force radiating from her. 'I've never taken anything from you.' She rammed into Steve's chair again. 'You don't deserve help,' she hissed at him, swinging her chair around and heading back to the still open door. She paused and looked back at him. 'You have a choice, you know. That's what Sharon was trying to show you. Life sucks, but it's up to you to choose whether you sink or to swim. If you're gonna sink, then get the fuck on with it and sodding well do it. But you don't have to take anyone else down with you.'

Jenny couldn't listen to any more. 'Get out,' she said, raising her voice. 'Leave him alone.'

'Count on it.' Melanie shouted back. 'And you should do the same.'

Steve closed the door. He looked down, defeated, and not at all the angry, defiant young man she was used to. 'She's right,' he said. 'You should go.'

'I don't want to go.' Which wasn't entirely true as at some point she had to go home, but no way was she going to leave him alone yet. He was vulnerable and struggling and he didn't need crazy young women coming into his home and verbally abusing him. He needed encouragement and support.

'I am shit and everything I touch turns to shit.'

'I don't know what her problem is, but she's wrong.'

'Is she?'

'Yes.' Jenny said firmly, taking his hand and squeezing it reassuringly. 'You are still adapting to your new reality. It sucks, and it's bloody hard. You are bound to suffer low points.'

He looked into her face and she felt his pain. He was lost, and she knew that feeling well enough. How do you carry on when every part of your life has been taken away? All of your hopes and dreams, and ambitions are gone in one fateful stroke. How do you find a new future that has promise and potential and isn't just a poor reflection of what you were before?

'That's it,' she said, as understanding and clarity suddenly struck her.

'What's it?'

She stood up and started pacing, holding on to the thought, trying to define and understand it before it disappeared completely. It was a hint of how life should be rather than a clear vision. It was hard to capture or define or even know or understand what to do with the thought. But she felt hope surge through her and knew that something deep inside her had shifted. A change in perception, a new understanding, and a new future full of promise rather than fear suddenly seemed possible.

'You'll wear a hole in the bloody carpets. Or at least you would if I had any.'

'Don't you see?' she said excitedly. 'That's where we've both been going wrong.'

'For fuck's sake, talk some sense, woman!'

She sat back down beside him, took his hands and smiled while trying to articulate her thoughts. 'We've both been looking back, trying to recapture some part of our previous lives. We think that the future is reliant on us being some pale parody of who we were before. But it's not true. Jenny Fisher died the day of the accident, as surely as if she had stopped breathing. I've been trying to resurrect her ever since. And that's the problem, jenny is dead but I am not.'

'You sound like you've been on the wacky baccy, Jen.'

'I've never been more lucid in my life. I know now what I have to do and I'm sure it is the same for you.' She didn't have all the details worked out yet, but she knew she was on the right track.

'You reckon?'

'Yes. Let go of old Steve. He is gone along with all his dreams...'

'Ain't that the truth?'

'Don't you see? You now have a blank canvas to start again.'

'In this?' he hit the side of his wheelchair.

'Yes. So you can't walk and I'm scared shitless of everything. But if we let go of the past and who we were before, then we are free to reinvent ourselves and create our new futures.'

Steve shook his head. 'Sorry sweetheart, but I think you're talking crap.'

'Think about it,' she said. 'I know I'm right and I intend to live a new and exciting life.'

'Meaning?'

'Not sure yet, but I'll let you know when I've got it all worked out.' She leant across and kissed his cheek. 'Looks like you've saved me again,' she said, feeling as though a huge and crushing weight had been lifted from her shoulders. 'I need to go home, but I'll come back later. How about I cook us dinner this evening?'

He nodded his head with a bemused expression on his face as he opened the door for her. She waved and hurried out. It was cold and bright and the path was full of puddles from last night's heavy rainfall. She focused on her house and refused to allow the customary fear to overwhelm her. She knew she would probably never be free from her anxiety, but everything would be different now because rather than fighting it and striving to be the person she was previously. From now on, she would embrace it as being a part of the new woman, the new Jenny. It made her feel in control of her life and her future for the first time since the accident.

All she had to do now was decide what she wanted to do with the rest of her life and whether Miles still had any part to play in her future.

MILES SLIPPED INTO THE HOUSE. It was quiet, and it felt empty, hollow, like his marriage, he thought bitterly. He screwed his nose up as the stench of stale sick and spilt beer hit him. The aftermath of the party was not pretty and the clearing up was down to him. Well, it could wait. Clearly Jenny didn't care, so why should he? He needed a hot shower, a change of clothes and some serious thinking time. The image of Tammy with her tumbling dark locks was embedded in his brain. He was concerned for the young woman. She had helped him, taken him in, out of the Close, and he owed her. Clearly, the girl had been worried, even scared, by the arrival of Annabel. He had no idea who Annabel was unless it was her mother, but then why didn't she just say, 'mum's home'? He could understand that no parent would appreciate finding a stranger in their daughter's bed. Maybe it was a step mum?

He turned the shower on and stripped out of his clothes. They smelt fragrant, and he smiled as he recalled Tammy's kindness. She must have put one of those softening sheets into the tumble dryer with his clothes. Jenny bought a box of them once. They looked like tissues and were supposed to make your clothes soft and smell like a summer's meadow.

Miles felt a stab of guilt when he thought about Jenny, although he had no idea why. He had done nothing wrong – well apart from spending the night with another woman, but it's not like anything happened and if it had, then it would be because she drove him to it. He had tried so hard to help her through the trauma. Jenny was the one who was destroying everything, not him.

He stepped into the hot stream of water and closed his eyes, letting the shower wash away his tensions.

Annabel walked into the apartment and knew instantly that Tammy was there. The girl was as subtle as a peacock, fanning its tail feathers.

'Hi Annabel,' Tammy said, smiling brightly and trying to look casual and innocent. A look that men found irresistible, but she knew the girl far too well and it had no effect on her.

'Last time I checked, you were living in a very nice and I should add a very expensive apartment in Bletchley.'

Tammy looked slightly guilty, but the moment quickly passed. 'It is a lovely apartment,' she agreed.

'So?'

Tammy flopped down on the sofa. 'I like it here, Annabel. Besides, I was in the centre last night. I'd had a few drinks and was feeling tired. Miranda had met up with an ex and they seemed to be reconnecting. I was bored with the view, no new talent to be seen, so I jumped into a taxi and automatically gave them this address. By the time I'd realised my mistake we were here and I really couldn't be bothered to get back in the cab and redirect him to Bletchley...' she glanced up through her lashes, looking young and vulnerable. 'I didn't think you'd mind.'

She didn't mind, really, at least not too much. It was annoying that she was paying rent on the Bletchley flat, yet it was such a struggle to keep Tammy there. Miranda was much easier to handle and had settled easily into the new place. But then Miranda was a very different character to Tammy, far more confident and mature. Annabel looked at the young girl; she should take the key away from her and put her in a taxi straight to Bletchley. She had Jack arriving soon. She had asked him to organise a van and collect the new desk she had brought in Staples. It had been her intention to remove the bed from the second room and set up an office in there. But she could have him move the sofa across a bit and put the desk in the corner of the lounge. It wouldn't hurt to have the room spare for now. If Tammy felt the need to keep coming back, then she could allow the girl a bit of time to adjust. She always felt as though Tammy was the one who needed mothering. She didn't know much about her family or her background, and Tammy never spoke about her past. 'Have you got any bookings this morning?'

'Not until twelve.'

'Cup of tea then?'

'Yes please,' Tammy said, her face lighting up with a wide smile.

. . .

Victoria hurried home. So much for never again! He looked into her eyes and the next minute; she was back in his arms. Apparently she had no willpower, at least not when it came to saying no to Brett Anderson. He smiled, and she melted quicker than a lolly in an oven. Pathetic, she thought as she pulled the handle to open the front door.

'That you love?' Dave said as she walked into the lounge.

'Yes, just popped into the shop,' she lied as he walked out of the kitchen, the unmistakable smell of bacon frying wafting behind him. He seemed more relaxed, although the bruise on his eye looked bolder, with several shades of purple and blue spattered across his eyelid and down to his cheekbone.

'What for?' he asked, glancing at her empty hands.

'Milk,' she answered. 'But they didn't have any.'

'Why? There's a new carton in the fridge.'

She wasn't good at lying, never had been. Right from being a small child, she would barely manage to utter an untruth before her mother was wagging her finger and telling her not to tell fibs. Her mum always knew, and she had no idea what it was that gave her away. Maybe it was sheer stupidity. What was the point in saying she'd gone for milk when they didn't need milk? Did she want to get caught out?

'It was hidden behind the new loaf,' he added. 'I'm always telling you not to keep bread in the fridge.'

It was an ongoing disagreement. He would take the loaf out and she would put it back in. 'Keeps it fresh for longer,' she replied, glad to move away from the milk issue.

He was about to retaliate when the doorbell rang. He left her to it. 'I'll get it,'she said. But the door swung open before she reached it and Gemma walked into the room, followed by PC Clarke.

'Gemma? Why are you at home? Are you ill?'

'As if you care,' her daughter snapped at her before stomping up the stairs.

'What's with her?' Dave asked, walking in to the lounge from the kitchen carrying a mug of coffee and a plate with a bacon sandwich on it. He stopped when he saw the uniformed policeman standing awkwardly near the front door.

'No idea,' Victoria replied, staring up the stairs. 'Dave, this is PC Clarke. I asked him to come and see you.'

'Why?' her husband asked, an icy tone in his voice.

'Victoria, that is Mrs Pickles, told me about the assault...'

'Stick with Victoria,' she said, smiling.

Dave sat down on the sofa and placed his mug on the coffee table. He bit into the bacon sandwich and ignored the policeman.

Victoria had no idea why he was being so difficult and rude. PC Clarke stood holding his notepad. With a scowl at her husband, she offered the PC a coffee, which he declined. 'Well, take a seat,' she said, pointing to one of the leather recliners. 'Dave will be ready for you in a minute.'

The two of them sat in silence while Dave finished munching on his sandwich. He licked his fingers and finally put the plate down. 'Sorry about that,' he said, not looking sorry at all. 'I was hungry.'

'That's okay, I understand. Must have been a tough night,' PC Clarke said.

'Yeah, bastards jumped me. But I don't know what you're doing here. I rang in and reported the attack last night and, like I said then, I don't know who they were. It was dark; I didn't get a look at their faces.'

'I did look for the incident report but couldn't find it. Did they give you a crime number?'

'Of course.'

'Well, if you let me have it before I go, I can go into the file and add anything we talk about today.'

'Nothing to add,' he said irritably. 'I was attacked and robbed, that's it.'

'So the attack was completely unprovoked. You had no prior interaction with them earlier in the evening and no idea who they were or why they went for you?'

Dave shook his head. 'This really is a waste of time.'

'They took his wallet.' Victoria said, wishing that her husband would be more communicative and cooperative.

'Did you have much in it?'

Dave glanced from her to the PC. 'Nah,' he said. 'Just a few quid, but obviously my cards were in it...'

'But you've cancelled them?' she checked.

He nodded his head.

'What time do you think you were attacked?' PC Clarke asked.

Dave shrugged. 'Not sure.'

'Why don't you tell me and the policeman exactly what happened step by step through the evening?'

Dave glared at her again. She got the uncomfortable feeling that he didn't want to talk, not in front of her, anyway. So it was true then. Sonia was right, and he was seeing another woman. Part of her wanted to get up and walk out, make it easier for him to speak freely. But a belligerent streak in her made her want to stay in her chair; she wanted to hear what he had to stay. Her own emotions were in over-drive and seriously conflicted. Would he lie to the policeman or was now the time for truth?

'I had to pop into work.'

Liar.

'Just had a few bits to sort out. I left there around six o'clock.' he looked at her again. 'I wanted to be back in time for the party in the Close. I stopped for a quick drink.'

'Where?'

Dave dropped his gaze and stared at his size ten boots. 'The Duck.'

'That's not your usual,' Victoria said, surprised.

'It's between here and the office. I don't go there often, but it's convenient for a a quick pint.'

'Were you on foot or in your car?' PC Clarke asked, making notes in his book.

'Car, but I only had the one.'

'You told me you were walking.'

He glared at her again, clearly annoyed by her interruption. 'I was, but a bit later.'

'Sorry,' she said, trying to work it all out in her head. Obviously, he wouldn't have walked home from work. His office is on the other side of the city. But then she didn't believe that's where he had been.

'I was on my way home when I saw a man lying on the redway,' he continued, 'he was back from the road and it was already dark, so I couldn't see much and I was almost home. I parked on the drive and was about to go indoors. But it worried me; I kept thinking he might have had a heart attack or something. So I ran back.'

'You ran?' she said, surprised. 'Why didn't you go in the car?'

He gave her the annoyed look again. 'Well, it was only back up the main road and you know how wide the grass verge is there.'

If he meant the redway to the local shop and school, then it was true the space between the road and the path was thirty, possibly forty feet at its widest.

'I wouldn't be able to see very well without getting out of the car and I thought it would be a dangerous place to leave the vehicle on the main road like that. It seemed more sensible to run back on foot. I didn't really expect to find anything. I thought maybe someone had slipped over and they'd be gone by the time I got back. Only they weren't. It was a man lying face down at the edge of the redway. I knelt down to touch him and I was jumped from behind. I guess the others must have been hiding in the bushes.'

Victoria hadn't realised how close to home it was, or how calculated the attack had been.

'You think the man on the floor was a rouse?' PC Clarke asked.

Dave nodded his head.

'We must warn people,' Victoria said. 'That's the main route to school and the shops. I'll ring Sasha, my reporter friend; get her to do a story. Someone must have seen something. That's a busy road.'

'Nobody saw anything. It was dark!' Dave snapped angrily, his voice rising. 'Why do you want to panic people?'

'It's not causing a panic; it's making them aware of a potential risk.'

'I'm sure it was a one off, so stop making it into a big drama.'

Victoria stood up. 'Well at the very least I'm going to tell Gemma not to walk along that way after dark, or do you consider me telling our own daughter to be cautious as me being a drama queen as well!' She had no idea why Dave was getting so angry with her.

PC Clarke glanced up at Victoria and gave her what seemed to be a part sympathetic and part reassuring look. 'Attacks like this are very rare and it's probably best to leave it to us to make any announcements to the press,' he said.

Dave also stood up. 'I'm going for a walk. I need to clear my head.'

'I do have some more questions, though.'

'Yeah, well, I've had enough,' Dave said to the policeman. 'I'll come down to the station when I feel better. Although I've told you everything all ready.'

Victoria gave PC Clarke an apologetic look as they heard the front door slam shut.

JENNY LOOKED AROUND HER. The place was a tip. The debris from the party hadn't been touched. A part of her wanted to leave it to her husband to sort out, being as he was the idiot who had thrown open the doors to their lovely new home to a bunch of complete strangers. But even though she was still annoyed with him, she also felt sorry for him. She knew that, however misguided, he must have genuinely thought that she would like a party. The logic of his decision eluded her completely. Even before the accident, she had never been a party loving type of girl and surprises had always seemed a bit overrated. She could only conclude that it was desperation on his part. So she threw the windows open to eliminate the stale stench of beer, sick, body odour and garlic, and then pulled out a black bin sack from the under-stairs cupboard. She'd start with the rubbish and then see what could be done with the carpets. She had already spotted a dark red stain on the floor near the stairs, which she was pretty sure was wine.

She had no idea where Miles was and didn't feel inclined to look for him. Eventually, he would have to be faced; she wasn't in any hurry to deal with his hurt and his anger. She piled the party debris into the sack and thought about the angry young woman who had barged her way into Steve's flat. What was that all about? Clearly, the girl was upset, but Steve was vulnerable, and still coming to terms with his new situation. He didn't need a stroppy wheelchair woman giving him a mouthful.

The front door opened, and Brett stood in the doorway.

'Another run?' she said, smiling at him.

'Best thing in the world for banishing the demons.'

'You have demons?'

He lent down to remove his trainers; they were damp and slightly muddy. 'We all have demons, Jen.'

He said it lightly, but it worried her. She always thought of her big brother as being confident and carefree. Had something happened? Was it the mystery woman?

'Better hit the shower,' he said.

She screwed up her nose. 'Can't argue with that.'

He paused on the stairs and turned to face her. 'Are you okay, Jen?'

'Yes,' she said. 'Surprisingly enough, I am.'

'I'm sorry I didn't tell you about the party.'

She shook her head. She knew what her husband was like. He would have made sure that Brett felt unable to do so. 'Do you have plans to go home anytime soon?'

'Oh God, I really have upset you.'

'Don't be daft. That's not what I mean. I don't want rid of you. I'm just deciding what I need to do next.' Which was the truth. A tiny seed of a plan was planted inside her; she just wasn't sure what it would grow into yet.

He came down the steps and pulled her into a hug. 'Go. Stay, I'll do whatever you need me to do.'

She pulled back and grinned. 'Well, right now, I really need you to take that shower.'

Jenny watched him go upstairs and then she returned to the

cleaning. She had a lot to think about and some big decisions to make.

Gemma went cautiously down the stairs. Dad had gone out, and the policeman had left, but she had no idea where her mum was and she absolutely, completely and utterly did not want to see her. She had pretended to be asleep when her mother came to see her a short while ago. She had nothing to say to her and couldn't even bear to face her. So she edged down each step, looking and listening. Maybe she had gone out? It was her day off, but she could have sneaked off to see the man whose face she was snogging earlier.

Her stomach did a strange somersault, and she felt as though she were about to throw up again. She stood still and took a few deep breaths, and the nausea slowly eased away. She needed a pregnancy test; she had to know. Why did her stupid mother have to ruin everything like that? Mums weren't supposed to cheat. They were meant to be strong and supportive and born again virgins. She shuddered at the very idea of her mother having sex. It wasn't right. Old people shouldn't do it, it was way too gross.

She heard the unmistakable click of the washing machine door as it closed, so her mum was in the kitchen. She ran quickly from the stairs across the hall and out through the front door. She wanted to slam it shut. There was something satisfying about the thud that a slammed door made. It was like shouting 'stuff you!' loudly at the world. But since that would result in her nosy, cheating mother, chasing after her and demanding to know where she was going, she resisted the urge and closed it carefully and quietly so it barely creaked.

Gemma ran up the Close and when she reached the apartment block, she pressed the buzzer, hoping that Tammy was home. She hadn't forgotten the last encounter with Annabel when the woman made it clear that she should stay away. But she was desperate.

Unfortunately, it was Annabel's soft voice that responded.

'It's Gemma...'

'Gemma, I thought we agreed you weren't coming round again.'

'I know, but please Annabel, I need help.'

Gemma could picture the woman as she stood beside the intercom, deciding whether to let her in. 'Please,' she repeated, glancing down the Close, afraid that any minute her mum was going to be out looking for her.

The door buzzed as the lock disengaged and with relief Gemma pushed it open and hurried to the open the front door of flat number two.

'Hey baby,' Tammy pulled her into a hug even before she was through the door. 'Are you in trouble again?'

She was relieved that Tammy was at the flat. Annabel smiled at her and there was kindness in her eyes, but Gemma knew that the older woman didn't want her there. 'I'm sorry,' she said, looking at Annabel. 'I didn't know who else to turn to.'

'Your mother is not at home?'

Gemma let the tears that she'd been fighting all morning finally fall. Tammy led her to the sofa, and she sat down. Annabel handed her a tissue. She dabbed at her eyes and then blew her nose. 'I think I'm pregnant,' she blurted out.

If she was expecting horror or shock or some kind of moral outrage, she quickly realised that she was in the wrong place. Tammy put a supportive arm around her shoulder and Annabel left the room, returning seconds later with a test kit.

'Only one way to find out,' Annabel said, handing it to her.

Gemma stared at the packet.

'You just pee on the stick,' Tammy said.

'I'm afraid...'

'No baby, it doesn't hurt.'

'Not of the test, of the result.'

Annabel's stance softened. 'One thing at a time,' she said. 'Test first, then we know what we're dealing with.'

Gemma stood up, and gripping the test kit tightly, she headed for the bathroom.

. . .

Victoria finished cleaning the kitchen and put the kettle on. She would make a hot chocolate and take it up to Gemma, to see if she felt any better after a sleep. She had no idea why her daughter seemed so upset, nor why she was at home and not at school.

Dave had gone. She had didn't know where. The car was still on the drive, so unless he'd called himself a taxi or jumped on a bus; he was somewhere close by. Did his other woman live locally? Was she someone who used the same local shop? Did they pass by each other in the chilled food aisle? What if she lived in Jasmine Close? Maybe Dave had met her, and that was why he changed his mind about buying the new house. It had nothing to do with the walks and getting a dog, but everything to do with the location of his mistress.

Annoyed with herself and her thoughts, she pulled a mug from the cupboard and poured the sachet of chocolate powder into it. Aside from the fact that she was being neurotic and silly, who was she to judge or complain? She was no longer a faithful, loving wife. She had cheated on her husband and spent the night with another man and it should be her that was full of guilt and remorse. But Brett had made her feel alive and special, feelings that had been long lost. Was that how it was for Dave? Had he turned to another woman because their relationship was stale and unsatisfying? She added mini marshmallows to the hot drink and picked the mug up. Everything had changed and she couldn't pretend otherwise. The real casualty would be their daughter; it worried her that Gemma wouldn't be able to understand how everything that gave her life stability was suddenly torn down and in tatters.

She knocked on her daughter's door and when she received no answer; she pushed it open and went inside. The room was empty.

Back downstairs she tried ringing Gemma's mobile phone, but it went straight to the answerphone. She decided that since she had been deserted by her husband and her daughter, she might as well take advantage of the car being available to her. Besides, she was worried that if she stayed alone in the house for too long, she might be tempted to go looking for Brett, and that was not a good idea.

She put her shoes on and grabbed a jacket from the rack in the hall. It was cold outside but MK shopping centre was completely enclosed. It was a huge Mall and when it was built it had been the largest in Europe, although it had been overtaken by newer, bigger centres since then. All she had to do was to get from the car park to one of the multiple entrances and then she would be warm, so no point in wrapping herself up in a thick coat and scarf.

Victoria reached into the bowl on top of the shoe rack cabinet for the car keys and was shocked when they weren't in there. It was the household key's home and Dave was always nagging her and Gemma to place their keys in the bowl whenever they came inside the house. He was certainly meticulous about putting his own in there. So where were they? She opened the door and looked outside to double check that his car was actually parked in the drive. Why take the keys and not the car? It wasn't even as though his door key was on the same ring.

Once upon a time, they had two keys for the car, a set each. But one was long gone, lost during a day trip to Brighton, a rare occasion when Dave had done something spontaneous and exciting. He woke up and saw that it was a beautiful warm sunny day, probably one of the first of the year, if she remembered rightly. He pulled a sickie and persuaded her to do the same. They kept Gemma off school for the day and they drove to the coast. It had been almost perfect until it was time to leave and come home and he discovered his keys were missing. A frustrating and frantic search of the beach and the amusements and the café they eat in failed to retrieve them. Luckily she had her keys in her handbag and so they were able to drive home, but his mood along with the day was ruined. Somehow, he had made it her fault that his keys were lost.

She shook away the memory and felt in his jacket pocket. His briefcase was on the floor, neatly pushed against the wall beside the shoe cabinet. She knelt down and pressed in the combination. At first the lock didn't release, so she tried again and this time it worked. He was so predictable if it wasn't her date of birth, then it was Gemma's. She clicked the latches and lifted the lid; the keys were there on top of a pile of work papers and beside his wallet. The same wallet that he told her had been stolen.

Why had he lied? It made no sense. She picked it up and opened it. There was no money inside but his cards, the ones that he said had been taken, were in there. So if he hadn't been robbed, was he even attacked? The bruises came from somewhere.

Victoria put the wallet and the keys back in the briefcase and closed the lid down. She had no idea what to do next. Did she confront him? Or was it best to wait and see how far his lies would take them?

Her desire to go shopping had disappeared. She put the kettle on and picked her phone up to text Sonia, hoping her neighbour would be free for a coffee. She really needed someone to talk to.

EPISODE EIGHTEEN
JASMINE CLOSE - SERIES ONE

Miles could hear his wife downstairs. She was cleaning and sorting out the mess from last night's failed party. He should really go down and help. He even got as far as opening the bedroom door. But he paused, torn between his desire to set things right with her and his anger towards her for making such a fool of him. Throw into the already confused state of his mind a heavy dose of guilt. He closed the door and retreated back into the bedroom.

After all, he organised the party. Surely it was only fair that she cleaned up after it. Of course, he knew he wasn't being fair. For some unfathomable reason, she hadn't appreciated the trouble he'd gone to at all. So Brett had been right. Her step-brother knew and understood his wife better than he did. What did that say about him or his marriage?

The image of Tammy flashed into his mind and he let it linger, savouring the moment fondly for a few seconds. He still didn't understand what had happened that morning. He wanted to talk to her, to thank her again for helping him last night and to make sure that she was all right and he was worried about her. Had she'd got into trouble because of him? He felt concerned that she had seemed so fearful of Annabel and the more he thought about it, the more sure he became that the woman couldn't be her mother. Maybe a flat mate or older sister? He really didn't know, and he needed to see Tammy again and talk to her just to settle things in his mind.

Of course, wanting to see her again had nothing to do with the fact that she was stunning and sexy and had shown an interest in him that had been flattering and exciting.

He heard the vacuum cleaner and hoped that Jenny had managed to remove the stain from the carpet. She could be a bit shoddy when it came to cleaning. He reached for the door handle again, but let his hand fall away. He wasn't ready to face her yet. How was he going to explain where he had been all night? He would have to think of a cover story to tell her. It wasn't really lying. Well, obviously it was. But it didn't count because he hadn't done anything wrong. It was just easier to make up a story than try to explain how he spent the night in a young woman's bed. It was a small white lie, a tiny untruth offered for the sake of his marriage, if he still had one. No need to hurt or upset Jenny any more than he already had.

He was surprised and relieved that she hadn't already sought him out to demand to know where he spent the night. Not that Jenny was likely to demand, not her style. She would ask him calmly while her beautiful eyes assessed him. She didn't like confrontation, but she was very perceptive and capable of seeing straight through any lie that he could come up with. He lay down on the bed and closed his eyes. He would go down soon, just have a rest first and work out what to say. If he was lucky, he might not have to tell her anything at all. It was possible that she had slept in the backroom and wasn't even aware of his all night-time absence.

VICTORIA KNOCKED ON THE DOOR, but the house was silent. Sonia obviously wasn't home. She listened carefully, but Casper didn't bark and the boy's laughter and chatter were absent. Maybe they'd gone for a walk.

She shivered and wished that she had grabbed a coat. What was she thinking coming out without one?

'Vic...'

Victoria turned and saw Barry waving at her. She didn't want to see him and certainly didn't want to chat, but he was a mate and he couldn't be ignored. She walked across the Close, hugging her arms around her to protect herself from the cold November chill.

'You alright love?' he asked, looking genuinely concerned. 'I saw the police car outside your house.'

She saw Tom hovering behind Barry. She smiled and waved, but he looked away. Maybe he hadn't seen her; Tom was always ready with a flirty smile or a cheeky wink. 'Dave was mugged last night,' she said, not knowing anymore if it was true or not.

'Nooo! That's terrible.'

Tom glanced her way again, just briefly, before hurrying off. Perhaps he was having a bad day, she thought.

'Is he hurt?' Barry asked.

'Bruised, but otherwise okay.'

'Shocking, isn't it? See, I said we should have gone to that desert island, no muggings allowed out there.'

Victoria smiled and shivered.

Barry pulled her into a brief awkward hug, then he let go and rubbed his hands on her arms, warming them.

'Blimey Barry, what was that for?'

'Just to let you know you're not alone, love,' he said gruffly.

She was touched, really touched, and smiled warmly back at him. 'Thanks,' she said, meaning it. 'But I'm okay.'

'Not working?'

'No, it's my day off. Mandy's covering.'

'That's lucky. Your husband is probably glad to have you around.'

'Yes, very lucky,' she said, thinking that since he had disappeared, there wasn't anything that she could do for him. Besides, she did not know what was going on. Clearly the bruises had come from somewhere, but since his wallet was in the briefcase, the multi-coloured addition to his face had not come from a robbery.

She said goodbye to Barry and saw Sonia walking down the redway. Casper was on a lead with no evidence of his limp, so at least he seemed fully recovered.

'Where are the boys?' she asked, crossing the Close to meet her neighbour.

'Just dropped them at the nursery,' Sonia replied. 'I get three hours' quiet time now. Coffee?'

Victoria nodded and followed her inside.

'Spill...' Sonia said as soon as they were through the door.

'How do you know?' Victoria replied, looking at Sonia as though she were a witch or a wizard with magical powers.

Sonia laughed. 'Vic, out of your work uniform, you are like an open book.'

Victoria frowned. 'Really?'

'Really. Right now you are wrestling with worry and guilt,' she grinned. 'And I bet I know what that's all about!' she walked into the kitchen and put the kettle on. 'But there's something else as well, something to do with Dave. You found out any more about his mistress?'

Victoria didn't know how Sonia saw through her so easily but the fact was she needed to talk and get another opinion about what was going on so she told her neighbour all about Dave and his black eye and the police and the mystery with the wallet.

'Well, it's obvious, isn't it?' Sonia said.

'Not to me.'

'She's married.'

'Who?'

'His bit of fluff. She's a married lady and last night, while they were enjoying a bit of illicit naughty nookie, her hubby came home and kicked butt...'

'No.'

'I reckon. I mean, it makes sense. Dave could hardly tell you the truth so he made up the story to cover his arse, only he hadn't expected you to call in PC Clarke or to go searching through his briefcase.'

Victoria sipped her coffee. Was Sonia right? It did make sense? Was his black eye from his mistress's husband? She finished her drink and returned home, hoping that Dave was back so that they could talk. But he wasn't, and neither was Gemma. As she was wondering what to do with her day, her phone rang. It was her sales manager, asking if she could work after all. Mandy, the woman who usually covered her days off, had just taken a call from the school to say her daughter was being sent home unwell. If Victoria was honest with herself, it was a bit of a relief to have something to do, so she agreed to do it. Feeling totally fed up with her family, she got herself ready for work and wrote a big note to her husband and her daughter saying that they needed to talk, then she went off to work.

JENNY LOOKED AROUND HER. It wasn't too bad. The stain was still visible, but only just and at least the awful smell had gone. She knew Miles was upstairs; she heard him in the bedroom and he must have been aware of the fact that she was home. If he hadn't heard her banging around, he certainly couldn't have missed the noise of the hoover. She didn't understand why he hadn't come down and demanded to know where she had been all night. It wasn't like him to sulk or to avoid the unpleasant. If he was angry with her, and surely he must be, then he would confront her immediately and usually forcefully. It wasn't that she wanted a showdown, but she knew he had to be faced at some point.

She heard a creak on the stairs and went out into the hall, but it was her brother, not her husband, who headed down towards her. She felt a mixture of relief and irritation.

'You okay Jen?'

She nodded her head, debating whether or not to march upstairs and force the issue.

'Can I do anything?'

'No, think I've finished in here,' she said.

'Yeah, so I see you've done a good job.'

She knew Miles wouldn't think so. He would fret and worry about the remaining non-stain and dash out to buy every available product, and if none of them worked, he would no doubt replace the carpet. She realised she didn't want to stay and see him. She needed to get out. 'You busy Brett? Will you take me shopping?'

He looked surprised. Probably not as much as she was, though. Where had those words come from?

'You sure?'

'Yes... No...' what she'd meant to ask him was if he would go shopping for her. But since the request was out there, maybe she should try. She usually ordered online or waited until Miles was home and sent him off with a list. But she needed stuff for dinner that evening; she wanted to do something special for Steve as she felt he really needed someone to show they cared for him.

Brett took her hand. 'no pressure,' he said gently. 'Give me a list and I can get whatever you want, or I can stay close and hold your hand if you feel up to getting it yourself.'

'I'll try,' she said, making a decision.

'Okay then,' he picked up the keys to her Beetle and smiled reassuringly. 'Where to?'

'M&S,' she said.

'The shopping centre?'

She thought for a second or two and then shook her head. 'No, let's go to the smaller centre at Kingston.'

'By Tesco's?'

She nodded. The food hall was nothing like as big, but it wouldn't be as busy as the main shops in the centre. She felt she stood more chance at Kingston. She took her coat from the hook in the hall and followed him out. She walked to the car and felt stronger and more confident than she had felt for many months. Whether she managed to get the shopping, it felt pretty momentous, and she even wanted to give it a try. One baby step at a time, she thought, strapping herself in.

GEMMA LET herself into the house and saw her mum's note straight away. She felt a surge of anger towards her mother, but remembering

Annabel's words, she tried to let it go. It wasn't easy. As she saw it, her mother was threatening to break up the family, and that scared her silly. Who would she live with? Would she have to choose between her parents? She felt the sting of hot tears behind her lids. They might be very annoying, but she loved them both. It simply wasn't fair. Why did the stupid running man have to come between them and ruin everything?

She heard her phone beep and pulled it out of her pocket. She had been getting calls and texts from Abby all morning. They were all the same, demanding to know the answer to two questions – had she done the test and what was the result? She checked the time on her phone. Abby would be in double English, no point ringing her now until lunchtime. Tammy had hugged her when she left. 'Go home baby and snuggle up in bed with a hot water bottle and a soft teddy bear.'

Gemma decided to take her advice. She was lucky to have Tammy and Annabel; she didn't know what she would have done without them. And even though the older woman didn't want her there, she had been really kind and helpful. The three of them had gathered together, waiting for the little box on the stick to do something. Both Annabel and Tammy had held her hands, and all three had let out a collective sigh of relief when it showed up as being negative.

'So why am I do I feel sick and dizzy?' she had asked.

'Probably stress, sweetie,' Annabel said, putting a comforting arm around her shoulders and hugging her tight. 'You've had a bit of a time of it recently and this could be your body telling you to take time out. Or it could be a bug, easy enough to pick up anytime, let alone when you're a bit run down.'

Gemma burst into tears, surprising them and her.

'What? You wanted to be pregnant?' Tammy gasped. 'But you're far too young…'

'Of course not.' Annabel answered for her. 'It's just the relief, isn't it?'

Gemma managed to nod her head while wiping her eyes and

then blew her nose. 'Mum's cheating on my dad,' she suddenly blurted out.

'I doubt that baby,' Tammy said screwing her nose up in distaste.

'Why?'

'Well, last time I saw her, she seemed pretty uptight and not at all like a woman who was getting plenty.'

Gemma stared at Tammy in shocked surprise. Her mum was just her mum. She couldn't get her head around her having sex. It really was too gross and way too weird.

Annabel gave Tammy a glare that seemed to say, 'shut up.' Tammy got the message and rested back on the sofa, her arms folded across her chest. 'Why do you think she is?' Annabel asked gently.

'I saw her kiss him.'

'Who?'

'Not sure, he runs a lot and I think he lives in the Close. He has an accent...'

'American?'

'I guess,' she said with a shrug.

Annabel and Tammy exchanged a look.

'What?'

'Don't read too much into a kiss,' Annabel said.

'It wasn't a peck on the cheek.'

'Even so, don't go judging too quickly or too harshly. Adults have their issues as well; romance and heartache aren't reserved only for teenagers, you know.'

'But what about dad?' Gemma said, not really getting what Annabel was trying to say. Surely she couldn't be suggesting that it was okay?

'Do your mum and dad get on?' Tammy asked.

'Of course,' she replied quickly enough. But a little worm of doubt crept into her mind. Did they? Dad seemed to be out all the time and mum was more stressed than usual. They never went out together, never even really stayed in together either. In fact, if she thought about it, they rarely even seemed to talk. She just assumed that was how marriage worked.

Annabel smiled at her. 'All I'm saying is that no one ever knows what really goes on inside a marriage. They might both be really unhappy.'

'Yeah, your dad could be playing away himself,' Tammy said cheerfully but unhelpfully.

'What?'

'We don't know that,' Annabel said, throwing Tammy the look again. 'But it is possible that he has someone else, just as it's possible that your mum has found a bit of romance with the mysterious American.'

'Oh, this is just too awful,' Gemma cried, feeling as though her world was collapsing.

'Hey, just remember that none of it is about you. Both your parents love you. If they are having marital issues, then it is for them to sort out. Parents make mistakes and screw up just the same as kids do.'

With Annabel's words still playing out loud in her brain, Gemma walked upstairs and into her bedroom. She slipped out of her school uniform and put her pyjamas on, then she crawled under the duvet and hugged the battered old teddy that she'd had since she was a baby.

'I'M SORRY I CAN'T,' Jenny said, clutching the trolley as though she were clinging onto a life raft while adrift at sea.

'It's okay,' Brett said with as much reassurance as he could manage. 'Come on, I'll take you back to the car.'

She paused, looking around her with a mixture of panic and determination. He could see how much she wanted to do this and wished he could make it easier for her. He hated to see her so conflicted. She was close to tears, but still she stood still as the battle raged on within her. He waited, not wanting to add to her turmoil. He wanted to get back and see Victoria, but no way was he going to rush his sister. She needed his help, and he was there for her, no matter how long it took. He felt a surge of anger towards his brother-in-law. Why couldn't Miles be more thoughtful and supportive?

'I so want to do this,' Jenny said.

'You've come this far. Why not be happy with that and try again tomorrow? Get a bit further each day and you'll soon have it beaten. If you wait in the car, I'll go in and get the shopping for you.'

'I felt ready. Besides, it's for Steve. I wanted to show him that we both still have lives worth living. Yet here I am, unable to step inside a shop.'

Brett hadn't realised that the trip was actually for the benefit of the wheelchair guy. He wondered what Miles would think of that. He could totally see how Jenny would feel connected to him. They both had demons to hide from. Miles was a fool for keeping them apart. The fact that she was trying so hard for Steve showed he was the one who could actually help her find a way through the maze of her suffering.

'I'm cooking him dinner tonight. He's a bit down. You can join us if you like. Looks as though you're going to have to get the shopping for me.'

Brett assumed that the invitation wouldn't be extended to her husband as well. He was curious about the guy in the chair, and he and would like to meet him, but he wasn't ready to commit his evening. He was holding out for Victoria, in the hope that she would let him take her out. 'This is really important to you, isn't it?' he said.

She nodded her head. She looked so disappointed in herself, and he wanted to help her. He looked around him. Even though the store was smaller than the one in the centre, it was still busy. It was alongside a Tesco superstore and a row of other high street favourites. The car park was packed and shoppers were dashing around. It was mid-November and people were buying for Christmas. It wasn't really surprising that his sister was struggling. 'Come on,' he said, prying her hands off the trolley. 'I've got an idea.'

He led her back to the car and started the engine.

'Brett, I need some shopping. You'll have to go in for me.'

'Not yet,' he said, indicating and pulling out of the car park.

'What are you up to?'

He glanced at her and smiled. 'wait and see.' He drove back towards the city centre.

'It'll be worse at the big M&S.'

He ignored her and went along the dual carriageway to the roundabout. Instead of turning right and into the approach road to the centre, he went all the way around so that he was going back the way he had just come from, but on the other side of the road. He indicated and pulled into a gas station or petrol garage, as the Brits called them. He didn't stop at the pump, but instead drove to the front of the forecourt and into one of the empty parking spaces. He turned to Jenny and grinned at her. 'Well what do you think?'

She looked at the entrance. It was a BP garage with a Marks and Spencer mini mart inside and other than one elderly gent paying for his petrol; it was empty.

'I know it won't have the same range as the bigger food stores, but anything you can't get here, I can run into the centre and pick up for you.'

'I think you are the best brother in the world,' she said, looking delighted.

VICTORIA OPENED the Show Home door and said goodbye to the couple that she hoped would come back tomorrow and sign up for an off plan apartment. She saw her husband as he drove past her out of the Close; he didn't even glance her way. She knew he couldn't have missed her note. She had stuck it on the bottom of the bannister, so it was in plain view the minute anyone went in the door. But he had chosen to ignore it and had driven off without bothering to say goodbye. Had he gone to work, or was he off to meet his mistress? Either way, it was time for her to face the fact that they could be heading for divorce. No way could she afford to stay in her lovely new home. It would have to be sold; she had no idea where she and Gemma would go. There might be enough money to look at buying a shared ownership property. They were lucky in Milton Keynes that there were quite a few around. With her share of the small amount of equity they had in the house and a modest mortgage, she could buy a thirty-percent share in a property and pay either the council or housing association rent on the rest.

They had a few small investments and modest savings that could be split and would help a bit. It wasn't what she wanted, but what choice did she have? She knew that shared ownership properties tended to be snapped up and their house would have to be sold first. She had a few contacts in the local estate agencies; maybe she should start putting out feelers.

Victoria picked up her mobile phone and tried ringing her daughter; she wasn't at all surprised when it went straight to answerphone. She still had no idea why Gemma was home from school or where she had disappeared to earlier. Things between them had seemed a bit better lately, and she was disappointed that her daughter was back to shutting her out again.

The door opened and Brett walked in. He didn't say a word, just strode straight up to her and kissed her firmly on the mouth. Of course, she wanted to push him off and step away, but she didn't. Instead, she leaned into him and kissed him back.

'That wasn't sensible,' she said several minutes later. 'Anyone could have seen us.'

'But they didn't,' he replied, pouring himself a coffee from the percolator. 'Besides, I've just seen your husband drive away.'

'My daughters at home though – well maybe,' she added, not at all sure. 'Anyway, that's not even the point. I work here. A customer could come in, or one of the workers or Barry the foreman.'

He sat down on the comfy chairs designed to make the customers feel at home. 'Okay, I get it. No more kisses at work; it's just that I'd been thinking about doing that ever since the brief kiss on the sidewalk this morning.'

She wanted to say no more kisses anywhere ever, but couldn't make the words form.

'I'm taking you out tonight,' he said as though it were a statement with no question attached.

'I can't...'

'Sure you can. You make up an excuse and you leave.'

'That easy?.'

'Yep, if you want it to be.'

'Where?' she asked, even though she had no intention of going out with him.

'You'll have to come and find out,' he said, standing up and handing her the coffee mug. 'And for goodness's sake, give me your phone number, woman.' He grinned and stroked her hand, his eyes darkening as they lit up with desire.

She knew that she shouldn't, but her fingers had written her number down and handed the paper to him as if her brain had no control over what they did.

She watched him go, and even before he was gone from sight; she had a text message from him with an x. It was madness. What was she doing? But it was also wonderful to have someone actually taking an interest in her. Was this what it was like to be addicted to something? You know you should stay away; you know it's dangerous and people will get hurt, yet you keep going back for more.

MILES FINALLY MADE the decision to knock on the door. Well, more accurately, press the intercom buzzer. He had to see her and make sure that she was alright. It took a while for anyone to respond and when they did, he knew the soft female voice that said 'hello' was not hers.

'Umm, can I see Tammy please?' he said, feeling like a stuttering schoolboy. His mouth had gone dry and his hands were sweaty. He told himself it was because he was concerned for her.

'Who is this?' the soft voice asked.

'Umm, just a friend.'

'Well, I'm sorry, friend, but she isn't here.'

'Really?'

'Yes, really.'

'Umm, where is she?'

'I'm sorry, but you'll have to contact her directly.'

The intercom went dead, and he was left staring at the wall. He thought of buzzing again and asking for her number, but if he was the friend he said he was, then he would definitely already have it. Then he thought about saying he'd lost her phone and her number along with it, but that sounded lame even to his ears.

He stepped away from the door and looked around him. The builders were all hard at work, making the most of a day without rain. A couple of the lads waved at him as if they knew him. They seemed to be sniggering, and he realised they were the workman he had seen from Tammy's window that morning. He looked away, embarrassed, but they did give him an idea.

Miles walked down the alleyway that separated the apartments and the houses and led to the wasteland at the back. There were no builders around and so he hurried quickly along the back of the apartments until he reached the back of flat two. The curtains were drawn and he could see that the lights were on inside. It was only mid-afternoon, but already darkness was creeping across the sky. He didn't believe that Tammy wasn't home. He wasn't sure what was going on, but he knew he had to see for himself.

The rear apartments had small patios and a fence panel between each one, offering six feet of privacy if the occupants wanted to sit outside. But beyond that, they were not fenced in. He had no idea if they were even allowed to put up more fencing. After all, they were flats, not houses, and so private gardens were not expected.

It made it easy for him to get right up to the windows. He knew from the morning which one was hers since she had made him climb out of it to escape Annabel. He pressed his face against the pane of glass and squinted into the room. It was empty; if Tammy was in the apartment, then she wasn't in the bedroom.

Tiptoeing, he edged along to the French doors, which he assumed led to the lounge. The curtains were closed, but there was a gap about half an inch where they didn't meet. Once again, he pressed his face up against the glass pane and stared into the room.

He saw a tall man with his back to him and his arms around a woman, and they were kissing passionately. It wasn't Tammy. The woman was tall, almost as tall as the man, and she was blond, not dark. He searched the room with his eyes until, accepting defeat, he returned to the kissing couple. Only they weren't kissing anymore. The woman had pulled back and was staring at the window and the gap in the curtain. She was looking directly at him.

Miles saw the man swing round as the woman shouted and pointed. He stood up straight, and he ran. He heard the key turn in the lock and the French doors slid open. He dived behind the fence panel at the end of the row as he heard footsteps pursuing him. He knew he was going to be caught and his mind was frantically searching for a valid reason for being what they would surely think of him as being a pervert or a burglar. Either way, he was in big trouble.

Then, just when he thought his embarrassment was about to peak, he heard the man swear and the unmistakable hiss from a cat.

Miles stood still and listened.

'What?' he heard the woman call out. 'You alright?'

'Yeah, nan's bloody cat leapt out at me and I tripped in a rut. Think I've twisted my ankle.'

'Bugger! Did you get him?'

'Nah, he's gone.'

Miles kept very still and as quiet as he could. He heard them retreating back into the apartment and when he thought it was safe, he slipped quickly back to the alley and hurried home.

JENNY PUT her small overnight case on the floor and the groceries on the kitchen unit. 'Hope you like steak?' she asked.

'Shit Jenny, you know I'm a vegetarian.'

She stared at him in horror, and then she saw the mischief in his eyes. 'You rotter,' she said. 'I nearly believed you.'

He smiled, and she was glad that she had gone to so much effort for him. However bad her situation was for her, she knew it was so much worse for him.

'Can I help?'

'No. I'm doing this as a thank you for letting me stay. You relax.'

He switched the TV on, and she got to work. She still hadn't seen Miles. He had been out when she got home from the shops. She had packed a few things into a bag, then walked up to Steve's with the shopping. She had thought about leaving her him a note but decided against it. She had a phone; he could ring her if he wanted to talk. Besides, he could work out easily enough where she was or he could ask Brett. She had told her brother that he didn't have to lie for her. If Miles asked him, then he could tell her husband where she was.

She looked up in surprise as the doorbell rang; surely she hadn't conjured him up with her thoughts. Steve opened the door and Mary's grandson Jack stepped into the flat.

'Sorry to disturb you, but I'm just telling everyone to watch out and lock up properly because I think someone was snooping around the apartments earlier.'

Jenny saw the look of pain and panic that flitted briefly across Steve's face.

'Thanks mate,' he said, quickly hiding it. 'I'll make sure I lock up.'

'It's probably nothing,' Jack added, as though he picked up on something in Steve.

'Yeah, better to be warned, though.'

'Thanks,' Jenny said, as Jack nodded his head and left through the still open door.

Steve closed it straight away with his remote button. He gave her a smile that she assumed he meant to be reassuring, but she saw his pain and felt a huge surge of anger against the bastard who had broken in and robbed him.

'Glass of wine?' she said, holding up a red Merlot.

'Hell yeah,' he said. 'Make mine a bottle.'

MARY FINISHED HER NIGHTCAP, then locked the door and turned the lights out. She climbed into bed and pulled the covers tight around her. She wasn't worried, not about some stupid, cowardly burglar. Jack had been round earlier and checked the apartment, making sure all her windows were properly closed and bolted. Obviously it had been good to see him, but of course she knew now how far the relationship with the flashy floosy had gone. He was practically living with her and apparently she had given him a job as well. But Mary hadn't liked the way he'd been so evasive when she asked what the job was.

'Just odds and sods, Gran,' he'd said. 'Helping out with stuff, that's all.'

Did he think she was senile? She knew what went on in the flat and who the woman was. 'Don't get hurt Jack.' She said seriously. She knew that he was normally the heart breaker but even he was out of his depth with this one. The woman was a Madam. What was he playing out? How could he get himself involved with a tart like her?

'Hey, don't worry about me Gran, I'm a big boy, I can take care of myself.'

'She'll eat you for breakfast!' she said sharply, unable to stop the words from tumbling out.

He grinned and gave her a hug. 'Lock the door behind me,' he said. 'I'll pop in and see you in the morning.'

Of course, that was the only good thing about his liaison, she thought. Having him so close meant he could drop in to see her more. She just hated the idea of him being hurt by the big-busted, cold-hearted hussy. She closed her eyes and let her tiredness wash over her. Life was an effort nowadays, and sleep was always welcome.

She had no idea how long she'd slept for or what the time was. All she knew was that someone was in her flat. While all her limbs and senses were ageing and fading, her hearing was still sharp and although she hadn't been in the flat very long, it was enough time to familiarise herself with the sound of the place, and something was not right. She knew every creak and groan that the apartment made. As she lay still and silent in the dark, she knew that someone was in her kitchen.

EPISODE NINETEEN
JASMINE CLOSE - SERIES ONE

Annabel couldn't sleep, a situation made worse by the terrible racket going on outside. It sounded like a cat fight, only worse. As if all the felines in the neighbourhood had gathered together for a night time bundle. She tried to bury her head in the pillow to block out the noise, but it didn't help anymore than Jack's snoring did.

She gave him a sharp nudge in his side, which made him stop for a moment, but a few seconds later, the annoying nasal cacophony started over again. She groaned and gave up remembering all the reasons why she was still single and why she enjoyed sleeping alone. At that moment, she felt tired and grumpy enough to dump him and if he opened his eyes, that's exactly what she would do. She walked around the bed and looked down at him, smiling despite her irritation. Snoring aside, she was having fun and enjoying him being around. So she pulled the covers higher around his neck and then left the bedroom.

The cat cries in the lounge sounded even louder. She walked to the window and opened the curtains, looking out into the darkness. She couldn't see very much since the area was still undeveloped, and clouds mostly obscured the moon and there was no street lighting.

She left the windows and put the kettle on. Maybe a camomile would help. She put the tea bag into a mug and realised she was kidding herself. The only way that she would get any sleep was if she shut the cats up. She debated waking Jack up and sending him out into the cold, but decided that since she was the one being disturbed by it, then she should deal with it.

She grabbed her coat and put it on top of her short silky nightdress, and pulled on her flat walking boots. She searched for and failed to find a torch and went out armed with the light on her mobile phone and the light that came on as she unlocked the patio door and slipped out into the dark. The chill hit her like a slap round the face and she almost retreated straight back inside, but the cat's cries were piteous and she needed to get some sleep.

Annabel hesitated for a second when she remembered the face at the glass earlier in the evening, but she was pretty sure it was a peeping Tom who had heard the stories about the goings on at the apartment and was hoping to grab a quickie free porn show. She didn't feel he posed any risk, although Jack had disagreed and insisted on warning all the neighbours. He didn't know the business of brothels like she did. Weirdos, stalkers, and peeping toms were all part of the package.

It was easy enough to follow the cries of an animal in distress. It sounded as though the fight was over and only the loser remained. She trod carefully, aware that the rain and the diggers had created an uneven surface full of ruts and crevices and she didn't want to end up with an ankle injury like Jack.

The noise was getting louder. She used her phone to see the way ahead and jumped, startled, as a beam of light caught the eyes of a fox. It was very close and staring straight at her. She was a bit taken aback. Weren't wild animals supposed to run away when they saw humans? She stamped her feet and waved her arms around, feeling like a demented scarecrow, and the fox slunk away. She had the feeling it left not because it was afraid of her, but through embarrassment by association.

She waved the phone around again and saw another set of eyes.

This time, they belonged to a cat. It was Jack's nan's cat, who, if she remembered correctly, was called Rex, or was it Roy? The cat was crying loudly and was cowering in a crevice; all she could see was its head.

'Had a run in with a fox, little puss?' she knelt down, annoyed that the ground was damp and no doubt muddy, and stroked the animal's head. 'Come on, let's get you home.' It wasn't stuck, just scared. She pulled him out and that's when she saw he was a bit battered. Running the light from the phone over him, he had several flesh wounds. It must have been one hell of a fight. 'You do know the fox is bigger than you?' she said, holding him tight and gently fussing round his chin. He seemed to like it and started purring. She smiled. She liked cats and had fond memories of the scruffy moggy her grandma had when she was a child. 'Come on Roy, or is it Rex I'll take you home?'

She walked carefully along the scrubland towards the opposite end of the Apartment block. Mary was in the last one. Obviously she couldn't go knocking on her door in the middle of the night, but she knew, because she'd read about it in the local paper, that they had fitted a cat flap with some funds raised from the rescued cat story. If she pushed Rex, no, she was sure it was Roy, into the flap, then hopefully he would have enough sense to stay there for the rest of the night. Then everyone, especially her, could catch some shuteye.

She edged her way down the side of the building until she reached the kitchen. Because it was at the end of the block, it had an additional window and Annabel was surprised to see a light on inside. The blind was down, and she could see it swaying in the breeze. She immediately realised that the window was gone. Looking down, she saw the broken glass and from inside the flat, she could hear someone moving around.

She pressed 999 and put her phone to her ear. She asked for police and gave them the address, and she hung up, put Roy down, hitched her nighty and dressing gown up and climbed in through the gap.

. . .

Mary was lying very still. If she'd been a few years younger and her knees in better shape, she would have climbed out of bed and boxed the cheeky bastard's ears. She wished she had a mobile phone, Candice had told her she needed one more times than she could remember, but she had always resisted. They looked complicated and fiddly to her. But lying in bed still pretending to be asleep while some no good hooligan ransacked her house was the worst torture imaginable.

She knew he would come into the bedroom. When he'd searched his way through everything else, he would come to get her handbag. Jack used to tell her she was a silly mare for always insisting she take it to the bedroom with her and the wisdom of his words wasn't lost on her now. If her purse had been in the kitchen, he might have taken it and buggered off.

She screwed her eyes up, trying to see around the room. Was there anything she could use as a weapon? She reached across to her bedside table, feeling for anything that could help.

She could hear footsteps and scuffling outside of her room. She would play old and senile, shouldn't be that hard to do. If he took her bag and left, she'd let him be, but if he wanted a fight – well, then he would discover that even a daft old bat like her could still scream loud and pack a punch.

The door opened with a squeak, and light from the lounge flooded into her bedroom. She kept her eyes squeezed tight shut and tried to make her breathing deep and even mimicking sleep. She heard and sensed him as he came close and leaned over her as if checking that she was really asleep. She could smell his breath. It was sour and unpleasant. She had to fight to stop her nose from twitching in disgust. He needed to quit smoking and invest in a decent mouthwash.

He stepped away, and she heard him moving around the room. Drawers opened, and she winced as the contents were tipped across the floor. Taking her purse was one thing. Wanton destruction of a lifetime's worth of nicknacks and memories was something else altogether. What gave him the right to violate her in her own bloody home?

She could feel the rage growing inside her. She tried to talk herself down and tell herself not to do anything stupid. But as her Jack used to say. 'Sometimes you have to stand up and be counted.'

Mary threw the covers off and willed her tired old bones into action. She hurled her glass of water at him and then, with a scream of anger and armed with her weapon, she launched herself at him.

ANNABEL CHECKED the lounge and tiptoed towards the bedroom. She heard someone moving around and knew that she couldn't wait for the police. She couldn't let anything happen to Jack's nan. She reached the bedroom door and ducked as a missile hit the wall beside her and she was showered in water and she heard the sound of glass smashing. Her hand reached out to put the light on and she saw the frail old lady leap up from the bed and onto the intruder's back with a wail and a scream that could have come straight from a Hammer horror movie.

The intruder threw Mary off as though she were weightless; her white feathery hair sticking out in all directions as she bounced across the bed.

Annabel charged at him, and they both fell to the floor. He managed to get to his knees, and she saw Mary battering him round the head with her hairbrush. Annabel lunged for him again, but he found his footing and he took a swipe at Mary, sending her reeling backwards. Then he placed a swift kick into Annabel's side before taking off out of the bedroom.

Annabel scrambled to her feet; she glanced at Mary, who waved her off.

'Get Jack,' the old lady cried.

She ran out of the door and into the lounge. Roy leapt across the floor in front of the escaping man and almost tripped him up. But somehow the man remained on his feet. He pulled the front door open and ran out into the Close. By the time she got to the door, he was nowhere in to be seen. It was as if he had simply vanished into the thin nighttime air.

Followed by the cat, she went back to the bedroom to check on Mary. The old lady had a nasty red blotch that would no doubt turn into a colourful bruise across her cheek. Her skin was thin and so pale that all the veins were visible on her bony arms. But remarkably, she seemed to be okay.

'What were you thinking taking him on like that?' Annabel said, unable to keep the touch of admiration out of her voice. She saw the old-fashioned silver hairbrush on the bed; she picked it up and smiled. 'What were you hoping to do? Groom him into submission?'

Annabel picked her mobile phone up and speed-dialled a number.

'Yeah?' a sleepy voice answered.

'Jack, you'd better get round here to see your nan.'

Mary looked at her in her muddy dressing gown and boots. 'What are you even doing here?' she asked.

As if waiting for his cue Roy the cat jumped up onto the bed and fussed around his mistress.

'You'll have to ask him,' Annabel said, leaving the room to meet the police, who were finally arriving.

JENNY WOKE TO THE LOUD, authoritative knock on her door. She opened her eyes, winced, and promptly closed them again. It took her a few seconds to work out where she was and why she was curled up on a sofa and not at home in her lovely, warm bed. She felt truly rough. Her mouth was dry and vile, and her head was heavy and painful and her limbs ached from the cramped sleeping conditions.

The notion of – leave them alone and they'll go away – was not working and so with immense irritation and reluctance she threw the duvet onto the floor, slid her feet into her slippers and padded across to the door. She swung it open and looked into the faces of the two police officers who had called after the marijuana complaint.

'You again?' she moaned with a shiver, realising that opening the door in just her PJs was a mistake. 'Has someone complained again? Because they are mistaken, there's no pot here.'

'Can we come in?' the male PC asked. He flashed his warrant card, 'PC Clarke and this is PC Lipton.'

She wanted to say no, go away so that she could crawl back into bed, but knew that wasn't an option. They wouldn't leave until they had done or said whatever it was they were there to do. So she stepped aside and let them in, then she closed the door, shutting out the harsh morning light.

'What's going on?' Steve asked, wheeling in from the hallway that led to the bedroom and the bathroom. He pressed a button on his remote and the blackout blinds slid up, bathing the room in the early morning sunlight. 'Not you lot again.'

'Heavy night?' PC Lipton said, looking at the empty bottles of wine lined up on the kitchen side.

Had they really drunk all three bottles between the two of them? No wonder she felt so sick.

'Sorry to disturb you so early, Mr Lance, Mrs Fisher,' PC Clarke said. 'Did you see or hear anything suspicious around three am this morning?'

Jenny shook her head. 'I was out cold.'

'Not surprising.' The female PC said, glancing at the bottles.

Jenny gave her a glare. What right did the woman have to judge them?

PC Clarke looked at Steve. 'And what about you, sir?'

Steve was frowning, clearly thinking hard. He didn't look great; his hair was sticking up at odd angles – a serious case of bed hair. He was pale and looked tired. Like her, he was still in his pyjamas. They were black with a batman motive on the front; he seemed vulnerable and very young.

'You alright Steve?' she said gently.

'Yeah.' He nodded at her then looked at PC Clarke. 'I woke up at around that time, thought I heard a door open and footsteps. I assumed it was Jenny using the bathroom; I went straight back to sleep. Why? What's this all about?'

Jenny was thinking hard. Did she go to the loo in the early hours? She had no memory of getting up, but then she couldn't really remember anything beyond eating dinner. The evening was a blur.

'Next door was burgled last night,' PC Clarke said.

'That's terrible. Is the old lady alright?' Jenny thought about the frail old woman who lived next door and felt a surge of anger against the cowards who preyed on the weak and the vulnerable.

'Yes, luckily the intruder was disturbed.'

'Was it the same man who broke in here?' Steve asked, a brittle edge to his voice.

'Hard to tell,' PC Lipton said, looking at him coldly. 'Being as you never cooperated by giving us a statement.'

'Hey, that's not fair. He was the victim.' Jenny jumped to his defence. What was the woman's problem with him?

PC Clarke sent a glare in his colleague's direction and turned to Steve. 'We can't say for sure, but it's certainly seems possible.'

They asked a few more questions and then left, leaving a card with a number to ring if they thought of anything else useful to add. Jenny felt like making a complaint against the female PC. Her attitude was aggressive and confrontational, surely not qualities conducive to being a good police officer.

She put the kettle on and started clearing up from the night before. Miles could never go to bed and leave all the cooking mess congealing in the kitchen. It felt liberating and rebellious to leave it last night, but she had to admit it wasn't much fun facing it all in the morning.

'Coffee?'

Steve nodded his head and then disappeared into his bedroom. She felt so sorry for him. He was only just getting over the break-in and now he had to deal with the fact that the thief was still around. She hoped the police were right and the old lady was okay and she wondered who had disturbed the burglar.

She washed up and made coffee. Steve returned to the lounge washed and dressed with his hair gelled into submission. Neither of them wanted anything to eat and sipped their drink in silence. Jenny rinsed the mugs and showered and dressed. She was surprised that Miles hadn't arrived banging the door down, demanding to know what she was playing at. It seemed like he had given up on both her and their relationship.

'Can I come back later?' she asked Steve.

He smiled and nodded, but it was a movement of the lips and it didn't reach his eyes. She bent down and kissed his forehead. 'Thank you for a lovely evening.'

She looked around for handbag and couldn't see it anywhere. She tried to remember when she last had it and decided that she must have left it at home. With a wave at Steve, she walked out the door, took a deep steadying breath and hurried home to face her husband.

VICTORIA WAS ALONE in the bed. She'd heard Dave arrive home at just gone midnight, but he never came upstairs. She assumed he must have slept on the sofa again. She glanced at her clock. It was eight thirty-five. She'd overslept, which was almost unheard of for her. She got up and hurried across the landing to knock on her daughter's door. There was no sound from inside the room, so she opened the door and went in. Gemma wasn't there, which she took as a good sign and hoped it meant that she had got up on time and had already left for school.

She had managed a brief chat with Gemma yesterday when she persuaded her to have a bowl of soup. But beyond the fact that she had a stomachache and felt sick, Victoria didn't really know what was wrong. Her daughter was definitely off with her, even more than the normal teenage traumas have with their parents.

Victoria went downstairs. Her husband wasn't there, but evidence that he had indeed slept on the sofa still was. The soft fleecy throw from the cupboard was on the floor alongside a half empty glass of water. She picked up the glass and carried it into the kitchen. She put the kettle on and grabbed a banana; she hadn't got the time for a proper breakfast.

As she made herself a cup of tea to drink while she got ready, she indulged in a brief fantasy and relived the feel of Brett's lips pressed against her own. She had resisted going out with him last night, even though she had been seriously tempted. It wasn't as though Dave would care. She hadn't seen him since he had run out on PC Clarke yesterday morning. It was Gemma who stopped her from going out on a date with Brett. Her daughter had been upstairs feeling unwell, so she had texted him and told him she couldn't make it.

Fifteen minutes later, after the quickest of showers and a spray of miracle dry shampoo, she was leaving her house. She glanced up the Close, hoping to see Brett setting off on one of his runs. She saw two police cars parked outside the Apartment block and was itching to walk up and find out what was going on but knew she ought to at least unlock the Show Home office and put her laptop on.

The postman handed her some letters. She glanced down at them and was just about to stick them through the letterbox to deal with later when one of them caught her eye. It was from the bank. She knew the address printed on the back and there were two copies, one addressed to her and one to her husband. She pushed his letter along with the other letters back into her house and, clutching her copy, she hurried off to work.

She turned on the computer, checked the answerphone, opened all the blinds and curtains, sprayed the odour neutraliser throughout the Show Home and put the percolator on. Then she sat down and opened the letter.

Idiots, she thought crossly, they've got the accounts mixed up. The letter was demanding immediate action to bring their financial affairs back into credit. She knew that after the move, their bank balance wasn't what it used to be, but no way were they wiped out.

Sonia came into the office. 'You heard Mary was burgled last night?'

So that's what the police cars were about. 'Was she hurt?'

'No, I don't think so. You okay?'

Victoria held the letter up while Sonia scanned it. She wasn't one to share the private details of her life, but somehow her new neighbour had broken down the barriers of her usual reserve. It was difficult to maintain a distance when Sonia was so open and friendly, and besides, she needed someone to talk to.

'Ouch, that doesn't look good. You better get busy and sell some houses.'

'But that's not the point. We have individual accounts, but this is our joint one where all the bills get paid from. Every month we both have money going into it to cover the mortgage, etc. We also have the joint credit card and a savings account.'

'Maybe the bank has screwed up the payments going into this account?'

Victoria shook her head. 'No, that's not it, I checked my account yesterday and the last standing order was definitely paid out of it. I don't understand. Neither of us ever uses this account. We don't even carry debit cards for it, they're kept in a drawer at home. We live on whatever we have in our individual accounts. That way, the money for the mortgage and bills is always available.'

'Very organised. Must admit our bank balance is always nearer the red than the black. Sounds to me like either the bank has screwed up big time or that lovely husband of yours has been syphoning off the savings. Maybe the mistress has expensive tastes.'

Sonia said it lightly enough, but the words were like a slap round the face to Victoria. 'He wouldn't,' she whispered, more to herself than her friend.

'Nah, course not,' Sonia replied, looking at her carefully. 'Best get on the phone and have it out with the bank. I'll get you a coffee.'

Victoria went into the Show Home kitchen to make the call, leaving Sonia in the office. She didn't want a potential customer to walk in on her conversation.

A few minutes later, she walked back into the office and dropped down into the chair at her desk.

'Alright?'

She didn't look at Sonia but instead stared at her hands. They were shaking. Tiny tremors running down through her fingers which she couldn't stop.

'Oh God Vic, what has he done?'

. . .

MILES WASN'T AT HOME; presumably he had gone to work. It was a relief that she didn't have to face him, but she knew he couldn't be avoided forever.

'Did you have a good evening?' Brett asked her.

'Yes lovely thanks,' she said, although since her memory was so foggy she couldn't be totally sure it was true. 'Did Miles ask where I was?'

'To be honest, Jen, I hardly saw him all evening. I think he went out.'

The red wine stain on the carpet was almost gone, so she knew that Miles had been home and busy at some point and in a way it was comforting to know that she could still understand and predict some of his behaviour. She wondered where he went. Not looking for her that much was clear. She wouldn't have been hard to find.

Brett took her hand. 'You know you can't kip on a mate's sofa for ever.'

'I know.'

'So what are you going to do?'

'I'm working on it,' she said seriously. 'I have a few ideas.'

'Well, I'm here, whatever you need me to do.'

She smiled, feeling lucky to have such a brilliant brother. 'Did your evening go as planned?'

He let go of her hand and shook his head. 'No, not really,' he shrugged his shoulders in a c'est la vie type way and turned around to make himself busy with mugs and tea bags. 'Want one?'

'Thanks,' she said, wondering who had got him into such a state. Most of his relationships were entirely on his terms. She often worried about him because he seemed unable to let anyone close or make any kind of commitment. But whoever it was that had captured his interest this time, she was running rings around him. 'You haven't seen my handbag around anywhere, have you?'

'No, didn't you take it with you yesterday?'

She thought she had, but it wasn't at Steve's and it wasn't in the hall or her bedroom. She definitely had it when they went shopping yesterday, but wasn't sure after that.

'I'll check the car for you,' Brett said. 'Maybe you left it in there after shopping.'

That would make sense. She followed him out to the door while he unlocked the Beetle and checked the floor in the front passenger seat. Nothing. 'Try the boot?' it was unlikely, but she was running out of ideas.

It wasn't there. Could Miles have moved it somewhere? She checked the study and looked again in the bedroom and in her balcony sanctuary. It was gone.

MARY NEARLY CRIED when she saw what the little bastard had done to her lounge. It was pure, wanton destruction, with no regard for anything that was precious to her. All her photos had been dropped on the floor like they were rubbish. Her favourite, a wedding photo of her and Jack, had been ripped from its silver frame. She bent down and picked it up, smoothing down the edges. If her Jack had been here, no robber would have dared set foot in the house. He was a man who took care of his own.

'He was a handsome young man,' Annabel said, looking over her shoulder at the picture. 'I can see a resemblance,' the woman added, glancing at her grandson.

'Like peas in a pod.' Mary agreed, fighting back the tears. Jack was beside himself with upset and anger; she didn't want him to see her crumple. She had to stay strong.

A tissue was slipped into her hand. She looked up, surprised, at Annabel, who gave her a smile that was reassuring and full of understanding. Maybe she had misjudged the woman.

Jack took the photo from her hands. 'I'll get this copied nan and get you a new frame.'

She could feel the anger oozing out of him. It was barely contained, and it scared her. It wasn't good for a man to bottle up such strong emotions. She knew he wanted to beat the hell out of the intruder and he couldn't, so the frustration was eating him up.

Roy stayed close to her as though he, too, had gone into protective male mode. She sat down in her chair and he jumped up onto her lap and she stroked his back, glad to have him in her life. She looked up at Sasha; the young reporter, as she came through the open door. The police had been in and out all morning taking statements, knocking on doors and dusting for fingerprints.

'I couldn't believe it when I heard what happened,' Sasha said, her eyes moving from Mary to Annabel. 'I understand you were the hero?'

Mary glanced up at her rescuer.

'Well, Roy is the real hero,' Annabel said, pointing to the cat. 'If he hadn't taken on a fox... well, who knows what the outcome would have been.'

Mary shivered.

'You alright, nan?'

She smiled at her grandson. 'Shut the door, love. My nipples are turning blue from the cold.'

PC Clarke came through the door before Jack hobbled over and pushed it shut.

'Sorry, we are nearly finished.' Clarke looked at Jack. 'Neighbours have told me you went around warning everyone about a face at the door yesterday evening?'

'Just a peeping Tom,' Annabel said.

'You can't know that for sure,' Jack responded.

'Can either of you describe him?'

Mary watched as they both shook their heads.

'It was too dark,' Jack said.

Mary hoped, whoever it was, that they had the good sense to stay away. She didn't want Jack venting his fury and ending up in court on an assault charge.

. . .

VICTORIA LOCKED the door and walked up towards the apartment block. She wanted to check that Mary was alright and hear what had actually happened. She could see Sasha's car parked outside, which meant that another negative story would soon be filling the pages of the local newspaper.

'You alright love?' Barry said, crossing the Close to see her.

She didn't really want to stop and talk, but she couldn't be rude.

'Terrible isn't it? Two break-ins in as many weeks...' he tutted, 'you don't look so hot.'

'Gee thanks,'

'Oh love, I don't mean it like that. It's just, well, you look as though you're carrying the weight of the world on those slim shoulders of yours.'

She forced herself to smile, not quite fake sales smile, but she knew it wasn't from the heart either. 'Busy, that's all.'

'You got a minute?'

'Not really.'

'Please, it's important.'

She didn't have much choice. He took her by the arm and led across the Close towards the cabin. He shouted out to one of the brickies as they went past. 'Tell Tom I need him in my office now.'

Tom? What did he have to do with anything?

Barry pushed the door open and stood back to let her pass. 'Tea? Coffee?'

She shook her head. 'I've got to get on Barry, what's this all about?'

'Your Dave, and his spot of bother.'

'The mugging,' Victoria said warily, knowing it wasn't truly a mugging but since she didn't know what the truth really was, what else could she say? 'Why?'

'Best wait for Tom.'

Right on cue, the door opened and the young builder walked in. He glanced at her and then looked at Barry, a question in his eyes.

'You need to tell her,' Barry said.

Tom looked a bit like a wasp trapped in a jar. His eyes darted all around, anywhere but looking at her. He wanted to escape, but he knew he couldn't. 'Not my place,' he mumbled.

'Tell me what?' she demanded, getting annoyed and concerned. 'Tom?'

'No choice mate,' Barry said, folding his arms across his chest and staring directly at the young lad.

Eventually, and clearly with huge reluctance, Tom looked at her. 'Your husband, he was in the pub the night he was attacked.'

'I know that,' she said. 'He stopped for a pint in the Duck on his way home from work.' Not that she believed he actually went to work that evening.

'It wasn't the Duck. He was in the Queens Head and it was more than a quick pint,' Tom said. 'Look Vic, I'm sorry but the truth is he was there all that Sunday afternoon and evening.'

She shook her head, 'No. why would he spend all those hours in the pub?' She knew he liked a drink, but that was ridiculous. Tom was staring at his sturdy steel capped work boots as though they were the most fascinating footwear in the world. He couldn't look at her and suddenly the penny dropped. 'He was with someone. Another woman.'

Tom did look up then. 'No,' he said in surprise. 'He was alone.'

It didn't make sense, none of it made sense at all. 'Well, what was he doing for all those hours, then?'

Tom glanced at Barry, who nodded his head. 'Just tell her.'

'He was playing the slots, the fruit machines.'

What? She frowned, trying to make sense of it. She knew that there were fruit machines in pubs, but she had never played them and had never seen Dave show any interest in playing them. Besides, surely they were harmless. They enjoyed a couple of quid's worth in the amusement arcade whenever they were at the seaside. It was just a bit of fun.

'He was like a man possessed,' Tom continued. 'Hour after hour, he kept feeding the machine, and not for the first time, he's always in there.'

Victoria was feeling sick; it was all beginning to make total sense.

Was Tom telling her that Dave had shoved all their money into the greedy belly of a fruit machine?

'That night he was losing, well in fact, he'd lost just about every penny he had on him. So he had to get cash from the ATM, which meant walking away from the machine...' Tom paused and looked at her with what looked suspiciously like pity. 'He ran, and I do mean he ran, to get the cash out, but when he got back, a couple of lads from the bar had started playing it and they got a big pay-out. He went mad, swearing and shouting that they had stolen his jackpot. The barman had no choice but to kick him out. The lads left soon afterwards. Your husband's a big boy, and what he does is none of my business. I didn't think anymore about it until the next night when I saw the lads back in the pub sporting a few bruises and boasting about how they saw off some nutter, then I heard you telling Barry about the mugging and I put it all together.'

So that was that. 'He was beaten up by the lads?' she said mainly to herself. 'They jumped him.'

'Not exactly.'

'Not exactly? What the hell does that mean?' she thought about Dave's wallet still in his briefcase. If they beat him up, they didn't rob him.

'It was the other way around. He jumped them, tried to take back the winnings from them.'

'But there were two of them?'

'I guess, but he was angry and desperate for the money.'

Victoria stood up and thanked Tom and Barry. Then she walked out of the Cabin. Her head was spinning, and the trembling had started in her hands again. She had been clinging to some hope that there still might be an explanation for the missing money. That Dave had simply taken it out and put it into a new account without telling her, an ISA or something. Now she knew the truth. There was no other woman. He had a gambling problem, and he had wiped out all their entire savings pot to pursue his obsession.

EPISODE TWENTY
JASMINE CLOSE - SERIES ONE

Brett saw her out of the window. She was walking away fast from the building site office. Her head was down; she looked as though she might be crying. He hurried out of the house and caught up with her as she hurried down the Close towards the Show Home.

'Victoria?' he touched her shoulder. 'What's wrong?'

She stopped walking and turned to look at him. He was right she had been crying. She was pale and clearly shaken; her eye make-up was smudged as though she had tried to wipe the tears from her eyes. He took her hand firmly and lead her back to the house.

'I have to get back to work.'

'Not in this state, you don't.' He took her hand and she went into the house with him. He closed the door and pulled her into his arms, holding her tight. She resisted to start with and then it was as if the fight went out of her and she let herself lean on him completely. He felt a stab of anger towards her useless loaf of a husband. He was in no doubt the man was the cause of her being so upset. He stood and held her for several seconds while she cried it out. And, as the sobs subsided, he stepped back to look at her. 'Better?'

She nodded and sniffed.

He took her hand and led her into the kitchen. He grabbed a tissue from the pretty pastel box Jenny kept beside the fruit bowl and handed it to her. 'Sit down; I'll make you some tea.'

'I don't...'

'Yes, you do,' he said, cutting off her protest. 'I learnt from my step-mum years ago that for Brits, they can solve any crisis with a nice cup of tea. Or if not actually solved, then it can definitely put it in a better perspective.'

'If only it were that simple.'

'You want to tell me?'

'No.'

'Okay, then tea and tissues it is.'

He pushed the box closer to her and pulled out Jenny's china teapot from the cupboard. He had a newly acquired taste for hot tea himself, but he usually just stuck a tea bag in a mug. However, he knew that part of the process was the ritual, and that included a teapot and a proper china cup. Even he admitted there was something soothing about making a proper pot of tea, he thought that the aroma probably played a part but also the china itself being so delicate and attractive added to the experience.

'I'm impressed,' Victoria said, watching him pour the amber liquid into the cups.

'That was the intention. Milk? Sugar?'

'Just the milk.'

He handed her the cup and saucer and was rewarded with a small half-smile.

They drank in silence. He didn't want to press her to confide in him and at least she had colour back in her cheeks and didn't look quite as distressed as she did before.

'Thank you,' she said when her cup was empty. 'I must get back to work now.'

'You sure?' He followed her out of the kitchen, through the lounge, and into the hallway. Of course, all he really wanted to do was take her upstairs to his bed and make her forget all about her idiot of a husband. Instead, he pointed to the cloakroom and gently touched the area just below her eyes, which were dark from the smudged mascara.

She ducked into the toilet and came out with the smudges removed and freshly applied lipstick that he immediately wanted to kiss right off her lips.

'Let me see you tonight?'

To his surprise and delight, she nodded her head. 'Not 'till later though, I have things I've got to do after work.'

He wanted to kiss her goodbye. No, that was a lie. He didn't want to say goodbye at all, knowing her well enough already to know that he wouldn't be able to entice her away from returning to work. He watched as she slipped quickly out of the front door and hurried down the road.

JENNY WATCHED Victoria go from the upstairs bedroom window. She was surprised at her brother's choice. She knew it wasn't the first time he had become involved with a married woman. In fact, she suspected that's how he preferred his ladies and assumed it was the old cliché of fear of commitment, probably tied up with his own insecurities and an attempt to protect himself from heartbreak. She knew that he'd been hurt in his younger days, when he was at college, but she had been a teenager, and too wrapped up in her own hormonal angst to take much notice. She had memories of him mooching around the family home while her mum fussed over him and made murmuring sounds about how time heals everything. Surely he wasn't still holding onto that hurt? She always assumed that he simply wasn't ready to settle down. That he was enjoying his freedom too much and married ladies were easy fun and even easier to walk away from when the thrill faded. She didn't condone his behaviour or his attitude, but who was she to judge? She could certainly understand now what it was like to be in an unhappy marriage.

She wondered what was going on in the Show Home woman's life to make her risk an affair right under her family's nose. She turned away; it was none of her business. Nobody really knew what went on behind the closed doors of a marriage.

Jenny looked around the room. She had looked absolutely everywhere that she could think of for her handbag. It was definitely gone. She went downstairs and into the study and sat down at the desk. She would go online and look up the procedure for reporting a lost bank card. Did she need to tell the police? Surely they would only be interested if it was stolen, and she certainly didn't believe that was the case. It was one of those silly situations that would eventually resolve itself. She would find the handbag somewhere unbelievably crazy like in the washing machine or tucked under a blanket in the understairs cupboard. Of course, she had looked in all those places along with every other possible and impossible place she could think of.

She logged onto her bank and jotted down the phone number she needed to ring. While she was on the site, she clicked on their main joint account and was surprised to see that the available balance was several hundreds of pounds less than the account balance. She checked the pending section and no direct debits or standing orders were waiting to go out, so it meant that the difference between the two was down to debit card payments.

Logging out again and wondering what large purchases her husband had made from their joint account, she rang the number given. It was easy enough to report it lost. The young man with an Indian accent on the other end of the line was polite and helpful.

'When did you last use your card, Mrs Fisher?'

'Yesterday at the petrol station.'

'Do you know at what time that would have been, Mrs Fisher?'

'Mid-morning, I guess around eleven-ish.'

'And you haven't used your card since?'

'No.'

'Not for any online transactions?'

'No. I haven't even been online, well, apart from a few minutes ago, to look up the bank account and get a number to phone you.'

'Please hold, Mrs Fisher.'

She didn't want to hold, but had no choice. Irritating music played into her ear, punctuated by a voice that kept telling her how valued she was as a customer, and repeatedly thanking her for holding. Her head was aching, and she was finding the entire experience of losing her card infuriating. The wider implications were also beginning to dawn on her. If her handbag was lost, then that meant her driving licence and her favourite designer sunglasses, along with her mini make-up bag and small hairbrush. The bag itself was a Prada that Miles had given her last Christmas. She knew that he would not be impressed when she told him it was missing. Still, a lost handbag was hardly in the same category as a lost wife, so maybe he wouldn't make too much of a fuss.

The music stopped abruptly, and a new voice came onto the line. 'Mrs Fisher, I'm from the fraud department. We are concerned that your card has been used without your consent. My colleague informs me you have not used your card since yesterday morning and the last transaction you completed was for forty-nine pounds and fifteen pence...'

'Yes, but my husband has a debit card as well. This is our joint account.'

'I understand, Mrs Fisher, but I can clearly see that it is your card that has been used to make several online payments this afternoon.'

Jenny was stunned. It was all so much more serious than she first thought. She had stupidly believed that she had mislaid her handbag and it would eventually turn up again in a silly and surprising place. Clearly that wasn't going to happen and if the card had really been used, then she had to assume that someone had stolen it.

The voice in her ear was still speaking, and she was trying to pay attention but her mind was busy re-enacting yesterday's actions and every time she pressed the mental replay she clearly saw herself hurrying up the Close to Steve's flat carrying her overnight bag and with her handbag slung over her shoulder.

'... you do understand Mrs Fisher?' the voice said into her ear.

'Yes, of course, thank you for your help,' she replied, realising that she didn't understand at all. If she took her bag to Steve's, where the hell was it now?

. . .

Victoria didn't know how she got through the rest of the day. She felt as though the ground beneath her feet had turned to quicksand. It was unstable and shifting and any minute now; she felt she could fall into a huge hole.

Many times she had picked her mobile up to call or message her husband and demand an explanation. Each time, she had stopped and put the phone down again. What was the point? He would only ignore her like he had been doing for weeks now.

She was struggling to deal with the realisation that he had gambled away just about every penny they had. Luckily, it had been a quiet day. She wasn't at all sure that even her fake sales smile would be able to shine today.

The minute the clock on the wall hit five-thirty, she locked the door and hurried out into a taxi that she had already ordered and was outside waiting for her. She gave the driver the address of Dave's workplace and sat back to prepare herself mentally for the confrontation that was to come.

It took nearly ten minutes to reach the industrial estate on the southwest side of the city and cost her seven pounds. She only had a ten-pound note and knew when she handed it to the driver that he was not intending to give her any change but she held her hand out expectantly and waited while he tutted and made a big play about how much effort it was to find her the three-pound coins as change. She didn't care how annoyed he was or how tight he thought she was, with the reality of her new negative bank balance every penny counted.

She took a deep breath and walked purposefully towards the building. It was large, modern and purpose-built. The reception area was light and spacious and Victoria knew that the front of the building housed the administration personnel and that the vast warehouse was at the back. Dave worked in one of the open-plan offices. He often complained about having to listen to the silly girls wittering on about their periods, their make-up and their boyfriends, and he'd demanded to know why they needed to clutter up their desks with pictures of babies and soft, fluffy toys. She knew that he had been left behind. The colleagues he started working with many years ago had all moved on. They'd been promoted either within the company or taken their chances elsewhere. But Dave had stayed stuck in the same job, in the same office, in the same building. She wondered if she should have taken more notice. Had he been struggling for a long time? Had stress led him to some sort of nervous breakdown? Was it her fault?

Victoria walked to the desk and forced herself to smile as the young receptionist said, 'hello, welcome to Harvey's Stationary Supplies. How may I help you today?'

'I need to speak to my husband, Dave Pickles.'

'I'm sorry,' the receptionist said, looking slightly uncomfortable.

'I know he's working, but this is important.'

'Umm, can you hold a minute?' she pointed to the comfy chairs positioned around a coffee table. 'Take a seat, please.'

Victoria didn't really want to sit down, but the young woman seemed quite put out by her wanting to speak to Dave, so she thought it was best to comply. She walked across and sank down, watching the door to the offices and waiting for her husband to come out.

Only it wasn't Dave who walked towards her. It was his boss, Malcolm, that emerged.

She stood up and took a few steps to meet him. 'Hi Malcolm, has he knocked off early?' she asked, annoyed that she'd missed him.

The man was looking at her strangely, a mixture of worry and pity. Not unlike the looks she was getting from Tom and Barry earlier in the day. 'You better come into my office.'

She shook her head and stayed where she was. 'Just tell me,' she said, knowing she wasn't going to like whatever it was he had to say.

Malcolm was a few years younger than her husband and had started working at Harvey's a year or two after him. Yet he had overtaken Dave and got first the team leader's promotion and then he was made office manager. They had met several times, a couple of work parties and once when he had a barbecue and he had invited all his work colleagues. He was nice enough, as was his pretty, slightly plump wife, but they were acquaintances rather than friends. 'I'm sorry Victoria,' he said. 'Dave doesn't work here anymore. I'm afraid we had to let him go last week.'

'So it was stolen?'

'No, well maybe, I don't know.' Jenny looked at her husband and realised that he had a huge talent for making her feel small and stupid. Had it always been like that, or was it only since the accident? She wasn't sure. What she did know, however, was that she'd had enough.

'How can you not know?' he didn't raise his voice, just his eyebrows, which rose so high they almost disappeared into his hairline.

She was getting flustered, and that made her annoyed with herself for allowing him to upset her, which made her even more flustered!

'When did you have it last? Think, Jen, retrace your steps. How hard can it be? When was the last time you had your handbag?'

She knew it was when she got to Steve's apartment. She had run through it again and again and the last time she saw it was at his flat early evening yesterday. When she arrived, she'd put her bag down on the floor beside the coffee table.

'Jenny!'

'I've told you I don't know,' she lied. No way was she going to give him an excuse to march down to Steve's and start making accusations.

'Well, let us go through it now, step by step...'

'I'm not a bloody child, Miles.'

'Then stop behaving like one. This is serious.'

'Of course it's serious, but it's also only money and whatever has happened nobody has been threatened, scared or hurt,' she said, thinking about the burglar who broke into Steve's and Mary's.

Miles paused then. 'Yeah I heard about the old lady. What about your druggy friend? He wasn't targeted last night?'

'No. We were fine...' she said, realising her mistake as soon as the words left her mouth.

'We?'

It occurred to Jenny that he didn't know she had stayed away for the past two nights. How was that even possible? She took a deep breath and decided that there was no point in hiding the truth. Their marriage was in tatters and way beyond saving, so no point in putting off the inevitable any longer. 'I've stayed at Steve's for the past two nights, and the fact that you haven't even noticed my absence says it all really, doesn't it?'

He winced as though she'd slapped him. He opened his mouth, but no sound came out. He gave her one last shocked look and then walked out of the house, slamming the door hard behind him.

MILES STARTED WALKING. He didn't really have a destination in his head. He just knew he had to get away while he absorbed the information she had just thrown at him. He went briskly down the Close, past the Show Home and along the redway. He reached the fork in the path and had a choice to either head up and over the bridge towards the local centre with its school, shops and pub, or to veer off to the left and walk up to the canal.

He felt in his pocket and realised his wallet was in his jacket back at home and all he had on him were a handful of coins that wouldn't buy a packet of crisps, let alone a pint of beer. So he turned left and upped his pace. It was very cold and already dark. He shivered and thought he was an idiot for storming out without a coat. November in England was scarf and gloves time and he was striding along in his work shirt and a jumper. He always took his suit jacket off when he was in the car and so he would put a sweater on over his shirt for comfort and warmth during the journey. Jenny used to laugh at him, saying his life was all about little rituals, well he was glad of it now as an icy wind cut through the thin barrier of his clothes and stung his skin. He had heard talk on the radio about a heavy winter coming and the possibility of early snow.

He would have to turn back, otherwise he would end up with hyperthermia. He pictured himself collapsed in a heap, stiff and frozen at the side of the water while the ducks waddled past him. Would Jenny be sorry then? It would serve her right if he died, and it was all her fault and she had to live with the guilt.

Miles knew he was being ridiculous. But he was feeling angry and bitter. He had tried so hard to do everything he could to help her through the past traumatic months, and now she was throwing it back in his face.

He was consumed by rage towards that foul-mouthed wheelchair man who had stolen his wife and somehow poisoned her against him. She had even slept at his house! How had he not known? Obviously on the party night he had been very drunk and rescued from the rain by the lovely Tammy. So while he had been worrying about Jenny thinking she was in their bedroom, she had been with stroppy Steve. And last night when he got home from trying to see Tammy, he went straight to the study and onto the laptop. When he finally went up to bed and found it empty, he assumed she was asleep in her back room where she spent so much time. It never, not once, occurred to him that she wasn't even in the house.

He realised he had gone a long way and was in unfamiliar territory. He had only walked up the canal a couple of times since they moved in and had never been very far. Now he had passed several bridges and was feeling a bit disorientated. He decided the best thing that he could do was turn around and retrace his steps. After a few minutes, he saw the lights from the apartment block over in the distance. He paused and looked through the gloomy darkness, wondering if he could cut across the wasteland that would eventually lead to the phase two building site.

It was a large area and looked muddy and uninviting and was mostly fenced in. He was very cold, and he was shivering so hard that his teeth were actually chattering noisily; he needed to get home and back into the warm. He found a gap where a fence panel was down.

By the force of nature, it had been windy lately or through vandalism he didn't know or care. He had to negotiate a way into the area through brambles and bushes and wished he had a torch so he could search out a better route.

He made his way cautiously along the fence, aware that the ground was uneven and full of crevices and ruts; he didn't want to add a twisted or broken ankle to his growing pile of misfortune. An animal darted out in front of him and he realised it was a fox as the long bushy tail disappeared into the undergrowth at the edge of the area.

Up ahead, he could see Tammy's apartment. The lights were on in the lounge and the curtains were open. He wanted to go and look inside, but he couldn't risk being chased off again. He was worried about the young girl and he wanted to see her again, just to make sure that she was alright. He didn't believe the Annabel woman when she said that Tammy wasn't there.

As he got closer, he could see her bedroom window and, as he approached, the room suddenly illuminated. Tammy was clearly visible and almost naked. She was wearing a tight black Basque, hold up stockings and high black boots. Her hair was loose, and he was close enough to see she was wearing full make-up. He could also see that she was not alone. A man pulled her into his arms and together they tumbled onto the bed.

He watched, unable to tear his eyes away for several seconds, until Tammy untangled herself from the man's embrace, climbed off the bed and closed the curtains, shutting him out.

Miles hurried on past the apartment and down the alleyway. The man was not young, and he had a receding hairline and a belly that was beyond middle-aged spread. What was she doing with an old guy like that?

He was tempted to ring the doorbell and try to see her again, but what could he possibly say? It was up to her who she chose to sleep with. Or was it? Some memory stirred. Wasn't there something in the local paper a few weeks ago about there being a brothel on a new estate? What if it was Jasmine Close, apartment two to be exact, and

Tammy was a sex slave held against her will and forced by Annabel to perform unspeakable sexual acts on sleazy old men?

The idea filled him with rage and horror, but underneath those feelings, a spark of hope and optimism flared. He could save her. He could be a hero and rescue her from Annabel. He paused outside the flat, thinking hard. He couldn't just bang on the door. He needed a plan, and he needed to do some research. Check the reports and find out what and who he was dealing with. He knew that the sex industry was linked with all kinds of desperados. They were run by organised crime gangs. He'd read reports about trafficking and sex slaves. If he tried to help Tammy, he could find himself facing drug lords and gangsters. It was terrifying and exhilarating. If Jenny was stupid enough to let him go, then he would make sure that she knew what type of man she was turning her back on. He could see himself in the future giving interviews, possibly even on the telly explaining how he rescued a poor helpless girl, and maybe her friends as well, from a life of drugs and prostitution.

But first of all, he had to deal with something else.

Steve knew who was at the door. He had expected the knock ages ago. It was nearly an hour since Jenny rang to warn him that Miles had left the house and was, she suspected, heading his way.

Clearly, the man had taken quite a detour. He was white from the cold, but his nose was bright red, almost glowing like the most famous of reindeers. Not surprising, since the idiot didn't have a coat or jacket on and just a few seconds with the door open was as intimate with the cold as Steve wanted to get.

'You better come in.'

Steve closed the door and waved towards the sofa. He didn't want the man to stay or be comfortable, but he hated Miles for having the advantage of looking down on him.

Miles had a strange look in his eyes, hard to describe. It was almost feral. 'What have you done to my Jenny?'

'All I've done is listen and tried to be a friend. What have you done?'

'Friend? You're not a friend, you little shit. You fed her drugs and lies.'

'Seriously? That's all you've got?' Steve wondered how Jenny had ever seen something worthwhile in the man.

Miles moved closer, looming over Steve threateningly. 'If you weren't in that chair.'

'If I wasn't in this chair, you would be flat on your back with a black eye right now. You don't deserve her.'

'What and you do?'

'Maybe not, but I do care enough to put her first.'

'You little shit. You've known her for a couple of weeks and you think you have it all sussed out. I've had to deal with her self-indulgent crap for the past seven months. She was on the mend until you and your drugs messed with her mind.'

'She never was. You're kidding yourself. That's your problem. You are delusional. You don't see the truth, only a version of it you want to see.'

'I'll tell you what I see right now. A bitter, foul-mouthed drug addict who pretends to be a friend to take advantage of a sweet kind heart.'

'You kidding me? How have I taken advantage?'

'You stole from her.'

'What?'

'Her purse.'

'As if! Why would I steal from her?'

'Probably to feed your disgusting drug habit.'

Steve wheeled right up against the man, his voice shook with anger. 'I have never stolen anything from anyone, and I certainly haven't taken anything from Jenny.'

'Liar. She had her handbag when she came here and it was gone when she left.'

'Fuck off.'

'I'm going.'

Steve pressed the remote and the door swung open. Miles paused in the doorway and looked back. 'You're wrong. You've taken everything from Jenny. Now she has nothing.'

Steve shut him out and took deep breaths to calm himself down. He knew the man was angry and lashing out, but was there any truth in what Miles said? Had Jenny lost everything because of him? And what was the stuff about her handbag? He knew she had been looking for it. She couldn't find it that morning, but he assumed that she had simply left it at home. Miles was suggesting that he had taken it.

He picked up the phone and rang her. He warned her that Miles had been to his, and she apologised on her husband's behalf.

'Nah, don't be soft,' he said, feeling better and calmer just at the sound of her voice. 'He seemed to think I'd nicked your handbag.'

'He's just pointing fingers,' she said. 'We don't know what's happened to it.'

'So it is missing?'

'Yes.'

'And did you have it at my house?'

The question hung in the invisible telephone wires that stretched between them. 'Yes,' she said softly, 'but Steve, I know you didn't take it.'

He didn't know what to say. He felt as though he had been physically assaulted. Even though she said that he didn't take it, the fact that she last saw it at his house made him the number one suspect. It was not a pleasant feeling. 'I'll look for it,' he managed to say before hanging up. There weren't many places to hide a handbag in his house. He knew it wasn't there. So what the hell was going on?

How many more shocking revelations did she have to hear? Her husband had lost his job and gambled away all of their savings. She almost wished he was having an affair. Somehow that seemed more reasonable or normal. She thought that a mistress was something she could at least try to understand. How could she deal with his reckless destruction of their financial stability? The money put aside was supposed to be for Gemma's future. They had been saving for years to cover their daughter if she chose to go to university. They wanted to be able to help her with the cost of learning to drive and buying her first car. They used to talk about having funds for her wedding and money to help with the deposit on her first house. Years and years of monthly savings gone, she struggled to comprehend how it was even possible to shove so much money into a slot machine. She knew that the new casino had opened in the city. Had he started going there as well?

Malcolm had not been very talkative and kept saying there was a confidentiality issue and she would have to discuss Dave's departure from the firm with her husband. She finally lost the plot along with her temper and called Malcolm a pompous jumped up prat who should get over himself.

Not that it helped her get any more information, but it made her feel better. What did she do now? And if he wasn't at work, where the hell was he? She was pretty sure he couldn't be at the pub because there was no money left. Just to make sure, though, she called a taxi and had it drive her to the Duck and then to the Queen's Head. In the Duck, the barman didn't even know his name and after a quick look around; she realised that there were no gaming machines there, anyway. It was more a gastro pub focusing on the food and offering an impressive list of wines and even some cocktails. The customers were mostly smart and upmarket; it clearly fancied itself as being more of a wine bar. She knew Dave had only said the Duck to misdirect her and PC Clarke. She would be surprised if he had ever set foot in the place and knew that if he had, he would have felt uncomfortable and totally out of place. The Queen's head, on the other hand, was more laid back, informal and all about the beer and the sports and, of course, the fruit machines that were guilty of pushing her family to the edge or bankruptcy.

'Hi,' she said, forcing a fake smile onto her lips.

'What can I get you, love?' the barman asked, looking at her in her work suit with some curiosity.

'I'm looking for Dave Pickles. Have you seen him?'

The man's expression changed. It wasn't friendly or curious any more. The man looked annoyed. 'You are?'

'His wife.'

'Sorry.'

'Have you seen him?'

'Not today, in fact, not since I had to chuck him out on Sunday evening.'

So it was true then. Everything Tom said about the fight. She turned around to leave.

'Wait up...' the barman said, calling after her.

'What?'

'He owes me for his tab.'

Victoria looked at the man and shook her head. 'Fat chance,' she scoffed, walking away and out to the waiting taxi.

She closed her eyes on the short drive home, feeling as though she was trapped in a deep sleep, a nightmare that she couldn't wake up from. Her phone beeped and jolted her awake with a message. It was Gemma saying she was having dinner at Abby's and would be home at ten.

Victoria thought of Brett and knew that her life was in freefall and he was a complication that she could definitely do without. But he wanted to take her out, and she had agreed. Well, why shouldn't she? Dave had trampled all over her and Gemma and their marriage. She was guilt free now. She could see Brett and for a few hours, to try to forget her husband and what he had done to them.

STEVE CLOSED his eyes and tried to make sense of it all. Jenny had her bag in his flat, and now it was gone. Therefore, someone must have taken it and that meant that someone had somehow got into his flat. What other possibility was there? Who and How? He never gave his keys out to anyone. Nobody had one. Could it be the builders or Victoria from the Show Home? Did they have spare keys for all the properties? Or had someone got through the window? He'd had it open for a very short time that morning. The apartment got stuffy, and he liked to air it out. But it was only open for ten minutes and if he remembered correctly, both he and Jenny were in the lounge. No one could climb through the window and steal her handbag with them sat there sipping their morning coffee.

Her husband believed he'd stolen it from her. Miles was a prat, and it didn't really matter what he thought, but it didn't make him feel great to be accused of theft, and that made him think about Melanie. He called her a thief, and she insisted she was innocent. What if she was telling the truth, and she hadn't taken his weed or his bank card? Or what if Melanie stole the handbag?

He groaned and wished he could undo the damage that he had done to her aunt. Sharon had only been trying to help him. Tomorrow he would ring adult social services and try to withdraw his complaint and say or do anything he could to help save her career.

He wheeled around his apartment, his tummy growling. He was hungry but too restless to eat. Was Jenny staying again? He didn't know. Maybe she was keeping away from him. Even though she said she didn't believe that he had stolen her purse, she might have a tiny dart of doubt.

Truth was he had failed her. She came to him thinking she would be safe and relaxed while she worked out what to do about her marriage. But if she was robbed in his home, then his apartment was no longer a safe place for her. He hated being so useless and vulnerable. Wasn't that what the policeman had called him? Weak and vulnerable. Useless to anyone.

Some fucking tea leaf was using his flat like their own personal cash machine. Flitting in and out whenever they felt like it.

He picked the phone up and was about to call the police and talk to that PC Clarke. He seemed like a decent enough guy. He paused. Realistically, though, what could they do? Telling them didn't change the situation. He was still the pathetic saddo in the wheelchair that was easy pickings for any criminal with a mind to rob him. It wasn't as if they would post a policeman at his door, and he didn't want that, anyway. Somehow, he had to take back control.

He pressed in a number and waited for it to answer.

'Steve, hello mate, I was thinking about you yesterday, 'bout time we hit the pub again. It's your round, I think...'

'Yeah, let's do that Danny,' Steve replied, 'but first I need your help.'

'Sure, what's up, mate?'

Steve took a deep breath. He knew it was a big decision and one that could have dire consequences, but he couldn't carry on like this, unable to protect himself and, more importantly, protect Jenny. He wasn't willing to let some thieving bastard carry on treating him like a mug. He was stuck in a wheelchair, weak, vulnerable, useless, but there was something that he could do to make the terms of any future encounter more equal.

'Danny,' he said. 'I need you to help me get a gun.'

EPISODES 21 - 25

JASMINE CLOSE - SERIES ONE

EPISODE TWENTY ONE
JASMINE CLOSE - SERIES ONE

Victoria looked across the table and smiled.

'That's better,' Brett said, reaching out to take her hand.

She sipped her chardonnay and let herself relax and forget for a few hours about the nightmare that her life had become. It had been a lovely evening, and he had seemed determined to make sure that she enjoyed herself.

'Dessert?'

She shook her head. 'I'm full thanks.'

He caught the eye of the waiter and nodded his head. A minute or two later, the bill arrived, and he handed over his credit card.

Victoria suddenly wondered if she should offer to pay half. Not having been on a date for years, she had no idea what the current etiquette was. She reached for her bag; she had money in her own personal account. Not much, but hopefully enough. The restaurant was tucked away in a village north of Newport Pagnell, and she wasn't sure exactly where they were. She had been so stressed and distracted with her anger towards her husband and growing panic as to what the hell she was going to do that the journey had barely registered with her. She had tried to cancel on him, but Brett had insisted that she needed to go out and relax for a few hours. He was right. She felt calmer and, if not actually stronger; she felt more resigned to her fate.

She pulled her purse out, but Brett put his hand over hers.

'Don't even think about it,' he said. 'My treat.'

Victoria hesitated. Part of her wanted to argue and insist, but she had a feeling that the meal did not come cheap. The ambiance in the restaurant oozed quality, and that usually meant expensive. She put her purse away and thanked him, wondering what she was doing. Just a few short weeks ago, if someone had told her she would find herself in another man's arms, let alone in his bed, she would have laughed out loud at the absurdity of it all. Her marriage to Dave had been the ultimate Howard and Hilda package. Mr and Mrs middle England.

'Victoria...'

She looked across the table.

Brett stood up and smiled at her. 'Let it go.'

'What?'

He bent down and kissed her forehead. 'The frown, for starters.'

'Sorry,' she said, meaning it. She knew she should pay more attention to him, and not be dwelling on her problems, at least for a short while.

'Come on,' he said.

'Where are we going?'

'To recapture that smile.'

TAMSIN WAS VERY quiet as they took the short walk to school, and Belle was worried about her daughter. As Christmas approached, the big Kyle shaped hole in their lives seemed to overshadow everything. She wanted to tell her daughter that it would be alright. That was what mums were supposed to do: reassure their children and keep them safe. It would be a lie, and they both knew it. Kyle was gone and if Mo had anything to do with it, they would never see or hear from him again. Lost in her thoughts, she jumped in surprise as a loud bell rang from behind her. She turned her head and quickly pulled

Tamsin back to allow two speeding electric scooters to go hurtling past. It was a couple of older school kids going much too fast to allow for the pedestrians that shared the redway.

A large Labrador tugged at its lead, its tail wagging excitedly as its owner approached them.

'Lovely morning,' the woman said, trying to hold the dog back as it sniffed excitedly around Tamsin's feet.

Was it? Belle hadn't noticed. She forced herself to smile. 'Yes lovely,' she agreed, realising that it was one of those bright crisp days when the wintery sun manages to shine in a cloudless sky. It was cold, very cold, and frost sparkled on the bushes and shrubbery that edged the path. Silvery spider webs formed filigree networks between the leaves, and drops of dew hung frozen into tiny icicles.

Sad that her hurting heart had blinded her to the surrounding beauty, she looked down at her daughter, who was fussing over the dog.

'What's his name?' Tamsin asked the lady, her face alight with the pleasure that had been missing for weeks.

'I'm Jane and this is Oscar,' the woman replied. 'He's a bit mischievous, and he's got a mind of his own.'

'We better go,' Belle said, tugging at her daughter's hand. 'Or you will be late for school.'

'Bye Oscar,' Tamsin called as they hurried on up the redway.

'Can we have a dog, mummy, please?'

Belle wanted to say yes. She wanted to see her little girl's face light up with excitement and joy. But she knew it wasn't possible. 'Not in the flat poppet. We're on the second floor and it wouldn't be fair to the dog.' Besides, she was pretty sure that the lease excluded dogs. They walked the rest of the way in silence. Tamsin didn't argue or plead. She just accepted disappointment as though it were the way of the world. It broke Belle's heart all over again. At that moment, she would give a lot to have a child who threw a tantrum to try to get what they wanted. Tamsin's resignation showed that she had no such expectations. Her daughter wore sadness like a cloak. It wrapped itself around her small frame and the Tamsin who used to laugh and smile and sing silly songs was hidden away, swamped by the mountain of upset and disappointment.

Belle hugged her daughter and watched as she walked into school. The slow realisation that it was her fault crept into her consciousness. She had allowed her own pain and sadness to seep like a poison into her daughter. They had lost Kyle. They were both grieving, but that didn't mean that they had to stop living. Because Belle was full of guilt at leaving her son behind, she realised she had been afraid to find any pleasure or happiness in anything and that same insidious misery had infected her little girl.

She walked briskly back towards Jasmine Close. It was December, yet she had done nothing for Christmas. She had no presents, no tree or decorations and she hadn't even got Tamsin an advent calendar.

Belle waved at Steve as he wheeled past her, heading up towards the canal. He nodded his head and mumbled a good morning back to her. They had barely ever spoken, and it occurred to her she knew none of the residents beyond saying hello. Several of the houses and flats were occupied now, and it was possible that other children had moved in. Her self-imposed isolation could have prevented Tamsin from having playmates on the doorstep. Although Mo had stolen her son away, he had also given her and her daughter the freedom to settle. It was time she acknowledged that fact. They wouldn't move now. The apartment was where Kyle knew they were and one day he would come back to them. She didn't know when or even how, but she needed to believe it was true. In the meantime, they could make it home. It was time they both made friends and reached out to engage with the surrounding community.

As she walked up the stairs and passed her neighbour's door, it suddenly occurred to her that she hadn't seen or heard anything from Natasha or Ed or even the baby for days.

STEVE FELT BETTER for the fresh air. He loved the canal, especially peering into the murky depths to try to catch sight of a fish. He'd seen a few whoppers; some of the pike seemed smarter than the fishermen who sat for hours trying to net them. It was a bright December morning and even the still dirty water of the canal looked clearer and bluer from the sky's reflection.

He wondered if Jenny was on her balcony watching him. He hoped not, as he was very close to the edge. She would panic if she saw him leaning over to look down. She hadn't stayed last night; did that mean her and her dickhead husband had made up? He couldn't see it happening, more likely that one of them had moved to the spare room. She had the biggest house on the Close, so plenty of space to avoid each other. His hands gripping the wheels, he edged back onto the grass; it was a bit slippy from the morning dew and his wheels span and slid a little. Back on the redway, he headed home. He had calls to make and was hoping for an update from Danny regarding yesterday evening's conversation.

He hadn't slept all night. He tried, hour after hour, and he'd kept his eyes closed shut, willing his body to slide into slumber, but it never happened. His useless body had ached and his mind had raced. He wished he had some dope to help ease the pain and the restlessness, and in the long, dark hours he decided to ring Lou and beg her for an early supply. He would tell her about the second break-in, she might not believe him, but it was the truth and his need was genuine.

It was still early when he wheeled back to Jasmine Close. Victoria was just opening up the Show Home and waved to him as he went past. He glanced at Jenny's house. The curtains were still closed, but her husband's car wasn't on the drive. He almost stopped, thinking he would knock and see how she was, but he didn't. He felt awkward. Even though she said she knew he hadn't taken her handbag, the simple fact that it had disappeared while she was at his house had opened a gaping chasm between them.

Steve pressed his button to open his door and wheeled himself in. He put the kettle on and picked up his land line phone. He would ring Lou first, and then he needed a number for a locksmith. He had no idea who or how, but if someone was letting themselves in and out of his flat, then he was going to put a stop to it. He turned his computer on and realised that he was lucky to still have it. When the bastard broke in and took everything from his weed to his mobile phone, they had left his computer. He wasn't under any illusions; it wasn't from some moral dilemma on the criminal's part. Had he of been in possession of a nice shiny new laptop, it would be gone. His computer was old, heavy, and definitely not worth nicking. He kept meaning to upgrade and update, but his mum brought it for him when he was at sixth form college. She never had much money, and it was a huge expense for her. He never really appreciated it at the time, wishing that he could have a top of the range laptop like his mates all seemed to have. After she died and he saw the true state of her finances, he felt every inch the ungrateful git that he was and so the computer and its big, heavy, hard-drive took pride of place in the corner of his lounge.

He waited for it to boot up, and then he began his search. Twenty minutes later, mission accomplished, he rang Lou.

The phone rang for a long time, and just as he was about to hang up, it answered.

'Lou? It's Steve Lance from Jasmine Close.'

'No.'

'No? Is that you Lou?'

'Yes, pet, and the answer's no.'

Despite her voice being weak and shaky the 'no' was incredibly firm and final.

'You don't know what I want,' he said, irritated by her assumption even if it was the correct one.

'I don't? So you're not asking for an early delivery?'

'Well, I am but...'

He stared at the phone in his hand. She had actually hung up on him.

BELLE POINTED to the apartment block. 'Just here please,' she said to the taxi driver. 'How much?'

'Four fifty please love.'

She wanted to point out that she wasn't his love, but stopped herself just in time. He was only being friendly, and she was the one lacking in Christmas cheer. So instead, she smiled and handed him a five-pound note. She was going to say keep the change, but he took that as already given. The note went into his wallet and the wallet went back into his pocket and he made no attempt at all to help her out with all her shopping bags and once again she had to stifle a snipe at him. His bottom was clearly stuck with superglue to the seat. Or was it the size of his arse that was wedging him in? Either way, she doubted he ever left it during his shift, unless he absolutely had to. No wonder he was so overweight.

She dragged all the bags out and couldn't resist a sarcastic 'thanks,' before closing the door, she didn't even know if he heard her because he was gone the second it shut leaving her with a pavement full of carrier bags and a four foot Christmas tree still in its box.

It took her two trips, but she finally managed to get it all up the stairs and into her apartment. She had debated all the way around the shops and on the journey home whether to put up the tree and the lights, so when Tamsin got home the place would be transformed in a Christmassy surprise. She would love to see her daughter's face as she walked through the door, but on the other hand, Tamsin might enjoy the fun of decorating the tree herself.

In the end she opted for a compromise, she would put the tree up and leave all the tinsel and baubles for Tamsin to do after school.

STEVE OPENED THE DOOR. 'Thanks for coming so quick,' he said to the locksmith. 'I need this changed...' he pointed to the lock. 'I want new keys for it.'

The middle-aged man looked at the door and looked at the lock, then back at Steve. 'You do realise lad, I can only replace it with the same simple system?'

He couldn't remember the last time anyone called him a lad. 'Yeah, I know it has to work with my remote opener.'

'It doesn't really improve security you need a deadlock for that.'

'All I need is a new set of keys,' Steve said. The more that he had pondered the problem, the more convinced he had become that one of the site workers or one of the Show Home women had taken and pocketed a key before he moved in. There simply wasn't any other explanation.

The man shrugged his heavy shoulders and set to work. Steve retreated into the lounge, away from the cold air. His telephone rang, and he picked it up.

'Yeah?' he said, expecting it to be yet another call from a machine telling him he was owed hundreds, possibly thousands, in compensation for mis-sold PPI, even though he had never had a loan or a credit card in his life.

'Alright then.'

'Lou?'

'Yes, it's me, pet. Sorry I was a bit short with you earlier, but you should know better than to ring an old lady so early in the morning. My bones were barely moving, and I'd not even had my morning cuppa to wake me up.'

'Sorry Lou I didn't think.'

'And why should you pet? The young don't need to fret about the ills of the elderly. So give me a good reason. And I do mean a very good reason why I should break my rules again and let you have an early supply.'

'I was robbed again.' it sounded lame even to his ears. 'The bastard came back, it's the truth Lou.'

'Well, either you're a big fat liar or the unluckiest sod in the world, or maybe I'm just a gullible old fool. I'll see what I can do.'

She hung up before he could thank her, and he closed his eyes. At least he could sleep again once he got the new supply. He had been told that some doctors would give it to him on a prescription for pain and spasm. But it was drops that went on the tongue and the 'drug' element had been removed, so really it was little more than a painkiller. He liked smoking it and he liked the effect it had on him. It made him forget what he was and what he had lost.

'All done,' the man said, handing him a ring with three keys on.

Steve took them and placed them on his lap. 'Are we all sorted?'

'Yeah, you paid online.'

'Great, and thanks again for coming around so quickly.'

The man was looking at him strangely, as though he wanted to say something more. 'You take care lad,' was all he said before walking away.

Steve closed the door and wheeled himself into the kitchen. Somewhere he had the keys to the old lock, and he didn't want to get them mixed up. He was sure he had put them in the top kitchen drawer. He went all through and found nothing. He tried the drawer below, riffling through the tea towels. He found no keys. He paused and cast his mind back to the day he moved in. he had professional removals that unpacked and put everything away. He could see in his head the young woman in her green company overalls filling up his kitchen cupboards with all the new pots, pans and utensils that his social worker had made him order in advance. The keys were almost the last thing that she did. She held them up to him, three on a ring almost identical to what he now had on his lap.

'What shall I do with these,' she had asked him with a smile.

He remembered her as being blonde, petite, and pretty. He was straight out of rehab and feeling scared, tired, and very grumpy. He had made some bitter remark along the lines of 'couldn't give stuff, luv.' He didn't know if she had taken offence or not.

'I'll just drop them in here then,' she replied putting them in the top drawer.

So where the hell were they now?

SONIA THREW the last of the bread into the water for the ducks and the swans. Not many were brave enough to come to the edge of the lake with Casper barking and running up and down the water's edge like a demented hound from hell.

'Come on, boy,' she called, walking away. He made one last barking charge and then ran to catch her up. He loved Willen Lake, and it was one of the few places she could let him off the lead and allow him to run free. His leg was almost completely healed. It just needed strengthening and running up and down the slopes beside the Peace Pagoda offered the perfect exercise for him.

She stood and watched him, a smile on her lips and the sun on her face. It felt like the lull before the storm. She'd seen the forecast, the temperature was set to plummet and there was snow was on the way. Of course, the experts didn't always get it right and even when they did, Milton Keynes was in a valley and often missed the worst of it. But just in case, she wanted to let Casper get as much running in as his old legs would allow.

She strolled slowly along the footpath, letting him chase around in huge circles of tail-wagging and occasional barking. She kept an eye open for other dogs; it was as popular with owners as it was with joggers, bikers and mums with pushchairs. As she approached the top of the north lake, she whistled for Casper to catch her up. He came bounding along and almost went straight into her with his excitement. She fussed over his head; he was panting hard, his tongue hanging out, his eyes looking with loving devotion at her. 'Time to go home, boy,' she said softly, slipping the chain back over his head before they turned from the path and into the cricket pitch car park.

As they walked away from the lake, she saw a familiar car. It was the Pickles' estate car, and it was stopped on the edge of the carpark right up against the trees and bushes. She walked up to it and peered inside, surprised when she saw that Dave was asleep in the reclined front seat. She tapped on the window. He didn't move. She put her face up against the glass for a closer look. He had his overcoat on top of him as well as a red and black checked car blanket, but he still looked cold, his breath exhaling like a trail of steam.

Sonia banged on the window again, louder this time and Casper barked helpfully. Dave sat bolt upright looking around him in confusion.

She pulled the door handle, but it was locked. He took a few seconds to register who she was and then, as recognition hit him, he unlocked the door.

'Hello,' she said, pulling it wide open and looking in at him. The stale stench of fish and chips and body odour escaping out of the door. She saw the screwed up paper from the takeaway along with an empty service station Styrofoam cup and wrappers from crisps and chocolate bars.

'What do you want?' he said clearly not happy to see her. He shivered and pulled the blanket round him.

Casper stuck his nose in the car to see what was going on but withdrew again quickly and settled down on the gravel to rest after his duck chasing and running around.

'Have you been here all night?'

'No.'

'You have. You look frozen, put the engine on for five minutes and warm up.'

'I'm fine,' he said looking shifty.

'Why are men such crap liars?'

'I don't need the engine on.'

Sonia assessed the situation and came to the only logical conclusion available to her. 'You've run out of petrol!'

He grabbed the door and slammed it shut.

Unperturbed, she pulled it open again before he had time to press the handle in and lock it. 'Come on,' she said. 'You're coming with me.'

'Where?' he said warily.

'Home.'

'No way, Vic will kill me.'

'Deserved, from what I've heard.'

'Sod off,' he grabbed the door again.

'No way sunshine. I'm not leaving you here to freeze to death.'

'You just said that's what I deserve.'

'True but that's for Victoria to decide. I don't want to deprive her of the opportunity by leaving you here to catch pneumonia. Besides, you stink and need a shower.'

'How to kick a man when he's down!'

'Just telling it like it is. Now come on, you can come to mine and get warm and cleaned up.' She thought he was going to go into male stubborn mode and refuse. She was wondering what to do, should she call Victoria?

'Alright, but only if you promise not to tell her.'

'I promise,' she replied crossing her fingers behind her back. 'Lock the car and I'll drop you back later with a can of petrol to get you moving again.'

'Why are you doing this?'

She shrugged her shoulders, 'I have absolutely no idea.'

'I HAVE A SURPRISE FOR YOU,' Belle said to Tamsin as they walked back from school.

'What is it mummy?'

'Wait until we get home.'

'There's Oscar.'

Belle watched as her daughter ran off up the redway to fuss the dog.

'Another walk?' Belle said to the woman who was approaching from the direction of the canal.

'Three a day,' the woman replied, looking tired and a bit breathless.

'Are you alright?' Belle asked.

'Yes, we're heading home now. I think we went a too far and I've got a bit too cold.'

Belle nodded in agreement. The woman's nose was bright red, almost glowing in contrast to her pale skin. She tapped Tamsin's shoulder, 'come on poppet, let them get on.'

They all stepped back as bike bells rang and some older kids raced past.

'They are a menace.' The woman said. 'I know they are safer on the redway than on the road, but why do they have to go so fast? And those damn bells, they make me jump every time.'

They said goodbye and carried on walking. Tamsin stopped at the Show Home to admire the tree and the lights that had gone on that day. 'It's so pretty mummy.'

Belle was so glad that she had been to the shops that day. It felt as though she were coming through a fog and now at last she could see the way out. Of course without Kyle her heart would never be whole, but she owed it to Tamsin to let laughter and happiness back into their lives.

At the flat she unlocked the door and pushed it open, letting her daughter run in ahead of her. Tamsin stopped and stared at the undecorated tree. She dropped to her knees and lifted up the decorations from the box and burst into tears.

MEET me in the pub tonight, I've got some news for you, mate.'

'What time?'

'Make it about eight-ish.'

Steve hung up and took a deep breath. He could hear his mum's voice in his head telling him to be a good lad and ring Danny back to say he'd changed his mind. He looked at the phone clutched in his hand and, making a decision, he put it back in its charger. Maybe he was being a prat, but a prat with a gun felt better than being a weak, pathetic, vulnerable loser. He'd played that part for long enough and it was time for a change. It wasn't as if he would ever use it and besides, with his new lock on the door, the thieving bastard wouldn't find it so easy to get in again. And if he did, well, then Steve would be armed and ready. He wouldn't fire the weapon, but he would certainly like to see the man piss himself with fear. Bastards like that were usually bullies and would cry and run when facing someone or something scarier than they were.

He was disappointed he hadn't heard from jenny. He hated the handbag coming between them. He missed her; he had few friends and no inclination to make more. He needed Jenny, and that was scary. He thought about Melanie and realised that he had thrown away and wheeled right over her offered hand of friendship. He was thinking it more and more likely that she hadn't stolen from him and he really ought to ring her and apologise. Trouble was, he knew she would tell him to sod off, which was what he deserved after all the trouble he had caused her aunt. He wished he could take it back and put it right, but as his mum used to say, 'what's done is done.' Or was it? He wheeled to fetch the phone as an idea hit him. He dialled the number and asked for adult services. 'Yes, hello, this is Steve Lance,' he said to the woman on the line. 'I need to talk to you about my former social worker, Sharon Stanza. I'm sorry to say that I made the whole thing up.'

'You made it up?'

'Yep, my accusation was false. It was all lies.'

BELLE HUGGED Tamsin and for a long time they sobbed together in each other's arms. She stroked her little girl's hair, and they clung to each other as the grief they both felt was finally released. Eventually the sobs eased and Tamsin pulled away and picked up the pack of Christmas tree chocolates. 'Can I eat one?'

Belle smiled and nodded reaching for the box of tissues on the coffee table and passing one to Tamsin. 'Do you like the tree?'

'Can we make it look pretty?'

'That's what the box of decorations is for.'

'And lights?'

'Yes poppet, I got us lots of lights.' She held up two boxes, one with coloured bulbs and the other pack, was plastic flowers that flashed intermittently. 'Let's do these first.'

Together they wound the lights around the tree and then they put all the decorations onto the branches, followed by the chocolate Santas and bells. They stood back to admire their handiwork. 'lovely,' she said.

Tamsin was quiet as she stared at the flashing lights.

Belle put her arm around her daughter's shoulders. 'He'll be alright,' she said softly. 'Your daddy will look after him.'

'I know. But he won't have a Christmas tree or any presents.'

Mo had always allowed them to have the Christmas traditions so long as there were no religious images on advent calendars or cards. But she knew it would be different in Pakistan and she doubted if

Kyle would be allowed anything Christmassy. Maybe she was wrong and Mo would do something special for their son. She had to believe that he was happy and well looked after. It was the only way that she could cope. 'We will think of him and send him all our love.'

'He misses us mummy.'

'Like we miss him.'

'Yes,' Tamsin said. 'He gets sad sometimes.'

'I expect he does.'

Tamsin looked up at her. 'But he is alright mummy. I would know if he was very unhappy.'

'You would?'

'Yes.'

She couldn't know for sure if Tamsin's feelings were real or wish fulfilment. Either way, it offered a ray of hope. Belle didn't understand the twin thing. She wasn't sure anyone could unless they experienced it themselves. She had witnessed their extraordinary bond, though. As babies, they cried and laughed in unison and as small children, they always went down with the same bug at the same time. It was when they weren't together that they most amazed their parents. She remembered one time when they were about five years old. It was just before Christmas and they were at the Brent Cross Shopping Centre. They split up to buy presents. Tamsin went with her, and Kyle went with Mo. They were in WH Smiths looking at the books when Tamsin suddenly cried out and dropped to the floor, clutching her leg. Within a few minutes, she received a call from Mo to say that Kyle was in the centre's first aid room because he'd hurt his leg. She rushed from the shop to find her son and was told by Mo that he had been climbing where he shouldn't be climbing and had lost his balance and fallen and landed awkwardly. The security guard who ran to help them was concerned it might be broken, so he sent them for an assessment at the first aid station. Luckily it was just a nasty bruise and when the drama was over and they were in the car driving home, Belle realised that Tamsin had felt her brother's pain at exactly the same time that he hurt himself. It was one of many such incidences, if one had an ailment like an ear infection, she had to take them both to the doctors to determine which of them actually needed treatment.

Belle wasn't sure if the invisible bond and connection between her children would make the separation easier or worse. It was comforting to think that Tamsin would know if he was in trouble or distress, and heart-breaking that they were to be split up when they should be close together. Mo was a monster for what he had done. It might make some logical sense in a twisted world without emotion or empathy. But Tamsin and Kyle were brother and sister and they needed each other.

Realising that she was crying again and not wanting to upset her daughter, she hurried into the bathroom to wipe her eyes and blow her nose. Then she returned to the lounge. 'I have one more thing for you.' She picked up an M&S bag that she'd hidden behind the sofa and gave it to Tamsin. It contained two advent calendars, hidden behind each door were small Percy Pig sweets that her children both loved.

Tamsin held them both up and grinned happily.

'I thought you could open Kyle's every day for him,'

'Yes, he'd like that.'

'We're going to have a lovely Christmas,' she said to her daughter, determined to make it come true.

STEVE WATCHED Danny as he took a long slurp of his beer. His friend looked nervous and uncomfortable. 'Suggest you don't take up a life of crime,' he said with a grin. 'You are crap at this stuff.'

'Yeah well I can't believe you've persuaded me to do it for you.'

'I appreciate it mate.'

'I bloody hope so. The scum I've had to talk to...' Danny took another long slurp, he shook his head. 'Seriously scary bastards.'

'But you got it?'

'I got it.'

'I won't forget this,' Steve said.

'I just hope neither of us regrets it.'

'You worry too much. I told you I have no intention of using it.'

'Shit, I hope not Steve. Don't think prison would be a good place for either of us.'

Steve had no wish to go to prison. His new acquisition was strictly for protection. If any thieving bastard dared to enter his domain, it would be them shaking with fear, not him. Just owning the weapon made him feel stronger, safer, and less vulnerable. Despite Danny's worried frown, he knew he was doing the right thing.

He grinned at his friend. 'Cheers, mate,' he said, raising his glass.

EPISODE TWENTY TWO
JASMINE CLOSE - SERIES ONE

Steve willed his body to relax and his mind to let go. He needed to sleep. He was beyond tired. Yet the soothing delights of dreams still eluded him. He hoped Lou would let him have more dope and, to his mind, it couldn't come soon enough. Of course, he could go to the doctors for a prescription of sleeping pills. When he had been at the Stoke Mandeville rehab unit, they were available to him and, on a couple of occasions, unable to face another night of wakeful torment; he had taken the pills. They certainly worked; knocked him out almost the instant his head hit the pillow. Trouble was, they left him tired and weak in the morning. He didn't appreciate the feeling of lethargy and didn't enjoy taking tablets. He had been offered antidepressants and painkillers as well. The first he refused, and the second he only took when he absolutely had to.

He glanced at the bedside clock. It was two twenty-five. He squeezed his eyes tightly shut. If he could drop off now, he could still get six hours' sleep and be up at a reasonable time. Well, reasonable enough for a man with no job, no purpose and very little hope.

He heard a noise and tensed, straining to block out all the

familiar nightly noises like the constant hum of his pressure relieving air mattress and the ticktock of his bedside clock. One by one, he isolated the sounds and identified them, the vibration from his fridge freezer, the slight rattle that the vent made in his wet room when it was very windy outside. He could hear rain tapping at the front window, the sound of the occasional vehicle on the grid roads. If he listened really carefully, he could even hear the distant sound of cars speeding along the M1 motorway. Aside from all the normal nighttime noises, there was something else - footsteps outside his door and a key in the lock.

Steve held his breath and reached his fingers under his mattress. The gun was solid and comforting beneath his hand. His new replacement mobile phone was next to him on the bedside cabinet. Should he phone the police? He reached out and held it ready. But then reasoned that by the time the plod responded, the bastard would be long gone and then he would feel like a prat. What could he say? He heard noises and panicked like a frightened child? He didn't need anything to make him seem even more pathetic than he already felt.

Whoever was out there, they weren't getting in easily. The key wasn't working in the new lock. He felt uncontrollable laughter rising up inside him, but he held it in and concentrated on listening. There was a brief thump on the door as though the would be thief hit out in frustration before Steve heard the footsteps retreating. His hand gripping the gun relaxed and the stress within him escaped as a burst of hysterical victory laughter. He had changed the locks and cheated the bastard. He still had no idea who had his key or how they had it, but at least they no longer had easy access to his home and his home was once again his castle.

'WHERE'S DAD?' Gemma asked, munching on a slice of toast. 'Has he left for work already?'

'Not sure, darling, I haven't seen him.'

Gemma paused, the toast held aloft and ready to bite into. 'Did he come home last night?'

Victoria thought about lying. She didn't want to face the questions or the fallout, yet she knew the truth had to be dealt with at some stage, so it might as well be now. 'No, he didn't. I'm afraid your father is having a few problems at the moment.'

'Oh, my god! He knows, doesn't he?'

'Knows what?' Victoria asked, bemused by her daughter's reaction.

'About the man.' Gemma dropped her toast and stood up, looking at Victoria accusingly. 'He's left you, hasn't he? You've driven him out.'

The man? She didn't really know what to say. The conversation wasn't going at all how she expected it to. 'I don't actually know if he's left, but I...'

'Don't lie.' Gemma shouted as angry tears edged out from between her mascara laden lashes. 'I saw you. I saw him. It was disgusting! I'll never forgive you for what you've done to me and dad!'

'Gemma?' she called after her daughter, but the kitchen door slammed on her words.

Victoria sat down and cradled her coffee mug. She pushed away her own toast, her appetite gone. What did her daughter mean by 'the man?' did Gemma know about Brett? It certainly sounded that way, but how could she?

The front door opened and closed and she knew that would be Gemma leaving to catch the bus for school. She thought about running after her, but decided giving her time to cool down would probably be more sensible. Besides, she wasn't ready to have the whole other man conversation yet. If Gemma had seen her with Brett, then life had just got even harder and more complicated than it already was. And where exactly was Dave? After searching the pubs last night, she rang all his friends who all claimed they hadn't seen him. In desperation, she even tried his mother, thinking that he might have gone there. But Jean hadn't seen her son since they last visited a few months ago and Victoria felt mean for worrying her. Maybe there was another woman after all; it could be the stress of keeping an affair secret had driven him to gambling. All she knew for sure was that he had no job, no money, and he hadn't been home. So where the hell was he?

Her phone beeped with a message. She opened it up and smiled. Even though it was wrong, Brett was the beacon of light in her otherwise very grey world. The simple X he sent her lifted her spirits, and she was glad that he was in her life while she dealt with the debt and chaos that Dave had created. She felt a surge of anger towards her husband. The lies and gambling were bad enough, but the fact that he had apparently bailed on her made everything even worse. He had caused their world to collapse and then buggered off, leaving her and Gemma to face losing their home and possibly, in fact, probably, bankruptcy. He was a coward, and that upset her more than anything else.

Belle unlocked her door and let herself in. The tree lights twinkled even though it was morning. Tamsin had insisted that they switch them on the minute she got out of bed. Belle turned them off. She would put them on again when she left to fetch her daughter from school later. The phone rang, and she picked it up. She knew the number on the display. 'Hello mum.'

'Hello love,' her mother said. 'How are things?'

'A bit better,' Belle replied, glad that it was true. She told her mother about the Christmas tree and the sobbing.

'Sounds like you're both ready to move on.'

'Sort of. We were both missing him and that won't change, but it was my guilt for leaving him that was making us both so miserable.'

'Love, you did what you had to do for Tamsin.'

'I know, Mum, and that's what I have to focus on. I can't undo what happened and at the moment I don't have any idea how to get my son back, so for now I need to concentrate on my daughter.'

'Would you like me to come down? We could go shopping buy some bits for Tamsin...'

'Aren't you busy?'

'Nothing that can't wait for another day. I'll be with you in a couple of hours.'

Belle put the phone down and smiled. It would be a lovely treat for Tamsin to see her nana when she got home from school.

She went into the kitchen to put the kettle on and then into the bedrooms to gather up the washing. Loading it into the machine, she found herself pausing to listen, although she wasn't sure what she was listening for. She could hear the workman outside and all the sounds of a busy construction site. She realised it was what she couldn't hear that was worrying her. There was still no sound from next door. The apartments were reasonably soundproofed but even so she heard doors opening and closing, occasionally the sound of the TV, raised voices and most clearly of all the sound of the baby crying. The baby that cried almost all the time and was now silent. So silent that Belle couldn't even remember the last time she'd heard it at all.

Deciding that her decision to engage with the community included the neighbour who had caused her so much trouble, she put her door on the latch and banged on Natasha's door. No one came. She put her head against the PVC and listened. Still nothing. Belle returned to her flat and opened her French doors and went out onto the balcony. She leaned over and peered around to try to see into the next apartment, but the curtains were drawn and she couldn't see or hear anything. She had to assume that they had gone away.

STEVE CHECKED HIS FRONT DOOR; there was nothing to show that what happened last night was real and not just his sleep deprived imagination going into overdrive.

'Everything alright Steve?'

He turned round; PC Clarke was standing a few feet along the road beside his marked police car.

'You back again?' he glanced next door. 'Is Mary alright?'

'As far as I know. I was just having a look around. Barry, the building site foreman, said that he picked up someone lurking suspiciously on the site security cameras in the night.'

'Really? Anything to identify them?'

'I'm just heading over to have a look. You didn't see or hear anything?'

Steve shook his head. 'Nah, I sleep like a baby.'

He watched the PC walk across the Close and wondered why he lied. The words just slipped out as easily as jam off a doughnut.

He went back indoors and made himself some tea and toast. He often went for a wheel up to the canal before having his breakfast, but he was tired and couldn't be arsed. He wanted to go and knock for Jenny and he really wanted to see her, but he knew he wouldn't do that either. It was clearly going to be a slob day. He thought about Melanie and how she would tell him off for not bothering with a wash or a shave. He wondered if his phone call had made a difference and whether Sharon had got her job back. He hoped so.

He switched the TV on and settled down for a few hours of mindless morning crap. He must have nodded off during the Jeremy Kyle show because he woke up to the sound of a very chavvy woman screaming at a very skinny tattooed man egged on by the studio audience. He realised his phone was ringing. 'Yeah?' he said, picking it up and pushing the mute button on the television.

'I'll be round this evening.'

'Thanks Lou,' he said as the phone went dead. His spirits lifted, he turned the television off and headed to the bathroom to clean his teeth. Maybe he'd take that walk after all, and maybe even a shower.

MILES HAD BEEN DOING his homework. He was right about the apartment. According to the local paper, it had been illegally operating as a brothel. The woman Annabel was in fact the infamous Madam Ella, who was believed to have run a string of similar properties not just in Milton Keynes but right across the region. The deeper he dug, the more material and evidence he found. Madam Ella had been splashed across the tabloids many times before. It looked as though she started out as a glamour model; she even made it to page three of the Sun newspaper. He looked at her image on his company laptop. He'd found it in the newspapers' online archives. She was a real looker, although he doubted that her assets were real.

He jumped guiltily when a brief tap on the door preceded his secretary Shirley bringing him his morning coffee.

He quickly closed the page, feeling a bit like a horny schoolboy hiding lad mags from his mum. He was being ridiculous. It was important research and besides, the work computer wouldn't let him access any of the porn sites that responded to his search for her name. He would have to look at them when he got home later.

Shirley looked at him with a worried frown on her forehead. 'Are you alright, Mr Fisher?'

'Of course I am. Just got a lot of work to get through.'

She put the coffee on the desk along with a china plate with two of his favourite chocolate biscuits.

'Thank you Shirley.' He forced himself to smile while wishing she would hurry up and leave so that he could get back to his research. He was worried about Tammy and about all the other young girls held against their will. He wondered what hold Annabel or Madam Ella had over them. Was it drugs? A lot of the articles and information that he read suggested that most working girls were addicts and were therefore easy to exploit. But Tammy hadn't seemed like she had a drug issue. Would he know if she had a problem? He thought addicts looked sick with teeth missing and lank, dirty hair, but maybe that was just how TV drama portrayed them. The small time he spent with Tammy she had looked strong and healthy, with no sign of needle marks or scabs. He realised his secretary was still there, standing beside the desk, looking at him strangely.

'Was there something else, Shirley?'

'Well, it's just that you asked me to go through the latest personnel reports with you. Mandy from HR sent them yesterday afternoon.'

'Right...' he didn't want to go through some personnel reports. He wanted to continue his investigation and research into Madam Ella and how he could rescue Tammy. 'Thing is, I have a load of emails to get through. We'll reschedule for later this afternoon.'

'Can I help with the emails? Filter them for you, Mr Fisher?'

Why was she still there? He fought down his rapidly increasing annoyance with her and forced himself to sound calm and patient. 'Leave me to it; I'll get through them soon.'

Still she hovered, looking at him as though he had sprouted an additional head.

'What?' he finally snapped, unable to control his feelings any longer.

She took a step back in surprise. 'Only that you always insist on dealing with the personnel reports as a priority.'

Priority! What was she nagging on about? How could anything be more of a priority than saving a young girl from a life of slavery and degradation? 'It will still be a priority when we do it this afternoon,' he said, making himself sound firm and confident.

He watched her until she left the office, and he opened up the laptop again. He needed to look into sex trafficking.

THE HOUSE WAS EMPTY. No Dave, no Gemma, and neither of them were answering their phones. She switched lights on and closed the curtains. It was very quiet and a stab of loneliness hit her like a punch in the gut. How had it come to this? She walked into the kitchen and opened the fridge. She planned to make spaghetti bolognaise for dinner. Would she make it just for herself? Why wasn't Gemma home and where the hell was Dave? She put the kettle on and picked up the house phone, staring at it as though if she looked long enough and hard enough, it could make the decision for her. She put it down again and made herself a mug of tea. She thought about how Brett got his sister's best china out for her and made a mental promise that next time she was at the shops, she would buy a pretty teapot and cup and saucer, no more mugs. Then she remembered she was broke and would have no money for such nonsense. Given the state of the bank balance, buying tea bags could soon be a problem.

She picked the phone up again and dialled a number. 'Hello, can I speak to PC Clarke please?' she swung round as there was a tap on the kitchen door. She walked over and unlocked it.

Sonia walked in and shivered dramatically. 'Reckon snow is on the way,' she said, heading straight for the kettle and making herself a mug of tea.

'Just tell him Victoria Pickles would like to speak to him, thanks.' She ended the call and looked at her neighbour, who had found the chocolate hobnobs she kept hidden in the tea caddy.

'Who's that?'

'Tried to ring Clarke...'

'What the coppa?'

'Yes.'

'Why?'

'To report Dave missing.'

Sonia sipped her tea. 'Missing?'

Victoria sat down and took a biscuit from the pack. 'I've no idea where he is. The selfish bastard has run away leaving Gemma and I completely in the crap.' She dunked her biscuit and waited until it was soft and dripping before pulling it out of the tea and taking a quick bite.

'It can't be that bad?' Sonia said, looking at her intently. 'I mean, I'm sure he's not gone far.'

Victoria dunked the remaining bit of biscuit back in the mug. 'Not that bad? He's wiped out every penny.'

'Oh.'

She lifted the biscuit out and watched as it dripped and dropped back into the cup. She pushed her mug away and, unable to hold back any longer, she burst into tears.

'Hey, don't cry Vic, things'll pick up.'

'No, they won't.' Victoria replied, wiping her eyes on the back of her hand.

Sonia grabbed a piece of kitchen roll from the side and handed it to her.

'My marriage is over, my daughter hates me and I'm going to have to sell up.' She took the kitchen roll and blew her nose.

'I better get going,' Sonia said, hurrying towards the kitchen door.

Victoria stared after her in disbelief. All the times Sonia would be round uninvited, and at times impossible to get rid of, now when she needed her neighbour, she was bailing. So much for friendship!

MILES DIDN'T BOTHER with dinner. He wasn't hungry, and he had no interest or inclination to sit at the table with his wife and stepbrother spouting small talk about nothing. He had something far more important to deal with.

He sat in the dark at the bedroom window, watching the road. He had a clear view of the length of Jasmine Close and, in particular, the entrance to the apartment. Beside him were binoculars which he didn't really need, and a pad and pen, which he most definitely did. Already he had logged several arrivals and departures into the block of flats, but so far, none of them interested him.

Behind him, he heard the door knock, followed by the handle being pulled down. He didn't bother to acknowledge the attempted intrusion. He had bolted the door and had no intention of letting Jenny in.

'I've made you a coffee,' his wife called through the closed door.

He ignored her and watched intently as a taxi drove into the Close.

'I'll just leave it outside then…'

What did she want from him? She had destroyed their marriage and turned him into a laughingstock. She preferred the company of that swearing druggie to her own husband. Well, it was her loss. If she wasn't sorry now, then she soon would be. He was going to be a hero, the saviour of the sex workers. Then when she came crawling back begging him to forgive her and give them another chance, he would smile at her and say no.

. . .

Victoria paced the floor. She had phoned all Gemma's friends, and no one was admitting to knowing where she was. She glanced at the clock for what seemed like the hundredth time. It was almost ten. Gemma always tried her luck by pushing boundaries and being late. But her daughter had never stayed out after school without telling her where she was and what time she would be home.

Victoria didn't know whether to call the police or not. At what point would they consider her missing? She was pretty sure that a teenage girl out past her curfew must be an everyday occurrence. She told herself it was nothing to worry about. That Gemma would saunter in and wonder what all the fuss was about. Or maybe Gemma was still angry and deliberately punishing her following their words that morning.

Her mobile phone beeped, and she grabbed it up and opened her messages. But it wasn't her daughter, it was Brett. She threw the phone down onto the sofa, not even bothering to open it or read it. She was far too worried about her daughter to swap illicit love notes with him. The clock edged relentlessly round. It was five past ten. She couldn't stand it any longer. She had to do something. She picked up the phone to ring the police and then she paused; there was someone she hadn't phoned. She slipped her shoes on, grabbed her coat, and hurried out into the Close.

It was dark and very cold. The moon shadowed by heavy, slow-moving clouds. The lights in the Close were wide apart, with only every other one lit, all part of the council cost cutting. As she walked past the alley between the terrace houses and the apartment block, a noise made her jump and gasp as a mobility scooter trundled up behind her.

'Don't mind me, pet.' An old lady called out as Victoria stepped back to let it pass.

The scooter and its occupant pulled up outside Steve's flat. Victoria pressed the bell for number two and waited for a reply.

'Hello?'

'I'm Victoria, Gemma's mum...'

The door buzzed, allowing her to push it open. She walked quickly round to the door. It opened as she approached, and Annabel stood waiting for her. Not waiting for an invitation, Victoria went straight into the apartment, looking all around her for anything that would indicate Gemma was present.

Annabel closed the door and followed her into the open plan apartment. In growing frustration and close to tears that no way was she going to let the other woman see, Victoria swung round.

Annabel was in the kitchen, holding the larder door wide open. 'Try in here...'

'What?'

'Well, you obviously think I'm hiding something, so be my guest and search.'

'No, not something, someone...' she said, barely holding back a sob. She was being rude and feeling silly, but she didn't care. Worry was gnawing at her stomach and she needed answers.

'Ahh, Gemma.'

'You've seen her?'

'Not today.'

'When then?' Annabel didn't look as though she was going to give up that information easily. 'Please,' Victoria said. 'We argued this morning, and she hasn't come home.'

Annabel passed her a tissue. It was pretty and scented and pulled from a pastel patterned box. 'She's a sensible girl. I'm sure she'll be home soon.'

Victoria took the tissue and blew her nose. She looked directly at the other woman suppressing in her own hurt. 'She confides in you?'

Annabel shrugged elegant shoulders. 'It's often easier to talk to someone you're not close to, someone who won't judge you.'

Victoria bit back the retort she wanted to hurl at the woman. 'Is she in trouble?'

'No...'

'Tell me, please,' she hated asking, let alone pleading with her, but clearly she had seen Gemma and she definitely knew something.

Annabel looked at her as if trying to decide whether to tell her what she knew. Victoria had no idea what to say or do to tip the balance in her favour. The woman was a madam. She sold sex for a living and represented everything that Victoria deplored and condemned. Yet, for some unfathomable reason, Gemma had chosen her as a role model.

'She came to me because she thought she was pregnant.'

Victoria felt as though all the energy drained from her body. As if someone literally pulled the plug and all her pumping blood and oxygen flowed out of her. Her baby going through all that fear and panic alone.

'She isn't,' Annabel said, pointing to the sofa. 'Think you better sit down before you fall down.'

'You're sure she isn't pregnant?'

'Yes, we did a test. It was clear.'

'Thank god,' Victoria said with feeling. She didn't want to think about why Gemma had turned to Annabel rather than her. It hurt. Until that morning, she thought things were better between them. She headed for the door. She would go home and hope that Gemma would be in and, if not, then she would have to call the police. 'Thanks,' she forced herself to say. 'For helping Gemma and for telling me.'

'There is something else you should probably know.'

Victoria paused in the doorway, not at all sure that she wanted to hear any more but knowing that she had to.

'Gemma saw you kissing that rather attractive American from down the end of the Close. She was a bit upset.'

Victoria felt sick and dizzy. She managed to get out of the apartment block and stopped to try to recover. She leaned against the wall and took a few deep breaths. To the left of her she saw the door to the Fishers house open and for a brief second, her spirits lifted as she thought it might be Brett. The feelings were quickly replaced by anger towards him for causing trouble between her and her daughter.

She knew she was being unreasonable. She could hardly blame him when she kissed him back. It wasn't Brett, anyway. It was his brother-in-law, Miles. He looked like a man on a mission. He was wrapped up in a thick parka coat with the hood up and a scarf around his neck pulled across his face. His head was down and he was walking fast towards her.

She stood up straight and stepped away from the wall. She started walking back down the Close. 'Evening,' she said, not because she wanted to be sociable and she certainly didn't want to stop and chat, however being rude never came easily to her.

He looked startled, as though she was an aspiration appearing from nowhere. 'Yes, yes,' he mumbled before dropping onto one knee to retie his shoelace.

She hurried on past and then it registered that he was wearing shoes that had no laces. She turned around, but he was gone. She reasoned that he must have gone into one of the houses. He wouldn't have gone down the alley as it led to nowhere.

Up ahead, beyond the Show Home, she saw a bus pull up and as it drove away again; she spotted her daughter.

Gemma was looking up and down the Close, preparing to cross. Victoria wanted to tell her off. The road was a busy dual carriageway and because of the unique design of Milton Keynes grid roads; it meant that the speed limit was seventy miles per hour. Pedestrians and fast cars were never a good mix. Since there was a bridge just two hundred yards one way and an underpass a short distance the other way, risking injury and limbs to save a few minutes was simply not worth it.

Even at half ten in the evening, there was enough traffic to prevent Gemma crossing easily. With relief, Victoria saw her daughter turn and head towards the underpass.

She watched as Gemma walked alongside the road. Victoria went past the Show Home and turned towards the underpass. She saw a figure approaching her daughter fast from the opposite direction. Something about them made Victoria uneasy. She reached the underpass on her side at the same time as Gemma got to the opposite end. It was wide and well lit, but even so, it was out of view from the road and the houses, and it was a perfect place for a mugger to strike.

She was making assumptions and reasoned that the figure was probably innocent and just heading home minding their own business and she was simply letting her imagination fuel her fears. But as Gemma walked into the wide tunnel, the figure suddenly ran at her, hands out poised to grab her rucksack.

'Oi!' Victoria shouted.

The figure veered away and Gemma grabbed her bag defensively.

She started running towards her daughter, although any threat seemed to be gone and she wondered if she had got it wrong, been mistaken. The figure rushed past her and out of the underpass. She saw that it was a male, tall and skinny and youngish, with a knitted beanie pulled down on his head and his jacket zipped up to his chin.

'Are you alright?'

'Of course I am,' Gemma replied. 'What are you shouting at?'

'He looked dodgy. Thought he was about to grab your bag.'

'Well, he would have been highly disappointed. All I've got in there is my maths book, a mars bar and a half-eaten bag of crisps. Oh, and my make-up and hairbrush, I wouldn't want to lose them. I think you were making a fuss about nothing. The poor guy probably thought you were the dangerous one yelling at him like that.'

They walked up towards Jasmine Close, an uneasy silence between them. Victoria didn't know how to begin; did she demand to know why Gemma was so late home and why she hadn't called? Or did she let that slide and ask about the pregnancy test? Or did she go straight into an admission about Brett and explain about Dave and how they had no money left? Did she tell her that her father had disappeared?

They reached the house, and she unlocked the door, holding it open to allow Gemma to go through first. Her daughter switched the light on, dropped her bag in the hall and made straight for the stairs.

'Where do you think you're going?' Victoria cringed as her own mother's voice came hurtling into her head. All she needed to do was add '... young lady' to the sentence and it would be history replaying itself.

'Bed. I'm tired.' Gemma folded her arms across her chest in a defensive pose.

Victoria shook her head and forced her voice to sound calm and neutral. 'No, not yet. I think we need to talk.'

Steve pressed the button to open the door for Lou. She looked even older and more frail than usual. 'Thank you for this,' he said, clutching the packet of marijuana like it was worth more than the crown jewels.

She nodded her head, that looked tiny and lost under the hood of her thick winter coat. 'Keep a tight hold on it this time pet, I can't let you have another early batch, no matter what sad tale you feed me.'

'I understand,' he said. 'Although it was the truth.'

She smiled, and it reminded him of his old granny. She used to look at him the same way when he was a child. As if she was supporting and humouring him even when he was naughty and in trouble with his mum.

The cold night air blasted through the door. It was getting windy again, and it felt as though it must be below freezing. 'Will you be alright Lou? I can call you a cab; you can leave the scooter here and fetch it tomorrow.'

'I'll be fine pet, I have me mitts to keep me warm and...' she pulled a small hip flask from her pocket, 'a drop of the good stuff if my bones begin to freeze.'

He laughed affectionately. She was a gem, and he was lucky to have found her. He wished he knew her story and the truth about why she did what she did, but he had been warned not to ask. So he sat in the doorway shivering while she climbed onto the scooter and then he waved as she drove away. He closed the door, his mind already unpacking the package and rolling up a nice, juicy joint.

. . .

MILES PEEPED INSIDE THE WINDOW. The room was empty. He wasn't sure if he was pleased or disappointed. He wanted to see Tammy, make sure that she was alright, maybe even tap on the window and talk to her, tell her that he would soon be able to save her. On the other hand, he was glad she wasn't there. He didn't want to see her being forced into having sex with some sleazy old man.

He edged quietly along the wall to the French windows. It was a risk. He didn't want to be seen again, but he knew he had to check. He had been watching the flat all evening and other than Victoria from the Show Home, nobody had been in or out of the apartment block. Unable to stand it any longer, he had to get out and see for himself if anything was happening.

As he pressed his face against the glass and peered through the crack in the curtains, he heard footsteps to the side of him. He swung round and looked, but saw nothing. Leaving the window, he crept along to the side of the building to the alley and popped his head around the side. There was a figure pressed up against the wall at the far end, just inches from the Jasmine Close pathway.

Since there was no lighting in the alley or the wasteland beyond it, he couldn't make out the figure very well. They looked tall and slim; it could be a man or a woman. He just wanted them to go so that he could get back to his surveillance. He heard another sound. Wheels on concrete. He watched bemused as the figure suddenly leapt out of the shadows and attacked a person sitting on a mobility scooter. He heard a shout and realised it was Steve yelling.

The attacker had hit the person over the head with a weapon of some kind and they had fallen from the chair to the floor. The attacker grabbed a bag from the basket in the front and then turned to look down the Close towards the apartments.

ALL STEVE WANTED to do was settle down with a smoke. But he saw Lou's new phone on the sofa, and since she had only just left, he grabbed it and hurried after her.

He couldn't comprehend what he was seeing at first. Lou was in a heap on the floor. A man was standing over her, clutching the old handbag that never left her side.

'What the fuck...' he wheeled as fast as he could, shouting as he went, 'bastard! Put that back...'

The figure turned and looked at him. It was a man, young, scruffy and cocky as hell. 'Yeah? What you gonna do about it?'

Steve thought of his gun tucked under the mattress. What fucking good was it to him there?

'It's your fault, locking me out.' the man threw a set of keys at him.

Steve looked down at Lou. She wasn't moving. He felt a surge of rage and wheeled as fast as he could to ram the man. But the bastard laughed at him and jumped out of the way, then swung round and barged sideways into Steve, sending him and his chair toppling over. He landed with a painful thump on the floor, his chair ending up on top of him.

The man slunk away into the shadows of the alleyway as someone shouted from down the Close. Lights above him went on and Belle hung out over the balcony.

He pushed the chair off his chest and tried to pull it round so he could get back in it. He saw that Lou was still lying unmoving and the path beneath her head was dark and wet. He cried out as he realised she was bleeding.

The man ran down the alleyway and into the wasteland beyond.

IT TOOK Miles a few seconds to take it all in. The man ran out of the alleyway and into the darkness. Miles leapt into action and dived after him, taking him down in a rugby tackle. His triumph was short-lived though as the man was surprisingly fast and strong and threw him off, and scrambled to his feet and ran.

There was noise and shouts and chaos behind him. He stood up, clutching the stolen handbag in small victory. It was hard to see what was happening. It was such a starless night, but he was proud of himself for at least getting the bag back, even if he hadn't managed to apprehend the thief.

'Here,' he said, holding it up as Mary's grandson charged towards him.

The handbag was wrenched from his fingers as a large fist smashed into face.

He heard the words, 'thieving bastard.' And then everything faded to black.

EPISODE TWENTY THREE
JASMINE CLOSE - SERIES ONE

Victoria made them both a hot chocolate and squirted thick cream on top. Gemma was sitting at the breakfast bar, avoiding eye contact and responding to anything she said with abrupt one-word answers. Victoria placed the mug in front of her daughter and decided the only way forward was through honesty. She took a deep breath and dived straight in.

'You saw me with Brett?'

Gemma looked up then, her eyes exposing her pain and anger.

'Your dad and I have been struggling lately; he's been out all the time and behaving strangely.'

'Well, he would, wouldn't he, since his wife is a cheating slapper!'

'Gemma!'

'What? You don't like the truth when you hear it?'

'You don't know what the actual truth of the situation is and speaking to me like that is totally unnecessary.'

Gemma pushed her chocolate drink away. 'Fine, then I won't speak to you at all.' She climbed off the stool and walked to the door.

'You can't keep running away. We need to talk about this, about your father.'

'Nothing to talk about. He's left because of you and the Yank.'

'It's not like that.'

'Oh, and I won't be here for Christmas. Abby and her parents are going to her aunt's house in France and they have invited me...'

'Gemma no.'

'I've already said yes.'

Her daughter left the kitchen, slamming the door behind her.

STEVE WAS SURROUNDED BY CHAOS. It seemed as though the entire Close was out and on his doorstep. Even Mary, wrapped in her dressing gown, was fussing round him. Then Roy, her darn cat, jumped up on his lap as though the feline had every right to take such liberties.

'Here,' Belle handed him a mug. 'It'll warm you up.'

Mary pulled a small bottle of brandy from her pocket and poured a liberal dose into the liquid. 'This is what you need for shock,' she said.

Steve glanced at the stretcher that Lou had been moved on to. 'Are you two related?' he said to Mary, his voice barely more than a whisper as he fought to control his emotions.

'Are these yours?' Annabel asked, picking up the set of three identical keys from the ground.

He nodded. One mystery solved. The bastard must have taken them on that first break in and then used them to let himself in and out whenever the fancy took him. Steve felt annoyed and stupid for not checking after the burglary. It never occurred to him to see if his spare keys were still safe in his kitchen drawer.

They all turned to look as paramedics, flanked by two policemen, wheeled the unconscious attacker towards one of the waiting ambulances. Jack followed close behind.

'Thieving bastard,' Mary was shouting at the attacker, and waving her fists. 'Should chop his balls off...'

'Mary!' Belle looked shocked.

'Well, he gets his jollies by robbing and attacking little old ladies.'

Steve agreed, although he hated being put into the same old lady category as Mary and Lou. But then why not? He was just as sodding helpless. He wheeled over to the nearest ambulance. The crew was loading Lou into the back. 'Will she be alright?'

'We'll do everything we can,' the closest paramedic said.

'Where are you taking her?' Belle asked from behind him.

'MK general. Does she have any family we can call?'

Belle and the paramedic looked at Steve. He shrugged his shoulders, 'I don't know,' he said, wishing that he did and realising he didn't even know where she lived. He didn't want her to be alone. Maybe he could call a taxi, try to get one that could carry him in the wheelchair like Sharon had organised for him when they went to basketball.

'I'll go with her,' Belle said, as if reading his thoughts.

'What about your little girl?' Annabel asked.

'My mum's still here. She won't mind staying tonight.' She looked at the paramedic. 'Is that okay if I come?'

The paramedic stood aside to let her climb in. She looked at Annabel. 'Can you let my mother know what's happening?'

Annabel nodded, and the doors closed. Both ambulances drove off down the Close.

As he watched them go, he saw the front door of the Fishers' house open. He hoped it was Jenny coming to see if he was alright but it was her brother.

Brett jogged up the Close and looked around the assembled group. 'What's going on?'

'He caught the burglar,' Mary said, pointing proudly at her grandson.

'Everyone alright? I saw the ambulances…'

'The thieving bastard will have a nasty headache when he wakes up.' Mary said again, looking at Jack as though he were a hero to rival Superman.

'He attacked a friend of mine,' Steve said, looking at Lou's scooter. 'Perhaps one of you can get that inside for me.'

Jack and Brett immediately turned to the scooter. Steve opened his door and headed home.

'Mr Lance?'

He swivelled his wheels and looked at the plain-clothes policeman flashing his warrant card at him.

'DC Jones, I need to ask a few questions, sir.'

'He's had a nasty shock love, can't it wait until morning?' Mary asked. 'Besides, he's the one you want to talk to. My Jack, he floored the thieving bastard.'

'It's okay, Mary,' Steve said, thinking he might as well get it over with. 'You can come in.'

'Thank you.' The detective turned to Mary. 'My colleague will be talking to your grandson.'

Steve wheeled into his apartment. His head was spinning as he tried to think about what he should or shouldn't say. He didn't want to get Lou into trouble. 'Can't really tell you much though officer, Mary just dropped in for a coffee and got attacked when she left.'

DC Jones followed him into his apartment. 'So what exactly do you know about the rolls of marijuana that we found in her handbag?'

JENNY WAS FLYING, soaring through clear blue skies above a turquoise sea. She was free and unafraid until she collided with some large unidentifiable object. She was falling, falling, falling...

'Jenny wake up.'

She landed with a bump and a yelp and opened her eyes. Her brother was gripping her shoulders and shaking her. Her head was swimming as she reluctantly moved from her dream realm and back into reality. It was still dark, so why was he waking her?

'There's been some trouble in the Close.'

'Steve?' she threw her duvet off and sat up. 'Is he hurt?'

'No, but an old lady was attacked and robbed just outside the flats.'

She could tell be the tone of his voice that there was more to come. 'What? What is it?'

'It's Miles. He's been arrested.'

'Miles? Arrested?' it didn't make sense. 'Has he attacked Steve?' It was the only thing that she could think of.

Brett shook his head. 'No they're saying that he attacked the old lady and stole her bag.'

'That's ridiculous.'

'That's why we need to get to the hospital…'

'Hospital?'

'Miles was punched and knocked out by Mary's Rambo grandson. I'll make you some coffee. You get dressed.'

Jenny nodded her head. Was she still dreaming? None of it made any sense. Miles would never attack an old lady or steal her bag. 'It must be a mistake.'

She dressed quickly, her mind trying to find answers to account for what had happened, like why was Miles even outside that late in the evening? She ran down the stairs. Her brother was in the kitchen.

'Here, I put extra cold milk in so you can drink it quickly.'

She took it and drank it gratefully. The caffeine helping her to shrug off the last haze of sleep. 'Let's go.'

She followed him out to the car and refused to allow her mind to race ahead to the horror of the hospital with all the noise, bright lights, and people that were bound to be there.

'You okay?'

She nodded, gripping her hands tightly together on her lap. 'I will be,' she replied while chanting over and over in her head, 'I am a calm and confident woman.'

Jenny stayed close to her brother as they hurried into the hospital Accident and Emergency entrance. It was a busy place; every blue plastic chair in the waiting room was occupied. The writing on the whiteboard informed the patients that the average wait to be seen by a doctor was two hours. Glad that it didn't apply to them, she tried not to let her eyes wander around because the panic was welling up inside her. Instead, she focused on Brett's hand, which she was gripping hard as though her life depended on it.

'We're looking for Miles Fisher,' he said to the receptionist. 'He came in by ambulance.'

'You are?' The tired-looking lady at reception asked.

'I'm his brother-in-law. This is his wife.'

'Through there...' the lady said, pointing to a door to the right of the reception desk.

Staying very close to Brett, she followed him into the treatment area. A large white board listed the patient's names and the cubicle numbers they were located in. Jenny didn't need to check the list because outside of the third bay along, there was a uniformed policeman standing guard.

She walked straight up to him. 'I need to see my husband.'

The policeman moved to block her way. 'I'm sorry mam, the doctor is with him at the moment, and he's not allowed to speak to anyone until we've taken a statement.'

'But he's hurt.'

'He's also here because he's accused of committing a very serious offence.'

'Rubbish,' she said firmly. 'He has many faults, but attacking old ladies is not one of them!'

The curtain opened, and a doctor emerged. 'Mrs Fisher?'

'Yes.'

'Your husband was knocked out, and he has a broken nose and concussion. He is sedated and will be kept in overnight for observation. I would expect him to be released tomorrow...' he glanced at the policeman. 'Although I have no control over whether he can come home at that stage.'

'Can I see him?'

The doctor nodded, and she pulled the curtain and went inside. Behind her, she heard the policeman objecting, but she didn't care. She sat down beside him and took his hand. 'Oh Miles,' she whispered. 'What have you done?'

STEVE OPENED HIS EYES; it was still dark and very cold. He realised that someone was banging on the door. He glanced at the clock. It was just gone seven a.m.

'Steve, it's me.'

He recognised Belle's voice and pressed the fob to open the door. He felt sick, and he ached all over and hardly dared to ask the question. But he knew he needed to know the answer, good or bad. He had to know.

'You've been up all night?' she asked.

'So have you.'

She nodded her head; she looked tired and dishevelled but not upset.

'Lou's okay?'

'Yes. A bit battered and bruised and a broken arm, but she might be allowed home later today or maybe tomorrow, although...' she paused. 'There was a policewoman hanging around wanting to talk to her about some drugs.'

Steve hadn't said a word to DC Jones last night. Especially not about the dope. He told him all about how he was burgled and that the thief must have taken his spare set of keys from the kitchen drawer and had been letting himself in and out ever since. The detective took it all in and seemed excited about the information since they had been after the perpetrator for months. As a distraction subject, it worked well, but DC Jones kept coming back to Lou. How long had he known her? Where did he meet her? Why did she have the drugs? All he could do was play the spasso card and remain vague and unaware.

'Thank you so much for going with her. Did she call anyone?'

'No, it seems she lives alone. The hospital staff seemed a bit concerned. I heard them talking about calling in social services.'

He didn't know much about Lou or her life, but he felt he knew her enough to know that she would hate having social workers sticking their sticky beaks into her business. It was all his fault.

'It's cold in here,' Belle said. 'Why don't you turn up the heating or perhaps go to bed and grab a couple of hours' sleep? You look like you could do with it.'

'Yeah, I will,' he said. 'Thanks again.'

He watched her leave, then wheeled himself into the bedroom.

He didn't think that he would be able to sleep, but a couple of painkillers and a lie down might help him face the day. He needed to help Lou, but he had no idea what he could do.

Miles opened his eyes and then promptly shut them again. It felt like someone was sticking red-hot pokers in his eye sockets. His nose felt thick and swollen, like he had the snottiest nose ever. He lifted his hand to touch it and winced as something cut into his wrist. What the hell was going on? He slowly forced his eyes to open again and tried to sit up. The pain in his head and across the whole of his face was truly horrible. He tried to remember what had happened. He looked down at his arm and was shocked to see that he was handcuffed to the bed. He quickly realised that he was in hospital and the memories rushed back into his mind. The last thing he remembered was grabbing onto the burglar before being smashed in the face. There must have been two of them, the one he was chasing and then the one who threw the punch. Although he thought he remembered Mary's grandson, Jack, being there. So what the hell was he doing in handcuffs?

'Hello, is anyone there?' he called, looking around him for a buzzer to summon help. He found a red button attached to a long cord and pressed it. He couldn't tell, because he was in a private cubicle, whether he was in Accident and Emergency or if he was actually on a ward.

A stout nurse popped her head around the door; she looked tired as though she was at the end of a very long shift. 'Awake now are we?' she walked in and cancelled the call bell. 'I'll get the doctor to come and see you and I'll inform the officer that you are back in the land of the living.'

'Officer?'

'Yes, the poor bobby who's had to hang around all night because you decided to rob an old lady. I sent him off to grab a quick coffee.' She pushed a tuft of grey wiry hair back behind her ear and looked at him as though he were a germ that she wanted to eliminate with a spray of antibacterial gel.

He was trying to make sense of it all and failing miserably. He had a feeling that pleading innocence or ignorance wouldn't get him very far with her, so he kept quiet and hoped that once the police officer returned from his coffee break, they could sort it out.

'Any hope of me getting a tea or coffee?'

She pushed her glasses up her nose and made a strange snorting sound that was a like a nasal tut. 'I guess even the likes of you can hope.'

'I'll take that as a no then, shall I?' he replied irritably. How the hell had he gone from hero to zero?

The nurse left without a backward glance.

He wondered if Jenny knew where he was and what had happened. Surely not because otherwise she would be there beside him during this awful ordeal. No matter how strained things were between them, he was sure that Jenny wouldn't leave him to cope on his own. Besides, he'd taken on the mugger, that had to count for something, didn't it?

The doctor walked in, followed by another man who flashed his warrant card and told him he was DC Jones.

'You have a broken nose, a bump on the back of your head and a concussion.' The young doctor said so matter-of-factly that he might have been reeling off a shopping list.

Miles lifted his one unrestrained hand to touch his nose. It was bandaged all the way across the bridge. No wonder he was in such pain. 'Has it been reset?'

'It was a clean break. It's settled back into position. Keep it bandaged and come back in a week when the swelling has gone down a bit.'

'That's it?'

'Take paracetamol if you have any pain, get plenty of rest...' the doctor turned to the detective. 'He's all yours...' and then he left.

Miles wondered if the bump on the head was worse than he thought. He felt as though he had been kicked into a parallel universe. One where heroes were treated like the villains. He looked at DC Jones. 'Did you catch the buggers?'

'Miles Lance, I'm arresting you on...'

'What! Are you mad? All I did was stop the thieving bastard!'

Steve opened the door and PC Clarke walked in, followed by DC Jones. 'Back again,' he said warily. He didn't want to get Lou into any more trouble than she was already in and he felt the more they dug around, the likelihood of him falling into a big fat hole increased.

'Sorry Steve, but DC Jones has asked me to come and talk to you. We need to clarify a few things regarding the attack on your friend Lou Sykes last night.'

Sykes. He hadn't even known her surname. 'You got the bastard, didn't you?'

'We have arrested a man we suspect was involved in the robbery.' DC Jones said.

Steve waved towards the sofa and the chair. They sat down. It wasn't that he wanted to make them comfortable, but he hated having them both look down on him. 'He was caught in the act, wasn't he?'

'Can you tell us what happened again?' Clarke said.

'Again?'

'I'm sorry but yes please, it's important Steve.'

'Lou came to see me. We had a coffee and chat and then she left. I saw that she had forgotten her mobile phone, so I went out after her. I saw the bastard leap out from the alleyway and hit her over the head with something I couldn't see what. Lou fell off her scooter and I shouted at him to stop...' Steve paused as he remembered the mocking, scathing tone of the man as he'd thrown the keys at him.

'Steve?'

'He turned to face me and he was just laughing at me. He said it was my fault for changing the locks on my doors He threw my spare keys at me and pushed me out of my chair. Then he grabbed Lou's bag and made off down the alley.' Steve felt the flush chase across his face, part anger, part deep humiliation at the memory.

'So you believe it was the same person who broke in and robbed you before?' PC Clarke asked, watching him intently.

'Yeah, I know it was.'

'You could describe him? Identify him?' DC Jones said.

'Of course. He was tall, probably six one, skinny…'

'Age?'

'Twenty-ish.'

'Are you sure?' Jones said interrupting, 'did you see his face clearly enough to see his age?'

'Face, voice, clothes, language, it all points to a man in his early twenties.'

The policeman and the detective looked at each other.

'What?'

'Do you know him?' Clarke asked.

'What, as in socially?' Steve replied in disbelief. 'Don't you think I might have mentioned it sooner if I knew who the bastard was?'

DC Jones glanced again at his colleague, some unspoken communication agreed, he looked at Steve. 'Do you know Miles Fisher?'

'Yeah, of course I do. He's Jenny's husband.'

PC Clarke leaned forward. 'Did you see Miles Fisher on the evening of the attack?'

'No, should I have?'

'You're sure?' Jones said. He didn't seem pleased by the information.

'Of course, I'm bloody sure. I might be dead from the waist down, but I'm not totally stupid.'

'Nobody is suggesting that you are Steve,' Clarke said, putting a calming hand up. 'It's just that it is a really important point and we have to be completely clear that we understand what you are saying.'

'The man who attacked Lou Sykes was not Miles Fisher?' Jones asked solemnly.

Steve looked from one to the other. Were they serious? It seemed they were. 'Of course not,' he replied. 'The man's a dickhead, but he isn't a burglar who goes round hitting old ladies. Why in the world would you think it was him?' he looked from one to the other and new tentacles of fear and anger slithered into his blood. 'You let the attacker get away, didn't you?'

PC Clarke looked a bit embarrassed. DC Jones stared at his shiny boots.

'I don't get it. Jack caught him, knocked him out...'

'That was Miles Fisher.'

'Well, what the fuck was he doing in the alley?'

'That's what we need to find out.' DC Jones replied.

'So the thieving bastard is still out there?'

PC Clarke nodded his head. 'I'm sorry, Steve, but it seems he is.'

JENNY SAT CLOSE beside her brother and focused all her attention on her shiny shoes. The police station was busy, noisy and chaotic and even more terrifying for her than the hospital had been. Brett was being amazing; she knew how lucky she was to have him with her. All she really wanted to do was go home; she had plans and preparations to complete. It wouldn't be easy, but she knew it was the right thing to do. Of course, she had told no one yet, and she couldn't until Miles was back at home. He needed to be the first one she told.

'Why won't they let us see him?' she whispered to Brett.

He shook his head. 'Sorry Jen, I've no idea how this all works. They told me...' he glanced at the desk where the young WPC was dealing with a distraught young woman who looked and sounded like she was from eastern Europe, while at the same time trying to cope with a drunk who claimed he had been mugged. 'That Miles was making a statement and you could see him after that.'

'Should I get him a solicitor?'

'I'm sure he would have asked if he needed one.'

Jenny closed her eyes as the drunken man, apparently bored now with harassing the WPC, swayed his way into the waiting area and plonked himself into the chair beside her.

She wanted to be caring and compassionate, but he was leering at her suggestively and his breath could ignite a flame from twenty feet away. So she closed her eyes and wished herself to be somewhere distant. Somewhere warm and private and safe.

'Jen.' Brett nudged her gently in the side. 'He's out.'

Miles appeared from a side room. He had PC Clarke and a plain-clothes detective she didn't know with him. He looked terrible, his face was many shades of black and blue with a dash of purple under his eyes. His nose was heavily bandaged and his clothes were dirty and blood splattered.

'Thank you for your help,' she heard the detective say to him.

'... and sorry about the mixup.' PC Clarke added.

'As if sorry makes it all right.' Miles snapped crossly back at him. 'I want him arrested.'

'Who?' Jenny asked, standing beside him, wishing she knew what was going on.

Miles touched his nose. 'That thug Jack...'

'Mary's grandson?'

'Yes, he did this to me.' He looked at PC Clarke. 'I want him done for assault.'

VICTORIA PICKED the up mail from the floor and flicked through it. Although they didn't have red banners along the top of the envelope, they might as well have. She knew they were overdue letters; she had been ignoring phone calls and deleting emails all week. Almost every standing order and direct debit that should have left their account over the past month had either been recalled or declined by the bank.

She dropped the envelopes onto the kitchen worktop and put the kettle on. She hardly ever went home on her lunch break. Often she didn't even take one. But she hadn't seen a potential customer all morning and there was very little expectation of things improving anytime soon. It was less than two weeks to Christmas and buying a new house was not on most people's priority list.

She knew she would have to deal with the overdue payments in the end, but not today. Her next pay packet would be a good one. Whilst sales were slow in December, it was a great time for completions. People would pester and harass both her and their solicitors to chase sales through so they could exchange contracts and get into their new homes before Christmas. Since her commission was paid on completions, this was a good time of the year for her. If she could just fend off the debt collectors until her next payday, they would be safe for another month. Victoria was under no illusions that it was anything more than a temporary reprieve. For the first couple of months in the New Year, her commission would be low and she didn't earn enough on her basic salary to cover the bills. Even if, by some miracle, Dave returned to face the crisis he had created, it wouldn't help, since he no longer had a job.

She went to the fridge to get the butter to make herself a sandwich. She knew that there was a pack of opened ham that needed to be finished up, but she couldn't find it. Confused, she closed the fridge and looked in the bread bin, surprised to find that all that was in there was a crust and some crumbs. She left the kitchen and ran upstairs. There were dirty clothes in the laundry basket and in the bathroom, the toilet seat was up. Dave had definitely been there, so where was he now?

BELLE TAPPED on Steve's door and waited for it to swing open. She knew he wouldn't like what she had to say, but also knew that she couldn't keep the information from him.

'Only me,' she called as the door opened and she stepped into his apartment. The blinds were still down. It was dark and untidy, and the air smelt stale. Steve looked dishevelled and tired. She thought what a tragedy it was that such a young man had to deal with disability.

'I popped back in to hospital this morning to see Lou.'

'How is she? I rang the ward, but they were busy and wouldn't tell me anything anyway because I'm not family.'

She went further into the flat and sat down on the sofa. She could see the kitchen was in a state and wondered if he would take offence if she offered to wash up the dishes for him. Surely he should get some help? The newspapers were always reporting cutbacks in services. Was he hit by the benefit cuts?

'She seemed a lot better, nasty bang to the head, and she broke her arm when she fell out of her chair and hit the pavement.'

'So she's conscious and talking?'

'Oh yes, she is. She said the tea tasted like cat's pee and could I be a pet and sneak her in a little bottle of brandy so she could add a drop and pep it up a bit!'

Steve laughed. 'Sounds like Lou.'

'She's certainly a character.'

'Yeah, she's great. How long are they keeping her in for?'

Belle knew she had to tell him the truth, even though it would upset him. 'They are saying she can't go back to her own place. Not with her arm in plaster and with no one to help her. They want her to go to a nursing home for convalescence.'

'She'll hate that. But hopefully it won't be for too long.'

'Looks like the police are going to charge her with possession and for dealing in the marijuana...' she paused; he was as upset as she knew he would be. 'I'm sorry.'

He shook his head. 'It's just not right. She only does it for medicinal cases.'

'Not sure the law recognises a distinction.' Belle replied, not at all sure how she felt about the situation. She had no patience for drug takers and believed that dealers were the lowest of the low. But was this different? Lou certainly didn't fit her expectations of a drug dealer and she seemed every bit the sweet little old lady who only wanted to help people. And looking at Steve, although she didn't know him very well, it was plain to see how tough life was for him. So who was she to judge him, for taking some pleasure and relief smoking the occasional joint?

'She's alright though, is she? I mean, they haven't charged her yet?'

'No, I don't think they are planning on dragging her off to the cells. I don't suppose she is considered a dangerous criminal.'

'I'll try to get in to see her tomorrow if I can organise a taxi.'

'I think she'd like that,' Belle replied, standing up and looking around. 'Can I do anything for you before I go?'

He pressed the button to open the door. 'Thanks for seeing her and for stopping by,' he said.

She smiled, nodded her head, and left.

MILES WAS SILENTLY FUMING INSIDE. He hurt all over and had endured a horrendous twenty-four-hour period in the hospital and at the police station. That thug Jack was to blame, charging in with his fists. As if being hit by a man gorilla and accused of mugging an old biddy wasn't bad enough, now his wife was accusing him of being vindictive and petty by pressing charges against the man. Why wasn't she supporting him? He was the one with the broken nose; did she really think the thug should get away with it?

Brett pulled into the drive, and they all climbed out of the car in silence. Miles glanced towards the apartment block and wondered if Tammy was there. He hoped that when the police arrived to arrest Jack, they would discover for themselves that the place was a brothel. That would be a great result. Almost worth taking a punch in the face for. Jack will be arrested for assault, the madam will be arrested for running an illegal sex den, and the place would be shut down and he could swoop in and rescue Tammy and all her young friends.

'Miles, we need to talk.'

He turned around as he realised his wife was speaking to him. 'Not now.' he said, heading straight upstairs. He wanted to settle down at the window and watch the show unfold. PC Clarke had assured him that they would be paying Jack the thug a visit that afternoon. He didn't want to miss it.

'Miles, it's important.'

He paused on the stairs as impatience and resentment grew inside him. Important? She didn't understand the meaning of the word. It was important to him that she dealt with her stupid fears which had destroyed their marriage. It was important to him that she stopped seeing the drug addled prat in the wheelchair. It was massively important to him to know he had his wife at his side believing in him and supporting him. Whatever her perception of the word, it clearly wasn't the same as his. 'I need a lie down,' he said, without turning around to face her.

He went into their bedroom and closed the door. He looked around him and realised that things were missing. Like all the dressing table paraphernalia, he assumed she had moved it all into the back bedroom. That was, after all, where she spent most of her time.

Miles settled himself down at the window. His head throbbed and his nose felt thick and heavy. He had to breathe through his mouth, which felt dry and made his throat sore. But if it worked out as he hoped it would, then Tammy could be free very soon.

VICTORIA WALKED BACK to the Show Home. She felt strangely lightheaded and a little nauseous. She unlocked the door and let herself into the office. Her phone beeped with a message and she pulled it from her pocket, hoping it might be from her husband. It wasn't him. It was Brett saying he had been busy dealing with family stuff, but would love to see her later.

She texted him back saying she would be free that evening, although she had no idea if that was true or not. She needed to talk to Gemma, and she had no idea if the girl would be home or even willing to listen. She also had the problem of what to do with Dave. Since he had been home, she couldn't report him missing. Yet she still had no idea where he was. There was something unnerving about him creeping in and out of their house while she was out. It didn't make sense since he had every right to be there, but it felt sinister and underhand. If she had anything valuable like jewellery or heirlooms, she would be hiding them away, and that was an uncomfortable feeling. There was a burning anger deep inside of her that was threatening to erupt. She wanted to change the locks and dump all his possessions out for rubbish collection. She fought hard to reason and rationalise the feelings to keep them buried and under control.

She listened to her office phone messages and turned the computer on. The office door opened, and she glanced up, a part of her hoping it might be Sonia. She could do with someone to talk to. It was Barry who walked through the door with a friendly smile directed at her.

'Everything all right?' she asked. He didn't often leave the building site to seek her out. 'Is number thirty-one ready? You know that the Hammond family is moving in tomorrow?'

'Yep all in order, I checked it myself this morning.'

'Good...' she stared at him expectantly.

He fidgeted and looked uncomfortable. 'Just checking on you, Vic.'

'Me?'

'Yes, I know it's none of my business but I wanted to make sure that you are alright and to say that if I can do anything to help...' He stopped talking and stared at her, an expression of horror on his face. 'Oh no love, I didn't mean to upset you.'

Victoria was crying. Or, more accurately, sobbing.

Barry looked frantically around the office until he found a box of tissues, then he rushed to her side, thrusting a handful of Kleenex at her. He put his arm awkwardly across her shoulder.

Victoria blew her nose and let her head lean on his chest until the sobs eventually subsided. 'I'm so sorry,' she said. 'I don't know what came over me.'

'No, I'm sorry. Do you know that even as a kid I made girls cry? I used to practise pulling faces in the mirror; they looked hilarious to me so I thought it would make them laugh. But I soon learnt that girls and boys have different ideas about what's funny.'

Victoria smiled as she pictured him as a bewildered little boy in trouble for scaring all the little girls.

'That's better,' he said.

'Thank you, Barry.'

'For what?'

'For caring. Besides, I think I probably needed that.'

'Do you want to talk about it?'

Did she? She looked at his kind face and knew she couldn't dump all her woes on him. She knew him well enough to know that he would feel compelled to try to put everything right for her, and that wasn't fair to him at all. 'No, but thanks, I've got to sort this out on my own.'

She watched him leave, and she sat still and thoughtful at the desk, thinking back over the past few days. She had been tired, emotional, lightheaded, and nauseous. Not surprising given all that had been going on. She pulled her diary from her handbag and flicked through the pages as a new fear crept into her mind. She kept a grip on the mounting panic and told herself that there were many possible reasons for her period being late.

EPISODE TWENTY FOUR
JASMINE CLOSE - SERIES ONE

Jenny had intended to leave after Christmas. Sitting alone in her room, staring out across the back garden and beyond to the canal, she knew that leaving now was the right thing to do. She couldn't stay any longer. She realised that telling Miles wasn't what was stopping her and filling her with dread. It was the thought of facing Steve.

She looked at her case, packed and ready to go. What was the point of delaying? Miles was wrapped up in his own bitter world of anger and revenge. He probably wouldn't even notice she was gone. Of course, her plan relied on Brett being willing, but she was confident he would help her. So all that was holding her back was Steve.

She stood up and left the room. She pulled a coat around her and stepped into her boots. It was cold outside, very cold. She shivered and pulled her collar up higher. The clouds were low and heavy and it was already getting dark, even though it was still afternoon. She ran quickly up the Close and knocked on his door. It opened immediately, and she hurried inside, glad to be within the confines of four walls and out of the chill air.

Steve's face lit up when he saw her, and she felt cruel and mean for what she was about to do.

'God, it's so good to see you,' he said. 'It's been a hell of a few days. Wanna tea or a coffee?'

'No, thank you,' she said, walking further into the room to be closer to him.

'You've got that look,' he said warily. 'The one that always comes before shit news.'

She took his hand and fought back her tears. 'I'm so sorry, Steve, but I have to go away.'

'Away? Why away? If you wanna leave, dickhead, you can do that without leaving MK.'

She shook her head and felt the tears welling up in the back of her eyes. She wished she didn't have to hurt him. 'This isn't about Miles, Steve, it's about me.'

He shook her hand away. She understood he was angry and upset. She sat down on the sofa. 'When I was a little girl, all I ever wanted to do was to help people. When I played with my dolls, they were always in a hospital or a school or an orphanage. I thought I would be a nurse or even a doctor or maybe a teacher. I don't really know how I ended up as a sales executive in a huge corporation. I got caught up in a consumer fuelled life and forgot all about my personal dreams and ambitions.'

'Jenny, you don't have to go away to help people. You help me...'

There was desperation in his voice and she felt terrible not only for him but for herself as well. She would miss him. They had helped and supported each other. 'I'm sorry Steve, but I have to do this; I don't want to be the old Jenny. I need to turn the tragedy into something positive and become a new Me. A Me that I can feel proud of.'

'Where?' he asked, his own voice thick with emotion.

'Romania.'

'What the fuck!'

'There's an orphanage...'

'No,' he shook his head. 'That's old news; they sorted it out, sent loads of money and expertise.'

'I think that was Albania.' She wiped away the tears that were openly flowing down her cheeks. 'Anyway, it's true that things are better now than they were, but the problems still exist and there are children in desperate need of care and support. They need an education. I'm going over to teach English to the staff and the older children.'

'You can do that from here,' he snapped back angrily. 'If you believe the papers, then in January when our borders open up, all of Eastern Europe will come flooding into the UK. You don't need to go over there to teach them English. Set up classes here and you'll have a queue a mile long.'

She stood up and bent down to kiss his forehead, but he pushed her away sharply.

'Sod off then.'

'I'll email you when I get there.'

'Don't bother,' he snapped, opening the door and wheeling away out of the lounge.

She left, pausing in the doorway, hoping that he would relent and come back to say goodbye. He didn't. He had helped her so much and she didn't want them to part like this. She understood how hurt he was and that he was just lashing out. She would still contact him once she was settled and hoped they could still be friends and stay in touch.

VICTORIA LOCKED the Show Home and hurried up the redway towards the local shops. Sitting in the office worrying was a waste of energy and the only way to know for sure was to do the test. She was confident it would be negative. They had used protection and although she knew nothing was one hundred percent safe, surely she couldn't be unlucky enough to be in the tiny percentage of women who falls pregnant despite using a condom. At least the test would reassure her.

Was this what her daughter had been feeling? She felt sad that Gemma must have gone through the worry and the fear alone, well not completely alone, she conceded. Upset that her daughter was more confident talking to the local Madam than she was to her. It made her feel a total failure as a mother.

'Hi, shouldn't you be working?'

Victoria looked up in surprise when she realised Sonia was speaking to her.

'Oh yes, just nipped out.'

'Bunking off, huh?'

'I needed a few bits at the shop, milk for the office and some paracetamol,' she touched her head. 'Can't seem to shake it off.'

Sonia was wrapped up warmly in a multi-coloured woolly hat on her head and a stripy scarf with matching mittens. Casper trotted along obediently beside her. 'We'll keep you company.'

'No, it's okay, you carry on wherever you were going,' she said quickly, probably too quickly.

Sonia's eyes crinkled up suspiciously. 'What are you up to?'

Victoria wasn't ready to confide in anyone, besides her fears would almost certainly prove to be unfounded. She forced herself to shrug her shoulders casually and kept her voice calm and neutral. 'I'm not up to anything; I just don't want to put you out.'

'We're just having a quick walk before I pick the monsters up from the nursery. We'll walk up across the bridge with you and then we'll head back.'

Victoria looked at the dog. 'His leg seems completely better now.'

'Yes, it is. He's healed really well, especially given his age. It was so lucky that Dave came along when he did.' Sonia said. 'Have you heard from him at all?'

'No. Although he was in the house earlier.'

'Really?'

'Yep. Well, either that or I had a break-in from a hungry burglar who needed a shower and a change of clothes. I was all set to report him missing, but I can't even do that now. I'm at a loss; I have no idea what to do next. I even thought of changing the locks.'

Sonia turned her head to look at her. 'You won't will you? I mean, it's still his home.'

'Well, if I did, then he would have to knock on the door and face me if he wanted anything instead of sneaking in and out like a miserable coward.'

'I'm sure it's not like that,' Sonia said. 'He's probably in a really bad space himself.'

'Why are you defending him?' Victoria was surprised by her neighbour's words. 'The stupid git has taken us to the edge of bankruptcy and I'm the one having to deal with the fallout.'

'I'm not defending him, Victoria; I'm just saying there are always two sides to everything. Maybe you should hear his before judging him.'

Victoria stopped walking. She was shocked and more than a little upset. It never occurred to her that Sonia wouldn't be supportive of her. 'How can I consider his side when he won't even talk to me?' she said, wondering why she was having to justify herself.

'Maybe he would face you if you were more approachable.'

'You're serious?' Victoria said, unable to believe what she was hearing. 'How can any of this be my fault?'

'Well, you're not entirely squeaky clean, are you? A certain American…'

'Get lost.' Victoria snapped, walking away.

'Those in who live in glass houses.' Sonia called after her.

THE SHOW HOME WAS LOCKED. Brett looked up and down the Close; his eyes searched the building site and then stopped at her house. All the lights were out, and he doubted she was in. He pulled his mobile from his pocket and sent her a message asking her to ring him when she was free. He wasn't going to be able to see her that evening after all. Jenny needed his help with something; she was going to help in an orphanage somewhere and needed him to take her. He wanted to see Victoria and tell her in person. He had no idea where Jenny wanted to go or even what time they were leaving. If Victoria got back soon, then he might still get to see her before he had to leave.

He walked back up the Close and let himself into the house. He was surprised to see two large suitcases in the hallway. He found his sister in the kitchen; she was loading tins and food packets into two large plastic storage boxes.

'What's going on?'

'I told you this morning, I need your help,' she said without pausing or turning to look at him.

He knew she was upset. The slight thickness in her voice suggested she'd been crying and her body language was defensive. 'Hey,' he said, putting his arm around her shoulder. 'Come on Jen, talk to me...'

She turned into his chest and rested her head for a moment, and then she pulled back and looked up at him. He was right she had been crying.

'I'm going,' she said with a sniff.

'Yeah, I kinda had that bit worked out.'

'Will you take me?'

'Of course. Where are you going?'

She looked up at him, her eyes pleading. 'Europe...'

'Europe? What like France?'

'A bit further than that.'

'So you're going to the airport? Will you cope with getting on the plane and the flight?'

Jenny shook her head. 'No. I wish I could, but realistically I know that the airport and the plane would be all too much for me. I need you to drive me.'

Brett was trying to visualise a map of the continent. He knew England was separated from Europe by the English Channel, and he'd heard that the channel tunnel offered a quick and easy way to reach mainland Europe. 'Where exactly?'

'It'll only take a few days,' she said, avoiding eye contact. 'We can stop at motels en route. It'll be fun.'

'Where?' he asked again, thinking he might not want to know the answer.

'Romania.'

He searched his memory banks for any visual images of Europe. He used to have a Globe at home that lit up on the inside, and he spent hours staring at it, dreaming of places he could visit. If his childhood memories were correct, then Europe was a small continent. He thought Romania must be somewhere in the middle, possibly heading towards Turkey. How far could it realistically be?

'Please,' she said. 'I can take so much more stuff in the car and they are desperate for food and supplies. I know it's a lot to ask Brett, but if we leave today, you could be back in New York for Christmas.'

He wasn't sure he wanted to return to America yet, but he knew he couldn't say no. An image of Victoria flashed into his mind. She would have to wait. When he returned, he would see her and decide if he was going to stay for longer or fly home for Christmas. Although with Jenny away, could he realistically stay at the house? He might have to find himself a hotel. His sister needed his support, so he smiled and nodded his head. His sister hugged him tight. 'Are you sure you're ready for this?'

'No,' she replied, 'but I know I have to try.'

'I'll go and pack,' he said. 'Does Miles know?'

'Not yet.'

'Best tell him before he guesses, the cases are a bit of a giveaway.'

He ran up the stairs and started to pack, but he still had no idea how many days or nights he would be gone for or how many miles they would be travelling. He could look it up once he'd got himself packed and ready. He needed to text Victoria as well. He was sad he wouldn't see her for a few days. He would miss her, but he was confident that she would understand.

VICTORIA STOOD STARING at the ridiculous little stick, her eyes not believing what it was telling her. She couldn't be. It wasn't possible. How could life be so unfair? People had affairs and sex all the time and didn't end up being pregnant. She had done it twice with Brett and now she was having his baby?

She threw the spent test into the bin along with the one she'd done a few minutes earlier. She could doubt the validity of one of these tests, but probably not two. She wished Sonia hadn't been such a cow to her earlier. She really needed a friend to talk to. Did she tell Brett? She thought that he probably had a right to know. And besides, she didn't want to deal with it on her own. She picked up her phone, but her hands were shaking so violently she couldn't tap in the message. She dropped the phone onto her desk and made herself a coffee, then wondered if she was even allowed coffee? Was tea better? She tried to remember, but her experience of expecting Gemma seemed like a very long time ago.

She got herself a glass of water from the Show Home kitchen and sipped it, closing her eyes and trying to calm herself. She picked the phone up again, but instead of texting or ringing Brett, she found herself calling her mother.

'Hello dear, everything alright? Why aren't you working today?'

'I am working mum, just thought I'd give you a quick ring.'

'Really? Why? What's wrong? Is it Gemma? You have to watch out for teenage girls, Victoria; you know how easy it is to get into trouble.'

'Gemma's fine, mum,' she replied, wondering what had possessed her to make the call. She loved her mother, but they had never had an easy relationship. If she thought her parent would offer a supportive sounding board, she was delusional. 'Oh, I've got a customer, mum, I've got to go.'

BRETT TRIED RINGING VICTORIA; the phone was engaged, and it took him straight to her answerphone. He didn't want to leave a message, and he wanted to talk to her and explain. He would try again in a few minutes. As he put the phone down to zip up his case, and he heard Miles shouting downstairs. He hurried out of the bedroom and onto the landing. He put the case down and lent over the bannister. Miles and Jenny were having an argument in the hall. He hesitated, not sure if he should leave them to it or go down and try to diffuse the situation.

'You can't even step outside the door without throwing a massive wobbly. What bloody use are you going to be to anyone else?'

'This will help me.'

'Huh!'

'Miles, I'm sorry, but I'm going to do this and you can't stop me.'

'I can and I will.' He grabbed one of her cases and unzipped it.

'Miles, stop it.'

He picked it up and emptied the contents all over the polished wooden floor. 'Huh!' he yelled with a note of triumph in his voice.

Brett decided he better go downstairs.

'Stop being so childish.' Jenny shouted back at her husband.

'Me! That's rich coming from the woman who's too much of a baby to even say hello to the neighbours who come around to wish her happy birthday.'

'That's enough, Miles,' Brett said to his brother-in-law. 'Can't you stay civil and wish her luck? It's an incredibly brave thing she's doing.'

For a moment, Brett thought Miles might take a swing at him. He tensed, ready to dodge or deflect a blow. Not that he had ever known Miles to be violent. Uptight, pompous, and occasionally arrogant, but never violent. Something about his stance and the gleam in his eyes made Brett wary. His brother-in-law seemed to have changed in the time that Brett had been staying with them. 'Come on Miles, mate, why don't we all sit down and have a drink together before we go? Jenny can tell us all about it.'

Jenny was on the floor repacking her suitcase. Miles kicked one of her jumpers and looked coldly at Brett. 'I'm not your mate.' Then he grabbed his coat from the hook and left the house, slamming the door behind him.

'You alright?' Brett asked, bending down to help her with the suitcase.

'Yes,' she replied, looking tired and dependant. 'Is he right? Am I just kidding myself that I can do this?'

He looked seriously into her eyes. 'Jenny, you are the sweetest and the bravest person I have ever known. Of course you can do this.'

She smiled. 'Okay, well, let's get going quickly now before he comes back and before I lose my nerve. You packed?'

'Yes,' he replied. 'I'll just grab my case.' He ran up the stairs and picked it up from the landing, then dashed back down again. Jenny opened the door and between them, they loaded the car with the cases and the boxes of non-perishable food and two large black plastic sacks.

'Spare sheets and blankets,' she said in answer to his unspoken question. 'We have way more in the airing cupboard than we ever use.'

They went back into the house and Jenny picked up her handbag, and she looked around the house.

He took her hand. 'Come on,' he said, understanding that she needed his help and encouragement.

She nodded her head and let him lead her to the car.

They climbed in and he started the engine. 'I'll have to stop for gas,' he said.

'There's one on the motorway we can fill up there.'

As he drove past the Show Home, he realised that he still hadn't spoken to Victoria. He would try calling her again when they stopped.

AFTER PACING up and down the carpet for several minutes, Victoria finally came to a decision. He had to be told. She would ring him and ask him to meet her urgently. She grabbed her phone and pressed on his number. It rang, but he didn't answer. She left a voicemail asking him to ring and then she waited.

After a few minutes, with no response, she rang him again. Same thing, it rang. He didn't pick up. This time, she didn't leave a message. Instead, she ended the call and texted him once again, asking him to contact her urgently.

Another five minutes passed with no response from him. The news was so hot, so terrifying that she couldn't hold on to it for a moment longer. It had to be shared. So she texted him again – I'm pregnant! - Two simple words that would surely bring him running to her side.

. . .

BRETT FILLED the tank and went in to pay. He picked up a couple of bottles of mineral water and two candy bars called Mars, and paid at the counter. He put his wallet back in his pocket and felt around for his phone, but it wasn't there. He checked his other pockets, but then he remembered he'd put his mobile on the bed before taking his case out onto the landing.

'I haven't got my phone,' he said when he got back in the car.

'I've got mine,' Jenny said. 'You can use that.'

He looked in the mirror. There was a queue waiting to use the pump. He turned the key and started the engine. 'I don't know her number. It's on my mobile.'

'Victoria? I can get the sales number,' she said. 'You can ring her at the Show Home.'

He drove down the slip road and joined the fast flowing motorway traffic. He glanced at the dashboard clock. 'If I wait until we get to the coast, she'll have gone home. Can you ring for me, Jen? Just tell her I've got to go away for a few days.'

VICTORIA FELT SICK. Her head was spinning, and her palms were sweating while her body was trembling with tiny shivers. Her mind kept racing through all the reasons why he hadn't called her back. Why he hadn't responded to the news that she was pregnant? Was he asleep, in the shower, in the bath, watching TV – phone on silent, in a coma, dead? Her reasons and excuses became ever more outrageous and ever more desperate.

She checked her phone again. Nothing.

She looked at the clock, she still had almost an hour to go before she finished work but since she hadn't seen a single customer all day and she felt sicker than a child stuffing sweets in a sweetshop, she decided to lock up and go home.

Victoria hurried around, switched off all the lights, and closed the door. As she turned the key in the lock, she heard the phone ringing on her desk. 'Sod's bloody law,' she snapped to herself. The first phone call all day. She thought about going back in and picking it up in case it was head office, but decided that whoever it was and whatever they wanted could wait until tomorrow.

Miles stood in the alleyway, waiting. He was furious that she was leaving but realised that, in a way, it might be a good thing. She would come back, of that he was certain, and in the meantime he was free to pursue his mission to save the lovely Tammy.

The police car was parked outside the apartment block. He'd seen it arrive from his bedroom window. But his confrontation with his wife meant he missed seeing them actually going into the apartment. It didn't matter; the main thing was that he would see them bring Jack out. He thought about going round the back to look through the window, but was a bit worried that if he were seen, it wouldn't look good for him. He hoped that Madam Ella was caught in the act and that the police would drag them both out in handcuffs. He also hoped that Tammy wasn't in there since he didn't want to see her arrested.

His ongoing research had led him to a site for punters that told tales about not only the different houses of ill repute, but also the girls that worked in them. The punters left ratings and comments and Tammy was a very sought after and highly prized young lady. She must earn Madam Ella a fortune. The site also gave up-to-date information about how to contact the ladies. It seemed that locations and phone numbers were regularly changed in an attempt to stay one step ahead of the law. He discovered that Tammy and another girl called Miranda worked out of a flat in Bletchley. He had already made a call and had booked himself an appointment for a 'massage' tomorrow evening.

The outer door to the apartment opened and DC Jones, along with another police officer he hadn't seen before, came out. He looked intently, eagerly expecting another policeman to come out with Jack in handcuffs, his head down in defeat and shame. But the door closed behind them. They were alone.

He ran out to meet them. 'Where is he? Did he get away?'

'Mr Fisher,' DC Jones said, acknowledging him. 'Did who get away?'

'Don't play games with me. You were here to arrest Jack for his vicious assault on me.'

'Yes, we have spoken to him about the alleged incident and he is helping us with our enquiries.'

'Alleged?' he pointed to his nose. 'Here's your evidence.'

'Our investigation is ongoing, Mr Fisher. I suggest you go home and get some rest for you and your nose.'

Miles stared at the departing car. Had the whole world gone insane?

VICTORIA WAS CONFUSED AND DISORIENTATED. She was on the bed but fully clothed. It was dark. She glanced at the illuminated clock and was shocked to see that it was just gone midnight. She reached onto the bedside table and grabbed her phone. She had no messages and no missed calls. So that was that then. Nothing Brett could have said or done would make the point more clearly. She told him she was pregnant, and he'd stood her up and hadn't even bothered responding to her. It was her teenage nightmare all over again. She turned the lamp on and squinted as the light hurt her tired eyes. She climbed off the bed and left the room. She hadn't seen or heard Gemma at all. She remembered going upstairs after finishing work early for a quick nap. That was over six hours ago.

Victoria opened her daughter's bedroom door and glanced inside, relieved to see Gemma curled up cuddling her tatty old teddy that she'd loved since she was a toddler. She quietly closed the door and went downstairs to get a drink.

She had no idea what response she had wanted or expected from Brett, but the idea of him ignoring her completely had never occurred to her. Tomorrow morning she would march up the Close, bang on his door and demand he talk to her. She sipped the water and realised that there was no point. Through his complete lack of response, he had already made his thoughts on the matter totally and unmistakably clear. He wasn't interested in her or the baby.

TAMSIN RAN AROUND EXCITEDLY, stamping her feet and skidding and sliding. There might not be much, but it was the first snowfall of the winter. 'Can we make a snowman when I get home from school, mummy?'

Belle looked at the light dusting on the ground and shook her head. 'Don't think we could scrape enough up to make a snowball, let alone build a snowman,' she laughed.

Enthusiasm undimmed, her daughter ran and then slid her way down the redway. Up ahead of them was Steve. Belle often saw him as she walked to and from the school. He seemed to spend a lot of time near the canal. She thought he must be lonely and decided that on her way back, she would go and talk to him. It was time she got to know the other residents better, and he had certainly been having a rough time of it all lately. Besides, she would like to know if he had heard from Lou. She hoped the old lady was feeling better was doing okay.

Tamsin let go of her hand to run on ahead when she saw Oscar and Jane walking along the path. Belle thought the lady didn't look well. She was wrapped up against the December chill, but even so, there was a bluish tinge around her lips and her face was very pale. Belle didn't know the woman at all and didn't feel that it was her place to fuss or pry, so they just exchanged pleasantries while Oscar rolled around the snow and Tamsin fussed over him and tickled his tummy.

'We better get going poppet, say goodbye to Oscar.'

'He would happily take that attention all day,' Jane said.

Belle wished she could let Tamsin have a dog, but it simply wasn't possible. Maybe they could visit the pet shop and look at hamsters or fish, something that could thrive within the confines of the flat. She thought it would be good for the little girl to have the care and responsibility of a small pet.

'Bye Oscar,' Tamsin called as they waved goodbye and carried on towards the school.

STEVE BOTH LOVED and hated the snow. He didn't like getting cold and in the chair, his wheels slipped and slid and he felt even less in control than he usually did. Yet there was something deliciously fun about snow. Probably partly nostalgic with childhood memories of snowball fights and sledging in the park. There was also something cleansing about fresh virgin snow. He wasn't sure what or why. It was the sort of thing that Freud might have an opinion on.

He wheeled up towards the canal, pushing hard to get the blood pumping. It might be pretty, but it was still bloody freezing. He had a bit of bread for the ducks, not something he usually did, but he'd grabbed the last of the loaf on an impulse. Seeing them huddled on the bank made him glad that he had. He tore it into small chunks and threw it all onto the snow covered grass. From the flurry of feathers and quacks, he assumed they were very hungry.

He watched for a few minutes until the last bite of bread was fought over and eaten and the ducks had dispersed, then he wheeled closer to the edge.

The water was frozen. Not a thick solid layer, but a thin flimsy topping of ice. He could see movement below as the fish swam around. It was as if they knew that the ducks and fishermen couldn't reach them and so were bold and confident, showing off beneath the covering of ice.

He edged closer; he could see his reflection and recoiled. Would he ever get used to the chair? It was all he saw when he looked at himself. It dominated everything and consumed him. At rehab, they had told him he should embrace the chair, as it gave him freedom. He didn't feel free; he felt trapped. Shut inside a body that no longer worked. He wondered if Jenny was watching. Was she up on her balcony soaking up the view before she bailed on him? Or maybe she had already left. The Beetle wasn't on the drive. She could already be halfway across the continent. He wanted to be happy for her, to wish her well and all that crap. But he was a selfish bastard and didn't want her to leave. He needed her and had no idea how he was going to cope without her. His loneliness engulfed him as a physical pain. He wished he'd never met her; never let her into his life.

Hands on the wheels, he went that little closer, staring into the deep icy water.

The sharp shrill ring of a bell right up alongside him made him jump. His hands, still clasping the wheels, moved as a physical response to the shock. He shot forward. Time seemed to slow down. He felt the movement of the front wheels slipping, unstopping, unstoppable over the edge of the bank of the canal. He heard the bikes sweep past him. He heard a dog bark and heard someone shout. He realised that the shouting was from him. He pulled back on the wheels and tried to save himself. But the ground beneath him was alive, and the forward momentum of the chair was far too much for him to stop.

The breath was sucked from his body as the full force of the freezing water swallowed him up.

BELLE DODGED out of the way to avoid the bikes hurtling at full speed along the redway. 'Slow down,' she shouted after them, pretty sure they didn't even hear her. There was a lot of noise coming from the direction of the canal. A dog was barking furiously and someone was shouting. She was at the point on the redway when it divided into two and the left path led to Jasmine Close and home. She knew something was seriously wrong, so she turned right and ran as fast as she could on the un-gritted pathway.

Oscar was at the edge of the canal, running furiously up and down and making a lot of noise. She couldn't see Jane. As she got closer, she realised that the surface ice that skimmed the surface of the water was disturbed, and just as she got to the edge, Jane's head popped up out of it. The woman took in great gasps of air but seemed to be being pulled back under. Oscar jumped into the water to help his mistress.

Belle dropped to the damp, cold grass and reached her arm out to try to reach Jane. But the woman's head disappeared under the water again. Oscar had something in his mouth and Belle quickly realised that the dog had his teeth in a jacket and was dragging a body to the edge. Jane's head came up again and Belle realised that mistress and animal were pulling Steve along together.

She reached out again, and this time she was able to make contact. Jane held her hand out and Belle pulled her in. Jane's other hand was gripping Steve under his shoulders and between them, they dragged him onto the bank. It wasn't easy. His sodden clothes added to his size and weight, and he was unconscious and non-responsive.

In the distance, Belle heard sirens and hoped that they were coming for them. Someone was running towards them and she could hear footsteps approaching fast from the direction of the road. The canal was a popular spot for dog walkers and several houses in Jasmine Close had windows that could overlook the area, even though they weren't exactly close. Please God, someone had seen it all and had called an ambulance.

A man dropped onto his knees beside them and started to examine Steve.

'Have you called for help?' she asked.

'Yes,' he replied, my wife saw what happened, and she's run down to the road to show them where we are.'

'He's not breathing,' Belle said with a sob.

The man was feeling his pulse and bent his head down onto his chest. 'Yes, he is.' He turned Steve onto his side and into the recovery position.

The sirens were very loud now. Help was nearly with them. Belle realised Jane was still lying on the grass bank where she collapsed, exhausted, after dragging Steve to the water's edge. Oscar was fussing round his mistress and whimpering.

Belle took her coat off, wincing as the freezing air hit her; she laid it over Jane, who was shaking violently.

The paramedics came running up the redway, two policemen followed, and she saw that one of them was PC Clarke.

Belle stood up and stepped back to allow them access to Steve and Jane. 'Come on Oscar,' she called him over to her and fussed him while the paramedics got to work.

'What happened?' PC Clarke asked.

'I'm not sure; when I got here Jane was in the water dragging Steve out.'

'I saw the man in the wheelchair topple into the water,' the man said.

'Accident?' PC Clarke asked.

The man pointed across the water and beyond the bridge. 'We were all the way back there. Not a canal side view. He seemed to be leaning over and all of a sudden he was in the water.'

'He cried out,' the man's wife said, linking her arm in his.

Two more paramedics arrived with a stretcher on wheels. Belle watched as Steve was lifted onto it and then rushed away back to the ambulance. She went to go after them, thinking she should go to the hospital with him. But Jane looked to be in a bad way and was staring at her pleadingly.

Belle moved closer. Jane seemed to want to say something, but the paramedics were busy with tubes and monitors and oxygen.

'Come in the ambulance with us if you want,' one of them said to Belle.

She looked at PC Clarke. 'This is her dog.'

The man looked at her. 'I'll take him for now if you want. We only live across the canal. You can come and fetch him later.' He looked at the policeman as if for confirmation that it was a good idea. 'I'll write our address and phone number down.'

PC Clarke handed the man a piece of paper from his notepad, along with a pen.

The woman leaned in closer to Belle. 'My Ted is a magistrate, you know,' she said proudly.

'Used to be,' Ted chided affectionately. 'Retired now.'

'Well, thank you,' Belle said. 'I'll be back as soon as I can.' Although she had no idea what she was going to do with a dog in her flat. She was hoping that Jane would recover quickly once they got her warmed up and then Oscar could go back home with his mistress.

Oscar whimpered as the man attached the lead to his collar and they watched as they loaded Jane on to the stretcher that had just arrived to take her to the waiting ambulance.

Belle turned to PC Clarke as a thought hit her. 'His wheelchair must be down there,' she said, looking into the cold dark canal.

He nodded. 'I'll see what I can do.'

EPISODE TWENTY FIVE
JASMINE CLOSE - SERIES ONE

'Welcome back to the land of the living.'

Steve looked up into the round moon face of Sharon Stanza and tried to remember what had happened.

'Suggest you wait for the better weather before you try wheelchair swimming,' she said. 'Although I'm not sure it'll ever take on as an Olympic sport.'

His mind filled with sounds and images as he recalled how he had fallen into the canal. 'Am I okay?' he asked, reliving the icy shock as he'd entered the water.

'Well, the jury is still out on that one. But apparently there shouldn't be any long term ill effects from your impromptu dip.'

He tried to sit up. He felt like shit and then he realised he was in hospital. The uncomfortable bed with metal bars to stop him from rolling off it and onto the floor. The thick infection barrier curtains that engulfed the area and the smell and sounds that brought back horrible memories from when he had his car accident. He groaned. 'When can I go home?'

Sharon grabbed the hand-held bed controller and gave it to him so that he could raise up the back of the bed himself. She looked directly at him. 'Depends.'

'On what?'

'On whether you're safe to be sent home? Or not.'

'You said I was alright.'

She tilted her head and several chins squished into her shoulder. 'I mean mentally.'

'It was an accident,' Steve said, realising how it must have looked.

'What, so you got too close and lost control of your manual wheelchair?'

He had to admit it didn't sound very convincing, and he couldn't blame her for her sarcastic tone. 'I was too close. I was watching the fish. Then something made me jump...' he thought hard, trying to remember. 'Yeah it was the bell from a bike. It made me jump and my hands were on the wheels and I shot forward. The ground was icy and I couldn't save myself. I did try...'

'You've been under a lot of pressure,' she said. 'It's been hard for you.'

'It was an accident,' he repeated. 'Please Sharon, you've gotta believe me.' He knew that if Sharon and the doctors believed he had tried to take his own life, they could transfer him to the hospital's psychiatric unit and keep him locked up there indefinitely. As his social worker, she could help him. Her word would carry a lot of weight. But he was also well aware that she had no reason to do him any favours and no one would blame her if she took this opportunity to make him suffer. 'I'm sorry Sharon,' he said, his voice barely above a whisper. 'For what I did.'

He saw something flash in her eyes. Was it anger? Bitterness? It went so quickly he couldn't be sure.

'You put it right,' she said eventually. 'Anyway, I'm here to assist you not to dwell on the past. I've got a load of tests and assessments organised for you today. I'll come back tomorrow and we'll discuss the situation then.'

He wanted to argue and insist that he should go home today. He hated hospitals. He knew he would hate the psychiatric ward even more but he wondered if he could get away with discharging himself.

'If you have any ideas about taking yourself off home…'

Was this woman a mind reader?

'Get rid of them now. The doctor is this close.' She showed with her pudgy little fingers just how close. 'To having you sectioned for your own safety under the mental health act.'

Steve closed his eyes, feeling defeated.

'I'll let you rest.'

He heard her pull the curtain that went right around his bed; he opened his eyes again and called after her. 'Sharon?'

She paused and looked at him.

'How is Melanie?'

She gave him a look that he couldn't fathom at all. Was it good or bad? He guessed it must be bad. After all, he was the one who had behaved appallingly.

'Melanie is very well, thank you,' she said in an overly polite voice that was very out of character for her, and then she was gone.

'IT'S HIM AGAIN,' Jenny said, looking at her phone in irritation. 'I'll have to switch it off.' She didn't know why Miles kept ringing her and then hanging up. There was no logical reason, so she had to assume it was just to torment her. She dropped the mobile into the glove box. 'There, he can play his little games all he likes now.'

It felt liberating to switch off the phone and put it out of sight. She was heading off on a new adventure and she didn't need to take his negativity and controlling behaviour with her.

'I'll need to get some gas soon,' Brett said. 'Maybe we should take a break and get some lunch?'

She smiled and nodded. So far, she was doing really well. They had stayed at a small B&B in Folkestone last night and then driven onto the channel tunnel train early that morning. She had even managed to go into the small, intimate dining room for breakfast. It felt as though she were leaving her fears and her problems back in

England, and a new and exciting future beckoned. Of course, she was realistic enough to know that it only worked like that in movies, but even so, she was confident that once she got to her destination, she would cope. How could she dwell on her own silly problems when she was with children who were so much in need of her help? She thought about Steve and hoped that he was alright and had forgiven her for leaving.

'Was it you?' Steve said to Belle as she walked towards the bed carrying a supermarket packed bunch of grapes and a bar of chocolate. The curtains had been pulled all the way back by one of the nurses, who had ignored his protestations and insisted that it was good for him to socialise. Not that any of the other patients seemed any more willing than he was to engage in friendly chitchat or banter. The guy next to him had slept all day, snoring loudly and farting frequently and the two men in the opposite bays had both been glued to some show on their over bed TVs. He would have liked to put the headphones on and watch his own television but he had no money with him to buy a prepayment card and even if did have any cash, he had no way of getting it into the machine, wherever it was, to get one. The nurses all seemed to be rushed off their feet. They were efficient and seemed caring enough, but clearly they had no time to stop and chat or even to pause and offer reassurance. He certainly couldn't ask them to fetch him a TV card. He was trapped in a bed in a horrible nightmare and seriously contemplating throwing his pillow at the snorer beside him when Belle walked in.

'Me what?' she replied, handing him the grapes and the Dairy Milk, smiling at him.

She really was very pretty and not as old as he had previously thought. They hadn't really talked much before and he assumed, probably because she had two sprogs, and that she was a lot older than him. But seeing her up close, he revised that thought and decided she was almost certainly under thirty. 'Did you pull me out?'

'Well, yes, and no,' she said, sitting down in the chair beside his bed. 'I reached in and grabbed you, but it was Jane who got to you first. She jumped in and dived under the water to release your lap strap and pull you to the surface. Then, with Oscar's help, they got you to the edge of the canal and I helped haul you in.'

'Shit,' he said, shaking his head as the enormity of the situation hit him. 'Thanks,'

'It's Jane and Oscar you really need to be thanking.'

'I will.' He frowned. 'Who the hell are Jane and Oscar?'

'A lady who was passing by and saw you go in.'

'A stranger risked her life for me?'

'Yes,' Belle said.

'As soon as I'm out of here, I'll thank her and Oscar.'

'Why wait?'

'They won't let me go home yet.'

'Are you hurt?'

'No, but they think I tried to top myself...'

'Did you?'

'No.'

She smiled. 'Good.' She stood up.

'You're going already?' he felt let down.

'I'll be back,' she called as she walked away.

The man opposite him pulled his headphones from his ears and grinned across at Steve. 'huh, looks like you have the same luck with women as I do, mate!'

Steve ignored the man and closed his eyes. He wasn't sleepy, but he was tired. Why did his life always have to be about so much pain and disappointment?

'Don't go to sleep now...'

He opened his eyes. 'You're back.'

'Told you I would be. Took longer than expected though. You'd think a hospital would have plenty of these, but it seems not. They are a very valuable commodity in here.' She pointed to a basic metal wheelchair and grinned at him.

'Where are we going?'

'To see Jane.'

'She's in here?'

'Yep, in a ward just down the corridor. How do I get you into this?'

Steve looked at the chair. It was lower than the bed, but it would be okay getting into it. Not so easy getting back onto the bed, though, but he wouldn't worry about that now. 'I need to get this baby bar down,' he said, gripping the metal bars. 'It will probably lift up, or maybe it drops?'

Belle looked underneath the bed and pulled and tugged until she found how to release and lower the bars.

'Now push the chair alongside the bed and I'll lower myself into it.'

His arms were strong even though his legs were useless. He swung his feet over the side and then leaned down onto the arm of the chair with his left hand and let the rest of his body follow. He almost missed, and she had to grab him to stop him from falling straight onto the floor.

'Bloody hell,' Belle exclaimed. 'I thought you said you'd lower yourself not sodding death roll into the chair.'

Lifting up with his arms, he wriggled his bottom back into the seat and placed his feet on the footplates. 'No worries,' he said, grinning. 'Let's roll.' He tried to wheel himself, but the chair wasn't designed like his own one was for personal use. It was heavy, and the wheels were large.

'Shall I push you?'

He bit back a rude retort because he knew she was being incredibly kind and helpful. He hated the loss of even that tiny bit of independence that he had previously enjoyed, but knew that if he said no, then they wouldn't get anywhere fast. 'Okay, thanks,' he said, the words uttered as barely more than a mumble.

It felt strange to be pushed, but he discovered it wasn't quite as bad in a hospital as it would be in any other situation, as even ablebodied people were regularly pushed around by porters, nursing staff and their relatives. He was glad and grateful to be out of bed. It occurred to him he was wearing pyjamas that weren't his own. Where they came from, he didn't know, but they felt stiff and starched and were a size or more too big. But they were definitely better than the hospital gowns that left your arse and your modesty on view to the world.

She pushed him into another ward, past the nursing station and into a bay very similar to the one he was just in. Only this was larger with four beds on each side, all occupied by women of varies ages. Belle pushed him to the last bed on the left. The curtain was partly pulled so they couldn't see until they got there that it was empty.

'Excuse me,' Belle called out to a nurse who was changing the drip for a patient two beds down. 'I'm looking for the lady who was here?'

The nurse paused from her task and glanced at them both. 'Are you family?'

'No, we are just friends.'

'She was taken to the intensive care unit early this morning.'

Steve felt as though he had been slapped hard in the face. 'She's okay though?' he said, his voice thick and husky with emotion. He didn't know the woman, but he knew the woman had saved his life.

'I'm sorry I can't discuss her situation with you.'

Steve wanted to argue or plead, but Belle was already pushing him back out of the bay and out of the ward. 'Where are we going?'

'Intensive care.'

She pushed him fast; they didn't speak until they reached the ward. It was very different to the other wards. The doors were locked shut, and they had to press an intercom to request entry. The nursing station was positioned like a barrier and you couldn't get to the beds and the patients until you had spoken to a member of the nursing staff.

Belle gave the name. The young nurse on the desk looked at them both and they were again asked if they were family.

'No, we're friends.'

The nurse began to shake her head and Steve butted in. 'Please,' he said. 'I have to see her. She saved my life, she pulled me out of the canal. I need to thank her.'

The young nurse looked at him with sadness and compassion. 'We heard about that,' she said. 'Wait here for a minute.'

Steve looked at Belle. 'Shit, it doesn't look good.'

They both looked expectantly towards the nurse, who returned with another woman who looked as if she were about forty but could be younger. Her eyes were red and puffy, like she'd been crying. She was expensively and smartly dressed, but her clothing was crumpled and creased, her hair out of place, her makeup worn off. Steve guessed she had spent the night at the hospital, probably in a chair beside a bed.

'This is Mrs King's daughter,' the nurse said before making herself busy at the other end of the desk.

'Is Jane okay?' Belle demanded.

The woman shook her head, new tears welling up in her eyes, which were fixed on Steve. 'She suffered a heart attack and died this morning.'

'I'm so sorry,' Belle whispered, her voice thick with emotion.

'You were a friend?'

'We passed her in the Close almost every day. My little girl loved Oscar, Jane and I often chatted while she played with the dog.'

The woman's face hardened. 'bloody dog, she should never have got him.'

'She seemed to love him...'

'Of course, she loved him, but she wasn't up to looking after him.'

'She was unwell?' Belle asked.

The woman was still staring at Steve, even though she was talking to Belle. He felt uncomfortable under her searching scrutiny and very emotional. The lady who saved his life was dead. Did she die because of him? He hardly dared to ask the question. Guilt was overwhelming him and emotion was choking him up. He couldn't have said a word even if he knew what words to say.

'She had a heart condition. She was told to take it easy, not go walking miles every day with that damn dog. And especially not to go diving into freezing cold water.'

'She saved my life,' he forced himself to say. 'I'm so sorry...'

'The question is, what are you going to do with the life that she sacrificed hers for?'

He squirmed under the piercing glare of her stare.

'Hey, that's harsh,' Belle said.

'Is it? From what I've heard, he might have put himself in the water deliberately.'

'It's okay,' he said to Belle. 'She has every right to be upset.' He forced himself to look at the woman. 'I didn't. I promise you it was an accident and I am very glad to be alive and sincerely grateful to your mother for saving me.'

The woman seemed to relax, as though she had held herself in tight control and could now let go. 'Okay then,' she said, finally unpinning him from her relentless gaze. 'Then she did the right thing and she would have no regrets, so neither do I.'

'Thank you,' he said, his eyes welling up with tears that he refused to let fall.

'That's settled then,' the woman said. 'I'll leave it for you to sort out. If you need me to sign any legal documents, let me know.'

Steve and Belle looked at each other in confusion as the woman turned and started to walk away from them.

'Umm, sorry... what's settled and what are we sorting out?' Belle asked.

The woman turned and frowned. 'The bloody dog. Oscar...' she glanced at Steve, 'He's your responsibility now.'

'Me? A dog?'

'Yes. I think it's fitting and fair, don't you?'

He slowly nodded his head. Not because he necessarily agreed, but because he couldn't argue. The woman had just lost her mother because of him. At that moment, he couldn't say no to anything she asked of him.

Belle pushed him back to his ward. After several minutes of silence while the new reality sank in, he finally spoke. 'What just happened?'

'Think you got yourself a dog.'

'For real?'

'Yep.'

'How the bloody hell am I going to look after a dog?'

'Tamsin and I will help you.'

'You will?'

'Yes,' she replied firmly.

Steve nodded his head. The woman was right. It seemed fair that since he was responsible for the dog losing its owner, then that in turn made him responsible for the dog.

'Okay then.' He could barely look after himself, but he made a decision to do his absolute best for the dog. He owed it to Jane, the lady he had never met but a lady who had given up her life to save him.

VICTORIA PRESSED the play button on the office answerphone again and listened as Jenny informed her that Brett would be away for a while. She had played the message over and over as though doubting its validity or maybe desperately seeking some hidden meaning or message that she'd missed the first ten times she' d heard it.

Given the timing of the recording, she was in no doubt he had received her text message. He had obviously freaked out so completely that not only had he run away, but he couldn't even tell her himself and he had to get his sister to do the dirty work for him.

She was beyond tears and tantrums. It was time she took control. She pressed the delete button and turned her attention to the laptop in front of her. On the screen was a list of clinics and health centres and in the search bar at the top it read 'Abortions, Milton Keynes'. She had no choice. She had to think about Gemma and what was best for her. Besides, she couldn't support a baby on her own. She was almost certainly going to lose her house, and she had no other savings. Dave had lost out every penny they ever had. Having a baby simply wasn't an option.

Victoria looked up as the door opened and Belle walked into the Show Home.

'Hi,' she said, 'How are you? I heard you were a bit of a hero.'

'No, it wasn't me. I just helped a bit.'

'Do you know how Steve's doing?'

'Yes, I've just got back from the hospital and he is doing really well. Thanks. I could do with your help, though.'

The last thing in the world that Victoria felt like doing was mercy missions for someone else. But she knew that being self-centred and self-pitying wouldn't alter her situation, so she forced herself to smile. 'Sure, what's up?'

NATASHA GROANED and turned up the volume on the television to block out the noise of whoever was knocking on her door. She concentrated her attention on the two men in blue t-shirts who were rummaging around the stalls at a huge indoor antique fair. As far as she could make out, they had to buy things that would then be resold at auction. Another couple, an elderly man and a much younger woman in red t-shirts were doing the same thing. It seemed that whoever made the most profit at auction was the winning team. Natasha knew nothing about antiques, had never been to an auction in her life, and had no idea why she was watching it.

Anything to while away the time and blot out the sad reality of her life.

The knocking paused, but only for a minute before her letterbox was lifted and the woman from the Show Home shouted through it.

'Natasha, open the door.'

She had no idea why the flats even had letter boxes. Downstairs in the lobby were mail boxes so what was the point in having the gaps in the door that allowed for noisy interfering busybodies to invade her space? She turned the volume even higher. The young girl on the screen squealed excitedly as she held up a small china cat. 'I think it's Royal Doulton,' she whispered to her teammate.

'Who sodding cares, you silly cow!' Natasha shouted at the screen.

'Please Natasha, let us in.'

She held her hands over her ears and closed her eyes tight. As a child, she would hide in the under-stairs cupboard when her mum and whoever was the latest boyfriend were arguing. She would drag a blanket off the bed and take it in with her, and curl up in a ball, close her eyes and cover her ears and pretend to be somewhere, anywhere else. Until one day one of the boyfriends locked the door. Cold, hungry and terrified, she was trapped in there all evening, all night and most of the following morning.

'Natasha, if you don't open the door, then I'm going to call the police and they will break it down. I need to know that you are alright.'

Alright? Of course, she wasn't alright. Silly cow.

'Last chance...'

If she opened the door and showed her face, would they go away and leave her alone? Surely they would have to. Her life, her flat. If she told them to sod off, then they would. She climbed off the sofa and walked towards the door, but she didn't want to open it. She didn't want to face them or anyone. But the idea of the police getting involved was even worse. So she unbolted the door and pulled it open.

VICTORIA STOOD up and stepped back as the door opened a slightly and Natasha's head appeared in the gap.

'Go away.'

Even though there wasn't very much of the young woman visible, it was enough to shock Victoria. Her skin looked sallow and her hair greasy and lank. The light had gone out of her eyes. She looked tired, washed out, and defeated. 'Natasha,' she said gently, 'let me in.'

'No.'

The door was closing, but Victoria was quick enough to jam her foot in the gap.

'Hey! You can't do that...'

'Natasha, where's the baby?' Belle said from beside her. 'Is she alright?'

'Please let us in,' Victoria said, keeping her voice as calm and soothing as she could. 'We only want to help you.'

Natasha pushed the door from the inside, trying to shut them out. Victoria looked at Belle, who nodded her head in silent agreement. Together, they pushed hard and forced the door open. Natasha jumped back, and they tumbled into the apartment.

'Come in, why don't you!' Natasha snapped sarcastically at them.

Victoria picked herself up off the floor, wincing from the pain in her knee where Belle had landed on her.

'You've no right to force yourself into my house. I'll call the police.'

'Yeah, you're good at that.' Belle threw back at her, nursing her arm, another casualty from the floor impact.

Victoria stepped between them. Belle had come to her because she was worried and with good reason. The flat was a mess, and not just the usual chaos that was inevitable with a baby on the premises. It was neglected, the home of a person who had lost the will to care.

'Where's the baby?' Belle asked, looking around her with the same surprise and disbelief that Victoria was experiencing.

The TV was very loud, and they all had to shout to make themselves heard above the auctioneer, who was driving up the increasingly excited bids on a china cat to ridiculous heights. She walked to the sofa and pressed the pause button.

'The baby?' Belle said again, looking around her as though she expected it to be hiding under a cushion.

Natasha folded her arms across her chest in a defensive pose and stared angrily at her neighbour. 'None of your damn business.'

Victoria looked at the young woman; she was only a few years older than her own daughter and clearly at, if not beyond, breaking point. She felt guilty that she hadn't done more to help her. She knew that Natasha was struggling and she should have been more persistent on her visits.

'Why don't you sit down Natasha,' she said soothingly. 'And I'll make us all a nice cup of tea.'

Natasha didn't budge; she stood stubbornly in the middle of the room. Victoria headed for the kitchen anyway and Belle disappeared into the bedrooms, presumably in search of the baby girl.

Victoria put the kettle on and ran some hot water into the sink. It looked as though the washing up hadn't been done for days, possibly even weeks. She opened the door of the fridge and wasn't surprised to find it was completely empty.

Belle came into the kitchen and shook her head. 'She's not here.'

Victoria was relieved. She had been a little afraid of what they might find. She showed Belle the fridge, and they looked in the freezer and the cupboards.

'What's she living on?' Belle whispered.

'The state of her, I'd say she probably hasn't eaten for a while.' Victoria picked up an empty crisp packet. 'At least nothing decent.'

The TV went back on, just as loud as it was before.

'What do we do?' Belle said, sticking her hands in the hot soapy water and washing up some dishes.

Victoria was pretty sure that Natasha needed professional help. 'Let's start with a hot drink and a meal,' she said. 'There's nothing here and I doubt she'll let us in a second time.'

'Okay,' Belle said. 'I'll go next door and cook her a nice omelette; you stay with her and see if she'll talk. I won't be able to sleep until I know the baby is safe.'

Sonia handed Dave a sandwich and sat down beside him on the soft, leather couch. 'If you don't go home soon, she'll get the police out looking for you.'

He took a bite and rolled his eyes. 'She always was a drama queen.'

'Listen to yourself,' Sonia said impatiently. 'You've been lying to her for weeks...'

She saw his guilty look.

'Maybe months.'

He shrugged his shoulders and took another bite.

'You've lost all the family money and then disappeared without a word or any remorse or explanation. Go home and talk to her.'

'I will,' he said. 'I'll just give her a bit longer to calm down.'

Despite feeling sorry for him, Sonia was losing patience. Besides, she was upset about her falling out with Victoria and wanted to put it right between them. It was difficult, though, when she was harbouring the errant husband in her house. He was pretty much living in her garage and that meant that she was not only holding out on her best friend, but also on her own husband. Sooner or later, Paul would wander into their garage and discover a strange car and an even stranger man dossing in it. 'Man up and bugger off home,' she said, taking the empty plate from him. 'You never know. If you ask nicely, she might even take you back.'

'Do you think so?'

Never in a million zillion years, she thought. 'Anything is possible,' she said.

'I will,' he looked at her and smiled.

He was an attractive man. She'd thought him interesting from the moment he scooped Casper up in his arms and done his mercy dash to the vets.

'Don't suppose I could have another sandwich first, could I?'

She took the plate into the kitchen and pulled the fresh uncut loaf from the bread-bin. He wasn't ready. No matter what she said or even what he said, Sonia knew he wouldn't be going home just yet.

NATASHA DIDN'T KNOW what to do about the unwanted visitor. At least the nosy bitch from next door had left, but Victoria was still in her kitchen. Even with the TV on full volume, she could hear the woman washing up. What must she think? What did it matter, anyway? She hadn't asked her to come in, and she certainly hadn't asked her to wash up the dishes. The pair of them just barged in. Who the hell were they to judge her? Whatever they thought of her, it couldn't be any worse than she thought of herself.

She fixated on the television when Victoria walked into the room and sat down on the sofa beside her. She didn't want to talk. Why would she? And more than that, why should she?

The woman took the remote and paused the programme. It

seemed there was no escaping from the nosy cow's unwanted attention.

'What?'

'Talk to me Natasha.'

'Why?'

'Because sometimes we all need someone to talk to.'

Natasha slowly turned her head and stared at the woman. 'Go away,' she said.

Victoria looked steadily back at her. 'I'll lay it out for you, Natasha,' she replied. 'Either you talk to me or I make a few calls to the police and social services or you talk to them when they come knocking, instead.'

Did she mean it? Did it even matter?

'Do you really want social on your doorstep checking up on your every move?'

'What can I tell you? Look around and see for yourself, I'm a screw-up, a failure. This is who I am. It's all in the genes. You can't fight genetics,' she spat back bitterly.

'Rubbish.' Victoria said. 'Self-pitying tosh!'

'No, you wanted the truth, that's it.'

'Listen to me Natasha, you are a young mum struggling from lack of sleep, not enough support and messed up hormones. We all need a bit of help from time to time and that's what I'm here to provide.'

'You're wasting your time,' she snapped, but a small ray of hope ignited within her. Was it possible that she wasn't destined to always be a screw-up?

'Where's the baby?'

Natasha felt the stab of angry tears. 'He took her.'

'Who? Your partner?'

'He said I was useless...' remembering the pain in their last row hit her like a physical blow. She looked at the woman coldly. What right did she have to make her explain and relive it all? She was doing okay being shut up in the house, hiding away from the world.

'I'm sure he didn't mean it. We all lash out sometimes.'

'He meant it,' she said bitterly. 'And he was right...'

Victoria reached out and took her hand and squeezed it gently. It took her totally by surprise that the simple show of kindness unleashed a torrent of tears.

The door, which was still on the latch, opened up and Belle came in carrying a tray with three hot drinks and a plate covered by foil.

'I haven't sugared the teas, and I put a squirt of tomato sauce on the side of the plate in case you like it.' Belle said, lifting the foil from the plate and handing it to her.

'I'm not hungry,' she lied, her tummy rumbling loudly as the smell of melted cheese hit her nostrils.

'Hungry or not, I'm sitting here until you've eaten it.'

'It looks and smells tasty,' Victoria said.

Natasha looked from one to the other. She wiped her eyes on her sleeve and took the knife and fork that Belle handed her. The omelette was light and fluffy and stuffed full with cheese, ham and mushrooms. 'Why are you doing this?' She was genuinely baffled by their interfering kindness.

'Told you,' Victoria said, smiling. 'We all need a little help sometimes.'

AFTER TWO DAYS in the hospital, Steve was delighted to get home. Sharon had supported his bid for freedom and her assertion that his untimely dip was an accident helped him to avoid the clutches of the psychiatric ward. He had no idea why she helped him. He knew that after what he put her through, no one would blame her for using it as an opportunity to get her revenge. He owed her and he knew it.

He thanked the driver of the non-emergency ambulance and let himself into his flat. He looked around him and realised that it really was where he wanted to be. Despite the break-ins and despite the recent dramas, it was his home.

He hated the chair that wheelchair services had supplied to him on loan. It was heavy and difficult to manoeuvre. With his own chair lying at the bottom of the canal, he had very little choice. Lightweight custom made wheelchairs didn't appear just by flashing the cash. He had to be measured and assessed and then it had to be ordered, manufactured and delivered. It would be weeks before he had a suitable replacement, and that was probably an optimistic estimate.

His doorbell rang, and he pressed the fob expecting to see one of the neighbours or possibly Sharon checking up on him. It was PC Clarke at the door.

'More questions?'

'No,' the policeman replied, 'I thought you might be needing this.'

Steve stared in delighted surprise at his wheelchair.

'We managed to fish it out. I didn't know if the cushion would be alright, but I put the cover through the wash and dried out the inside. The gel seems okay but you might want to get someone who actually knows about these things to take a look.'

Steve could have hugged the man, instead he moved back to let PC Clarke push his chair into the lounge. 'Unbelievable. Thank you so much.'

'You're welcome. Do you need help to get into it?'

'If you put it next to me and make sure the brakes are on, I can do a sideways transfer.' He lifted the arm up and, using the strength in his upper body, he heaved himself across and then lifted each leg and put them on the footplate. 'You have no idea how good this feels.' Even a gel cushion that had been dragged up from the dirty depths of the canal was better than no gel cushion.

PC Clarke folded the loan chair up and pushed it into the corner for him before saying goodbye and leaving.

Steve switched the computer on. Tomorrow Belle was delivering the dog to him and he needed supplies. He was both terrified of the responsibility and thrilled by the prospect of owning a pet. As a child, he'd always wanted a dog, but all he ever had was a goldfish and that went belly up within weeks of him winning it at the visiting fairground.

Knowing that a stranger had given her own life to save his had changed him. It was as if he'd been given a kick up the arse. Told to let go of all his self-pitying crap and do something useful with his life. Was this what Jenny felt? He had no idea what he could possibly do, but for the first time since his accident, he felt he wanted to try. Find a place for himself in society and find a purpose.

Oscar the dog would be the first step. He would care for the animal and love it like its former owner had. He put 'dog stuff' into the search bar and then got busy with his credit card.

ANNABEL UNLOCKED the door and walked into the flat. Tammy was snuggled up on the sofa, playing a game on her mobile phone.

'Didn't you give me the key back?'

'Yes…'

'So how?'

Tammy glanced up at her. 'I got a copy cut before I gave it to you.'

'A copy?'

'Of course, otherwise I wouldn't be able to get in, would I?'

'Um, that was kind of the point,' Annabel said, wondering why she let Tammy get away with it. The girl wasn't half as daft as she made out.

Tammy turned the game off and looked at her. 'You don't want me to be here?'

'It's not that,' Annabel replied. 'It's just that you have your own place, which isn't cheap, and, well, Jack and I need some privacy sometimes.'

Tammy stood up in a huff. 'I'll go now then,' she said, letting a small sob escape her lips.

'Don't be daft, you're here now. You might as well have a drink first.'

'Hot chocolate?'

Annabel smiled. Why could she never say no to the girl? 'Haven't you got any bookings today?'

Tammy's gaze dropped. 'No.'

'Tammy?'

'Oh okay, one later. But I don't like him Annabel, he gives me the creeps.'

They both turned as Jack came in through the door. 'Oh hello,' he said, clearly as surprised as she had been to see Tammy there.

'How is Mary?' she asked, sprinkling mini marshmallows on top of the hot drink.

'Yeah, she's doing okay, although that break-in has shaken her up more than she likes to admit. I've never seen her so nervous and jumpy like this, although she tries to hide it.'

'She's tough, and we're close by.'

'Yeah, I know.'

Annabel handed the hot chocolate to Tammy. 'You know some of our clients are not always quite as...' she paused, searching for a word, '... cute as we would like them to be.' It wasn't unknown for girls to get picky, and while she tried to keep them happy and certainly wouldn't ever expect a girl to do something she didn't want to do. She couldn't and wouldn't start turning clients away. At least not for most of the reasons her girls would come up with, like bad teeth or body odour. On the other hand, their safety was always her main priority and so she never dismissed their moans or complaints without listening and assessing their concerns first.

'I know that,' Tammy said. 'I don't expect them all to look like Brad Pitt,' she giggled. 'If I did then poor Mr Smith would never get any fun, and you know how much I love him.'

It was true; many of Tammy's regulars were older gentlemen who came back to her again and again. 'So who is he and what does he want you to do?'

'Well, it's more what he doesn't want,' Tammy said. 'It's that man from down the road. You know, in the big house?'

Jack looked across at them. 'Miles Fisher?'

Tammy nodded.

'I didn't realise he was a client,' Annabel said.

'He's new.'

'He's the bastard who's trying to get me done for assault. Has he hurt you?'

Annabel put a calming hand on Jack; she didn't want him to go into his super macho mode.

'He hasn't touched me,' Tammy said. 'That's the problem.'

'I don't understand,' Jack replied.

'He makes the appointment, pays the money and sits and talks to me for forty-five minutes, then he gives me a big tip and he leaves.'

'What does he talk about?' Annabel asked, trying to make sense of it all. Some punters did just pay for the company and the companionship and didn't want sex. Maybe he's one of them.

'I dunno, I don't really listen...'

'Helpful.'

'Well, he does my head in. He keeps banging on about saving me from all this, says he'll give me money and I can live at his house. As if!'

Suddenly, it all made sense. She'd come across a few of them over the years. They were the men who wanted to save the working girls, even if the girls didn't want to be saved.

'I'll go and have a chat with him,' Jack said, heading for the door.

Annabel shook her head. 'No, I'm sure he's harmless and he no doubt means well. I'll put the word out that he's barred.' She smiled at Tammy. 'You won't have to see him again.'

VICTORIA WALKED past Sonia's house and felt a flush of guilt. She had thought about inviting her neighbour on a shopping trip, but then decided against it. They hadn't spoken since the heated exchange a few days ago, and Victoria was still feeling hurt.

Belle and Natasha were already outside the apartment block waiting for her, and the taxi drove past her and stopped beside them. It seemed strange to see the two young women together without sniping at each other. If they weren't actually friends yet, Victoria was confident they soon would be.

Natasha looked stronger and more relaxed, although the sadness in her eyes was still there and would no doubt remain until she saw her baby again. The doctor had put her on medication to treat the post-natal depression and Belle had gone on a mission to feed her up. The difference was already showing.

The three of them climbed into the taxi and headed off to the shopping centre. When she had suggested they go on her day off, it had seemed like a good idea, but now she was wishing she had kept her ideas to herself. Not that she didn't want to spend the day with them both, but she tired easily and she had almost no money, which might be awkward.

Payday simply couldn't come quickly enough for her. They were living off the contents of the freezer, which luckily had been pretty full. Christmas was approaching at an alarming rate and she had no presents for Gemma and no idea how she could buy any, even after her pay went into the bank. She couldn't even put a Christmas tree up. They threw their old one out along with all the decorations when they moved. New house, new start, new tree! She would give a lot to have the tatty old one that went to the dump along with the temperamental lights that seemed to have a mind of their own.

'Oh wow,' Natasha said when they reached the Christmas display in Middleton Hall. 'This is amazing.'

Victoria looked around the newly created winter wonderland and watched the animated characters bobbing their heads and twisting and turning. There was a little bridge over a wishing well where people threw their coins and whispered their secret wishes. Everywhere sparkled with twinkling lights and there were little log cabins for vendors, a carousel and a castle.

'I thought about bringing Tamsin to see Father Christmas.'

'You should, she'll love it,' Victoria said, smiling as she remembered visits to the grotto with Gemma when she was small. She missed those days. It had all seemed so simple and straightforward when all she had to do to keep her daughter happy was hold her hand and smile. Looking around the displays, she realised she couldn't deny Gemma a proper Christmas. The two of them sitting in the house with no tree and hardly any presents wouldn't help their relationship. Selfishly she wanted her daughter with her for the festive season, but the best thing she could do as a mother was allow Gemma to go away with her friend Abby and her family.

'Except I know what she'll say when he asks what she wants,' Belle said.

'Kyle?' Natasha said softly.

Belle nodded her head. 'Yep, and even Christmas magic can't make that happen.'

Natasha put her arm around Belle and gave her a friendly hug. Victoria watched in delighted amazement.

'We should do that,' Belle said, pointing to a group of schoolchildren singing carols while the teachers walked around with collection buckets. 'We should have a carol singing party.'

'In Jasmine Close?' Natasha said uncertainly. 'Where?'

'At the tree outside the Show Home,' Belle said excitedly. 'We could have mince pies and mulled wine. A chance for everyone to come together…'

'Didn't work so well for the Fishers' party,' Victoria said.

'Well, I wouldn't know. I wasn't invited. But I heard it was well attended, even though the party girl did a runner.'

'I suppose we could ask around, see who would be up for it.'

'Great, I reckon there are several residents who could do with a bit of a singsong and some friendly company,' Belle said. 'We'll do it on Christmas Eve.'

DAVE LET himself into the house. He knew it was Victoria's day off and he had seen her go out in a taxi with a couple of other women from up the Close. Sonia had nagged him into submission, although he still wasn't sure he was ready to face his wife.

He went upstairs and into the bathroom. Sonia had told him, brutally and bluntly, that he needed to smarten himself up. So shower and shave were the first tasks on his list, then he would settle down and wait for Victoria to get home. He didn't expect her to be long. Although she liked the shops, she was never one of those women who disappeared all day. Two, maybe three hours were her limit.

The hot, steamy water was cleansing and comforting. It had been a horrible few weeks for him. Losing his job, being mugged, having to leave his home and dossing in his car. It was alright for Vic, she still had the house and Gemma. He'd missed their daughter and her smile and the occasional hug that she would give him. She'd always been a bit of a daddy's girl.

Sonia said that Victoria was saying they would lose the house, that they were almost bankrupt. It was a total exaggeration, a distortion of the truth. So he'd had a few financial problems. Who didn't? It wasn't the end of the world. They could come back from it. He knew that his wife always had a few quid tucked away in her own account. If he could persuade her to let him have that, then he could soon win back what he'd lost.

He had a feeling that she might not see it the same way as him, though, which was why he had stayed away. She never had been up for any excitement or risk taking. She always played it safe. Who could blame him for wanting more? She had stifled him over the years. In a way, she was partly to blame for the trouble he found himself in. He splashed himself with shower gel and rubbed it over his body, feeling happier than he had done for a while.

VICTORIA KNEW he was there the minute she walked through the front door. His shoes were in the hall. The smell of Lynx aftershave drifted down the stairs and the television was switched on to Sky Sports, even though nobody was in the lounge watching it.

She found him in the kitchen, staring into the fridge. 'Hello love,' he said, as though it were the most natural thing in the world for him to say. 'Are we out of bacon?'

'That and just about everything else,' she snapped. 'Where the hell have you been?'

'I'm home now,' he said. 'I'm sorry if I worried you.'

'Worried?' She couldn't believe how calm he was; speaking as though he'd been away on business for a few days, instead of hiding out after bankrupting them.

He closed the fridge door and crossed the floor in a couple of quick, easy strides and pulled her into his arms. She tensed and pushed him away.

'What's up Vic?'

She stared at him incredulously. Was he for real? Was he playing some weird game?

'Look, I know I've been a bit silly.'

'Understatement of the century!'

He looked irritated but carried on, anyway. 'I should have told you I'd lost my job. I'm sorry, but you know I always hated it there. They did me a favour, really.'

She stared at him as though he were an alien just landed from Mars. he might as well be for all the sense he was talking. 'Dave, we are flat broke.'

'A blip. Don't worry, I'll soon have us back on our feet again.'

'How?'

He smiled, although it didn't reflect in his eyes. 'I'll get another job. I already have a few possibilities lined up, seriously love, lighten up. It's nearly Christmas.'

'Yes, and we have no tree, no lights and no presents!'

She saw a flash of anger, but he quickly controlled it and smiled again. 'Trust me,' he said. 'Have I ever let you down?'

She opened her mouth, but he talked straight across her.

'I mean, other than this temporary problem. In all the years that we've been together, haven't I always been there providing for you and Gemma?'

She had to give him that. It was true.

'I screwed up Vic; everyone deserves a second chance, don't they?'

She thought of Brett and the way he had run out on her. She didn't want to be alone. She looked into his familiar face. Did he mean it? Was it possible that they could go back to their previous lives?

'I don't know,' she said.

The front door opened and Gemma hurried into the house and the kitchen and straight into her father's arms. 'Daddy.'

Across Gemma's head, their eyes met. She nodded. He grinned. What choice did she really have? She owed it to her daughter.

. . .

BRETT FELT the excitement grow within him. Despite his exhaustion, he wanted to see Victoria. The few days that the trip should have taken had turned into weeks. He had driven through the night to be back in Milton Keynes for Christmas. Of course, he had no idea if she would be able to spend any part of it with him. Had she kicked her idiot husband out or had they sorted their problems? He had no idea. The time spent away from her had made him realise how much she meant to him. The fling had become something far more serious for him and although it scared him since he didn't do serious, it also excited him.

As he drove into Jasmine Close, he looked towards the Show Home. It seemed to be closed, which was annoying. He glanced at the clock on the dashboard. It was four forty and Christmas Eve, so maybe it was inevitable that she would shut up early. He had tried to ring her at the Show Home when he was waiting for his time slot at the channel tunnel. He had an hour to spare, so he parked up at the huge shopping centre in Cite Europe and found a public phone and rang the Show Home. It went straight to the answerphone, and he left a short message just to say he would be in MK later that day. Disappointed and with time to spare, he found a jeweller and brought her a Christmas present.

Brett had no idea what reception he would get from Miles, or even if his door key would still work. The lock might have been changed. Since most of his clothes and his mobile phone were in the house, that would be a disaster, besides he really needed a shower.

He put the key in the door and relaxed with relief when it turned. The house was in darkness, so he assumed Miles wasn't at home. He felt awkward going in but reasoned that despite their problems, Jenny still owned half the property and he had her permission to be there.

The phone was still on the bed where he had dropped it, but not surprisingly, the battery was completely dead. He found his charger and plugged it in, then headed for the bathroom and turned on the shower.

. . .

Victoria checked herself in the mirror and smoothed down her hair. She didn't feel like going out in the cold and being sociable. Nor did she want to sing carols. Her Christmas spirit had gone with their daughter across the channel. The idea of spending the next couple of days shut in the house with Dave filled her with horror. She might have let him back into the house and her life, but he was in the spare bedroom and that's where he was staying. He might think that the troubles they faced were an insignificant bump in the path of their marriage, but that certainly wasn't her view. He had a lot of making up to do for them to stand any chance of getting back to normal.

She ran her hand down over her stomach. It was flat, well, not exactly flat, but certainly no more rounded than normal. Looking in the mirror, it was easy to think that the pregnancy was not real. The constant nausea she was experiencing was not so easy to ignore.

The smell of sweet mincemeat wafted up to her as she walked down the stairs. But even the lovely golden pastry of the mince pies couldn't lift her mood. She cooked them because in a mad moment she had promised Belle that she would. She put the two trays onto the glass protector on the worktop and glanced at the clock. It was ten past five; Belle would be banging on the door any minute. The plan was to have a glass of warm mulled wine and a hot mince pie around the tree outside the Show Home. Natasha had showed a design skill that surprised them all and had made invites for every house and flat in the Close.

The doorbell rang; she paused for a minute to see if Dave would answer. He didn't. She had no idea where he was. She pulled the oven gloves off and went into the hall to open the door. Belle, Tamsin and Natasha grinned at her. The three of them were wrapped up warmly, and Belle was carrying a portable CD player. 'All the favourites on here,' Belle said, holding it up. 'Paul from next door has put a pasting table up and Sonia has laid a cloth out with some candles on it.'

'It's all sparkly and pretty,' Tamsin said excitedly.

Victoria looked at the expectant faces and found herself smiling. How could she not? The little girl looked so happy. Belle and Natasha had become friends and had worked so hard to organise the sing-song.

'Better get the mince pies then,' she said, glancing up the stairs and wondering again where Dave had disappeared off to. 'Does someone need to push Mary down?'

'I knocked,' Belle said, 'but Mary told me it was too cold for her to come outside and she would open her window and listen from her flat.'

BRETT FELT as though he had rejoined the human race. He had been living out of an overnight bag and sleeping in small hotels where often hot water was a bonus. It definitely made him appreciate the wonder of modern plumbing. He had spent over a week with Jenny at the orphanage, helping her to adjust and settle. He had helped by doing some basic repairs and maintenance jobs that were way overdue on the property. As a result, he now had a keen understanding and appreciation of how privileged his own life was.

Dried and dressed, he picked up his phone and switched it on. The charge wasn't complete, but it had enough on it for him to see that he had several missed calls and text messages. Some were from business contacts, including his lettings agent who handled his property portfolio. He knew that he had neglected his company for far too long and no matter what the situation was with Victoria, he would have to return home to New York soon.

He scrolled down and opened the last message received from her. He blinked and re-read the two simple words that jumped and jumbled, his head swimming as though he were totally inebriated.

STEVE JOINED in with the Close rendition of 'Holy Night' while Oscar sat beside him wagging his tail. Tamsin's little gloved hand rested on the dog's head and she kept stroking and fussing him, which he clearly loved. Steve reckoned if Oscar was a cat, then his purring would be so loud it would drown out the singing.

He saw a man approach pushing a buggy and recognised him as being Ed, Natasha's partner; he knew from Belle that the couple had been having problems. He nudged Natasha, who was standing on his left. She turned towards him and whispered. 'What?'

He didn't need to answer. Her face lit up as she saw Ed and her little baby. Were they married? He didn't know. She ran up the Close to meet him and dropped to her knees to look into the buggy.

Steve smiled; it was good to see everyone enjoying themselves. Of course, he knew that when he got home and closed his door, he would be alone again and stay that way all over Christmas and New Year. He watched as Natasha stood up and Ed pulled her into his arms. He wished he had someone to love and to love him back, but he knew it would never happen. What did he have to offer?

He thought about Melanie and her dreams. She wanted to marry and have children. Was it really possible? No, he thought she was delusional, but he also knew that he still owed her an apology and he had put it off for long enough.

The carol finished, and he turned to Belle. 'I'm just popping home,' he said.

'Everything alright?'

'Fine,' he replied. Just something I need to do.'

VICTORIA WASN'T ANSWERING her phone. Brett could hear music and singing and a quick glance out of the front window confirmed the Close had gathered for carol singing. He searched the assembled crowd until his eyes rested on Victoria. She seemed to be alone. Or at least alone with the rest of Jasmine Close beside her. No sign of the husband or the daughter.

He put his shoes on and opened the front door, then grabbed his coat and ran down the Close. He saw Steve heading back to his flat. Jenny had asked him to check the man was okay, and he would, but not yet. He needed to talk to Victoria.

She saw him coming. So did everyone else. Not surprising since he was sprinting like a madman, being chased by a monster.

He expected her to part from the crowd and walk up to meet him, but she didn't. He expected her eyes to light up and her lips to upturn in the smile that he loved so much, but that didn't happen either. He realised that the text had probably been a plea for help and reassurance from her and his lack of response must have hurt her terribly. The message from Jenny saying he would be away could have been interpreted as abandonment.

He stopped running and weaved his way through the small crowd. Still, Victoria made no move towards him or acknowledged him in any way. In fact, the opposite was true as she looked determinedly in the opposite direction and carried on singing Away in a Manger.

Brett moved up close beside her. 'Please Victoria, we have to talk.'

'Too late,' she whispered back without turning her head.

He touched her arm. 'Don't say that, I've only just seen your message.'

Her singing faltered, and she turned her head to look at him.

'I didn't know until a few minutes ago.'

She didn't look as though she believed him.

'I left my phone here. I've driven over fifteen hundred miles all through the night because I wanted to see you before Christmas. I charged my mobile and checked it just a few minutes ago.' He paused and looked deeply into her eyes. 'I promise you I would never have left if I'd known.'

Her expression softened, and he saw sadness and regret in her beautiful eyes. 'It's too late,' she whispered and then turned away and carried on singing.

He didn't know what to do or say. What did she mean too late? Surely she hadn't aborted their baby, not without talking to him first.

'You haven't?' he whispered, hardly able to get the words out. His throat seemed to have seized up completely, as if he were being strangled.

'Go away Brett,' she replied. 'I have a husband and a daughter and you and I were a huge mistake.'

He didn't want to go away, but he couldn't bear to stay either. He couldn't comprehend the idea that she had so callously aborted their baby. Did he mean so little to her? Couldn't she at least have waited until he got back to discuss it?

Up ahead, he saw a sports car pull up and Annabel and Jack climbed out of the car. He saw his brother-in-law dart down the alley that lead to the back of the apartment block. Then the stupid cat that Mary took in ran across the path in front of him. He stumbled but kept on his feet. Behind him, the singing became louder as they launched into a chorus of 'We Wish You a Merry Christmas'.

He would book a flight home. If he hurried, he might even get an evening flight back to America. He felt homesick for the busy bustling streets of New York. He wanted a big fat pizza from the Italian takeaway just around the corner from his apartment, and he missed the smell of strong Americano coffee and the sight of yellow cabs.

He felt in his pocket for the door key and instead pulled out the gold necklace that he had brought for Victoria. With a burst of fury, he threw it into the bushes.

VICTORIA CARRIED ON SINGING. Anything to stop her from running up the Close after him. Was it true? Had he really not seen her message before he left? It didn't matter. Sending him away was the best thing to do for them both. What she said to him was right, she was married, and she already had a child. It was her job to keep her daughter safe and happy and she had risked it all for a fling. Holding the family together was what mattered now. The appointment at the clinic was booked for January and nobody need ever know.

Of course she would know. She would have to live with the knowledge forever.

Across the twinkling lights of the tree, she saw Sonia watching her. Their eyes met briefly before Victoria looked away. It was alright for Sonia; she had her happy little family. Paul had his arm resting across his wife's shoulder and the boys stood on either side of them. Her neighbour had no right to judge her.

She glanced up the Close and saw Brett at the driveway of the Fishers' house and, as though he could feel her gaze, he turned and looked back towards her. The distance was too great to see his expression in the dark, yet she was sure his hurt and anger and pain were visible. She wanted to run to him and say she was sorry, that she wanted to be with him and they should keep the baby. But of course she didn't.

She watched Brett go into his house, sure that she saw Dave lurking near the apartments. She squinted into the darkness but realised she must have been mistaken.

The singing reached its climax, '... and a Happy New Year.'

Belle was handing out glasses of wine when a shot rang out.

A loud crack shattered the calm and the peaceful ambience of the evening.

Belle dropped the tray she was carrying. Glasses shattered on the concrete, and everyone looked towards the apartments.

Then all hell broke loose.

To be continued ...

You can sign up to *Linda's* newsletter and read a FREE bonus episode introducing a new family into **Jasmine Close** here:

https://BookHip.com/LZJTMMN

Individual Ebooks in Series Two and Three are available on Amazon. A paperback version for each Series will be coming soon.

ABOUT THE AUTHOR

Linda Dunscombe is an experienced author who loves creating characters and weaving stories. You can find her books on Amazon and you can connect with her on Facebook.

facebook.com/jasmineclosecrew

You can sign up to her newsletter and read a FREE bonus episode to introduce a new family into Jasmine Close here:

https://BookHip.com/LZJTMMN

You can find all the Ebooks in Series One, Series Two and Series Three on Amazon.

If you are already a follower of *Jasmine Close*, I thank you for your continued support, it is very much appreciated.

New episodes will be coming soon.

facebook.com/jasmineclosecrew

Printed in Great Britain
by Amazon